Praise for bestselling author Cathy Gillen Thacker

"Thacker's superb characters
are wonderfully entertaining and lovable.
You'll root for both couples."
—*RT Book Reviews* on *Wanted: One Mommy*

"This Texas version of *When Harry Met Sally*
is an amusing contemporary romance
starring likable lead characters and eccentric,
somewhat zany secondary players... Readers will
enjoy this lighthearted romantic romp."
—Harriet Klausner on *The Rancher's Christmas Baby*

Praise for bestselling author Laura Marie Altom

"Laura Marie Altom's quirky characters, innovative
plotline and humorous storytelling combine for a
truly memorable read in *Blind Luck Bride*."
—*RT Book Reviews*

"Altom's story is a modern romance
loaded with tension, today's problems
and a sizzling sexual tension."
—*RT Book Reviews* on *A Wedding for Baby*

CATHY GILLEN THACKER
is married and a mother of three. She and her husband spent eighteen years in Texas and now reside in North Carolina. Her mysteries, romantic comedies and heartwarming family stories have made numerous appearances on bestseller lists, but her best reward, she says, is knowing one of her books made someone's day a little brighter. A popular Harlequin author for many years, she loves telling passionate stories with happy endings, and thinks nothing beats a good romance and a hot cup of tea! You can visit Cathy's website at www.cathygillenthacker.com for more information on her upcoming and previously published books, recipes and a list of her favorite things.

After college (Go, Hogs!), bestselling, award-winning author **LAURA MARIE ALTOM** did a brief stint as an interior designer before becoming a stay-at-home mom to boy/girl twins and a bonus son. Always an avid romance reader, she knew it was time to try her hand at writing when she found herself replotting the afternoon soaps.

When not immersed in her next story, Laura teaches art at a local middle school. In her free time, she beats her kids at video games, tackles Mount Laundry and of course reads romance!

Laura loves hearing from readers at P.O. Box 2074, Tulsa, OK 74101, or by email, BaliPalm@aol.com. Love winning fun stuff? Check out www.lauramariealtom.com!

CATHY GILLEN THACKER

The Ultimate Texas Bachelor

LAURA MARIE ALTOM

Blind Luck Bride

TORONTO • NEW YORK • LONDON
AMSTERDAM • PARIS • SYDNEY • HAMBURG
STOCKHOLM • ATHENS • TOKYO • MILAN • MADRID
PRAGUE • WARSAW • BUDAPEST • AUCKLAND

Recycling programs for this product may not exist in your area.

ISBN-13: 978-0-373-68820-3

THE ULTIMATE TEXAS BACHELOR & BLIND LUCK BRIDE

This edition published by arrangement with Harlequin Books S.A.

For questions and comments about the quality of this book please contact us at Customer_eCare@Harlequin.ca.

www.eHarlequin.com

Printed in U.S.A.

CONTENTS

This book is dedicated to Joshua Douglas Gerhardt,
ultimate flirt and total heartbreaker.
Welcome to the family, little one.

THE ULTIMATE TEXAS BACHELOR

Cathy Gillen Thacker

CHAPTER ONE

"COME ON, LAINEY. Have a heart! You can't leave us like this!" Lewis McCabe declared as he pushed his eyeglasses farther up on the bridge of his nose.

Aside from the fact she was here under false pretenses—which she had quickly decided she couldn't go through with, anyway—Lainey Carrington didn't see how she could stay, either. The Lazy M ranch house looked like a college dorm room had exploded on moving day. Lewis needed a lot more than the live-in housekeeper he had been advertising for, to bring order to this mess.

Lainey studied the nerdiest—and most technologically brilliant—of Sam and Kate McCabe's five grown sons and wondered how anyone so rich could still be so out of step with popular culture. Where had he gotten those clothes, anyway? From some 1980s-style shop?

"What do you mean *us?*" she asked suspiciously. Was Lewis married? If so, she hadn't heard about it, but then her knowledge was spotty at best since she hadn't actually lived in Laramie, Texas, since she left home for college ten years ago.

The door behind Lainey opened. She turned—and darn near fainted at the sight of the man she had secretly come here to track down.

Not that she had expected the six-foot-three cowboy, with the ruggedly handsome face and to-die-for body to actually be here. She had just hoped that Lewis would give her a clue where to look, so that she might help her friend Sybil Devine hunt the elusive Brad McCabe down and scrutinize the sexy Casanova celebrity in person.

"Brad, of course, who happens to be my business partner," Lewis McCabe explained.

"Actually, I'm more of a ranch manager," Brad McCabe corrected grimly, shooting an aggravated look at his younger brother. He knocked some of the mud off his scuffed, brown leather boots, then stepped into the interior of the sprawling half-century-old ranch house. "And I thought we had an agreement, Lewis, that you'd let me know when we were going to have company so I could avoid running into 'em."

Lewis shot Lainey an apologetic glance. "Don't mind him. He's been in a bad mood ever since he got done filming that reality TV show."

Lainey took the opportunity to gather a little background research. "Guess that didn't exactly have the happily-ever-after ending everyone expected it to have," she observed.

Brad's jaw set. Clearly, he did not want her sympathy. "You saw it?"

Obviously he wished she hadn't. Lainey shrugged, not about to admit just how riveted she'd been by the sight of Brad McCabe on her television screen. "I think everyone who knows you did."

"Not to mention most of America," Lewis chimed in.

Bachelor Bliss had pulled in very high ratings, especially at the end, when it had taken an unexpected twist. Which wasn't surprising, given how sexy Brad had looked walking out of the ocean in a pair of swim trunks that had left very little to the imagination. He'd been equally appealing on the back of a horse, riding into the mountains at sunset, or dressed in a tuxedo while enjoying a night on the town.

The only thing she hadn't liked was the sight of him kissing one pretty woman after another…and he had done an awful lot of that.

"You shouldn't have wasted your time watching such bull," Brad muttered, his scowl deepening as his voice dropped a self-deprecating notch. "And I know I shouldn't have wasted mine filming it."

Lainey agreed with him wholeheartedly there. Going on an artificially romantic TV show was no way to find a mate. "For what it's worth, I don't think they did right by you," Lainey said.

Brad's brow arched as if he dared her to go on.

Lainey gulped but held her ground. "The way they depicted you was not very flattering," she continued bravely, knowing that if she was going to convince him to open up to her, he was first going to have to realize she did indeed believe he had gotten a raw deal. And more importantly, that she wanted him to be able to tell his side of things. Which, to date, he had not done.

"Gee." His gaze clashed with hers. "You think?"

"I agree," Lewis put in genially, seeming not to notice the sparks arcing between Brad and Lainey. "Those producers did make you look like a womanizing jerk with the attention span of a flea."

Brad folded his arms over his chest, frustration coming off him in waves. "Maybe I *am* a womanizing jerk with the attention span of a flea," he said.

Somehow, Lainey didn't think so. For one thing, the McCabes—who were known for their honesty and integrity—would never have let him get away with that in real life. She knew he'd tried it as a kid, shortly after his family moved to Laramie, Texas, and had gotten reined in quickly, both by family and by the girls he had triple-timed. And for another thing, Brad had not appeared to be enjoying himself on the TV show as he tried to decide which of fifteen eligible women to take as his bride. Instead, he had seemed…impatient with the entire process. Restless. Except when with Yvonne Rathbone, the flame-haired beauty he had eventually paired up with. Then, he had seemed genuinely love-struck. Until the end, anyway.

"And maybe you're not," Lainey countered calmly.

Not that her opinion was widely shared. Thanks to the brouhaha that had followed the finale of the eight *Bachelor Bliss* episodes featuring Brad McCabe, he had been a fixture in gossip columns and celebrity magazines. Everyone wanted to know why Brad had done what he had, but Brad wasn't talking—at least not to the press.

And thus far, those close to him weren't talking, either.

It was Lainey's task to see what she could do about changing that, and letting the whole truth and nothing but the truth finally be known. Not that it looked to be easy.

She had heard from mutual acquaintances that Brad McCabe's experience as the sought-after bachelor on *Bachelor Bliss* had turned him not just into *persona non grata* where the entire viewing public was concerned, but also into a hardened cynic. Judging by the scowl on his face and the unwelcoming light in his eyes as he swept off his straw cowboy hat and ran his fingers through his gleaming dark brown hair, that assumption seemed to be true.

The Brad McCabe that Lainey recalled from her

youth had been two years ahead of her in school, cheerful and charming as could be. He had been more city kid than cowboy back then. Full of charm and life, always ready with a wink and a smile and a witty remark.

Now, he appeared ready to bite her head off. His brother's, too, as Brad surveyed them both with shadowed, sable-brown eyes.

Lainey swallowed hard and tried not to notice how nicely the blue chambray shirt hugged his broad shoulders and molded to the sculpted muscles of his chest, before disappearing beneath the waistband of his worn, dark blue denim jeans.

"Not that I expected to see you out here, in any case," Lainey continued truthfully, forcing her eyes away from his rodeo belt buckle and gazing back up at his face. "Since word is you've been hiding out from just about everyone."

"I'm not hiding." Brad looked ready to kick some Texas butt. Hers, specifically. "I'm getting on with my life. And there are plenty of people in Laramie who know exactly where to find me."

Lainey shrugged as another shimmer of awareness sifted through her, weakening her knees. "The press can't seem to locate you."

"And that's exactly the way it's going to stay," Brad enunciated clearly, looking deep into her eyes. "I have nothing to say to them."

Which was a problem as far as Lainey was concerned, as she was currently trying to fulfill her long-held dream of becoming a reporter.

"Brad figures too much has been said about him as it is," Lewis confided to Lainey. Lewis tried to adapt some of his older brother's inherent cool as he slouched against a low wall of moving boxes, but instead he knocked several over. They tumbled to the scuffed wooden floor with a clatter. Lewis scrambled to pick them up while Brad, shaking his head in silent exasperation, leaned forward lazily to lend a hand. "The past is over," Lewis continued. "He's looking toward the future. Which is why he agreed to start up this ranch with me—"

"You have to pay in half to be a partner," Brad interrupted, looking irritated again. "I haven't done that. Therefore I'm the ranch manager." Brad turned back to Lainey. He looked her up and down suspiciously, from the top of her carefully coiffed chin-length blond hair, to her casual suede slides. "And you are…?"

It shouldn't have surprised Lainey Carrington that Brad McCabe didn't recognize her. Brad was two years older than she was. It had been a good ten years since they had run into each other in the halls of Laramie High School. And she hadn't been back to Laramie much in the last couple of years since her parents died.

She touched the strand of pearls around her neck. Wishing for some odd reason that she was wearing something other than the demure, pale blue sweater set and knee-length khaki skirt, she smiled. "I'm Lainey Carrington."

To Lainey's frustration, Brad still had no clue.

"When I was in high school I was known as Lainey Wilson," Lainey explained. "Greta Wilson McCabe, who runs the Lone Star Dance Hall—"

"Our aunt by marriage." Lewis beamed.

"Right." Lainey nodded. "Well, Greta's my cousin."

"Lainey was one of the princesses on the Homecoming Court, when she was a senior and I was a freshman," Lewis explained. "I remember because the dress you wore for the parade…"

Had caused quite a scandal. Lainey felt herself flush bright pink.

Brad looked at Lewis and lifted a brow, waiting for him to finish.

Lewis started stammering and staring at the toes of his Birkenstock sandals. Obviously, he wished he had never started the story.

Figuring she might as well own up to it—Brad McCabe was going to hear all about it later anyway—Lainey put in dryly, "Suffice it to say, the dress I chose for the festivities was a little too 'adult' for the occasion." She had picked it up at a secondhand shop in nearby San Angelo that was run by the Junior League. The black velvet dress had been beautiful, no doubt about it, and at ten dollars, quite a steal. But the plunging neckline, short clinging skirt and five-inch stiletto heels had been more suited for a sophisticated cocktail party than a high-school football game.

Lainey had known this, of course, even as she had accepted a dare from her friends to wear it. She had worked to disguise the deep V neckline, front and back, with an embroidered white-and-black silky evening wrap that she had worn with movie-star grandeur. Until a strong gust of Texas wind had ripped it off her shoulders and under the wheels of the junior-class float behind her.

And there she had been, her décolletage exposed nearly to the waist for all the world to see. A terribly embarrassed Lainey had had no choice but to finish the parade, sans wrap. When the floats had reached the stadium, the entire Homecoming Court had been whisked off the backs of their borrowed convertibles and onto the football field for the crowning ceremony during the pre-game festivities. The principal, seeing Lainey being walked across the field by a gawking football player, had been apoplectic, as had many of the other parents, at the amount of cleavage exposed. Lainey's equally ostentatiously dressed mother was the only one who hadn't thought it a big deal.

"You got suspended for violating the school dress code, didn't you?" Lewis asked.

Lainey nodded, her humiliation complete. She hadn't thought about any of this since Chip Carrington had taken her under his wing and made sure she knew what suitable attire was. Ten years had passed and she'd never worn anything the slightest bit risqué since.

Brad threaded his way through the boxes and furniture stacked here and there, and made his way into the kitchen. He pulled a soda can out of the refrigerator, seemed to think about offering one to Lainey, then didn't. Probably, she figured, because he didn't want to give her an excuse to linger.

She watched as he popped the top.

Wordlessly, Lewis walked over to the fridge and got out two cans of blackberry-flavored soda. Lewis brought one back to Lainey, still talking to Brad over his shoulder. "The reason you probably don't recall any of this is that you had already graduated from Laramie High School two years before, and gone on to...well..."

"Flunk out of college," Brad said, finishing yet another sentence Lewis never should have started.

Visibly embarrassed, Lewis pushed his glasses up on his nose again. He shoved a hand through his spiky, light brown hair. "Yeah. Guess you two have that in common, since you both were always in trouble back then."

Only because she hadn't had the guidance she needed, Lainey thought resentfully. "Well, not anymore," she said firmly. "I have an eight-year-old son now." She was a pillar of the community in the Highland Park area of

Dallas. Or at least she had been, until she had agreed to drive out to the Lazy M Ranch, to see what she could find out for her friend, Sybil.

Brad and Lewis both glanced at her left hand, checking out the wedding and engagement rings she had recently stopped wearing. "I lost my husband, Chip Carrington, two years ago."

"Sorry to hear that," Lewis said.

Lainey nodded, even as she noticed the flash of sympathy in Brad's eyes that disappeared almost as quickly as it had appeared.

"That why you're looking for a job as a housekeeper?" Brad asked with a look of utter male supremacy.

Lainey didn't even want to consider what her blue-blooded in-laws, Bunny and Bart Carrington, would think about her taking a position as a domestic. Financially, she didn't need to, thanks to Chip's trust fund. Emotionally, intellectually...well, that was something else. She wasn't sure how much longer she could go on living a life that didn't even feel like her own. There were too many hours in a day, not nearly enough for her to do—and with her son, Petey, needing her less and less... Not that loneliness and boredom were any excuse for what Sybil had asked her to do, or offered in return, Lainey chided herself. Even if such action was the gateway to the career she had always yearned for and had never had the opportunity to go for. At least not yet.

Aware Brad was waiting for her answer, she said, "I'm not here to apply for a job."

Suspicion hardened the ruggedly handsome features on Brad's face. "Then what are you doing all the way out here?"

Sybil had been right—this man had turned into quite

a handful. "I was on my way back from Laramie and heard Lewis had bought a ranch out here. So I thought I would stop by and say hello."

"And yet you two were never friends," Brad stated suspiciously.

Lewis glowered at Brad, then turned back to Lainey. "I'm glad you stopped by and I'd be even happier if you'd agree to help me out here. Forget him." Lewis indicated Brad with a telling glare.

Brad stepped between Lainey and Lewis. He gave Lainey a slow, deliberate once-over that had Lainey's pulse racing before addressing Lewis again. "I'm merely pointing out I think it's mighty peculiar that Lainey here stopped by out of the blue. After what? Some ten years or so?"

"What are you insinuating?" Lainey asked coolly, her soda halfway to her mouth, not sure whether she was angrier with Brad or herself for getting into this predicament. Surely there was an easier story she could have started with to jump-start her career!

Brad flashed her a crocodile smile that didn't begin to reach his battle-hardened eyes. "That Lewis is not what you are in search of."

BRAD HAD BEEN HOPING—in direct contradiction to the knot in his gut—that Lainey Carrington's sudden appearance at the Lazy M had been innocent in nature. The look on her face, when he voiced his suspicion, told him it was anything but.

Yet another female he couldn't trust.

Why did that surprise him?

Was it her angelic beauty that had him wanting to believe he could trust her? Her fair, perfect skin and the ripe peach hue blushing across her high, elegant cheeks? The silky cap of neatly arranged honey-blond hair around her oval face? The straightness of her pert, slender nose and the determined set of her feminine chin? Or was it the enticing curve of her bow-shaped lips and the warmth in her long-lashed, forest green eyes? Brad couldn't say for sure what it was that attracted him to her so fiercely. All he knew was that he had been around beautiful women all his life and been chased by more than he could count, but none had stopped him dead in his tracks the way Lainey Wilson Carrington had. None had made his heart stall in his chest, to the point he felt frozen in time. Like this moment was something he would always remember.

Which was maybe why he should continue giving her a hard time. To keep the walls up and prevent himself from succumbing to such cornball sentiment. Brad gave her his kick-butt glare. "I'm still waiting for that explanation."

"Maybe you should back off," Lewis said, looking ready to rumble for the first time Brad could remember. That didn't surprise Brad—something about Lainey, some inherent sense of vulnerability, had brought out the knight in him, too, before he had come to his senses.

Lainey turned to Lewis with a reassuring smile. "I don't mind explaining what brought me here." She drew a breath and turned back to Brad. "I stopped by because I wanted to talk to Lewis about the computer-software video games his company puts out. I heard some of the companies used kids to focus-test new products before they are actually marketed and that Lewis had built a new facility in Laramie for his company, McCabe Computer Games. I wanted to know if it would be possible to have my eight-year-old son, Petey, participate in a trial of a new computer game. I thought it might be a fun thing for him to do this summer while school is out. But when I arrived and saw the chaos, and realized Lewis was in the process of interviewing household managers, I knew that it wasn't a good time to be stopping by after all."

Brad's gut told him that as truthful as Lainey was obviously trying to be, she was also leaving out some mighty important parts. The deliberate omissions were what concerned him most. "And you have no interest whatsoever in me," Brad surmised.

The color on her cheeks deepened self-consciously, even as her chin lifted a challenging notch. "Why on earth would I be interested in you?"

Brad answered her with a lazy shrug. "The same reason everyone else in America is. Because I am the villain du jour."

Lewis added, "You wouldn't believe how many people—folks the family hasn't heard from in years—have called up, wanting the inside scoop on what happened with Brad on that TV show."

Lainey flushed and didn't meet Brad's probing gaze. Another sign, Brad thought, that she was nosy as charged.

Lainey defended herself with an indignant toss of her head. "Believe me, I had no idea you were out here, Brad McCabe. Never mind in such a cantankerous mood!"

Not one to take an insult lying down, Brad narrowed his eyes at her. "What is that supposed to mean?" he demanded.

Lainey glared at him, sipped her drink, and didn't reply.

"I think that's pretty clear." Lewis stepped between Brad and Lainey. "She's telling you that you're rude."

Brad wasn't about to apologize for that, darn it all.

"I don't want company," he announced bluntly. Hers or anyone else's."

Lewis arched his brow. "Fine by me. Then leave. 'Cause I want to talk Lainey into helping me out here."

Lainey sighed and tore her gaze from Brad's. "I told you, Lewis. I am not in the market for a job as a housekeeper. I need to be at home with my son this summer."

Lewis was undaunted. "Your son could come to work with you. Test out new games here at the ranch and at my company's new facility in Laramie. He'd have a blast!"

It was all Brad could do not to groan as Lainey hesitated, clearly tempted.

"I'm not asking for much. I just need help getting settled," Lewis continued persuasively. "All of my stuff unpacked and organized, along with Brad's."

Lainey tilted her head. "Your moving company should have offered that service."

"They said they'd unpack it for an extra fee," Lewis explained. "They also wanted me to tell the workers where to put everything. I couldn't do that because I don't know where it goes. I don't have time to think about stuff like that. Never mind figure out how to get a kitchen put together and all that."

Lainey looked at Brad as if expecting him to help. "Don't look at me," he said gruffly. "I've got my hands full trying to get the stable, pastures and barns ready to go."

Sighing, Lainey turned back to Lewis. "Don't you have a girlfriend who could help you?"

Lewis flushed beet-red and shook his head.

"What about your little sister or your stepmom?" Lainey insisted.

"They both think he should be doing it himself, and they're right," Brad said. "It's best to be self-sufficient."

"Spoken like a die-hard bachelor," she muttered just loud enough for them both to hear.

"The truth is," Lewis said, "Laurel and Kate probably would help me out, but Brad doesn't want them around right now. 'Cause they ask too many questions. You know...about how he's *feeling* and stuff."

Brad rubbed his jaw. "I think Lainey Carrington can do without the play-by-play."

"Well, it's the truth!" Lewis countered.

Brad's temper flared. "Sometimes the truth does not need to be told!"

"Sounds like you have a pretty complicated situation," Lainey told Lewis sympathetically.

"So will you help me out?" he asked eagerly. "I'll give you one hundred dollars an hour to help me get organized. Because that's what professional organizers charge. At a few weeks—let's say three—that would be twelve thousand dollars, give or take. If you decide you want to cook for us, I'll pay you for that, too."

To Brad's chagrin, Lainey seemed intrigued.

Lainey blinked. "What were you planning to pay a housekeeper?"

Lewis shrugged. "If she lived in, fifty thousand, with free room and board. Like I said, I'm planning to make the guest house into the housekeeper's quarters."

Lainey cast a look in the direction Lewis was pointing. Her soft lips pursed thoughtfully. "How much room does it have?"

It was all Brad could do not to groan out loud as his

brilliant but clueless brother answered. "Eleven hundred square feet—a kitchen, living room, two bedrooms, one and a half baths."

"She already told you no," Brad interjected, knowing the last thing he needed was a nosy female underfoot. Lewis would be gone all day. It was Brad who would be here at the ranch, dealing with Lainey one-on-one, running into her every time he turned around!

Lainey scowled at Brad. "Excuse me. I don't believe either of us was talking to you."

Brad closed the distance between them, not stopping until they were nose to nose. "Well, I *am* talking to you. And let's be serious here." He paused to let his gaze drift over her in an insulting manner before returning to her green eyes. "A woman like you isn't cut out to live and work on a ranch." She was clearly pampered and city-chic. She even had pearls and earrings on. No woman on a ranch wore pearls and earrings and suede shoes with the heels and toes cut out. Plus, she had sensational legs! How was he supposed to get any work done when she was walking around in a skirt, showing them off?

Lainey folded her arms and leaned toward him. "Oh, for heaven's sake!" she scolded him fiercely, oblivious to the way her stance was lifting the soft curves of her breasts. "He isn't asking me to dig ditches!"

Brad frowned, refusing to let the alluring fragrance of her perfume distract him. With difficulty, he kept his gaze away from the fabric stretched across her breasts. He'd already had one glimpse of her shapely form, he didn't need another. "Those hands don't look like they've done any hard labor indoors, either," he continued.

Lainey released a long-suffering sigh. "I use hand cream," she explained as if to a moron, then turned back to Lewis, all smug self-confidence. "You say I can bring my son to work with me?"

This time Brad did groan out loud.

Lewis perked up. "Heck, yeah. You can even bunk in the guest cottage if you like. That way the two of you wouldn't have to drive back and forth to—"

"Highland Park."

Which was, Brad thought, one of the most exclusive neighborhoods in Dallas.

"This is the worst idea I've ever heard," Brad said, figuring the last thing they needed was some small-town-girl-turned-society-mama out here.

Lainey and Lewis turned to Brad. "No one asked you!" they declared in unison.

Lainey said to Lewis, "You understand it would only be for a few weeks?"

Lewis grinned, looking ridiculously slaphappy. "Unless I can talk you and your son into staying on permanently."

"You don't even know if she can cook!" Brad practically shouted.

Lewis shrugged. "If she doesn't, she can learn. Can't you, Lainey?"

Lainey took a long drink of her soda, then set the can down. "I certainly could. You've got a deal, Lewis. In the meantime, I've got to get back to Highland Park."

Which still wasn't saying if she did or did not know how to cook, Brad thought. Which in his view was an absolute necessity, since it was a twenty-minute drive to the nearest restaurant and the appeal of frozen dinners, sandwiches and prepackaged food—the only stuff he and his brother were capable of fixing—was already wearing mighty thin.

"But you'll be back?" Lewis asked anxiously.

"Oh, yes. Tomorrow." Lainey stared at Brad, all stubborn defiance. "First thing."

CHAPTER TWO

"No."

"Excuse me?" Lainey stared at her sister-in-law, sure she hadn't heard right.

Bunny Carrington touched a hand to the glossy black chignon at her nape. "Bart and I cannot let you take Petey out to some godforsaken ranch for the next few weeks."

Bart, Bunny's henpecked attorney-husband, hadn't said anything thus far. But that wasn't surprising to Lainey. According to Lainey's late husband, Bart had traded away his say in most everything when he agreed to marry Bunny and take her last name of Carrington, instead of have her take his.

Like Lainey, Bart's roots were decidedly blue-collar. In marrying Bunny, he had married up. And now, twenty years and a pair of twin girls later, he was still letting Bunny run the show.

Lainey sat down on the edge of the plush, ultra-suede sofa in Bunny and Bart's family room. Through the plate-glass windows, she could see Petey romping in the lagoon-shaped pool with his eighteen-year-old cousins, Becca and Bonnie. Relieved he was not privy to any of this, Lainey stated calmly, "I think you misunderstood me. I wasn't asking your permission." Any more than she was asking their permission to work as a reporter. "I just wanted you to know where you could contact us."

Bunny glanced at Bart. He looked troubled, too, but not necessarily in agreement with his wife. Obviously, Bunny wanted Bart to say something.

Finally, the tall gangly man with the perpetually defeated expression on his face, cleared his throat. "I think what Bunny is trying to say here is that some changes may need to be made."

A chill ran down Lainey's spine. No one had to remind her that thanks to the terms of the trust Chip had set up for Petey, which Bunny oversaw, all of Lainey's finances were controlled by her sister-in-law. Which was another reason why it was so important she start making some money of her own—soon. "What kind of changes?" Lainey asked suspiciously.

"Bunny thinks that it's impractical for you to be incurring such steep mortgage payments every month."

It hadn't been Lainey's idea to have a ridiculously high mortgage payment every month. Chip was the one who had insisted they purchase a home in Highland Park. Lainey began to relax, ever so slightly. "I'm glad you brought this up," she said, relieved. "I've been wanting to sell the house. It is much too big for just Petey and me."

Not only was it an unnecessary expense, but also the home had too many memories of her and Chip. Lainey was finding it impossible to move on, when everywhere she went she saw and felt her late husband's presence. Lainey had loved her husband terribly. She saw Chip's good qualities in Petey every day. But now that she and Petey had gone through the mourning process, it was time to build a new life.

Lainey smiled at her in-laws. "Petey and I would be happy with something much smaller and less expensive.

Which is why I've been thinking about relocating back to my hometown of Laramie, Texas."

Lainey had no family ties there any longer, since both her parents had passed on years ago, but Laramie was still as friendly and laid-back as ever. When she had driven out there earlier this morning, she had been surprised to discover how much it had felt like home.

Bunny and Bart regarded each other tensely.

"You misunderstand us," Bunny said finally. "Bart and I want you and Petey to move in here with us."

BRAD WAS ON HIS WAY OUT to the barn to begin unloading bundles of PVC pipe from his pickup when a familiar dark green SUV turned into the lane leading to the Lazy M ranch house. The vehicle zipped toward the parking area and stopped just short of the guest house. Seconds later, Lainey Carrington was stepping out of the driver's side.

She was wearing an open-necked hot-pink silk shirt with three-quarter sleeves, a trim black skirt that failed to reach her knees, and open-toed sandals that, like the rest of her outfit, were hardly suited for life on a working cattle ranch. Despite the eye-catching hue of her blouse, her outfit was conservative enough to be worn in a corporate setting. The way it hugged her slender curves was another matter indeed.... Just looking at her made Brad's mouth water.

The knowledge of his own desire made him frown. He had promised himself at the end of the TV show that he was swearing off all women for at least a year. It hadn't been a problem—until now. Unbeknownst to the producers who had hired him for *Bachelor Bliss*, his rep as a bed-hopping ladies' man was a hell of a lot more fiction than fact.

She went up to the ranch house door, rang the bell, pressed it again and again. Finally, she came back down the steps and looked toward the barn, where he was busy unloading the back of his pickup truck.

She got back in her vehicle, drove the short distance to where he was, and got out of her SUV again.

Apparently remembering all too well the way they had parted, Lainey gave Brad a cool glance. "Lewis around?" she asked, stepping nearer in a drift of remarkably alluring perfume.

"Nope." Brad lifted one bundle onto his shoulder, then another.

She marched closer yet, her sexy shoes tapping across the blacktopped ranch driveway. She seemed to be spoiling for a fight. Although, not necessarily with him, Brad noted.

"Care to elaborate?" Lainey asked tightly.

"Nope." Carrying the bundles of pipe, Brad headed for the newly painted beige barn.

She skipped to keep up with his long strides. "Don't be such a—"

Curious as to what she would call him, Brad prompted, "What?"

"Donkey's rear end!"

He grinned. Somehow, he hadn't seen her cussing. At least not out loud. Not that her verbal imagery hadn't done the trick in getting her message across.

Lainey danced across his path, forcing him to detour around her. "Just tell me where he is and I'll leave you alone," she said.

Grimacing, Brad set the bundles down on the cement floor of the barn with a loud *clank*. Then he straightened to face her. "He went to Laramie, to work at his facility there."

Her expression fell and she took a step back. Sunlight poured down from the blue Texas sky, illuminating the honey-gold strands of her hair. "How long is he going to be gone?" she asked.

Brad shrugged, noting the flush of color across her cheeks, the mist of perspiration at her temples. "You'd have to ask Lewis, but he usually puts in a twelve-hour day, if not more." So did Brad.

Frustrated, Lainey raked her teeth across her lower lip. "I really need him here, to tell me where he wants me to get started."

Determined to be as ornery as possible, in hopes she would get ticked off and leave, Brad tipped back the brim of his hat and regarded her with an indifferent gaze. "You'll have to take that up with him."

To his disappointment, Lainey looked undeterred. "I guess I could go ahead and move my stuff into the guest house."

Brad looked back at the SUV. The rear seat was down and it looked packed to the gills with stuff. Even the front passenger seat was heaped with belongings. Brad frowned. "Where's your son?" Not that it mattered to him, but the other day, Lainey had sounded like her son Petey was a very important part of her life.

"Obviously, he's not with me today."

She didn't look happy about that. Which made Brad ask before he could stop himself, "Everything okay?"

Lainey folded her arms in front of her. "You really care?" she asked.

He shouldn't, Brad knew. Not if he was going to keep his distance from the lovely blonde.

"That's what I thought."

Suddenly, she looked near tears. Brad, who had never been much good in the comforting-others department, had an insane urge to take her in his arms. Instead, he remarked, even more matter-of-factly, "If you want to go around looking like you lost your best friend, that's your business."

Lainey swallowed hard, her eyes moistening. "How about if I go around looking like I am losing my only child, then?"

"What are you talking about?"

"Nothing." Lainey sighed and shoved her hands through her hair. "It's none of your business anyway."

"True enough." Brad was silent. What was going on here? It wasn't like him to get involved in anyone else's private business. He had enough trouble managing his own. "Still, if you want to talk..." he found himself saying.

Lainey's voice grew turbulent. "He's at the theme parks in central Florida with his two cousins, aunt and uncle."

"Why didn't you go?"

"Because I wasn't invited."

Ouch. "That was rude."

Lainey's slender shoulders stiffened. "I'm sure Bart and Bunny didn't mean anything by it. They thought I needed some time to myself."

She didn't *look* like she needed time to herself. Brad strode back to the pickup for another load. "When will they be back?"

Lainey remained in the shade of the barn. "The end of the week, which will give me enough time to get settled in and have everything ready for Petey here—so it's probably for the best, anyway."

She didn't look as if she believed that, Brad noted. Not that it was any of his affair.

"Is the guest house unlocked?" she asked.

Brad dropped the second load of pipe next to the first, then fished in his pocket for the key. He dug it out and handed it over, knowing the reason why Lewis had made himself scarce when Lainey would be moving in. Not that it was up to Brad to deliver the bad news to Lainey. It was her fault. She should have investigated further before taking the short-term job with his brother. "Lewis asked me to give this one to you."

"Thanks."

Years of ingrained training had Brad asking, albeit reluctantly, "Need any help unloading your SUV?"

"Nope." She swung away from him, and walked to her vehicle, spectacular legs flashing in the bright June sunlight. As he watched her go, Brad couldn't help but notice she looked more like a well-to-do suburbanite, out for a day of shopping, than a housekeeper or—what was it Lewis had called it—personal organizer?—about to embark on the massive task of making the Lazy M ranch house livable.

Telling himself to quit thinking about her and concentrate on the installation ahead, he continued unloading his pickup, laying pipe, sprinkler heads, fans and linear heat sensors on the cement floor of the freshly scrubbed-out barn. He was nearly done when he heard the first scream. Shrill and terrified sounding, it split the air with the intensity of an air-raid siren.

"What the…?" Brad dropped the box in his hand.

Another scream pierced the air, louder and longer than the last.

He took off at a run.

LAINEY WAS STILL SCREAMING when Brad charged through the open front door and found her crouched, still shaking and scared, atop the kitchen counter.

His expression went from panicked to amused in an instant.

"Look, I know the place is a mess, and you must feel frustrated as hell, but don't you think you're overdoing the drama just a tad?"

Lainey wished that were the case. Not that Brad didn't have a point. Perhaps she shouldn't have yelled like a banshee when she discovered the state of her quarters for the next few weeks.

Unbelievably, the guest cottage was in even worse shape than the Lazy M ranch house. Instead of being crowded with boxes, though, it was heaped with old furniture of various kinds and all sorts of odds and ends. In short, it looked the way many people's attics looked after being neglected a good ten, twenty or thirty years. But that wasn't why she'd been yelling her head off for the past two minutes.

"Follow your nose, cowboy!" She pointed to the source of the foul odor that had prompted her to head for the kitchen in the first place. "And get those...*creatures* out of here!"

"Huh?" His expression perplexed, Brad swaggered through the maze of belongings and stared down at the five exceedingly ugly creatures on the other side of the counter. "Armadillos?"

"Nine-banded armadillos." Lainey shuddered, not about to admit how glad she had been to see Brad charging to her rescue. Not that she considered herself a damsel in distress, of course. "A whole family of them."

Brad braced his hands on his waist. "I can see that."

"I hope that's all of them, anyway!" Lainey shuddered again. She didn't know what she would do if she found other creatures in the guest house, as well. The four baby armadillos, weighing about five or six pounds each, were backed into the corner of the U-shaped kitchen, toward the sink. The mama—a behemoth the size of a terrier and a lot less friendly—was guarding the only way out.

Brad flashed her a bad-boy smile that was enough to make her stomach drop. "It is."

"How do you know? You just got here!" She was the one who had been crouching uncomfortably on the kitchen countertop, her skirt hiked up around her thighs, for what seemed like an eternity as she screamed for help.

Brad's glance slid from the floor, to her legs, and then to her face. "Because armadillos always have four identical offspring—every time," he told her in a husky voice that soon had her tingling all over. "They all come from the same egg, hence they are the same sex."

She couldn't believe she was talking reproduction with one of the sexiest bachelors alive. "Well then, let's hope Papa Armadillo isn't around here somewhere, too," she declared.

He shrugged his broad shoulders, unconcerned. "Oh, they never hang around for the birth. He probably took off months ago, shortly after, uh, getting her in the family way."

She felt herself flush. "Do we really need to be talking about the mating habits of armadillos right now?" she muttered, trying to no avail to bring the hem of her skirt down, just a little. Unfortunately, the fabric was too tight and she lacked maneuvering room.

"You brought it up. What did you do to rile Big Mama up, anyway?"

Telling herself Brad's scrutiny was not sexual in

nature, Lainey explained, "I walked in and almost tripped over one of her babies. Next thing I knew, I was surrounded by scurrying...screeching...beasts." She shuddered again, recalling the panic that had ensued.

He reached over and gave her bare knee a warm, companionable squeeze. "Given the way you were screaming and leaped up here, they probably think the same thing about you."

Trying not to think about the way her skin was tingling from just that brief casual contact, Lainey frowned at him. "Very funny."

He folded his arms in front of him. "I suppose you want me to remove them."

Lainey rolled her eyes. He was enjoying her discomfiture and dragging this out on purpose! "Duh."

"Okay." Brad pivoted on his heel. "I'll be right back."

"Wait!" She reached out for his shirt, missed. "You can't leave me here!"

But of course he already had.

She looked back at the armadillos nervously. She hadn't seen one of them since she was a kid and living in rural Laramie. And she'd never viewed one this close. The mother had a pointed face and large pointy ears that stuck straight up. A hard brown shield covered the mama's shoulders, another her rump. Between the two were nine bands, hence the name. Her tail was long and tapering, sort of like a rat's tail, only this was completely covered with disgustingly bony rings. She had scattered yellowish hairs across her body, particularly around her face, and wicked-looking claws on all four of her feet. Lainey had no doubt Big Mama would fight to the death to protect her young—Lainey would, too.

She did not want to tangle with the animal.

What seemed like an eternity later, but was really only a couple of minutes, Brad strode back in, carrying a large metal animal cage and wearing heavy-duty elbow-length leather ranch gloves. "Just so you know," he warned her, eyes twinkling, "this probably isn't going to be pretty. Or quiet."

Unsure whether it was excitement or annoyance speeding up her heartbeat, Lainey said in a strangled voice, "Just get them out of here!"

Brad moved a couple of boxes to block any exit attempt the five armadillos might make, then waded into the kitchen, trap in hand. When the baby armadillos scattered, Big Mama ambled away from Brad and then broke out into an awkward run, slamming into the side of one cupboard, then another. For a while it was kind of like trying to catch a greased pig. As soon as Brad would get near Big Mama, she would head off in the other direction. Unperturbed, Brad stalked the mother armadillo calmly, until he finally had Big Mama cornered, then reached down and grabbed her swiftly by the base of the tail. Big Mama squawked in terror and spun wildly, but Brad held on and somehow managed to drop her into the metal trap and shut it again without getting scratched or bit. The other four babies were caught in the same manner. Once all five were in the trap, Brad locked the lid.

Lainey breathed a huge sigh of relief. She hadn't realized until that moment how glad she was to have Brad there, saving the day. "Now what?" she demanded.

"Depends." Brad gave her an assessing look. "You like armadillo meat?"

"You're kidding."

The corners of Brad's lips twitched as he said drolly,

"Guess that's a no." Brad picked up the cage of animals and swaggered for the door.

"Tell me what you're going to do with them!" Lainey called after him, belatedly feeling just a tad sorry for the cornered creatures. She was sure, after thinking about it a moment, that they hadn't meant to intrude or scare her to death.

"You want to know?" Brad's dark brown eyes held a dare. "Come along and see!"

LAINEY THOUGHT ABOUT IT for a minute, then declined his invitation with a shake of her head. Accepting dares was what had always gotten her into trouble. It was enough of a risk just accepting a job here without disclosing what she hoped to gain for herself, and do for Brad in the end. "Thanks, anyway," she said.

"Suit yourself." He headed amiably out the door.

Lainey heard the sound of metal on metal as he put the cage into the back of his pickup, then he climbed behind the wheel and drove off.

When she was sure he and the "uninvited guests" were gone, she climbed down from her perch and started to explore. But no sooner had she cleared the kitchen than a sound near the door had her spooked again… and climbing right back up onto the kitchen counter. Surely Brad McCabe wouldn't be gone that long, she told herself.

Fifteen long minutes later, he returned. He pushed back the brim of his Stetson. "Any particular reason you're still sitting up there?" he asked with a curious lift of his brow.

Lainey was beginning to feel pretty darn foolish, but better safe than sorry…. "I thought I heard something over there."

Brad frowned. He seemed to know instinctively that she wasn't joking around. "Where?"

Lainey pointed toward the living room window she had opened soon after she arrived. She could handle just about anything except wild animals. Those scared the heck out of her.

Looking more bored than scared, Brad strode over to investigate. He reached the antique sideboard that blocked Lainey's view, stopped dead in his tracks. "Well, I see the problem," he said eventually, backing up slightly and rubbing his chin.

"What is it?" she demanded, feeling even more alarmed.

He leaned over. When he straightened he held a half-burned pillar candle in his hand. "What do you think? Look dangerous to you?"

Lainey regarded Brad skeptically, aware her knees were still shaking a little. "That's all it was?"

He glanced around, looking puzzled. "I don't see anything else over here. This, however, was on the floor, lying on its side."

"Why would it just fall off like that?" she asked suspiciously.

"The wind?" He set the candle on top of the sideboard and lazily made his way toward her.

Lainey's heartbeat kicked up a notch. "You're sure there are no more wild animals in here?"

"Well, I don't see or smell anything else," Brad drawled as he walked through the combination living room and dining room, past the kitchen and half bath, and through the back hall, where the two bedrooms and full bath were located. He returned to stand in front of her, grinning wickedly. "Now, are you going to continue sitting up there or are you going to get down so we both can get back to work?"

Swallowing hard around the sudden dryness in her throat, Lainey moved toward the edge of the counter. "First tell me what you did with the party of five," she countered curiously.

"I drove them to a distant pasture and turned them loose next to a stream."

Sounded good to her. "Are they going to come back?" she asked nervously.

He taunted her with an impudent smile. "After the way you were carrying on?"

She tossed her hair—something she hadn't done since high school. Maybe college. "I'm serious."

"It's doubtful." He regarded her, eyes alight with interest. "Since there are numerous places for them to burrow and there's plenty for them to eat where I let 'em loose."

Lainey scooted to the end of the counter. "What do they eat?"

"Grubs, earthworms, insects, sometimes berries and bird eggs. Not that I saw any bird's nests in the area."

Lainey realized there was no way to get down off the counter gracefully. She fervently hoped Brad would realize that and turn away—but he didn't. "How did the armadillos get in here in the first place?" she asked, carefully swinging her legs over the side of the counter.

Brad watched as her skirt slid higher than she would have liked.

Wordlessly, he reached for her. Hands on her waist, he lifted her down to the floor. He held on to her just long enough to steady her and make sure she had her balance. That was all it took for Lainey to feel a surge of desire more potent than anything she had ever felt.

She sucked in her breath, stepped back.

He stepped back, too, looking just as stung, as they struggled to claim the threads of the conversation.

"We were talking about how they got in here," Lainey prodded, trying to appear cool.

"Beats the heck out of me." He shrugged, the powerful muscles in his shoulders straining against the fabric of his shirt. "I didn't see any holes in the wall. The guest house sits on a cement slab, so they certainly didn't burrow through that."

Lainey bit her lip as she noticed the flush of sun on his face. And something else…something interesting… in his eyes. "And they're too big to come up through the plumbing," she said.

Clearly enjoying toying with her, he looked her over from head to toe. "They don't like water anyway."

So full of facts, he was practically an encyclopedia of Texas life. "So how *did* they get in here?" Lainey challenged. If he knew so much, he must know that.

"Must have walked in last night."

Lainey regarded Brad skeptically.

Reluctantly, he explained. "The place had a musty smell, so Lewis propped open both doors and a few windows to get a nice cross-ventilation going. It was after dark, and armadillos are generally nocturnal this time of year. Big Mama probably thought this looked like a good shelter, or maybe she was just foraging for food with her babies and got shut in here when Lewis closed up."

Lainey walked over to survey the place where the candle had fallen. She did not appreciate having the wits scared out of her for the second time that afternoon.

How was she ever going to sleep in here tonight? "Well, don't open up the place to whatever might inadvertently wander in here again," she warned him haughtily.

Brad angled a thumb at his chest. "I didn't do it the first time."

Lainey swung around to face him, bumping her face on his shoulder in the process. "You weren't concerned about the musty smell?"

Once again, Brad put out a hand to steady her. "Why should I be when my brother already was?" he asked, his capable fingers radiating warmth through her shirt to her skin. "Besides, *I* didn't hire you to help us get organized."

"And why is that?" Lainey demanded tartly.

"I don't see any sense in paying someone for something you can do yourself."

Lainey pushed away the ridiculously romantic fantasies his nearness was evoking. "Except you two *haven't* done it yourselves," she pointed out.

"So?" he shot back. "We would have gotten around to it eventually."

She smirked, not about to let him get away with that whopper. "How long have you been living out here?" she asked.

He stepped toward her. "We closed on the property two weeks ago."

She felt a completely uncalled-for fluttering in her middle. "And continued to live in this chaos?"

He poked the brim of his cowboy hat up with maddening nonchalance. "Why not? Doesn't bother me any more than armadillos, field mice, snakes and porcupines do." He lifted a brow. "Course if *you're* not comfortable coming face-to-face with wild animals, *you* could always head on back to Dallas."

That sounded like a dare. Lainey stepped toward him this time, not caring that her move left them mere inches apart. "Excuse me?" She angled her head up at him.

"This is a ranch, you know." He leaned toward her ear and whispered conspiratorially, "Animals of all sorts are supposed to be all over the place."

It was the stalking males that worried Lainey.

"I know where I am, thank you very much!" Not that she would ever let herself fall prey to someone as demonstrably fickle as Brad McCabe. Even if she had always wondered just how ardently he could kiss….

"Good." He paused, gave her a self-assured, faintly baiting look. "'Cause for a moment there, you bein' so surprised and all, I was beginning to wonder just how much you remembered about life out in rural Texas."

"Enough," she replied sweetly, "to know a great big pile of horse bucky when I see or hear it."

"Excuse me?" He mocked her earlier reprimand to a tee.

Finally, for Lainey, everything fell into place. "I know what you've done here, Brad McCabe. And I am not amused," she told him heatedly. "Not in the least!"

CHAPTER THREE

WELL, THAT WAS GOOD, Brad thought with no small trace of irony, because he sure as heck didn't have a clue what she was talking about.

"You planted those armadillos in here to chase me away!" Lainey declared with an indignant toss of her head.

"Now why would I go and do a darn fool thing like that?" he demanded right back, furious at being once again erroneously suspected of being the bad guy, and at the same time amused because she was so far off track in her assumption.

Lainey ran a hand through her tousled blond hair, pushing it off her face. "You made it abundantly clear yesterday afternoon that you did not want me here!"

Brad adapted a no-nonsense stance, legs braced apart, arms folded in front of him. He figured he would let her make a fool of herself first, then set her straight. "So?"

Lainey's green eyes glimmered hotly. "So I accepted Lewis's job offer anyway."

Brad released an exasperated breath. "An action I am sure you will quickly come to regret, if you haven't done so already."

"Well, these silly little hijinks of yours are not going to work!" She stomped closer yet.

Brad hooked his thumbs through the belt loops on

either side of his fly and rocked back on his heels. "Sure about that?"

"I have just as much right to work on this ranch as anyone else."

"Maybe so. But can you handle it?" Brad stepped closer, purposefully invading her space, not stopping until he had backed her against the sideboard in the center of the room. "Can you handle me?" Not sure why he had started this, except somebody had to set her straight, Brad flattened a hand on either side of her, caging her between his arms, and leaned in close. "You know my rep." He let his glance drift lazily over her softly parted lips before returning, ever so deliberately, to her eyes. "I'm bad news with all the ladies."

To Brad's surprise and grudging respect, Lainey inhaled deeply and stoically stood her ground. "A fact that makes no difference whatsoever to me, since I am a widow."

And thereby off the market—perhaps forever—in her estimation. Not in Brad's. Lainey may well have felt she had already been there, done that, but he hadn't. And being around Lainey, even for a short period of time, had him thinking all sorts of crazy things. Like what it would be like to have her in his bed. Or his life. And not as a thorn in his side. But as a lover, confidante, friend.

Not that this was even a possibility, he reminded himself sternly.

He was in the business of getting her out of here as soon as possible. Before he got in over his head and she got hurt.

"Well, yee-haw."

She lifted a brow in wordless inquiry, her cheeks turning an even deeper pink.

He smirked in a way meant to infuriate. "If memory serves, a lot of young widows I've come across in this town have been hot to trot." And he was reputed to be randy as could be. If that combination didn't send her running…and get her safely and quickly off the Lazy M Ranch…he wasn't sure what would.

Unfortunately, Lainey wasn't taking his hint.

She lifted her chin, ice in her smile. "I am not in the least bit sex-starved, I assure you, Brad McCabe."

He felt a stab of jealousy as unexpected as it was intense. He hadn't heard anything about Lainey having a boyfriend. Nor had she mentioned that as a potential problem yesterday when Lewis had been talking to her about moving to the ranch for a couple of weeks—or longer. Surely if there was a man in Lainey's life important enough for her to bed, she would have wanted to run the possibility of her moving out here with "the most loathed bachelor in America" with her beloved, if only as a courtesy. Or, at the very least, asked Lewis if it would be all right if she had "visitors"—meaning a territory-staking male friend—at the ranch to see her while she was here. Instead, the only person she had seemed concerned enough about to mention was her eight-year-old son. Who was, coincidentally, also the person in her life most likely to prevent her from kicking up her heels and having a little fun.

Somehow, looking at the stiff way in which she was holding herself, and the defenses that were in high gear, Brad didn't think Lainey had been kissed in a good long while. Too long, actually.

"Yeah?" He leaned in even closer and lowered his mouth to hers, prepared to have a little fun. "Well, let's just put that declaration to the test."

Lainey hadn't thought Brad was really going to kiss

her. She'd thought he was only trying to scare her off the ranch, and out of his way, by pretending to put the moves on her. But there was nothing feigned about the feel of his lips pressing against hers. Nothing fabricated about her reaction to the imprint of his tall, strong body pressed warmly against hers.

She hadn't felt this alive, this much a woman, since… well, she couldn't remember when. And though she repeatedly told herself she really had to stop this now, with every shift in pressure of his warm wonderful lips, every stroke and thrust and parry of his tongue, she felt herself sliding deeper and deeper into the mystery that was him. And heaven only knows what might have happened next, had she not heard a discreet feminine exclamation of dismay, and a throat clearing—loudly—behind them.

Lainey and Brad broke apart at the same time, and turned in the direction of the sound. Right away, Lainey recognized Brad's uncle, Travis McCabe, and his wife, Annie. The handsome couple had both owned ranches before they married some fifteen years ago—since then, the Rocking M Cattle Ranch and the Triple Diamond had been combined.

"Lainey! I don't know if you remember me," Annie Pierce McCabe said, stepping forward, looking much younger than her forty-five years.

They had never been friends—there was too much of an age difference—but Lainey had admired the moxie Annie had shown, creating a new life for herself and her three sons after her divorce. "Of course I do." Lainey accepted the slender, red-haired woman's welcome. Annie was one of Lainey's role models, and one of the reasons why Lainey had been thinking about moving back to Laramie permanently, once her job at the Lazy M was done. "I've been using your barbecue sauce since it first came out." Lainey smiled.

"She's famous for it, all right." Looking fit and strong as ever, Travis wrapped a hand affectionately around his diminutive wife's shoulder, then greeted Lainey, too.

"Travis...Annie." Brad nodded at them both.

"Brad." Travis glared at Brad in scolding fashion even as he shook Brad's hand.

"We came to help!" Annie said, in an effort to let them both off the hook.

But Lainey knew that unless they addressed the ardent clinch that Annie and Travis had just witnessed, it would be like trying to ignore the elephant in the middle of the room.

She wrinkled her nose, pretending to misunderstand, while at the same time transferring her embarrassment—and the blame for the romantic fiasco—squarely where it belonged, onto Brad McCabe's handsome shoulders. "You knew Brad would be putting the moves on me?" Lainey asked their company innocently.

Brad gave Lainey a surly look that let her know he had expected her to get him back; he just hadn't known—until this moment—how she was going to do it. "Hey," he chided amiably, clapping a calloused hand across his broad chest. "I saved your life, sweetheart!"

Sweetheart. Why did that sound so good coming from those lips, even if it was in sarcasm, and not a true endearment? Determined to demonstrate she was not intimidated by Brad McCabe, no matter what he dished out, she stood her ground. "I hardly think that's the case, since those armadillos were not going to bite me."

Brad chuckled. "You never would have known that by the way you were screaming," he countered.

Lewis came in behind them, as eclectically dressed as always. "What did I miss?" he demanded, looking about as unsuited for ranch life as was possible.

"Nothing," Brad and Lainey said in unison, while Annie and Travis shook their heads and stifled grins.

Lewis frowned. "Doesn't look like nothing," he murmured.

"Your brother was harassing her," Travis explained helpfully.

"I thought I told you not to do that!" Lewis reprimanded Brad.

And just that quickly, the balance of power in the room shifted. Lewis hadn't meant to remind Brad that Lewis, not Brad, actually owned the Lazy M.

"Right. *Boss*." Brad slapped his cowboy hat back on his head and stomped out. Travis shot a look at his wife, and then followed Brad.

"I—I didn't mean—" Lewis stammered, upset.

"I know you didn't and so does he," Annie said gently, before turning back to Lainey. "You remember my three older sons?"

"The triplets?"

"Teddy, Tyler and Trevor are twenty now. They're all working the ranch for the summer."

Lainey could hardly believe it. "They're in college now?"

"Yes. Tyler's planning to be a vet, Trevor a cattle rancher, and Teddy wants to breed horses. They all just finished their sophomore year at Texas A&M. They're on their way over. They're going to help us move furniture and try to make the guest house livable for you and Petey. Speaking of which, where is your son?"

Regret swept through Lainey. "Petey is on a trip with his relatives. He'll be joining me this weekend."

"Oh. Our two youngest boys will be so disappointed. Kurt is nine and Kyle is eight and they were so excited to hear there's going to be another guy roughly their own age, on the next ranch over."

Two boys came in. They were followed by three strapping young men who did indeed look all grown up. All five had rusty red hair and freckles, just like their mother. "They're bein' strict with us!" the taller boy, soon introduced as Kurt, said.

"Yeah, and that is not their job," his slightly smaller brother Kyle pointed out. "It's yours and Daddy's."

"They were headed for mischief," Teddy told his mother.

"If anyone would know it when we see it, it'd be us," Trevor grinned.

Tyler's eyes twinkled even as he claimed, "We weren't that bad."

Lewis and Annie groaned as Brad and Travis came back in. Lainey had been just a teenager when Annie and Travis's romance began, but even she remembered the triplets—who had been four at the time—had caused lots of havoc in the months and weeks before, during and after Annie and Travis had gotten together.

"Really?" Travis countered, his eyes twinkling, too. "Because I seem to remember, among other things, some 'flying' eggs…"

A chuckle resounded through the group at the memory. "All right, all right, maybe we were that mischievous, but we've grown up okay," Tyler claimed.

That they had, Lainey noted admiringly. It was clear all five of the brothers loved one another dearly. She had so wanted for Petey to experience the love and camaraderie of siblings, too. Instead, he was growing up an only child, just the way she had….

But there was no more time to think about that, because Annie had had enough of standing around. She clapped her hands together, looking every bit as anxious to get on with the "organizing" task ahead as Lainey was. "Okay, guys," Annie told the assembled crew, "now that we've got all of you here to do the heavy lifting, let's get busy and start moving this furniture where Lainey thinks it should go…."

"LET ME GET THIS STRAIGHT," Brad said early the next morning when Lainey came face-to-face with him and his brother in the Lazy M ranch house kitchen. "It's only your second day on the job and you already want time off?"

Lainey ignored Brad—who looked unbearably attractive in jeans, boots and an old chambray shirt—and spoke directly to her real boss, or at least the only person she planned to take any orders from. "I wouldn't ask if an old friend of mine weren't in Dallas today, on business." *With me.* "I haven't seen Sybil in a couple of years and she has enough time to have lunch with me. I'd really like to go."

Clearly aware he was annoying her, Brad looked her over, taking in the fit of her pale yellow, linen sheath dress, matching cardigan and shoes, before returning ever so slowly to her face. "Must be nice to be a dilettante," Brad mumbled under his breath, just loud enough for Lainey to hear.

"Better than a smart-mouth any day of the week," she muttered right back.

Lewis stepped between them. He looked annoyed at Brad, too. "Will you leave her alone before she quits on us?" Lewis demanded.

"So what?" Brad finished the second half of his

orange juice in a single gulp. He set the glass down on the counter with a *thud*, as determined to rile Lainey as ever. He shrugged indifferently. "Then we'll simply hire someone else who will work more than one day in a row."

"Keep it up," Lainey told Brad, walking around Lewis to confront him, "and I'll be tempted to kick you in the shin." It would serve him right for kissing her the way he had, when she knew he hadn't meant it. And she, unfortunately for her, had.

"Not going to hurt much with those fancy sandals you're wearing," he said in a tone sexy enough to make her want to kiss him all over again. "And speaking of footwear..." He pretended to study her carefully. "This being a ranch—with free-roaming wildlife and all—"

Oh, brother. Like she was going to fall for that again. "Not to mention one very big and ornery beast," Lainey added sweetly, hoping to shame him into behaving.

"—don't you think it's time for you to start dressing a little more practically?"

Lainey had been thinking about it—until he mentioned it, anyway. Clothes that were just right in Dallas seemed a little too fancy here. Lainey had been dressing the way Chip had expected her to for so long, she had no idea how she would dress if it were up to her. Deciding she did not like the presumption in Brad's eyes, she said, "I suppose you'd like to see me in boots and jeans?" The question was, what would she like to see herself in?

"Depends on how much leg you intend to keep flashing. Yesterday, for instance, when you were climbing up on that kitchen counter, I could see..."

The heat of a self-conscious blush warming her face, Lainey headed for the door before she was tempted to smack Brad McCabe's ornery face. She couldn't believe he had kissed her, and she had kissed him back. What in the world had she been thinking, even letting him come to her rescue?

"When are you coming back?" Lewis asked hopefully, as he followed her to the back porch.

Lainey turned around and smiled at Lewis. He at least was truly one of the nicest guys she had ever met. "Later tonight. And don't worry. Beast or no—" she glared over Lewis's shoulder, at Brad "—I'll be here working the rest of the week."

LAINEY JOINED HER OLD FRIEND Sybil for lunch at The Mansion on Turtle Creek, and typically Sybil got right to the point. "Were you able to find out where Brad McCabe is right now?" she asked as soon as their iced teas had been served.

Lainey knew it would serve the Texas cowboy right if she were to put the most tenacious magazine editor in the country on his tail, but Lainey couldn't do it. And not just because of the way Annie and Travis's crew—and Brad and Lewis, too—had pitched in to help her begin the task of organizing the Lazy M Ranch and guest houses the previous afternoon.

Pure and simple, ratting out Brad would be the wrong thing to do. Even if doing so would help her old friend and former college roommate. "I have to tell you, Sybil, from what I learned, Brad McCabe is in no mood to be interviewed."

"So?" Sybil ran a hand through her short jet-black curls. "Be persuasive. Change his mind. You're a pretty single woman. He's supposed to love pretty single women."

One would certainly think so, given the way Brad had been portrayed on the reality TV show. "Even if I were able to get an interview with him—a feat which it is doubtful I'll be able to perform—I can almost guarantee you that he wouldn't answer a single question about what happened on *Bachelor Bliss*. Nor is he likely to agree to be photographed for *Personalities Magazine*."

Sybil frowned, disappointed but not defeated. She leaned across the table, looking as lithe and trendy as ever in her designer pantsuit. "I need that cover story, 'America's Most Loathed Bachelor,' if I am going to prove myself worthy of the editor-in-chief position."

Lainey knew Sybil was in hot competition with another senior editor for the post. The July first edition of the bimonthly celebrity magazine was Sybil's chance to prove herself. Her competition was working on the June fifteenth edition. Whoever had the highest sales would win the post. Lainey wanted Sybil to win, but she did not want to sacrifice the privacy of her family and friends to make it happen.

Even though, Lainey added sarcastically to herself, it would almost serve Brad right if she did expose his whereabouts. Where had he gotten off thinking he could haul her into his arms and kiss her as if there were no tomorrow? She wasn't one of the babes who had lined up to win his heart on the show!

"His family won't tell anyone where he is," Lainey said, sticking to what she could—in good conscience—reveal. "And the citizens of Laramie are just as protective of him." Had she not stumbled across him, and been hired to organize the Lazy M, she still wouldn't know where he was currently residing.

"Maybe they'll change their minds," Sybil said as the waiter returned with two bowls of tortilla soup.

"I doubt it. Brad is very well loved in his hometown.

More than one person told me they didn't know who that was on the reality show, but it sure as heck wasn't the Brad they knew, before or since."

"So they think he was screwed by the producers."

Lainey nodded, savoring the spicy mixture of flavorful broth, tender chicken, crisp tortillas, creamy avocado and cheddar cheese. "At the very least, portrayed in a deliberately unflattering light."

"Except that doesn't make sense, since the producers very much want their bachelors to be extraordinarily heroic."

And Brad had been portrayed as the world's biggest cad.

"Viewers won't watch if they don't like the bachelor," Sybil continued between spoonfuls.

Except they had watched, in record numbers, if only to see the handsome lothario get what was coming to him.

"Look, you knew him as a kid, right?"

Lainey made a seesawing motion with her hand. "Sort of. He and his family moved to Laramie when Brad was sixteen, a few years after their mother died."

Sybil leaned forward impatiently. "My point is, you have an insight into this guy—a personal connection—that none of my other reporters have. If you can find him, you have the ability to get close to him."

At least in theory, Lainey thought. Right now Brad was so prickly she couldn't see anyone getting close to him, man or woman. Even his beloved younger brother Lewis was giving him wide berth.

"This could be your big break, Lainey. A cover story that could catapult you into the big time and erase all those years when you didn't work as a writer. Getting this story for me would make your lack of journalism degree a moot point. And if I'm hired as editor-in-chief, largely because you got the story of the summer, I promise you a job as a staff writer."

The waiter cleared their plates and returned with warm lobster tacos for Sybil and Texas crab cakes for Lainey. "I told you—I don't want to live in New York City. I want Petey to grow up in Texas, the way I did. Maybe even in Laramie."

Sybil rolled her eyes. "Two weeks out in the sticks and I guarantee you will change your mind about that and go running back to Dallas."

Maybe, and maybe not, Lainey thought. She had already been there a few days, and already she felt calmer, more relaxed, more in touch with her true self than she had in years.

Being back—even temporarily—was like having a fresh start in her life.

Sybil sat back in her chair. "How many times have you said to me, on the phone or in e-mail, that you wished you'd had the chance to work for a while before you got married, to see if you had what it takes?"

Lainey sighed. "Hundreds." Whenever Chip or his family had made her feel small and inconsequential, she had wished she had more of a sense of herself, more inner strength. She had wished she had a life apart from her husband and son. Something to call her very own.

"If you don't want to leave Texas, that's fine. You could work for *Personalities Magazine* as our southwest stringer."

Sybil didn't know how tempting that sounded. "That would still mean travel." Lainey forced herself to be practical.

"Day flights. You could hop on a plane in the morning, interview someone and be home in time to cook Petey dinner. I promise."

Which would make the situation workable, Lainey knew. And the job would fulfill Lainey's long-held dreams of being a reporter and challenge her in ways she hadn't been challenged in a long time. Certainly, being a staff reporter for *Personalities Magazine* would be a lot better than trying to make it as a freelance reporter, selling stories here and there.

"The point is, Lainey, you and I both know that the story the producers presented to the viewing public was not the *whole* story. If Brad McCabe is the wonderful guy at heart that his family and the entire citizenry of Laramie, Texas, think he is, then other stuff *must* have happened behind the scenes that maybe only Brad—and the woman he ended up first choosing and then unceremoniously dumping at the end—know about." She took a sip of water. "And you've read the stuff Yvonne Rathbone's been spouting. That he was a Jekyll and Hyde, her heart was shattered all to pieces…and she will never ever get over what happened in a million years."

"I saw her on one of the morning news shows, after it happened," Lainey admitted reluctantly. Yvonne had been crying her eyes out. "She appeared credible."

Sybil looked cynical. "You and I have both known women who are capable of twisting the truth. It's up to you to discover what really occurred and write it up, so everyone knows what happened, instead of the lies and the half-truths Yvonne and the producers are putting out. In the meantime, I've got some standard contracts and releases for you to sign."

She handed them over. Lainey perused them while they waited for their dessert and coffee. The documents were fairly straightforward. Until Lainey got to the amount being offered for the article. She glanced up. "You're willing to pay me five thousand dollars for one three-thousand-word article?"

"If we publish it," Sybil concurred. "And we won't publish it unless you can come up with something new, factual and fairly sensational."

And therein lay the challenge, Lainey thought, as she kept reading the terms of the contract. How could she become friends with the McCabes, while at the same time secretly investigating—for public disclosure—the true character of one of their own? If what she found out flattered—and freed—Brad from this nightmare of bad publicity, she could very well be a hero in their view. But if the worst happened, if Brad actually had been a cad, for absolutely no reason, as his ex alleged, what then? If Lainey were the bearer of news like that, the citizens of Laramie would not be happy with her. And that resentment could prevent Lainey from returning to Laramie—with Petey—to live.

"You'll notice we have the exclusive right to publish whatever you do find out," Sybil pointed out.

"As well as make any editorial changes you see fit," Lainey noted, all of which was standard.

Sybil handed over a pen. "I'll need you to go ahead and sign this agreement—and then we'll get down to the brass tacks of what the magazine expects from you on this assignment."

Lainey complied and Sybil countersigned, then handed a contract to Lainey and slid the other back into her carryall.

"So this is what I am proposing," Sybil said as they sipped their coffee. "I want you to use your knowledge of Brad and anything else you can find out about him and his family that is not currently known. And then I want you to interview Yvonne Rathbone for the magazine and use that intimate knowledge to try to trip her up, see if you can catch her in some obvious lies. And maybe, just maybe, get her to at least give you a clue, if not an outright confession, about what really happened behind the scenes at *Bachelor Bliss*. Maybe if you get her to admit enough, you'll be able to use your desire to clear Brad's name and rep to get his family to tell you where you can find him for a sit-down interview. That way, he'll see how much you want to help him, and he will fill in the rest for you."

Did she want to help him? How could she not? Certainly, she wanted to know the truth of what had happened, and be responsible for getting that truth out for everyone to know! "That's a lot of ifs," Lainey said finally.

Sybil dipped her spoon into the raspberry sauce on top of the crème brûlée. "I remember very well how tenacious you are when you're on a story. I have faith you will be able to get the job done."

Lainey admitted to herself that she wanted all the answers as much as Sybil did—if not more. Thinking about the task ahead, knowing she was up to the challenge, she savored her chocolate cake. It was time to prove she had what it took to be a reporter, time to build a new life for herself and Petey. "What's the time frame?"

"You have the rest of this week to prepare and do your digging. I've set the interview with Yvonne up for Sunday afternoon. She's going to be in town this weekend to appear at a charity gig—and she agreed to meet with you and a photographer from the magazine at the Fairmont Dallas, where she'll be staying. I'll need the article on her and Brad one week from today."

Seven days. "That's not much time."

"It's enough for a pro. You're a pro, Lainey. You know it and I know it. You've just been off the job for a while. Now it's time to get back to the work you were born to do."

"What if I can't get Brad to talk to me and tell me his version of events? I mean, it's been almost three months and he hasn't told anyone what happened thus far."

Sybil shrugged. "You'll still have the article you write about his ex—Yvonne Rathbone—after you interview her. And you can write the article about Brad whether or not he allows you to interview him. That fact alone might induce him to cooperate." She continued. "And even if it doesn't, you still have your Laramie connections. You'd be surprised what little tidbits you can pick up here and there when people feel comfortable enough to open up to you. Once compiled, they could make a hell of a story, or at least lend powerful insight to what happened to make Brad change his mind about proposing to Yvonne. I'm counting on your intimate knowledge of the family and the town where he spent his teenage years to give you an edge and an in that no one else has had to date."

"Because unless there's something new to be told about the breakup, you don't want it."

"Right. No sense in rehashing what has already been said a hundred different ways. That won't sell magazines. Readers want to know how Brad McCabe could seem so head over heels in love with Yvonne Rathbone one minute, and then treat her like dirt the next."

It was a puzzle.

Brad was ornery but he didn't seem cruel. And yet on the show he had abruptly seemed so cold, irrationally angry and bitter. Lainey paused. "Everything you've said thus far makes sense."

"And—?"

"I have to tell you," Lainey sighed, wishing she didn't have such a guilty conscience. It would be so much better for her career. "It doesn't feel right going after the story in such an underhanded manner." It felt like a betrayal. To herself, to the McCabe family, and especially to the target of her story, Brad McCabe. To the point that at least part of her was already regretting signing that publishing contract.

Sybil studied her. "All I am asking you to do is discover the truth and help Brad McCabe regain his reputation as a good and decent guy."

If Lainey did that, maybe the brooding look would disappear from Brad's eyes. Maybe he would regain his innate good cheer and the optimism he'd once had about love and life. Maybe then all the McCabes would rest a little easier. On the other hand, if he didn't, he could easily end up like her late father—embittered, angry and resentful the rest of his life….

"I'm sure all Brad McCabe needs is a journalist to whom he can tell his side of things and he will open up," Sybil continued.

But how could Lainey get Brad to trust her now, when she had gone out to the ranch to hunt him down? If she told Brad the truth, he would kick her off the ranch so fast her head would spin. If she didn't, she would be staying there under false pretenses.

"I think I understand where you're coming from," Sybil said gently.

Lainey didn't see how *that* was possible, given all she hadn't told her old friend.

"You're scared. You haven't had to work in a long

time, whereas a lot of women our age have done nothing but gain experience and devote themselves to their careers the past ten years. But you have to start somewhere if you want a career, Lainey. And I have to be honest with you—offers like mine are going to be few and far between."

Lainey toyed with the last of her dessert, feeling torn between her own ambition and her loyalties to those she had grown up with. "I know that."

"Then be sensible and take me up on this wonderful offer. Put your personal feelings aside and act like the tenacious reporter you were when we were in college! Find the facts. Put them in an article. And to help you get started—" Sybil opened her carryall and extracted a trio of DVDs.

"What's this?"

Sybil smiled. "Copies of the episodes that featured Brad McCabe and Yvonne Rathbone. I know you've seen them, along with the rest of the country, but watch them again, slowly and carefully this time. I guarantee you will see things you didn't see the first time, and that—plus your nose for news—will lead you to the truth about Rathbone and McCabe."

CHAPTER FOUR

SYBIL HAD BEEN RIGHT, Lainey thought late that evening as she watched the DVD on her laptop computer screen. Being able to watch the show again—thoughtfully—was going to be a huge help to her as she prepared a list of questions that would need to be answered if she were ever to find out what happened behind the scenes at Bachelor Bliss.

And the people who had known Brad forever were also correct in their assessment, Lainey noted. The Brad on TV was different from the smart, sassy, challenging man in real life. His actions, as he was introduced to each of the twenty women vying for his heart, were stiff, almost scripted, as were his deadly dull remarks. Except when it came to Yvonne Rathbone. When Yvonne approached him on the terrace, sumptuous curves spilling out of a glittering evening gown, flame-red hair flowing over her shoulders, something definitely clicked.

Lainey backed it up, and watched again as Yvonne sashayed toward Brad. Instead of simply clasping his hand or kissing his cheek in the same nervous, formal way all the other contestants had done, Yvonne went up on tiptoe and, covering her microphone with one hand, whispered something in his ear that the viewers couldn't catch. Brad's eyes lit up and he grinned, as if he hadn't expected Yvonne to say whatever it was she had whispered to him. And just that simply and quickly, a connection of some sort was made.

Question #1, Lainey wrote. *What did Yvonne say when she and Brad first met?*

Question #2. Was Yvonne the only woman in the bunch Brad was physically attracted to?

Because upon closer inspection Lainey realized that he hadn't looked as if he was enjoying himself with the others.

And if he were the selfish Casanova they had painted him as, Lainey thought as someone knocked on the guest house door, he should have been having fun with all the ladies.

"Who is it?" Lainey called, hurriedly stuffing her paper and pen beneath the sofa cushions.

"Brad McCabe."

Lainey swore as she switched off the DVD, hid the covers for the other two disks beneath that day's *Dallas Morning News,* and moved back to the picture of Petey she used as a screen saver. "Just a minute!"

Satisfied she'd left no clues as to her mission, she hurried to the door.

Brad's expression was impatient. He got straight to the point. "I need printer paper. I know it's late—"

"No kidding." She was already in her pink-and-white-striped cotton pajamas.

For once, he didn't look at her breasts. Not that he would have seen much. They were covered in the demure fabric. "But I saw you were still up—and Lewis said he knows he has some good quality stuff. He thinks it might be over here in a box marked 'Pencils and Scissors.' I've already looked through the ranch house from top to bottom, and I have to have this thing I'm working on done by seven-thirty tomorrow morning, or believe me, I would not be bothering you."

He did look stressed. Lainey realized this might be a good time to get started on gathering her background information from him. "Come on in. You can help me look for the 'Pencils and Scissors' box," she said casually, leading the way past the boxes that were stacked four-high along one wall of the living room, behind the conversation area formed by the green Naugahyde sofa and two easy chairs. A round oak table for four sat beneath the window in the square country kitchen. There were boxes there, too, again pushed against the wall. Lainey noticed Brad had showered sometime that evening. He still smelled of soap and cologne, and his gleaming dark brown hair had the soft, rumpled look that comes from running a towel through just-shampooed hair and letting it dry any which way. Clamping down on her awareness of him—it wouldn't do her story any good to get distracted by his irresistible male presence—she asked, "What are you working on?"

"A business plan for the Lazy M. I've got back-to-back meetings with all three of the town's bankers tomorrow morning. I'm hoping one will be sufficiently impressed to want to lend me the money I need to get the cattle operation up and running. What are you doing?" He glanced at her personal computer sitting on the coffee table. Lainey tried not to feel guilty—and failed. She knew some reporters lied routinely about everything under the sun as they went undercover to ferret out stories that could not be dug out any other way. Lainey was not one of them.

She planned to get Brad's cooperation in the *Personalities* story. That would be a lot easier to do if they were friends and he understood from the get-go that she was there to help him clear up any misconceptions and restore his good name, not malign him as so many others had done. "I was catching up on my e-mail, and doing a few other things on my laptop." *That I can't tell you about...just yet,* Lainey added silently. *But I will, I promise, just as soon as I think you trust me enough to understand.* "Before that I was lining the kitchen shelves."

Brad studied the vintage Fiestaware she had bought at a tag sale the previous month. The rainbow-hued stoneware had been too colorful for her late husband's taste—he'd preferred things subdued and understated—but she loved it because it reminded her of her youth and her flamboyant mother.

"Are those our dishes?" he asked her.

Lainey blinked. "I didn't know you and Lewis had any dishes. Other than paper plates and cups."

"Actually, uh, we don't, as far as I know, which is why I was asking. We could use a few plates and glasses and stuff in the kitchen."

Lainey made a mental note to work on that. "Actually, these dishes are mine."

It was his turn to look surprised.

"I'm going to need them when Petey comes out to stay at the end of the week."

He regarded her with an unreadable expression. "You thinking about taking the job here permanently?"

Was she?

Certainly it would be far enough away from Bunny and Bart that she wouldn't have to worry about them pressuring her. Room and board wouldn't be a factor, either, since that was free as long as she was out here. The fifty-thousand-dollar salary Lewis had talked about paying a housekeeper would go a long way toward

Lainey's other expenses, while she made a name for herself as a reporter, either at *Personalities Magazine,* under Sybil, or elsewhere, as a freelance journalist.

But all that depended on Brad understanding what she ultimately had to do here. And, of course, Petey liking it out at the ranch.

His eyes narrowed. Misunderstanding the reason for her hesitant look, he continued wryly, "Don't worry if you are. I won't make a pass at you."

Lainey scoffed as she headed back to the bedroom earmarked for Petey. Brad followed.

"I know what you're thinking about."

The kiss...

"But that wasn't a pass." He stepped past the twin bed with a rough-hewn frame and the bureau, to review the boxes stacked against the wall.

"It wasn't," she deadpanned, looking over at him.

"That was just a kiss." Brad was the picture of lazy male assurance. "If and when I ever make a pass at you, you'll know it."

Lainey's heartbeat quickened. "I expect I would. So it's a good thing you're not going to do it because I'm not one of the women who signed up to compete for your attention."

"Thank heaven for that," he muttered beneath his breath, his lips taking on a brooding slant once again.

Lainey edged closer. "Mind answering a question for me?"

He lifted an indolent hand. "Depends."

"How come you were so...sort of gallant but humorless on *Bachelor Bliss,* at least in the beginning? I mean, I've just been around you a few days and you're always full of witty remarks—"

"Or full of something," he said with comically exaggerated seriousness.

"But you weren't funny on the TV show like you are in real life. Tell me the truth. Did they make you rein in your natural—"

"Don't you mean wicked?"

"—sense of humor while you were on camera?"

Respect glimmered in his brown eyes. "You're the first person who's ever asked me that."

Aha! She'd known it! "So it's true," Lainey said, ignoring the tingle of awareness starting up inside her whenever Brad was near. "The show's staff told you to rein in the repartee. What'd they do?" She regarded him with all the directness she could muster. "Write your dialogue on cue cards or something?"

"Not all of it," he allowed reluctantly.

"How much?" Lainey pressed.

He shrugged. "I don't know. Maybe...ninety-eight percent or something."

Lainey found this distressing. She figured the *Personalities Magazine* readers would, too. "But the TV show is supposed to be reality."

Brad grimaced. "There's nothing real about that particular reality TV show. Everything on *Bachelor Bliss* is a setup, whether it's the circumstances you're in, or the person you're with."

Interesting, Lainey thought. She wished she could dig out her notepad and pen. "Was the breakup with Yvonne part of the script?" Because from what Lainey recalled, it hadn't looked that way. Yvonne had appeared really stunned by what Brad had had to say, or not say, to her that evening during the final proposal ceremony.

An unreadable emotion shuttered Brad's eyes. "I don't know how we got on this," he said gruffly.

"Or in other words, you're not going to tell me," Lainey said, disappointed. Not yet, anyway….

"You got that right." He stalked out into the hall and across to the bedroom where she was bunking. A queen-size brass bed dominated the center of the room. Lainey had outfitted it with a ruffled white spread and several satin throw pillows. The clothes she'd been wearing earlier—including her lacy pink bra—were strewn across the bed.

She blushed as Brad's eyes touched on her lingerie. Silence fraught with sexual tension fell between them as they both turned to scan the writing on the sides of the moving boxes.

"That box must be here somewhere," Brad complained.

"You've got a lot riding on these meetings, I take it," Lainey said, still not finding anything marked "Pencils and Scissors."

Brad pulled a box from the middle of the wall that appeared to have no marking on it and turned it every which way.

Finally, the one they wanted!

"Let's put it this way," Brad muttered as he ripped it open. "I used every bit of my savings to repair the existing pasture fences, purchase the equipment I need for sprinkler and heat-detecting systems in the barn, not to mention what it cost to get a new roof put on the barn, repair the termite damage that had started on one end, and repaint the whole darn thing."

He began taking out wads of packing paper, handing them over to her.

"I've been meaning to ask you about that," Lainey said as he dug deeper and deeper.

"Yeah?" Brad emerged, victorious, with a ream of high-quality printer paper.

Lainey dropped the wads of packing paper back into the box. "Was the barn that color when you bought the place?"

Brad led the way out of her bedroom. "No, I painted it." He paused at her front door. "Why? Don't you like it?"

"It's a nice guy color, I guess." Lainey stepped out onto the porch with him.

"But?"

She turned her glance to the buildings located behind the house. "I thought most barns were either red or white or weathered gray."

Brad grinned and shook his head, suddenly appearing in no more hurry to leave her side than she was to see him go. "See. That just shows how much you don't know about ranching."

Lainey looked back at the barns and stables. In the moonlight, they didn't look so bad, but in the daylight they were so deadly dull they practically faded into the landscape. "There's a reason they're all golden tan, right down to the corral fence?"

"Yep."

And here she'd thought Brad and his brother just had no color sense whatsoever. "I'm dying to hear," she prodded dryly.

"It calms the cattle."

"You're joking."

"Nope. Texas A&M has done studies on color and cattle management. That particular color is very soothing to cattle. They don't know why exactly—seems the cattle aren't talking," he quipped, "but whenever cattle are around that color they are very calm and relaxed, which in turn makes them a lot easier to handle."

Lainey studied him. "You must have some theory as to why that's so," she observed softly.

Brad nodded, more sober rancher now than flirting cowboy. "It probably has something to do with the fact that animals don't see colors the way humans do. Their depth perception is different, too. This particular hue of tan eliminates shadows and blends well with the landscape, and hence the cattle are more apt to stay calm, less prone to balk, when you're leading them toward either a barn or a fence painted this color."

"So how come all the ranches out here don't have their barns painted this color?"

Brad shrugged. "Maybe they haven't done their research."

Lainey regarded him with respect. Obviously there was much more to Brad than he usually let on. "The fact you have should help you with your loan."

"I hope so. I really need a bank to back us."

BRAD SEEMED genuinely worried, Lainey realized. More so than he should be given the circumstances. She asked the questions that would tell *Personalities* readers what Brad planned for his future. "Couldn't Lewis just lend you guys the cash? Given the success of his computer-gaming company...he's supposed to be rolling in dough."

Brad frowned. "He's already put up the entire down payment for the ranch."

Determined to keep him off guard, Lainey pushed on. "You must have known this was going to be the case when you two decided to purchase the ranch together."

Tired of holding the ream of printer paper, evidently not ready to leave, Brad set the package on the rough-hewn cedar table next to the cushioned glider. He took a seat and stretched his long legs out in front of him. "We purchased it before I headed off to do *Bachelor Bliss*."

Lainey sat down on the other end of the glider and turned to face him. "They paid you to end up so miserable?" she said as they moved back and forth.

Looking even more handsome in the soft glow of the guest-house porch light, Brad replied, "They gave all the contestants five thousand dollars to appear on the show. The real money for me—and the female contestants the public took a shine to—was to come later, in endorsements. The last bachelor, for instance, made over two million in television commercials when the series wrapped up. They had close to three million lined up for me."

Another fact the show's viewers would be interested in learning. "Only now, because of the way the series ended, you're public enemy number one," she guessed.

"Right."

"Hence the sponsors want nothing to do with you."

"Right again." Brad sighed. He brushed the flat of his palm down his jeans. "Not that I had any business doing those commercials anyway."

Lainey's hair was still damp from the shower; she wouldn't style it in the usual sleek bob until tomorrow. She could see Brad noticing—maybe even liking—the natural waves. Self-consciously she tucked a curl behind her ear and tried not to notice him tracking the movement. "Didn't you believe in the products?"

Brad held her gaze. "I would never endorse something

I didn't believe in. The problem is," he confided, frowning, "it's not real work."

Lainey caught the snobbery in his tone. "I think the people who vie for and film those commercials would disagree with you."

He made a face. "It's just not the kind of thing I do."

What was it Chip had said to her, whenever she had talked to him about her ambitions? *Reporting? Come on, Lainey! Get real! That isn't the kind of thing we Carringtons do.* She hadn't liked his snobbery then. She didn't like recalling it now. A person was not defined by his or her profession. Her mother had not been low class just because she worked in a bar and wore the provocative outfit the establishment management demanded during her work hours, and equally flamboyant and sexy clothing when she was off. Her mother had been sweet and gentle and hardworking, beloved by all who knew her and bothered to find out the person behind the ensemble.

"I disagree," she said. "Work is work, and there is value in work whatever it is."

Her irritated tone brought a provoking smile to his lips. "You really think so."

"Yes. I do."

He paused to consider that and seemed to be searching for the exception to the rule, if only to get her goat. "Even for something like—say—stripping?" he asked her playfully.

How had the situation gotten back to sex again? What was it about the two of them that sparks flew whenever they were together? "Okay. You got me there," Lainey replied dryly. "I would not take my clothes off in front of a bunch of leering strangers for money. But that's still work, and if someone chooses to do it to earn a living, then that's their business. It's not up to you or me to judge them."

"You only say it's real work because you've never been in a situation where you've been leered at that way."

Close enough, Lainey thought, and before she could stop herself the words came tumbling out. "Oh, yes, I have."

Brad looked as ready to continue their argument as she was. "Ah, yes. That homecoming parade Lewis was talking about."

Lainey flushed. Why had she started down this road? "That was my fault for letting my friends dare me into wearing that dress." She'd been young, foolish. Reckless to a fault in a way she wasn't now that she was a mom.

Brad stretched his long legs out in front of him. "Well, this was my fault for letting the producers talk me into appearing on that TV show."

"You didn't sign up for it?"

"No." He settled more comfortably on the bench seat of the glider and laid one arm along the back of it. "They came to me. Apparently, cowboys are heroes and Texans are sexy and they wanted a bona fide Texas cowboy for their bachelor this time around. So they looked at rodeo standings, saw my picture and thought I was just handsome enough to be the star of the show."

"What'd you say?"

"Hell, no." Brad turned to her, dark eyes sparkling. "I was already thinking about talking to Lewis about buying a ranch. The last thing I wanted to do was fly to Los Angeles and spend a month on an estate in Santa

Barbara with fifteen contestants all vying to be the first Mrs. Brad McCabe."

"So why did you?"

He scowled, his frustration with the situation apparent. "The commercial money afterward. Since I'm not a computer genius capable of starting my own company like my dad or Lewis, I knew it was the only way I'd ever get the kind of cash I needed, so quickly. I should have known a plan like that would backfire on me, and stuck to real work, instead of trying to take the easy route."

Lainey saw his point about that. In a lot of ways, her life had taken a wrong turn when she married money and let the demands of that kind of life control her. "I don't think there is anything wrong with doing commercials for products you believe in," she said, repeating her earlier assertion.

"Moot point now," Brad said.

Just then Lainey's cell phone rang. Alarmed—it was unusual for anyone to call her after midnight—she uncurled herself from the swing and went inside to get it, then came back out onto the porch to stand with him.

"Hello?" she said, nodding at Brad.

"Mom?" Petey's thin voice trembled in her ear.

"Hi, honey," Lainey said, her voice dropping to the gentle tone she reserved just for him. She turned her back to Brad. "Is everything okay? Are you having a good time with your cousins, Aunt Bunny and Uncle Bart?"

"Yeah. We saw fireworks in the shape of cartoon characters tonight. It was pretty neat."

"I bet." He sounded homesick.

"I want to ask you somethin'."

"Go right ahead," Lainey encouraged softly.

"Are you proud of me—for being so big and brave?"

Where had that come from? Lainey wondered, momentarily taken aback. "Honey, I am always proud of you."

"Lainey?" Bunny's voice came on the phone, crisp, businesslike as always. "Sorry to call so late, but Petey wanted to tell you about the fireworks."

"Is he okay? Because he sounds awfully homesick...."

"He's doing fine! What?—oh! I've got to go! We'll check in with you tomorrow, okay? Love you!"

Lainey heard a *click* as Bunny cut the connection. The dial tone sounded in her ear. Frowning, she ended the call on her phone, too, but left it plugged in and turned on in case Petey called back again.

"Everything okay?" Brad asked.

Lainey wasn't at all sure how to answer that.

"I'M SORRY, BRAD," Tommy Johnson, branch manager of Laramie Savings and Loan, said. "Your business plan looks excellent. But without some sort of collateral..." He hesitated. "If you wanted to have Lewis co-sign for you or put up part of the ranch, well, that would be a different story."

"No." Brad lifted a hand to cut off the discussion. "I was looking to stock the ranch on my own."

"I understand. But it's not like the old days, where a handshake or a man's word would suffice. We're all owned by big companies now, and we have guidelines we have to have follow."

No one had to tell Brad it was a conglomerate world. Bigger had always meant better in Texas. But bigger did not always mean better in business. The loss of the personal touch also meant the loss of good service and ample opportunity. Still, maybe there was something he could do, some way to fix this. First, he had to know if lack of collateral was the only reason he was being turned down. "Answer me this. If I hadn't been on *Bachelor Bliss,* would my chances be better?"

"Not for obtaining a loan. But it would probably help you be taken more seriously in this new venture of yours. The last thing any businessperson wants to be thought of is fickle and unreliable."

"And because I didn't propose to Yvonne Rathbone, that's the view of me now."

Tommy made a face and rubbed his knuckles on the underside of his chin. "Actually, it goes a little further back than that."

Brad lifted a brow.

"Unfortunately, your work history speaks to the same sort of problems," Tommy explained. "You dropped out of college, hit the rodeo circuit off and on, and worked ranches here and there."

"For good reason! To supplement my income and learn as much as I could from as many top-rate sources as possible."

"The point is, you didn't stay in any one place for long. Then you signed up to do that reality TV show, and reneged on that at the end."

He'd had a damn good cause for that action, too. Not that he planned to tell anyone what it was. Bad enough he'd been humiliated that way without letting the rest of the world in on it, too.

"And now you're in business with Lewis, a person who knows a lot about computer software but nothing about raising cattle. As much as the people around here love you, it's going to take time and a lot of stability on your part for you to be taken seriously as a rancher."

Which meant, Brad thought later as he drove back to the Lazy M, it was either start very small and let the ranching operation grow slowly over a number of years, or go back to the fallback plan of letting Lewis pay for everything—the land, the cattle and the operating costs, even Brad's room and board. The two were going to split the profits right down the middle, but it would be years before those amounted to much.

Brad was still scowling as he parked his pickup next to the ranch house and walked inside.

He followed the lilt of Lainey's soft, feminine laughter and the eager sound of his brainiest brother to the formal dining room that was being retooled as Lewis's home office. Brad was claiming the former formal living room as his study, since neither of them planned to give any parties that couldn't be held out on the lawn, or, in inclement weather, in the kitchen and family room.

"The chandelier is going to have to come down and be replaced with another light fixture," Lainey was saying. "Otherwise you'll be in danger of bumping your head on it every time you get up from your desk."

Brad stopped in the portal, shocked by what he saw.

Lainey had only been working on this room since this morning, but already it had been transformed from a mess of boxes with a trio of bookcases and large U-shaped desk into an organized work environment. She'd taken down the dusty drapes that had come with the house, and removed the outdated drapery rod from the wall. Lewis's three computers, fax, two printers, copier and speakerphone were all organized in a way that made sense, with the computers set up equidistant from one another in his workspace for easy access, the other equipment placed on the shelves. They had also brought in the beat-up green leather reclining chair that had been with Lewis since his college days and put it in the corner, along with a pole lamp that made a cozy reading nook.

Lainey and Lewis both had their backs to Brad as Lainey pointed out places on the ceiling. "I think you're going to want to add some track lighting around the perimeter," she was saying, "to really brighten up the space. And maybe a nice rug? And those posters you bought during your travels would look nice on the walls, if you had them framed."

"Can you help me with that?"

"Sure," she replied.

"I never know what to buy."

"You've done just fine so far."

Lewis beamed at her compliment.

Brad's scowl deepened as Lainey and Lewis belatedly seemed to realize they were no longer alone and turned to face him.

"So, how'd it go?" Lewis asked cheerfully. "The banks give you everything you need to get the cattle operation up and running?"

Brad shook his head. He only wished it had been that easy. But he wasn't going to hide from the truth—at least not in this regard. "Seems like we're back to the original plan," he stated matter-of-factly.

Lewis looked disappointed but not surprised.

His brother might not know how to dress or dazzle the ladies, but he had business sense—and instincts about what would or would not fly. Which was why Lewis had tried to keep Brad from going to the banks in the first place.

"No problem." Lewis reached into his desk and took out a business checkbook. He tossed it to Brad. His eyes were filled with the respect that, thanks to the lies that had been spread about Brad, was in short supply nearly everywhere else. "I had your name added to the account. So you can write checks for whatever you need."

"Thanks," Brad said, grateful for the trust, even as he felt like he was choking on his pride.

An awkward silence fell. "Listen, if you two want to talk business, I can get busy elsewhere," Lainey murmured.

Brad had nothing further to say on the matter. Lewis knew where they stood as well as he did. Lewis was the family's biggest success story, and Brad was the family's biggest failure.

BRAD SPENT WHAT WAS LEFT of the day toiling over the sprinkler system in the barn. He was still working on it as dusk approached, and Lainey appeared in the doorway. Deliciously tousled from a day of working hard, she was clad in a trim peach skirt and a sheer white short-sleeved shirt, embroidered with peach-and-green flowers, over an opaque white tank top. Her only concession to the hard physical work she was doing was the white socks and sneakers on her feet, instead of the usual sandals. As she moved toward him, a strong breeze wafted through the open barn doors on either side of the twenty-four stall facility, mussing her blond hair. Brad liked the way she looked. Womanly, purposeful, mouth-wateringly feminine, and flushed with the heat of the June day.

When he had ended his stint on *Bachelor Bliss,* Brad hadn't thought he would want anything to do with romance ever again. Lainey made him reconsider. And it wasn't just her looks, or the way she sassed and challenged him. Or even the way she had kissed him back, all the while swearing the lip-to-lip contact meant nothing. It was the way she listened to him. The way she knew what questions to ask, when to push, and when to back off.

She wanted to get to know him, the real him. Not the stud on TV or on the cover of magazines. More surprising still was the fact he wanted to really get to know her, too.

Not that it was going to be easy. She seemed a lot more comfortable asking the questions than answering them.

She tilted her head back to regard the PVC piping that ran the length of the barn's center, then spread out over each of the stalls. Four-foot fans were placed forty feet apart. Sprinkler heads were mounted eight feet over the floor above each stall. "Wow. This looks state-of-the-art," she said as she walked across the scrubbed cement floor.

"Pretty much." Brad continued mounting the thermostat and timer control on the wall just to the left of the door.

Lainey stood, legs braced apart, hands on her hips. "Have you ever done this before?"

He couldn't say why exactly—usually Brad didn't care what people thought of him—but he wanted Lainey to be impressed with his accomplishments. "I helped put in a system on a ranch in Colorado," he told her matter-of-factly.

She turned around slowly to get a full 360-degree view of his handiwork, and gave him one of her in return. Brad's mouth went dry as he noted the perfection of her curves. "Is it all for fire safety?"

"There is an overheat- and fire-detection system in here." Tearing his gaze from her breasts, Brad pointed out the components to her. "And the sprinkler system will be hooked up to that, as well. But what I'm installing right now is a cooling system that will protect animals against heat stress."

Lainey wrinkled her nose. "Is that a problem?"

"It can be," Brad replied soberly, "especially for newly weaned calves, or animals that have just been transported from one ranch to another."

"I guess you've had experience with that, too."

Brad nodded. "I worked a ranch in west Texas a couple years ago where they would have lost half their new calves if they hadn't had a system like this." He came down the ladder, thinking that standing there face-to-face with her would prompt him to knock off the romanticizing. It just made it worse. That close, he could see the softness of her lips, the flush of color in her cheeks, the clear interest in her forest green eyes.

As the moment drew out, with neither one of them saying anything, the awareness between the two of them increased. Finally, Brad cleared his throat, knowing it was either get back to business or kiss her. "Did you need something?"

Lainey blinked, clearly coming back to reality as slowly and reluctantly as he was. "Um, yes. Lewis is going into Laramie to pick up some pizza for us—apparently your supply of frozen dinners has dwindled precariously and I haven't had time to buy any groceries, either—and he wanted to know if you had any requests."

Brad wasn't sure whether to thank Lewis for the interruption sent his way—or damn him. One thing for sure, he'd be thinking about Lainey, and the way she looked right now, for days and nights to come. Pizza. What did he want on his pizza? "No anchovies on mine," Brad said finally.

Lainey grinned. And still didn't leave. "Okay, that covers what you don't want," she teased. "What *do* you want?"

You, Brad thought, almost as shocked by the thought as he was aroused. *Beneath me. Hair spread across my pillow. Arms and legs locked around me. And me so deep inside of you I don't know where I end and you begin.*

Not that he had any right to be thinking that way.

He had no intention of getting intimately involved with any woman again anytime soon. And Lainey Carrington was the kind of woman who would demand emotional involvement.

Lainey Carrington was a forever kind of woman. And he was, as had been pointed out to him more than once today, a short-term kind of guy. At least as far as everyone else was concerned.

But that didn't mean he couldn't want to make love to her. Wanting was not out of the question.

Acting on those desires was.

"Well?" Lainey's impatient prodding brought him out of his reverie. "What do you want on your pizza?"

Brad straightened. "Whatever you and Lewis want is fine with me," Brad said, distracted at the sight of the Lexus pulling into the driveway. Instead of stopping at the house, as most visitors did, the driver appeared headed directly toward the two of them. "Friends of yours?" he said.

"Oh, my!" The paper in Lainey's hand fluttered to the ground as the rear door of the SUV opened and a towheaded kid sprang out and dashed toward her.

"Mommy!" The little boy threw himself into Lainey's arms.

"Petey!" She hugged him to her tightly. He hugged her back just as hard.

Seeing the resemblance—and the affection—between the two made Brad smile. Lainey's son had her intelligent eyes and warm smile. Even the stubborn way they held their chin was the same.

"Who's this?" Petey asked, looking at Brad.

"This is Brad McCabe. He and his brother Lewis live here at the Lazy M Ranch. Brad—my son, Petey."

Brad shook Petey's hand with the same courtesy and respect he'd offer a grown man. "Nice to meet you, Petey."

The little boy looked awestruck in the way city kids who have never been on an actual ranch usually do. He tipped his face up to Brad's. "Are you a real cowboy?"

"Yes."

"Do you ride horses and everything?"

"I will as soon as we get some, later this week. Right now, we're still in the process of fixing up the stables and corrals to get ready for 'em."

Petey gazed at the barn and pastures wistfully. "I always wanted to ride a horse."

Brad recalled the joy he'd felt when he first sat a horse at his uncle's ranch. It was an experience no boy should miss. "Well, maybe if your mom says it's okay, I can teach you how." Brad looked at Lainey for permission.

Obviously embarrassed, she tucked Petey closer to her side and said, "We didn't mean to put you on the spot."

"It'd be my pleasure," Brad replied, meaning it. There

were some things he could still do without a bank loan or a gentleman's reputation.

Petey beamed, thrilled.

Brad cast a surreptitious look at the couple who had driven Petey out to the ranch. They were still in the car and appeared to be deep in some sort of serious discussion that his gut told him spelled trouble.

"So are you surprised to see me?" Petey demanded, going back into Lainey's arms for another exuberant hug, as the elegant-looking couple finally emerged from the front seat of the Lexus. The woman had carefully done hair and makeup. She was wearing an expensive white linen dress, and a sweater tied around her shoulders. Her companion had thinning hair and a slight paunch. He was wearing a grass-green golf shirt and plaid slacks that belonged on a country club tee-off area.

"I sure am," Lainey said, ruffling her son's hair.

Lainey paused just long enough to introduce her sister- and brother-in-law, Bart and Bunny Carrington, then asked them, "What happened? I thought you weren't coming back until the end of the week!"

"Petey was a little homesick," Bunny said.

"Actually," Bart added, "the twins wanted to come home, too."

Bunny's smile looked frozen. "Suddenly they feel they're too old for family vacations," she said, unable to completely disguise the hurt in her tone.

Bart shrugged. "I think they just wanted to be with their friends. They want to spend as much time as possible with each other since they're all going off to different colleges in the fall. And I can't say I blame them—they have big changes ahead."

"For you, too," Lainey returned perceptively. "I'm sure you're really going to miss the girls."

"It's time for them to spread their wings," Bunny claimed with a smile. "And besides, we'll still have Petey."

Except, Brad thought, Petey was not their son. He was Lainey's. Hence, it really wasn't the same, no matter how much they tried to tell themselves it was.

The back door of the ranch house banged open and Lewis came bounding down the steps, car keys in hand. In his '80s slacks and tie-dyed McCabe Game Company T-shirt, he looked more like the proverbial slacker than the wealthy CEO of his own company. A fact Brad knew Lewis used to sort out the people who would treat him well no matter who he was, from the hangers-on, who were only interested in him for his newfound wealth.

Lewis smiled as he reached the group, and went straight for Lainey's son. "You must be Petey."

Petey cocked his head. He looked at Brad, then back at Lewis. "How'd you know that?" Petey asked Lewis, perplexed.

Lewis ran his hand through his spiked hair. "'Cause your mom talks about you constantly."

"Oh, yeah? What does she say?"

"The usual. That you're the smartest, cutest, nicest kid who ever lived."

Petey looked at Brad for confirmation. Brad nodded. "It's true," he said. It had been obvious from the first that Petey meant the world to Lainey. A fact that pleased her son no end.

"And guess what else?" Lewis continued affably, while Bart and Bunny watched, their expressions wary, almost jealous. "I heard you like playing computer games." Oblivious to the looks he was getting from Petey's aunt and uncle, Lewis bumped fists and slapped palms with Petey in the multistep greeting currently popular with kids. "And as it happens, I'm designing some for eight- to ten-year-olds that I want you to help me test."

"Really?" Petey looked as if he couldn't believe his good luck. First, horses, and now this.

"Meantime," Lewis said, as soon as he, too, had been formally introduced to Bart and Bunny Carrington, "I'm starving. So what do you all want on your pizza?"

CHAPTER FIVE

BUNNY BLINKED. "You're making pizza?" Obviously pizza wasn't a staple of her high-class life.

"Heck, no," Lewis retorted cheerfully, before Lainey could stop him. "We don't have the makings for that in the house. We hardly have any groceries."

Thanks, Lewis, for thoroughly alarming my sister-in-law. Lainey smiled at Bunny and Bart reassuringly. "I'm going to remedy that first thing tomorrow," she said.

"Meanwhile," Lewis continued affably, "we've got to eat, so I'm driving in to Laramie to pick up a few pies at Mac Callahan's Pizza & Subs. And, of course, you're welcome to stay for dinner."

"Pizza is hardly a proper meal," Bunny countered, her expression stiff with disapproval.

Brad shrugged, siding with Lewis. "I don't know why you'd say that," Brad said lazily. "It's got all the food groups."

"Yeah, and I like it a lot!" Petey piped up, eager to be one of the guys.

Bunny looked at Lainey. "Perhaps Petey should return to Dallas with us, now that he's seen you," she said sweetly.

"No!" Petey grabbed on to Lainey's waist and held tight. "I'm staying with my mommy!"

Bart—who looked like he didn't want any

trouble—headed back to the Lexus. "I'll get his suitcase."

Bunny turned her withering glare on Bart.

"Does this mean you're not staying for dinner?" Lewis asked, still looking eager to get on the road to town.

Bunny narrowed her eyes at him. "Obviously not," she replied coolly.

Lainey wrapped her arms around her son's shoulders and tried desperately to end this encounter on a pleasant note. "Petey, did you thank your aunt and uncle for the lovely trip to Florida?"

"Thank you. I had fun even if I did get homesick and miss my mom," Petey said sincerely.

Bunny's expression gentled. She leaned down so she and Petey were face-to-face. "We had fun, too," she told Petey warmly, giving him a hug.

Bart returned with Petey's suitcase. "Here you are, sport."

"Thanks, Uncle Bart." Petey hugged him, too.

"Thank you, both," Lainey said. "I appreciate everything you've done for us."

"Yes, well, we're going to have to sit down and talk soon," Bunny said.

Lainey felt a shiver of unease. Bunny's tone could only mean trouble.

Fortunately, not tonight.

Bart took his wife's hand and drew her away. He appeared as determined to end this conversation as his wife was to prolong it. "We'll see you all later," he said.

"PIZZA FOR BREAKFAST, TOO!" Petey said early the next morning. "This is so great!"

"Don't get used to it," Lainey warned. "Starting tomorrow, we're back to the usual eggs, cereal, fruit and pancakes."

"Is that what cowboys eat?" Petey asked as Brad entered the ranch house kitchen. Lainey was already hard at work lining shelves, while her son sat on a stool at the counter, eating off a paper plate.

Brad flashed one of the smiles that was all too rare these days. "Cowboys usually eat whatever is around." Brad peered into the fridge, sighed, and brought out the pizza box. "Which in this case is not much."

"I know. That's how come I'm having soda with my pizza this morning instead of milk or juice. Mommy says we're all out and we have to go to the store."

"I know." Lewis came in, coffee cup in hand. "Sorry about that." He helped himself to a slice of pizza and ate it cold. "Guess I should have picked up some last night when I got the pizza and wings."

Lainey waved off his apology. "It's fine. I need to run into town and get groceries today, anyway."

"What would you think about cooking for all of us?" Brad asked.

Surprised, Lainey turned to him.

"I know it's not in your job description," Brad said. "But while you're here, it sure would help out."

"No problem," Lainey said. "I love to cook."

"Yeah, my mommy is real good at that," Petey said between mouthfuls. He swung his legs back and forth. "You just got to tell her what you want and she'll make it for you."

Lewis and Brad grinned, seeming both amused and touched by Petey's enthusiasm. Lewis looked at Lainey. "As long as you're going into Laramie, you want to bring Petey by the McCabe Game Company testing facility for a session?"

"Can I, Mom?" Petey practically bounded off his stool he was so excited by the prospect.

Lainey looked at Lewis. "You're sure it's okay?"

"He can stay all day and come home with me tonight, if you like," Lewis said. "We have a group of eight- and nine-year-olds coming in today to play some of the prototypes, and to talk to the focus-group leaders about what they think. Annie and Travis's sons, Kurt and Kyle, are going to be there. If Petey would like to participate, it would be great."

"Thank you." Lainey smiled. She looked at her son. "Sounds like you've got quite a big day ahead of you, then."

Lewis said to Brad, "You okay with helping Lainey with the groceries?"

Brad practically spit out his coffee he was so surprised. It was all Lainey could do to keep her face expressionless. She couldn't imagine a more unlikely partner.

"We need a lot of stuff," Lewis continued. "We can't expect Lainey to carry it all herself."

If Lainey hadn't known better, she would have felt Lewis was matchmaking. As Brad and Lewis stared at each other, a challenge seemed to pass between them. Over what exactly, Lainey wasn't certain.

"Sure," Brad said finally. "Why not?"

"YOU DON'T HAVE TO DO THIS," Lainey told Brad, outside the supermarket. Although, it would help her cause—and his attempts to put the *Bachelor Bliss* fiasco behind him—if the two of them did become friends.

Brad tossed her a look that quickly had her heart

racing. He pulled out a cart for them. "You think I'm not capable of a little grocery shopping?" he teased her.

"I didn't say that." Feeling she had no choice but to brazen her way through this sticky situation, Lainey led the way toward the fresh produce aisle once they were inside the store.

"But?" Brad tossed a bag of baby carrots into their cart.

Lainey perused the lettuce, finally deciding on Boston, red-leaf and romaine. Her breath hitched in her chest as she turned her face up to his. Just being near him like this made her blood heat and played havoc with her objectivity. Not good for a reporter on a story. "It's not really most men's idea of a good time." And it certainly didn't fit his reputation.

"I don't know about that." Brad stopped to inspect the tomatoes. "Personally, I like perusing the persimmons."

Lainey grinned at his joke. How did an ordinary summer morning suddenly end up feeling so much like a date, albeit an arranged one? "Have you ever even eaten a persimmon?" she asked, putting bags of oranges, apples, lemons and limes into the cart.

"I'm not sure." Brad loaded a ten-pound bag of potatoes and a five-pound bag of onions onto the bottom of the cart. "What exactly *is* a persimmon?"

Lainey looked around and didn't see any in the store just then. The Dallas markets would have had them.

"It's sort of like a plum," she said finally, aware how cozy and domestic this felt, how unlike her marriage to Chip. There, the lines had been strictly drawn. He was the one in control, she was the subordinate. Chip had never done anything remotely domestic. Chip had hired people for that. Brad just seemed to do what needed to be done, without giving too much thought to whether he was "too good" for it or not. Lainey liked that about Brad. She wanted to see it revealed in what was written about him. And if she had anything to say on the matter, it would be.

"Oh. Well." He swaggered closer, his steps long and lazy. "Maybe I have tasted a persimmon, then."

"And maybe not?"

He shrugged, looking amused. "I don't always know what it is I'm eating."

Lainey hadn't, either, when she first married Chip and moved to Dallas.

Brad leaned closer. His warm breath whispered past her ear. "What's so funny?" His voice was sexy, self-assured.

She shrugged and stepped back. She had to keep some distance here. And she couldn't do that when they were close enough to feel each other's body heat. "Just thinking about my first taste of escargot." She forced her tone to be casual, unlike her thoughts.

His gaze moved over her in disbelief. "You ate snails?"

"Only because I didn't know what they were."

His brown eyes lit up merrily. "And when you did?"

Lainey rolled her eyes. She struggled not to notice how good he looked, with a cowboy hat pulled low over his brow, how ruggedly at ease. "Let's just say I never acquired a taste for them."

"Or armadillo, either, apparently."

They grinned, recalling her first day on the ranch. Lainey was aware they were flirting. And that Brad suddenly seemed like the old Brad she remembered. Carefree, happy-go-lucky, flirtatious. It was good to see.

Their exchange was putting her in a reckless, lighter-of-heart mood, too. “What’s put you in such good spirits?”

Brad’s smile broadened. He shrugged. “The thought of a home-cooked meal tonight?”

It had to be more than that, Lainey thought. “You haven’t tasted my…” Lainey stopped as she saw a man in a tropical-print shirt, Bermuda shorts and straw hat snapping photos of them through the plate-glass window in front of the store.

BRAD SAW THE COLOR DRAIN abruptly from Lainey’s face. Instinctively, he moved closer, cupped a protective hand on her slender shoulder. “What is it?”

Lainey’s face grew even paler. “That man,” she whispered. Standing stiff as a statue, she nodded toward the front of the store.

Brad turned in the direction of her gaze. “I don’t see anything.”

Lainey swallowed. “I could have sworn that tourist out there was taking pictures of us inside the store.”

“Looks like he is with his family,” Brad said, as the man directed a woman and two teenage girls—also tourists—to stand in front of the windows, just beneath the sign.

“I’m sorry. For a moment there, I thought we were being stalked,” Lainey said.

Brad took their basket and guided it toward the dairy aisle at the rear of the store. “It wouldn’t be the first time.”

“Since the show ended?”

He nodded grimly. “You wouldn’t believe the number of people trying to make a buck off me. The first couple weeks after the last show aired were the craziest. We had tabloid reporters everywhere. Harassing my family, friends, trying to find out where I was."

This wasn't the place or time Lainey had figured on having this conversation. But never one to look a gift horse in the mouth, she said, "It's probably not going to stop, you know."

He looked over at her.

"As long as there are questions, there will be reporters and writers trying to find out the answers to them. The quickest way to end it is to find someone you trust, and just tell them your side of the story."

IF BRAD DIDN'T KNOW BETTER, he'd think she was one of *them*. But that was ridiculous. Lainey was a homemaker, and temporary-professional-organizer-slash-household-manager. Not a bloodthirsty reporter. "They're never going to go away."

"They will once the real story is out there," Lainey persisted, as she added a selection of cheeses, milk and butter to the cart. "Haven't you heard the saying? The only thing worse than no news is old news."

Brad added eggs and fresh corn and flour tortillas, too. "People will forget," he insisted, wishing she would do what everyone else who knew him had finally done and just drop it.

"No, they won't." Lainey continued pestering him. "Not around here. Fifty years from now, everyone who knows you will be still be wondering why you dumped Yvonne Rathbone in front of an audience of seventeen million people."

"So it will be one of the great mysteries of all time. So what?" Brad's expression hardened as he pushed the cart toward the meat case.

"So I would think you'd want to get on with your life," Lainey told him passionately.

"In case you haven't noticed? I am."

Lainey fell silent. She seemed to have realized, Brad noted, that she had overstepped her bounds by a whole hell of a lot.

The rest of the shopping was done in relative silence. Eventually, Brad had to go back and get another cart. They filled that one to overflowing, too, then headed toward the checkout lines.

"I want to split the groceries with you," Lainey said as they reached the conveyer belt.

"Not necessary. Lewis said room and board was included, so he and I will pay for them."

Lainey got out her billfold at the same time as he did. "We'll put it on my card—you and Lewis can reimburse me for half later."

Brad knew he had offended—or maybe just disappointed?—her with his refusal to go public with his side of the story. But she seemed to be taking it awfully personally. Too personally. Which was odd, he mused as their groceries were scanned and sacked. He had never figured her for one of those women who always had to be right….

Finally, the total appeared. Lainey removed the bank card from her wallet and slid it through the machine mounted on the counter. "Debit or credit?" the clerk asked.

"Debit," Lainey said.

The clerk punched in a few numbers. Frowned. Punched them in again. "I'm sorry." She looked at Lainey. "It won't take it—insufficient funds."

Lainey did a double take. Her cheeks grew pink. "Try the credit, then," she said finally. Turning to Brad, she murmured, "There must be some screwup at the bank. I've got plenty of balance in there to cover this transaction."

Brad nodded.

"I'm sorry," the clerk said again, "it won't take the credit card, either."

"Now I know there's some mistake," Lainey said, visibly upset.

Brad pulled out his wallet, handed over his bank card. "Let's try mine."

It went through like a charm.

LAINEY FUMED about the mistake with her card all the way back to the ranch. She was still stewing as they carried the groceries inside and put them away. As soon as they were finished, she pulled out her cell phone, dialed her bank in Dallas and asked to talk to Customer Service. "What do you mean my account was emptied this morning?" she said, aghast. She listened some more, her face growing first a stunned white, and then an angry red. "I see. No. Thank you." She hung up the phone. Her hands were trembling.

"Anything I can help out with?" Brad asked.

She shook her head and picked up her cell again.

Feeling like he would be prying if he stayed, he went to check on his own phone messages. He had several. By the time he returned those calls and made his way back to the kitchen, she was off the phone again. She looked very upset.

He knew it was none of his business. He had tasks that needed accomplishing, too, but he couldn't just leave her like this. For the first time in a long while, it looked like someone close to him was having a worse time than he was. "Anything I can do to help?" he asked gently, his heart going out to her. She had been terribly embarrassed at the grocery store.

Lainey stared straight ahead. "Bunny has cut all my funds," she said, her tone as tense and upset as the look on her face.

"What do you mean?" he asked, moving closer yet.

"She called the bank this morning and had all the money transferred out of my account, and a hold put on my credit card."

Brad pulled up a chair and sat down at the table opposite her. "I don't understand. How can she do that?"

She steepled her hands. "She is the executor of Chip's estate. She controls all the funds he left for Petey and for me."

His glance dropped to the visible softness of her entwined hands. "Has Bunny done this before?"

Her lower lip formed a resolute line. "She's quarreled with me about money and decisions I've made about Petey before, but she's never done anything like this."

He paused. "Why would your sister-in-law be doing it now?"

"Easy." She sighed, discouraged. "She doesn't want us to move to Laramie."

"She said that?"

She bit her lip. "Not in so many words."

Brad edged closer, wishing he had the right to put his arm around her and offer the kind of physical comfort she obviously needed. "What did Bunny say?"

A bleak light came into her eyes. "That she was going to do some financial restructuring where the money being doled out of the trust was concerned, and that she and I should probably sit down to talk it over as soon as possible. She said if I wanted to bring Petey back to Dallas this afternoon, she'd make time to talk with me."

"Whoa."

Her expression was grim as she nodded. "Definitely a shot across the bow."

And a hell of a warning at that, he thought sympathetically. What was Chip thinking, to have left Lainey and Petey in a situation like this? Shouldn't he have foreseen his sister's irrational tendencies? "There's no way you can rearrange things so that you're in charge of the trust?" he asked.

"No. The beneficiaries of a trust are never the executors, too. Someone else always controls the money. And the person who sets up the trust—in this case, Chip—also decides who will control the dispersing of the trust's funds."

Not good. Brad sat back in his chair, drew a deep breath. "What are you going to do?" he asked.

Determination lit Lainey's eyes. "I'll tell you what I'm not going to do." She looked Brad straight in the eye. "I'm not going back to Dallas. And I'm not going to grovel. Not anymore."

"THAT'S SOME MEAL my big brother just missed," Lewis said, as Lainey cleared the plates and returned with a golden peach cobbler, still warm from the oven. She got out the ice cream and several dessert plates.

"My mom makes the best fried chicken," Petey said with a contented sigh.

"Don't forget the mashed potatoes and cream gravy and the green beans," Lewis said.

"And the salad," Petey added.

Lainey grinned, glad her efforts had been appreciated.

"Brad is going to be sorry he wasn't here," Lewis continued warmly. "Where is he, anyway? Did he say where he was going?"

Lainey shook her head. She regretted that Brad had missed the sit-down dinner in the ranch house kitchen, too. And not just because it would have helped set the stage for her eventual request for an interview with him.

"A couple of ranches to look at cattle. I'm not sure where exactly. He borrowed a livestock trailer from Travis, though. He expects to be coming back tomorrow with some of the herd."

"I can't wait to see that," Petey enthused. "I like trucks and animals as much as I like video games." Petey looked at Lewis shyly. "Thanks again for letting me be a tester."

"You're welcome, Petey. You and the other kids had some really fine ideas on how to improve the new prototypes."

Petey grinned and turned to Lainey. "Aunt Bunny said I wasn't going to like being out here, but she was wrong. This place really rocks!"

"I'm glad you like it," Lainey said quietly, doing her best to keep her temper in check. She was still angry at her sister-in-law for the stunt she'd pulled with Lainey's sole bank card. Lainey also knew she had only herself to blame for allowing herself to be in such a predicament. She could have gotten a job and her own money a long time ago. She hadn't.

She would now.

"I'm glad you enjoyed yourself, too," Lewis said, oblivious to the dark nature of Lainey's thoughts. "It's fun having a kid around here. Reminds me of when I was growing up."

"Were there a lot of kids in your family?" Petey asked.

"Five, besides me," Lewis said. He launched into tales of growing up one of five boys, with only one baby sister, Laurel. Petey was spellbound all through dessert, and dishes.

Lainey hung up the dish towel and checked her watch. Eight o'clock.

"You've done enough for today," Lewis said, reading her mind. "Why don't you knock off?"

Lainey looked at the rows of moving boxes stacked in the utility room and back hall. "I didn't get as much done as I had hoped to."

"So you'll stay a few days or weeks longer." Lewis winked at Petey. "You won't mind, will you, sport?"

In answer, Petey beamed.

Exhausted from the excitement, Petey was showered and tucked in bed by nine, and asleep by ten. When she was certain it was quiet, Lainey curled up with her computer again, and the DVDs of *Bachelor Bliss*. Lainey watched two more episodes. The closer she looked, the easier it was to see that Brad was not enjoying himself. The smile he wore was plastered on his face. He was genial, easygoing, gallant. But only around Yvonne Rathbone did he seem at all genuine. Yvonne appeared as if she was enjoying Brad's company just as much during the half-dozen or so outings that the two had.

Their last evening alone together was particularly romantic. Brad appeared totally smitten.

So what had happened to change that? Lainey wondered.

Why had he gone in the next day, clad not in the tux he was supposed to be wearing, but a pair of jeans and a Western shirt, stuck his hands in his pockets and told her, "You know what? This isn't working out. So what do you say you and I just do ourselves a favor and call it quits here and now?"

Yvonne—wearing a beautiful evening gown—gasped and broke into tears.

Brad turned and walked out.

The camera cut back to Yvonne, and her gasping, wrenching sobs.

Frowning because once again it seemed like Brad was a real cad, and not the quick-witted, warmhearted man she was getting to know, Lainey went back to the menu and clicked on the last episode of the series of shows featuring Brad. Brad and Yvonne were seated with the show host, discussing what had not happened during the final "ceremony."

Yvonne was tearful and obviously hurt by the fact Brad hadn't asked her to marry him. Brad didn't care. He was alternately ignoring or glaring at Yvonne as they "discussed"—or, to put it more aptly, *didn't* discuss—the situation. His anger was subtle, but there nevertheless.

Obviously, Lainey concluded as she watched it over and over again, Yvonne had done or said something to really anger Brad. Maybe not in front of the cameras, but away from them. The question was, *what?*

CHAPTER SIX

"MOMMY, LOOK!" Petey ran into the upstairs hall, where Lainey was organizing the linen closet early the next morning. Bypassing the snap-together building block set he had been playing with, he took her by the hand and dragged her to the window. Out in the yard, Brad was backing his pickup, and the livestock trailer behind it, toward the pasture gate.

"You think he's got another horse in there?" Petey asked.

Lainey hadn't seen such pure excitement on her son's face in a long time. She put her arm around his shoulders. "I don't know, honey."

"Can we go see? Please, Mommy!"

"All right." Lainey smiled. "But on one condition. We have to make sure we don't get in the way, so I want you to stay right by my side."

Petey nodded eagerly, already latching on to her hand. "I will, I promise."

By the time they reached the yard, Brad was out of the pickup and opening the rear doors of the trailer, which were situated inside the fence. "Whoa, there!" Brad said. "No. This way. Come on, fella. That's it. Right this way…."

Seconds later, a large rust-colored bull with horns at least four feet wide came lumbering down the ramp and onto the pasture grass. Brad followed, apparently unafraid, as the bull hit the ground and kept right on going, out onto the pasture. When he reached the watering hole in the center of it, he bent his head and began to drink.

Brad closed up the rear of the trailer, got back in the truck and moved it forward enough that he could go back and close and latch the gate.

As soon as that was done, Petey broke away from Lainey and ran toward Brad. "Wow!" Petey said. "Is that a real cow?"

Brad grinned. "It's a bull, Petey. And his name is Tabasco Red."

It also weighed a good thousand pounds. Lainey had only to look at her inquisitive little boy's face to know what he was thinking. "You aren't to go near him, Petey."

Petey frowned, disappointed and upset. "But Brad went near him," he complained.

"Brad is a grown-up. When you're a man, you can go near bulls, too. Not until then," Lainey said firmly.

Brad looked at Lainey. He appeared ready to differ with her. She sent him a look, letting him know that would not be wise. He remained blessedly silent.

"Are you going to get more bulls?" Petey asked.

"We've got twenty virgin heifers being delivered tomorrow," Brad told her son matter-of-factly.

"What's a virgin hecker?" Petey asked.

It was all Lainey could do not to cringe and cover her face.

"Heifer," Brad repeated, seeing Lainey's embarrassment and leaving out the "virgin" part this time. "And it's a young female cow who has never had a baby cow—or calf," Brad explained seriously.

"Oh." Petey mulled that over. "Are they going to be

out in the same place?" He pointed to the pasture closest to the house, where Tabasco Red stood chewing on grass.

"Not right away, no."

"Okay. That's enough questions, Petey." Lainey smiled, doing her best to pretend she wasn't the least bit discomfited by the conversation. She made a show of looking at her watch. "It's almost nine o'clock."

Petey perked up. "Time to go to my play date?"

"Yes," Lainey said.

Brad shot her an inquiring look.

"I got invited to go to another ranch," Petey informed Brad excitedly, "where there are two boys almost my age. Kyle and Kurt McCabe. They're supposed to be your cousins—I met 'em at the game company yesterday. They were testing stuff, too."

"That sounds like fun," Brad said, suitably impressed.

"It's going to be," Petey told Brad. "They have a swimming pool and a basketball hoop."

"If you want, I can drop Petey off," Brad said. "I'm on my way into town to buy feed, anyway. I'll go right by there."

Lainey looked at Petey. "That okay with you?"

Petey nodded. "Do we get to ride in the pickup?"

Brad slapped his hand on Petey's shoulder. "You bet!" The two swaggered off, side by side, with Petey doing his best to imitate his new hero.

LAINEY HAD MOVED on to Lewis's bedroom when her cell phone rang, shortly after noon. She continued hanging up clothes with one hand even as she answered.

"So, how's the search coming?" Sybil asked, shifting into editor mode the moment hellos had been said. "Have you been able to talk to Brad McCabe yet?"

"I'm working on it," Lainey said, frowning as she looked at a suit of Lewis's that would have been better suited to the Beatles, circa 1965. "I have to tell you, though, Brad McCabe is still in no mood to be interviewed."

"I assume you're working on getting him to change his mind."

Not as hard as I should be, Lainey thought guiltily, aware if truth be told that she was more interested in getting to know the man he was now, than what had happened on Bachelor Bliss.

"You've got a great opportunity here," Sybil stressed.

"I won't blow it," Lainey promised.

"That's what I wanted to hear," Sybil countered cheerfully. "In the meantime, I've been using my contacts in the business to see what I could uncover, too."

"Got anything?" Lainey switched into reporter mode.

"I just got off the phone with Yvonne Rathbone's manager. Apparently, she's been hired to do guest spots on two of the network's dramas. The episodes are going to air early in the fall." There was a rustle of paper on the other end. "I managed to get you a telephone interview with the producer who hired her. Call this number—" Sybil paused to read off a ten-digit number and extension, while Lainey wrote it down "—at precisely two o'clock Pacific time, and Rocco Talmadge will speak with you. Have your questions ready. Five minutes is all you've got."

Lainey was alone in the ranch house, working on Brad's bedroom, when the time came to make the call.

She perched on the edge of the bed, notepad of questions in hand. As promised, she was put right through to Rocco Talmadge, the producer who had hired Brad's ex.

"Were Yvonne Rathbone's appearances on two network dramas part of the deal when she signed on to do *Bachelor Bliss?*" Lainey asked.

"No. This was arranged after that stud broke her heart and the whole country fell in love with her."

"So, it's just a publicity stunt, then, to attract viewers?"

Rocco sighed. "Could have been. That's what I figured it would be—if we hired her. But that was before she came in to do a screen test for us last week. Yvonne was just flat-out amazing. She nailed her dialogue and conjured up all the right emotions at just the right time. She even had the camera work down, although I guess that's not surprising given the fact she just spent six weeks filming *Bachelor Bliss*."

Lainey recalled Yvonne had been a copier sales rep before she quit to do reality TV. "Has Yvonne acted before?"

"No. She's just a natural, I guess."

Interesting, Lainey thought. Had Yvonne's stellar "acting" ability somehow played into the breakup with Brad, his reasons for wanting to dump her, regardless of what was expected of him? "Do you think Yvonne will have other acting opportunities after this?"

"If she manages the actual taping as well as the auditions? Absolutely! Listen, I've got to go. Thank the people at *Personalities Magazine* for mentioning this. It's bound to boost our ratings."

Lainey knew a little free publicity never hurt. "No problem."

Still musing over what she had learned, Lainey cut the connection and put her phone back on her belt, just as a door slammed downstairs. Quickly, she put her notepad and phone into the deep slash pocket of her skirt and went back to hanging up jeans.

Seconds later, Brad strode into the room. His hat was off and his shirt was unbuttoned to the waist. He seemed surprised to see her standing there.

"What?" he said abruptly, looking her up and down. He took off his shirt and tossed it into the hamper Lainey had put in the adjoining bathroom.

She blinked, unable to take her eyes off his broad shoulders and nicely muscled chest. The satiny smooth skin had been shaved when he was filming *Bachelor Bliss*. No more. The suntanned flesh was covered with sable-brown hair that spread across his pecs, and arrowed down past his navel to disappear beneath the waistband of his jeans.

"What do you mean—what?" she mocked.

He strode closer, smelling like sweat and man. "Why do you have that look on your face?"

The one that indicated her heart was racing, her knees were weak, and there was a fluttery, melting sensation in the middle of her tummy? Knowing it would irritate him, Lainey played dumb. "What look?"

Brad's brown eyes narrowed as he studied her intently. "I don't know. Guilty, maybe?"

Of course—since she was here under at least partly false pretenses. But unable to tell Brad any of that yet, Lainey shrugged. "I'm uncomfortable, definitely."

His brow furrowed. "Because?"

"I was in here, in your bedroom, working, when you came striding in, tossing off clothes right and left."

"I wouldn't call one shirt 'clothes.'"

Lainey ignored his joke. "I would. And I think I should be leaving now…." She started to step past, heart racing all the more.

"Don't you want to know why I'm undressing?" Brad called after her in the low, sexy voice that had broken so many bachelorettes' hearts.

She turned, discovering Brad had his boots, belt and socks off, too.

"We've all been invited to Annie and Travis McCabe's for dinner." He disappeared into the bath, returned with a can of shaving cream in hand.

What was it about a man in nothing but a pair of jeans, and whatever he had under them…? "Thanks for letting me know." She folded her arms in front of her and watched as he spread lather over his face. "But I'm not sure I can go. I have an awful lot of work to do here." And an awful lot of research and interviewing to do, too….

Brad plucked his razor off the sink and began running that through the cream, disappearing from view from time to time to watch what he was doing in the mirror. "Petey will be awful disappointed if you don't show up. He's having a great time over there. I think he wanted to share the ranch with you."

Put like that…how could she say no? "Well, maybe for a little while." She wanted her son to be happy as much as she wanted the truth about Brad and Yvonne and their *Bachelor Bliss* experience to be known.

Brad rinsed his face and blotted it with a towel. "Be ready to go in an hour?"

"No problem." She edged toward the door, reluctant to leave, knowing she had no apparent reason to stay.

"Something on your mind?" he asked curiously, moving with her.

Damn him for being so intuitive. "I was just thinking," she said finally.

"About?"

How someone so obviously sensitive to others could be so cruel to a woman he had—at least on TV—fancied himself in love with. But aware this wasn't the moment to bring that up—that it would take a lot more subtlety to work the question into the conversation—Lainey said, instead, the first inane thing that came to mind. "I was just wondering about those cows you are having delivered tomorrow," she fibbed. "They're not going to be in the same pasture as that bull, are they?"

Brad gave her a bemused look as he went to his closet and flipped through the Western shirts Lainey had just ironed, organized and hung up. "That's kind of the point of buying twenty virgin heifers," he told her drolly.

She cringed. It was all she could do not to cover her ears. "Please don't call them that." It conjured up thoughts of sex. And sex was the last thing she needed between her and Brad.

"What would you like me to call them?" he asked, mischief turning up the corners of his lips. He leaned against the bathroom door frame, brawny arms folded in front of him.

Lainey knew her eyes were suddenly sparkling, too. "Cows?" she guessed timidly, knowing her lack of knowledge about ranching matters was endless.

"How about longhorns?" he said dryly.

"Fine." She took a deep steadying breath and tore her eyes from the sleek masculine contours of his chest. She was not going to wonder what it was like to touch him. There. Or there… "Back to the, uh…um…" Oh, dear heavens. Couldn't she keep her mind on the conversation they were having for one second?

"Inseminating?" Brad asked helpfully, even more mischief in his eyes.

"Yes." She steeled herself not to be so attracted to him. She had a job to do here, she reminded herself sternly. Two jobs! "Can you please not have the longhorns mating in front of Petey."

His chuckle filled the air. "Where would you like me to take them? A bedroom?"

Lainey failed to contain the blush rising upward from her neck. "How about the barn? Couldn't they, um, do it there?" She couldn't believe she had just said that. And judging from the look on Brad's face, neither could be.

"These are longhorns," he told her matter-of-factly. "They need room to maneuver and the freedom to—how should we say it…engage?—when they feel like it."

Lainey sputtered, "But Petey—"

"Probably knows a lot more than you think," Brad interjected.

Lainey scoffed and folded her arms over her chest. "He doesn't know about this," she stated firmly.

Brad straightened and sauntered toward Lainey. "Then maybe it's time he did."

Lainey watched as Brad carried the jeans and shirt he had selected into the bathroom and hung them on the hook inside the door, then returned to his bureau to search for the black knit Jockey shorts she had also put away. "I'm not prepared to talk to him about the birds and the bees just yet."

He took his socks and underwear into the bathroom and plunked them down on the nicely organized black ceramic tiled counter. "Then just talk to him about bulls and heifers," he said.

Lainey paced back and forth, her slides echoing

against the wooden floor. "That might lead to other questions," she said.

He looked down at the hot pink polish she had put on her toenails the evening before. "Yes, it certainly might," he drawled.

She struggled not to react to the way his glance was slowly moving up her bare legs. "You're not being at all helpful!" she scolded.

For lack of a better place to sit, Brad went back to lounging on his bed, legs spread, arms resting on the mattress on either side of him. He looked at her and slowly shook his head. "You're not being at all realistic if you think a kid can be around animals and not eventually get some idea of how Mother Nature works."

Lainey didn't know whether to slug him or kiss him. Truth was, she wanted to do both. "So you won't help me out with this?" she asked, piqued.

Brad rubbed the underside of his jaw, testing the just-shaved smoothness of his skin. "I'll talk to Petey, and explain to him what's going on and why, if you want," he offered, all cocky male.

"That wasn't what I meant!" Lainey threw up her hands in exasperation and stomped closer.

He offered an engaging half grin. "I know what you meant."

Lainey moved even closer. "You can be very aggravating," she told him, even as she was aware a chance like this might not ever come again.

"So I've been told," he admitted rakishly.

"Is that why you broke up with Yvonne Rathbone the way you did, just to be aggravating?" Lainey asked.

THE QUESTION CAME out of nowhere, and spoiled the playful mood that had sprung up between them. "Why do you care?" Brad asked her, aware she was one of the most natural beauties he had ever seen in his life. Everything about her was extraordinarily fine. From the top of her honey-blond hair to the tips of her toes, she was one memorable woman. Which of course made her unprecedented nosy question all the harder to take.

Lainey shrugged. A self-conscious flush darkened her cheeks but she didn't back down. "I'm curious."

"Curiosity killed the cat."

She kept her eyes on his. "I'm no feline."

Brad sighed, not about to argue that point. "You're all woman, all right." Palpable tension arose between them as Lainey edged closer.

"So what happened?" Lainey pushed him deliberately. "Did the two of you sleep together? Did Yvonne disappoint you in bed? Is that what happened to make you walk away?"

Brad's gut told him two things. One, Lainey didn't look as if she wanted him to have that kind of past with Yvonne. Two, he had the feeling Lainey had said that just to get a reaction. He and his brothers used to do that to each other, when they were growing up, whenever they wanted to dig out the truth. They'd say something so outrageous that the target of the innuendo would have to say something to defend himself. Before they knew it, the real story was out there.

But the two of them weren't kids.

They were adults. Who were ready to cross a boundary from which Brad sensed there would be no turning back.

"You're aware you're really out of line, here," he informed her.

Lainey tilted her head. "At least I'm not afraid."

She headed for the door. Brad was on his feet before

she could take two steps. He clamped a hand on her shoulder and swung her around to face him. "What does that mean?"

Her slender shoulders lifted in a shrug. "I just don't understand why you refuse to talk about what happened with Yvonne."

Back to that again. "Maybe I like my privacy."

"And maybe you're embarrassed."

"What do I have to be embarrassed about?" he demanded gruffly. Aware her skin was heating where his fingers rested, he dropped his hand.

"Your behavior?" she countered sweetly. "I mean, it's not every day that a guy dumps a perfectly nice woman without provocation on national TV."

Anger roiled inside him once again. "My actions weren't without provocation," he defended himself hotly.

Her teeth worried the softness of her lower lip. She searched his face and asked the question Brad had already heard a thousand times, from family and friends. "What did Yvonne do that was so bad?"

He hadn't answered anyone else. Maybe it was time that changed. He knew if he didn't tell someone at least part of what happened soon, he was going to explode. "Yvonne led me to believe some things that were not true. And then she made damn sure I'd find out what kind of person she really was fifteen minutes before the taping of the final ceremony was to start."

Brad had hoped Lainey would leave it at that. Of course, she didn't.

"I don't understand," she said slowly. "Why would Yvonne do something like that when you were about to propose to her and she was in love with you, and you both could have walked away with lucrative endorsement contracts if only you had stayed together?"

He sighed. "Yvonne wasn't in love with me."

Lainey lifted her brows. "She sure looked like she was on TV."

"Well, she wasn't," he said harshly.

"That still doesn't answer the question as to why she would do something guaranteed to make you break up with her, at the very time she was set to win everything," Lainey persisted.

"Maybe," Brad said harshly, "because Yvonne got a lot more attention playing the victim after she was dumped than she would have had if she rode off into the sunset to live happily ever after with me."

Well, that much was true, Lainey had to admit. The story of Brad and Yvonne's live on-air breakup had captivated the media for weeks. Still, the smitten way Yvonne had looked at Brad as "their love" unfolded had certainly seemed genuine enough. Which meant Lainey had to ask the hard questions, even if Brad didn't want to hear them. Shifting into full reporter mode, she continued her probing. "So you're saying what—that Yvonne was just pretending all along?"

"Who knows." He shrugged.

Once again, Lainey had the sensation he was withholding tons more than he was telling.

"All I can tell you is that she sure had me fooled."

Not to mention the rest of the country, Lainey thought. She sat down on the edge of the bed. "I guess that explains why you acted so cold and hostile and uncaring toward Yvonne during the last show." If Brad had felt personally betrayed—duped—by Yvonne, his actions made sense.

He exhaled. “It was all I could do to get through that Heart Ceremony.”

“Then why did you?” Why stride in there, hell for leather, and treat someone badly on camera when you knew millions of viewers were watching? she wondered.

He shoved his hands through his hair. “I went because I’d signed a contract. And the show’s producers told me they’d sue me for five million in damages if I walked. So I met my obligation.”

Now that was a scoop. “The producers must have been unhappy.”

“Are you kidding? That was exactly what they wanted. Ratings had been going down on all the *Bachelor Bliss* shows. The novelty of TV romance was wearing pretty thin. The show’s creator, Gil Hewitt, knew the only way to keep the show on the air was to create some real-life drama.”

“But you weren’t in on the game,” Lainey said carefully.

“I wouldn’t have cooperated had I known what kind of behind-the-scenes minidrama Gil Hewitt had planned.”

A drama Brad still hadn’t fully explained—and he didn’t look likely to, either. “Were all the women in on this?” Lainey treaded carefully, wary of scaring him off with questions that were too pointed and probing.

“I don’t know for sure, but I don’t think anyone witnessed what happened except me, Yvonne, and the person on the show who made darn sure the grand finale all happened according to plan.”

And that was the way Brad obviously wanted it to stay, Lainey realized in mounting frustration. “So the big reveal wasn’t on camera?” she guessed, wondering why the *Bachelor Bliss* producers had stopped short of showing that, too. Unless doing so would have tipped the hand as to what would happen next.

"No. Thank God. Although—" Brad stopped, shook his head and didn't go on.

Frustrated but not defeated, Lainey persevered. "And you never suspected...during the show's filming...that anything was amiss?"

He shrugged and took on a brooding expression. "Looking back, I see the way the show's staff kept pushing me toward Yvonne as a mate," he allowed finally.

"And you were okay with that." Lainey knew it had sure looked that way on the TV screen.

"It sounds crazy now, knowing what I do about the conniving...sneak, but at the time, I thought Yvonne might very well be the perfect woman for me. She appeared to be everything I had ever wanted."

Lainey pushed aside a flare of jealousy. With effort, she stayed professional and zeroed in on his suspicions. "You don't think that happened by chance, do you?"

Brad shook his head. "No. I think someone gave Yvonne advance access to the questionnaires that we filled out when we were accepted as contestants. There were pages and pages of them, plus interviews with psychologists to make sure we were emotionally fit to be in this type of program."

"And Yvonne used the information she gleaned to—?"

"Simultaneously undercut other contestants and make herself into a persona that fulfilled my every fantasy."

For reasons Lainey preferred not to examine too closely, she didn't ask what precise "fantasies" were fulfilled. "That's a pretty hefty accusation," she stated calmly, wishing she weren't thinking about taking Brad in her arms again and claiming him as hers and hers alone.

"But true, nonetheless."

They sat there in silence. "Now do you see why I want nothing to do with the show or anyone on it ever again?" Brad said finally, meeting her eyes.

Lainey nodded sympathetically, understanding that he had been humiliated and betrayed, and was—as most men would be—still very reluctant to talk about an incident that had so damaged his pride. But he needed to talk about it, and get it all out, as much as she needed for him to do so.

Unfortunately for her, Brad hadn't yet divulged the details that if disclosed would make Lainey's story a sensation. Which meant she had to try harder to help him, and herself, and her friend, Sybil. Most of all, she wanted to set the record straight. Get the truth out there once and for all. End the innuendo, the lies, and most of all, the damage to Brad's reputation.

"The thing is, Brad," she said, looking deep into his eyes, "ignoring what happened is not going to make it all go away."

CHAPTER SEVEN

BRAD KNEW HE SHOULDN'T have started down this road. He wasn't even sure why he had. Except, there was something about Lainey, the way she asked questions, the way she wanted to understand everything about him, that held him spellbound. She fascinated him in a way no other woman had.

"You should tell your side of the story, and I mean every bit of it, Brad, and clear your name," Lainey said.

So everyone said. Trying not to notice how pretty she looked in the late-afternoon sunlight streaming in through the windows, Brad turned his gaze away from her and removed his boots. "I'm tired of explaining myself," he stated gruffly.

"Then let someone else do it for you," Lainey persisted. "Someone you trust."

Annoyed, Brad leaned forward, elbows resting on his thighs. "And who would that be?" he demanded, giving her an arch look.

For a second, Lainey looked as if she had a very specific idea who that might be but was afraid to suggest it. The moment passed, and she shrugged. "There are a lot of different venues," she said carefully, coming closer, so they might continue talking in the low intimate tones that fit the situation. "Magazines, TV shows, even newspapers. But the avenue that would benefit you most financially would be a book deal."

"A book," Brad repeated.

"Yes. A tell-all." Lainey remained directly in front of him, her body braced in challenge. Knowing she wasn't going to back down kicked his heartbeat up another notch.

"Forget it." He stood, restless as ever. Then made the mistake of looking at her again. For the life of him, he couldn't figure out why she persisted in dressing so nicely for such rigorous work. Most people wore old clothes—shorts and T-shirts—when they unpacked moving boxes. Lainey was clad in a sunny yellow cotton skirt and matching white-and-yellow diagonal-striped top. Her legs, arms and shoulders were bare, the exposed skin soft and silky looking. Facts that only added to her appeal. And his bad judgment for noticing. Hadn't he determined after the *Bachelor Bliss* debacle that he wasn't going to get involved with a woman again for a good long while? And a woman like Lainey would, by definition, require emotional involvement.

"You're such a hot commodity right now that with the proper agent you could probably get a deal well into the six figures. Now, that may not be what you would have earned doing commercials after the show, but it's still a lot of money, and it would go a long way toward helping you buy into this ranch as a full partner the way you had planned."

That did sound good. Baring—no, *selling*—his soul did not. Deliberately, he kept his eyes on her face. "For starters, I can't write."

She offered a tantalizing half smile. "I'm sure the publisher could pair you with an excellent ghostwriter."

The thought of furthering his public pillorying was

unacceptable. "No. My private life remains private." He started toward the bathroom.

Lainey followed, looking just as determined as he felt. She leaned a slender shoulder against the door frame as he bent to splash cold water on his face. "You're fooling yourself if you think what happened will remain secret forever. Someone is going to find out about it, and then they'll benefit, and you won't. Again!"

She was calling him a chump. And maybe he *was* one for letting the conversation go on this long. Brad dropped the towel onto the sink. "You want me to benefit from all this?" he said, his mood shifting as he moved toward her.

Pique flashed in her eyes. "That's what I've been saying, isn't it?"

"Then how about you help me out?" Brad retorted as he stopped in front of her.

Giving her no chance to respond, he wrapped his arms around her and pulled her close. He heard her soft gasp of surprise as his head dropped, and then his lips were on hers, their mouths fusing as one, their bodies pressing close together. Heat flooded through him. Lower still, blood pooled into an insistent ache.

Brad hadn't meant to do anything but shut Lainey up in the most shocking way possible. He hadn't expected her to melt against him, or to open her mouth to the plundering pressure of his, or to kiss him back. He'd figured he deserved a slap across the face. Not this sweet, gentle, loving invitation to dally.

Lainey knew it was a mistake pushing Brad, just as it was a mistake to allow him to take her in his arms. She should be fighting for what she wanted here, instead of devoting herself to helping him. But she couldn't help it. Something about his stubborn male pride, the hidden vulnerability in his heart, combined to draw her like a moth to the flame.

And full of fire, he was.

She'd never been kissed like this. With such fierce possessiveness and total mastery. Nor had she ever allowed herself to melt into anyone so completely. Always before, there had been that careful wall of restraint. The veneer of cool sophistication she had worked so hard to achieve.

There was nothing reserved about the way he was dancing her backward toward the bedroom wall. Nothing subtle about the way he held her there, arms flattened on either side of her head, body pressed warmly against hers. Brad was kissing her as if she were already his woman, and damn if she didn't feel like that just might be the case.

But deep down she knew that if she allowed him to make love with her, then and there, it would mean no turning back. Brad McCabe would have not just her body, but her heart. That truth brought Lainey crashing down to earth. Realizing she had no other choice, she removed her arms from about his neck, tore her mouth from his and pushed him away with all her strength.

BRAD WATCHED HER MOVE a short distance away. Sauntering closer, he girded his thighs and crossed his arms as if for battle. "What? No slap?"

"Not that you don't deserve it." Feeling heat in her cheeks, Lainey spoke as if underlining every word.

"But?"

Not about to let him get the better of her, now or at any other time, Lainey held her ground, despite the fact they were now uncomfortably close. Close enough to start kissing again. Close enough for her to inhale the musky scent of man and sweat clinging to his skin. Close enough to see the speculation gleaming in his brown eyes. "If I'm going over to Annie and Travis's for dinner with Petey, I need to get cleaned up."

A devilish smile tugged at the corners of his lips. "I like you the way you are," Brad said. Bracing his legs a little farther apart, he skimmed her provocatively with his gaze. "All mussed up."

When he looked at her like that, Lainey felt sexy and powerful, in a very decadent and satisfying way. Unwilling to consider what it would be like if someone as used to having his own way as Brad McCabe became part of her life, Lainey drew an unsteady breath. "I'm not one of your women," she said. Although, she noted in dismay, she had been acting as if she were—advising Brad to seek a book contract instead of an exclusive interview with her.

Times like this she had to wonder if she possessed the necessary single-mindedness required for her profession. An ace reporter destined for fame and fortune would have been focused on the story they were trying to research, not looking out for the best interests of others to her own detriment.

"Women?" he repeated with a look of utter male supremacy, drawing her back to their conversation.

Finding his low, seductive voice a little bit too disarming, Lainey turned away. "You know what I mean."

"I know what you think you mean." Ignoring her resistance, he pulled her back into his arms. "And just so you know—" he leaned forward and whispered in her ear "—I never thought you were one of my women."

Heart pounding, she studied him. He wasn't hitting on her, wasn't attempting to kiss her again. He was just playing mind games with her. Giving her reason to stay away from him and not bring up the subject of his experience on *Bachelor Bliss* again.

Still, the embrace, and her reaction to it, stayed with her all through dinner at the neighboring Rocking Diamond Ranch. She was still distracted by the searing memories as she, Annie and the other adults—Lewis, Travis and Brad—took their coffee out onto the wraparound porch. The three boys were out in the side yard, playing fetch with Duke, the family's big black Lab.

"So, how's Tabasco Red doing? Has he settled in okay?" Travis asked Brad.

Brad nodded. "So far, he's doing fine."

"I've got a heifer in the barn you might want to take a look at," Travis said. "A little on the scrawny side," he continued as the three men set their coffee cups aside and ambled down the porch, "but good bloodlines and I'd be willing to let her go cheap, if you're interested...."

As soon as the men were out of earshot, Annie kicked back in her rocking chair. "So, how is the organizing going?"

Relieved to think about something other than the man who had her totally fascinated...and confused, Lainey smiled. "I've got the kitchen and two offices downstairs done. Today, I've been working on the bedrooms."

"Lewis said you've been amazing."

She flashed Annie a look of gratitude. "Thanks to your help getting the furniture in the right place, and some of the extraneous junk cleared out, I got off to a mighty fast start." Almost too fast, as she was going to be finished in no time. And once she was, she would have no more excuse to stay on. She didn't want to think about how depressing that was. She was enjoying being back in Laramie, living on a ranch for the first time in her life. Petey liked it, too. "Besides, all I really had to do was unpack boxes and put things away. It hasn't been all that hard."

Annie poured more coffee, then set the carafe back on the white wicker table between them. "You wouldn't know it to hear Lewis talk. He thinks you're a miracle worker. And speaking of men in need of miracles..." Her smile widened. "My nephew—Lewis and Brad's brother, Riley—is moving back to Laramie in August. He just finished his residency and has taken a position at Laramie Community Hospital. Anyway, he's going to need some similar work, and he'd like to hire you to help him get organized, if possible."

"No problem." Lainey planned to take on as much work as she could handle.

"You ought to start your own business as a professional organizer," Annie continued.

Was that what she wanted? Or did she want to continue to pursue her long-held dream of being a journalist? All Lainey knew for sure was that she had some serious choices ahead of her. Like how far she was willing to go to uncover Brad McCabe's secret.

Annie studied Lainey. "Is that frown related to our discussion—or to the man who has you tied in knots?"

Lainey wasn't used to talking about her personal life, but heaven knows she needed to confide in someone. "It's that obvious?" she asked wearily.

"Let's just say I recognize the particular type of tension flowing between you and Brad because it used to flow like the Rio Grande between Travis and me before we hooked up."

Lainey recalled Annie and Travis had enjoyed the kind of high-profile romance that'd had the whole community buzzing, yet they had come out of it with a relationship that only seemed to get stronger and more loving every year. Lainey gazed at the rosebushes Annie had planted next to the porch.

"Is Brad the kind of womanizer everyone says he is?"

"There's no shortage of women pursuing him. He's so handsome and charming. I just don't think he's allowed himself to get caught very often, if at all."

"A good-time guy," Lainey paraphrased, her mood as careful and wary as it should have been earlier.

Annie sighed, worry coming into her pretty eyes. "Let's just say, before Brad did *Bachelor Bliss*, he never minded entering a party with a pretty woman on his arm. Now, he's lucky if he gives any female the time of day."

That was certainly how Brad had behaved when Lainey had first showed up at the Lazy M to talk to Lewis. But lately, Brad had been giving her a lot more than the time of day. But then, she had kind of gotten in his face, in her efforts to get the real story out of him. If Lainey were half the reporter Sybil seemed to think she was, she would have told Brad right away who she was working for and pressed a lot harder to get him to 'fess up. Instead, she was letting Brad's comfort level—instead of her own pressing timetable—dictate her reporting. She was easing off on the scoop of the summer, wishing instead that she could spend more time with Brad, just for the sake of their getting to know each other. How crazy was that?

Annie shook her head at Lainey. "He's really gotten to you, hasn't he?"

Whoo, boy, had he. Lainey had never been this distracted—and fascinated—by a man before. She pushed out of her rocking chair, and moved to the edge of the porch. Abruptly, she realized the ranch had gotten awfully quiet. Never a good sign where kids were concerned. She peered around to the side yard. No boys. No dog. Uh-oh. "Do you know where the kids went?" she asked.

Annie's brow furrowed. "They're supposed to be right there."

Worry slid to panic. "They're not."

Annie leaped out of her chair. She was halfway down the front porch, with Lainey right after her. At the same time, Travis, Brad and Lewis emerged from the barn closest to the ranch house. Annie cupped her hands around her mouth and yelled at Travis, "Are the boys with you?"

Travis shook his head.

In the distance, there was a bark.

Then another.

And another.

They all turned in the direction of the sound.

In the distance, Duke could be seen leaping and bounding through a pasture of four-foot-high grass, bordering a thicket of cedar trees and juniper bushes.

"Oh, no!" Annie said, frowning.

Travis frowned, too. "I'll get 'em," he said.

"YOU BOYS KNOW BETTER than to go out there in shorts and tennis shoes," Annie scolded, as the boys and their dog returned to the yard where they were supposed to be hanging out.

"We were just playing ranchers and rustlers," nine-year-old Kurt explained to the five grown-ups who had been worried about them.

"Yeah." Eight-year-old Kyle chimed in, more

interested in the game they had been playing than the safety issues in question. "Kurt stole Rocco—he was pretending to be our prize bull—and me and Petey had to go and get 'em."

"That's all fine and good," Travis said sternly. "But you need to play that game in the yard where we can see you."

Brad nodded in agreement, looking sober indeed. "Those woods are deceptively deep. You guys could get lost out there."

"Or at the very least come down with a good case of poison oak or ivy!" Lainey said, belatedly aware she hadn't once thought to caution Petey about that. But she hadn't expected him to run off, either. "You don't have jeans and long-sleeved shirts on," she explained, more to her son than to the other two boys who lived on the ranch and knew the precautions necessary. "You're in shorts and T-shirts."

Abruptly, Petey's temper flared. "I don't even have any jeans here, Mom!" he fumed.

Lainey stared at her son in shock, embarrassed by his sassy tone. "Since when do you talk back to me?"

Petey folded his arms and glared at Lainey petulantly. "Since you treat me like a baby instead of a grown-up guy."

Well, maybe that's because you're not a grown-up guy, Lainey thought, aware this was not a discussion she wanted to have here. "I think we need to go home," she said, plastering a cordial smile on her face. She knew she was being abrupt, but it had been a very long day and she could see Petey was close to a meltdown. "Thank you so much for a lovely dinner and play date."

"I don't want to go home!" Petey shouted in a manner that was completely unlike him.

His two playmates, who might be prone to mischief but knew better than to talk back, fell silent, looking shocked, too. Duke lay on the ground at their feet, panting hard after his exertion in the heat of the summer evening.

"We're going," Lainey said firmly. She put her hand on Petey's shoulder.

Petey jerked free. He was already scratching furiously at his neck, legs and arms.

Brad's expression went from sympathy to concern. "Better get him in the shower as soon as possible. Lots of soap and water everywhere he might have come into contact with poison oak, ivy or sumac."

"You guys, too." Annie herded her two youngest sons toward the house.

Travis nodded before turning to follow his wife and boys. "And be careful handling his clothes," he told Lainey. "They could have the oily residue from the poison weeds on them, too."

"Thanks," Lainey said. She knew all this, but it had been so long since she'd been out in the Texas countryside and had had to deal with it that she had almost forgotten.

"You can't make me do anything I don't want to do!" Petey continued to shout ferociously.

Tired of fooling around, Lainey took Petey by the arm, her manner no-nonsense. "We'll just see about that, young man," she said, already guiding him in the direction of their SUV. "Now march!"

LAINEY PHONED THE RANCH HOUSE as soon as Petey was out of the shower. "Do you guys have anything for chigger bites on hand?" If they didn't, she was going to have to pack Petey in the car, pajamas and all, and drive to town.

"Be right over," Brad said.

He was at the guest house door two minutes later, bottle of Listerine mouthwash in hand, looking ready, able and eager to help.

"The insect bites are on his arms, legs, neck and face, not in his mouth," Lainey said dryly, feeling ridiculously glad to have him there as backup. She ushered him inside.

"Oh, ye of little faith," Brad said dryly. Petey emerged from the bathroom, clad in a pair of cotton sleep shorts and a Texas Rangers T-shirt.

Brad knelt in front of Petey. "Pretty miserable, huh?"

Petey glared at Lainey, like she was the worst mother on the entire planet, then looked back at Brad with a sad little nod. "I itch so bad," Petey whispered, as if Brad were his only friend left in the world.

Brad gave Petey a reassuring pat on his shoulder, letting Petey know with a look that things were going to be all right very soon, then asked Lainey quietly, "Do you have a small bowl or something I could pour this into?"

Lainey went to get it. Brad followed, her son in hand, and hefted Petey onto the kitchen counter as if he weighed five—not sixty-five—pounds. "This seem strange to you?" Brad asked Petey as he dipped a cotton ball into the minty-smelling mouthwash and began daubing it on the red welts on Petey's legs.

Petey nodded.

"Well, give it a minute," Brad advised.

"That feels kind of good," Petey said, after a

moment. He looked at Brad gratefully. "It doesn't itch no more."

"Anymore," Lainey corrected.

Petey glared at her again.

"Forgive me for being a mother," she muttered under her breath.

Brad grinned. He gave Petey a commiserating look as he dipped the cotton ball in mouthwash and began attending to the angry red bites on Petey's arms. "Women." Brad shook his head. "What are you going to do?"

Petey mimicked Brad's droll gesture and heaved a great big sigh. "I don't know," he said.

Grateful to Brad not only for making her son more comfortable, but for defusing the potentially explosive situation, Lainey leaned against the counter, watching. Chip had loved Petey dearly, but he had been a hands-off father when it came to anything practical. Chip had never changed a diaper, or gotten up with Petey in the middle of the night, or helped him learn his spelling words. She sensed Brad would do all that for any child of his, and more.

"Where did you get the idea to do this?" she asked.

"My brother, Riley."

"The physician who is coming to town soon?"

"Right. He learned it in medical school. I guess they did some studies and found that the herbal ingredients in Listerine have both antifungal and anti-itch properties. It kills the chigger, soothes the site of the bite, and voilà...you're better before you know it." Brad daubed Listerine on the spots on Petey's neck, then stood back. "Okay, cowboy, do you feel like I missed any? Are you still itching anywhere?"

Petey shook his head. "Thanks, Brad."

"You're welcome." Brad held out his hand. "Put her there, pardner."

Petey shook his hand.

Lainey hated to break it up, but she knew Petey was tired to the point of exhaustion. "Okay, sport, thank Brad and then head to bed."

Petey turned to Lainey, the anger gone. In its place was the need to make up with her, at least most of the way, before he went to sleep. "Can I read for a little bit?"

Lainey doubted he'd get past two pages, but she never discouraged reading. She knew it was the key to his future success. "Yes."

Petey turned back to Brad. "Thank you for helping me out. My mommy wouldn't have known what to do to make me stop itching so fast."

Lainey's jaw dropped. That wasn't quite true. And the glint in Brad's eyes as he glanced at her told her he knew it, too.

"Anytime you need anything you let me know." Brad ruffled Petey's head. The boy grinned and started back to his bedroom. Lainey was about to say something when her son turned back, gave her a brief, sorrow-laced hug, and then departed once again. Brad returned to the kitchen. He capped the bottle of Listerine. "You want to keep this? I've got an extra bottle at the house."

"If you don't mind, I think I will. And thanks—for helping and coming over." Lainey walked him out to the front porch. Darkness was descending. It was going to be a clear, pretty night, with lots of stars in the velvety Texas sky overhead.

"I'm sorry he was upset earlier."

"He was just overtired," she said.

"Sure that's all it is?"

Leave it to Brad to hit the nail on the head. Lainey bit her lip. Who would have thought he could be this easy to talk to? "He's having a hard time lately."

Brad's expression gentled. "Because he lost his dad?"

Lainey hesitated, more unsure of herself than ever. Something else that was unusual. Her ability to mother was the one thing she had always been confident about. "I don't know. It's been two years."

"Yet—?" He studied her, guessing there was more.

Lainey perched on the porch railing, her back to the yard, and ran a hand down the sturdy wooden post that supported the roof. "He was doing so well. I mean, initially, when Chip died, he had trouble concentrating at school, cried a lot and missed his father terribly during holidays. But as time wore on and almost two years passed, he seemed to be coping great. Then, suddenly, this last spring, he wasn't coping so well anymore. The things that used to make him so happy—spending time with his cousins, going on family outings, even going to the playground at the park—have left him tense and irritable."

Compassion crossed Brad's face beneath the warm glow of the porch lights. "Because he misses his dad?"

"And because he's growing up without one and thinks I treat him too much like a baby."

Edging nearer, Brad stood with his legs braced apart, hands in the back pockets of his jeans. "You don't. I've seen you with him. You are remarkably gentle and respectful, even when Petey's in the midst of having a meltdown."

"Thank you." She ducked her head. "But I don't feel so competent." She lifted her head again and looked into his eyes. "That's why I wanted to spend some time in Laramie this summer and let him participate in the game-testing program at Lewis's company. And be out here at the ranch, too. I thought a change of pace might lift his spirits. Take the quarrelsome edge, that occasionally seems to appear with no warning or reason, off his demeanor. I thought it was working, that he was really happy again. Now, I'm not so sure."

Brad moved to perch beside her on the railing. He reached over and took her hand in his. "He's just a little kid, Lainey. He's going to have his good days and his bad, regardless of how you mother him."

She tried not to think about how good it felt to have her hand clasped in that warm, strong palm. "And how would you know that?" she probed.

Brad grimaced, the brooding look back in his eyes. "Because I lost a parent, too."

CHAPTER EIGHT

COMPASSION FILLED Lainey's heart. "How old were you when your mom died?"

"Fourteen. But she was ill for months before that."

"Breast cancer, right?" Lainey asked, aware this was the first time Brad had allowed himself to be really vulnerable to her.

He nodded. "I was a lot older than Petey. Old enough to understand that life isn't always fair, and sometimes people get sick and they die. But it was still hard for me and my siblings and especially my dad, because he loved my mom so much. We all did."

Lainey had been married with a family of her own when she lost her parents. That had been difficult enough. She tightened her grip on Brad's hand. "As a kid…as a family…how did you cope?" Did the McCabes have some lessons they could impart to her?

"At first we were just so numb," Brad allowed reluctantly. His eyes took on a distant look. "I think to outsiders it looked like we were doing better than we were because everyone was still going through the motions, just the way we had when Mom was alive. But then as time went on the charade got harder and harder to maintain and everything began to fall apart. We went through nanny after nanny. Finally, in desperation, Dad moved us here, and that's when Kate Marten—my step-mother—came into our lives and made us deal with our loss."

"That's just it, though, Brad," Lainey said softly. "I'm almost certain Petey has already worked through his loss."

"Then what could be causing this difference in his behavior?"

She shrugged, averting her gaze from the tempting proximity of his chiseled lips. "My sister-in-law, Bunny, thinks it's growing pains combined with the lack of male influence in his life."

He cupped her hand in both of his. "But you don't agree."

She studied their clasped hands, aware of how natural this felt. "I know he misses being around Chip. All you have to do is look at how he perks up whenever you, Lewis, Travis and all the other guys around here pay him attention."

"He's a great kid. We enjoy being around him."

"And he, you."

An awkward silence fell between them. She knew she should either end the evening now…or risk kissing again. Deciding she needed her wits about her to complete the story she'd been assigned, she stood.

Before she got more than two steps away, Brad caught her wrist and tugged her back.

She pivoted to face him.

"I feel like I shouldn't have to say this," he stated seriously, "but what I told you earlier about Yvonne pretending to be one kind of person when she was really another…that stays between the two of us. I don't want anyone else—even my family—suspecting how I was duped."

Guilt flooded her. Much more than just Brad's pride

was at stake here. "Until you tell me otherwise, absolutely," she promised, meaning it.

"I'm not changing my mind about this, Lainey," he warned gruffly, closing the distance between them. "My private life, the way I was deliberately set up, is not for public consumption."

Well, there went her article for *Personalities* and the chance to jump-start her journalism career at the national level, Lainey thought, depressed. Unless she could convince him to change his mind, of course.

Did she want to?

Brad picked up on her confusion. And misjudged the reason for it.

"About earlier," he said after a moment.

She had only to look into his eyes to know he was talking about the passionate clinch that still had her insides humming with unslaked desire. Embarrassed at the lack of restraint she had shown when he pulled her into his arms, she moved to the edge of the porch and glanced away. "We don't have to talk about that."

He followed her, standing so close she could feel the warmth of his body and hear the slow, steady meter of his breath. "Suppose I want to?" he said quietly.

If she let her guard down, she knew what would happen. She couldn't risk falling head over heels in love with a man she was trying her best to remain objective about. She knew full well that business and pleasure did not mix. So she pretended this was about something other than what it was, too. "Look, I know you're more experienced in that particular arena than I am," she said, focusing strictly on the highly sexual nature of the encounter.

"Don't bet on it. I haven't been married or had a child

with someone—both things that I am guessing lead to greater intimacy and satisfaction."

Lainey didn't want to admit how lacking her previous marriage had been in that regard. She paused, worrying her lower lip with her teeth and looked deep into his eyes, finding all the understanding—and respect—she ever could have wished for. "But I don't mess around for sport," she noted softly. "When I kiss someone it means something."

Too late, she realized how insulting that sounded.

To her surprise, Brad didn't seem to mind. Or even disagree.

He leaned toward her intimately, looking sexy as hell. Every bit the intimidating bachelor he had been on TV. "Maybe that's the problem," he said, grasping her by the shoulders. "Whenever I've kissed someone, prior to you, anyway, it's never once meant anything close to what it should."

The gentle warmth of his fingers penetrated her skin. "What are you trying to say?" she murmured, wishing she didn't recall quite so vividly how passionately he'd kissed, or how tenderly he'd held her in his arms.

His gaze drifted over her as he favored her with a rakish smile. "It's high time my kisses did mean something." He took her all the way into his arms and tilted his head over hers. "It's high time," he told her, mouth lowering, "I felt something more than simple desire."

He gave her an instant to pull away if that was what she wanted. When she went toward him instead, he murmured a soft sound of approval and took her mouth deliberately, kissing her deeply. She clung to him, kissing him back, savoring the scent and feel and taste of him. Sensations swirled through her. His hands moved down her spine, working their magic.

"It's time I let myself feel what you and I were both meant to feel about each other," he whispered, probing her mouth with evocative thrusts of his tongue.

The kiss turned sweeter, more tender. "Brad, I—we—really shouldn't do..." Her will faltered.

"Do what?" he prompted lazily, kissing her again and again and again.

"This," she said, kissing him back.

When he finally let her go, she was so dizzy she could barely stand. Her insides were humming.

Brad smiled as he stroked his hands through her hair, caressed her face. "I know we have to say good night," he told her reluctantly. "I know Petey is sleeping inside and we have to set an example, but something is happening here, Lainey. Something good."

As much as she wanted to, Lainey could not deny it.

"I NEED TO KNOW you're making progress," Sybil said, early the next morning.

Lainey was certainly trying. She wanted nothing more than to get this assignment behind her. She had been up half the night, researching Yvonne Rathbone and Brad McCabe and everything she could find that had been written about the Bachelor Bliss episodes starring them. The Internet was full of previously published articles about the couple. But no one knew even a smidgen of the truth about what had happened to break them up—except Lainey. And unfortunately, Brad had not yet consented to tell Lainey everything or let anyone else, even his family, in on the secret.

Lainey still hoped that would change.

The secrets were eating him alive.

In the meantime, she was between a rock and a hard place, trapped between a man who was quickly becoming very important to her, and the job she had been contracted to do.

Aware her boss was waiting, Lainey briefed Sybil on the telephone interview with the Hollywood producer who had hired Yvonne to guest-star in two prime-time dramas.

"She certainly hasn't lost out on anything since Brad McCabe broke up with her on national TV."

Sybil was right, Lainey thought. Brad had been the one who had done all the losing, who'd had his reputation trashed. The unfairness of it all bothered her immensely. "I tracked down the phone numbers of the other female contestants on the show. I've been talking to them one by one."

"And?"

"Let's just say Yvonne was not well liked by the others," Lainey said.

"That could be shrugged off as jealousy, since Yvonne won more time alone with Brad and the chance to win his heart."

Which Yvonne hadn't. "Somehow, I think it's more than that."

"But no one's told you why Brad McCabe pulled the Jekyll and Hyde act," Sybil said.

"No, so far everyone has been very diplomatic," Lainey admitted reluctantly. "But I watched the DVDs of the show on my laptop again last night." After Brad had left and she was sure Petey was sound asleep. "And I zeroed in on the three most emotional women of the group. I'm hoping one of them will tell me something everyone else has been too discreet to say."

"You know you've got less than a week left to pull this off."

Lainey did not need reminding.

"I'm counting on you, Lainey," she persisted, sounding every bit as determined to succeed as she had been in college. "My winning the top slot at Personalities depends on my being able to pull this off. A lot is riding on my all-Texas issue," Sybil finished emphatically.

Including, Lainey thought, her own future.

"CAN I, MOM? PLEASE?" Petey asked over breakfast that morning. "It's my big chance to be a real cowboy, just like Brad."

Lainey grinned at the exuberance in her son's voice. How long since he had shown such enthusiasm for anything? Months, she knew.

Lainey looked at Brad. "You're sure you want to take Petey with you to pick up the heifers this morning?"

He nodded. "The Triple T isn't that far. Only about an hour from here."

"You're sure he won't be in the way when you're loading the animals?"

"The cowboys at the Triple T will be putting them on the truck. All Petey and I will be doing is making sure that the animals they are loading are the ones I bought last week."

"How are you going to do that?" Lainey put platters of scrambled eggs, crisp apple-wood-smoked bacon and piping hot blueberry muffins on the table. "Don't they all sort of look alike?" They did to her, anyway.

"The animals are tagged with numbers on their ears," Petey explained. "Brad says it's sort of like cattle earrings."

"Good thing they're female, then," Lewis teased.

"Steers have 'em, too," Petey explained importantly. "That way the cowboys can tell 'em apart when they get to the rodeo."

Lainey looked at Brad in surprise. She knew she should be accustomed by now, but she couldn't get over how ruggedly handsome Brad looked in the morning, even with rumpled hair and in need of a shave, as he was right now. She'd been around long enough to know that he showered twice a day but used his razor only once, in the evening after work. He wore nicer clothes in the evening. The jeans and shirts he wore during his ranching hours were worn and clung to the muscled contours of his tall body.

When he had come into the kitchen, she'd caught a whiff of soap and man and cool mint mouthwash. Just that easily, her motor began to race. Doing her best to ignore her awareness of Brad, Lainey asked, "These animals are slated for the rodeo?"

He nodded, digging into his breakfast with enthusiasm while Petey watched and followed suit. "The steers we get from the breeding operation will be sold to the rodeo when they're fully grown. I'm keeping the female cattle for breeding more rodeo stock."

"And that means nearly every year the size of Brad's herd will practically double," Petey explained. He looked at his mother seriously. "You hafta know your math, if you want to be a rancher."

Lainey smiled, glad Brad was having such a positive influence on her son. "When will you be back?" she asked.

Brad shrugged. "Noon, probably." He paused. "Sure you don't want to go? We've got room in the truck."

Lainey was tempted. "I've got work to do here." Reporting work. And because she was uncomfortable doing it, she'd just as soon get it over with. The sooner she got this writing assignment over, the better, as far as she was concerned. Never again was she going to sign a contract to clandestinely investigate anyone she knew, or had personal ties with on any level. It was just too darn hard. But she had sworn she would do this one article, so she had to follow through. Because she owed it to herself—her friend Sybil, too.

"Next time," Lainey promised. If you still want me to go. There was no guarantee that would be the case after the *Personalities* story came out.

As soon as the men cleared out, Lainey got right down to work doing the sleuthing that would allow her to expose the truth of what had really happened between Brad and Yvonne to the public without ever involving Brad.

First up was Susie, a bubbly brunette from Kansas City. The charming elementary-school teacher had been fourth from the last in the elimination, and had struck Lainey as being a very pragmatic, as well as beautiful, woman. "Are you asking me to be honest?" Susie asked.

"Nothing but," Lainey replied, holding the phone closer to her ear.

"I think the outcome was rigged from the first."

Lainey scribbled down Susie's exact words. "What makes you think that?"

"The rest of us had to make do with the outfits we brought with us, or what was on the wardrobe racks. Yvonne Rathbone came in with a whole suitcase full of designer clothing. And you can't tell me she could afford Prada and Marc Jacobs on a copier sales rep's salary."

Interesting, Lainey thought. "Did anyone ever ask Yvonne where she got her clothes?"

"Oh, yes. She just smiled and said it was all in who you knew."

Lainey paused, her pen resting just above the paper.

"Are you saying that the *Bachelor Bliss* producers gave her this clothing, and didn't make similar accommodations for the rest of you?"

"All I know is that when Yvonne didn't like the way she looked in something, another designer garment magically appeared for her to wear," Susie concluded. "It was always found on the wardrobe rack. Yvonne always waltzed in just in time to claim it as her own, before anyone else ever even knew it was there."

Up next was Abigail, a ski instructor from Idaho. Abigail also felt Yvonne Rathbone had received special treatment from the beginning. "Several times during the filming of the show, there was a shortage of rooms where all the contestants were quartered and she got bumped to another hotel."

Lainey wrote furiously. "Were the accommodations the same quality?"

"Are you kidding? The room she was moved to was much nicer!"

Lainey followed the lead. "Was anyone else from the show staying there?"

"Yes, the producers, and the show's creator, Gil Hewitt."

"But no other contestants."

"No. Just Yvonne."

Last on Lainey's list to telephone was Shelley. The gregarious travel agent was even more direct when asked if she thought Yvonne Rathbone had ever been given special advantage over the other contestants. "I just found it odd how Yvonne always seemed to know stuff about Brad—like which type of rodeo contests he did—before Brad even told us. Yvonne said it was because she followed the sport. She even claimed to have seen one of his events in Wyoming a few years ago."

Lainey zeroed in on the skepticism in Shelley's voice as she continued taking notes. "But you didn't buy it."

"No."

"Any reason why?"

"Yes!" Shelly replied emphatically. "Yvonne had a real aversion to stable smells. She almost threw up the day Brad took us all riding, on that first group date. I just couldn't see her willingly sitting in the stands in the heat and the dust, the smell of manure wafting up around her."

Lainey smiled as the pieces began to come together. From what she had seen on TV, she couldn't see Yvonne doing that of her own volition, either. "Mind if I quote you on that?" she asked Shelley.

"Sure. Why not? It's not as if the outcome of the contest for Brad's heart is still in question."

But it had been then. And it was becoming more and more clear that Yvonne had cheated to win. The question was, who had helped her get the edge? And what had that person stood to gain?

"DID YOU SEE ME on the horse, Mom? I was up in the saddle and everything!"

"I did see." Lainey smiled down at her son. Petey's day "helping" Brad had obviously thrilled him to no end. "You looked great!" She gave Petey a big hug, then looked over at Brad. "Thanks for giving Petey his first riding lesson," she said sincerely.

Brad radiated contentment, too. "Glad to do it."

Lainey led her son over to the kitchen sink. She handed him the soap and watched as he washed his hands. Petey babbled on in excitement. "Brad is teaching me how to be a cowboy. Cowboys are the strongest, smartest kind of grown-up guys, right, Mom? I mean, cowboys always know what to do in every situation. That's what Tyler, Trevor and Teddy McCabe said."

"Not surprising since they're all cowboys," Brad said with a patient smile. When Petey had finished, Brad went to the sink.

Lainey worried what would happen if Petey got too attached to Brad and then things did not work out between Brad and her. Momentarily distracted, she watched as Brad rolled up his sleeves. His forearms were muscular, feathered with sable-brown hair. She knew...from some of the swimming and beach shots done on *Bachelor Bliss*...that the rest of him was just as beautiful.

She really had to stop watching those DVDs....

Petey wrinkled his nose as Lainey handed him a towel. "Huh?"

"There are other jobs, too, like Lewis's," Lainey explained. "You think Lewis's job is a good one, don't you? And the one your father had?"

"Daddy mostly got on airplanes."

"He traveled a lot for business," Lainey explained to Brad.

"I don't think Daddy's job was a lot of fun, at least he didn't act like it. What I want to be when I grow up is a cowboy who makes up computer games."

"Could happen," Brad allowed with an admiring smile, as his brother Lewis strolled into the house via the back door, the canvas carryall containing his laptop computer slung over one shoulder.

"Something smells good in here," Lewis said.

"Dinner will be ready in about thirty minutes."

"I have a new prototype of the game you tested the other day," Lewis said to Petey. "Want to take a look at it and tell me if you think it is any better?"

Petey looked at Lainey. "Can I, Mom?"

"Sure."

They ambled off, chattering all the while.

Brad remained. Feeling far too aware of him for comfort, Lainey went back to cooking dinner. "Thanks for letting Petey hang out with you today."

Brad came up behind her. Placing one hand on her shoulder, he took the lid off a saucepan. "I enjoyed it. He's a great kid."

Warmth swept through Lainey in undulating waves. She knew he was not thinking about the food she was preparing. He was thinking about the way he had been kissing her the evening before. An embrace she was still reeling from. Something is happening here, Lainey. Something good.

Lainey gave the spicy shredded chicken a stir. "I also noticed you put the heifers in the barn instead of in the pasture with the bull. Is that so Petey wouldn't see, um, you know…"

Brad leaned in closer, the front of his thighs pressing the backs of hers as he lifted yet another lid. "Any mating going on?"

Lainey swung around quickly, as the steamy aroma of Mexican rice filled the air. She pressed her index finger to his lips. "Shhh. I don't want him to hear."

Brad grinned down at her, eyes twinkling. "He's going to figure it out sooner or later."

Feeling warmth everywhere their bodies touched, as well as where they didn't, Lainey flushed. "Do you really have to let them do it before we leave?" she whispered, embarrassed. "We're only going to be here another week." She slipped by him and went to the cutting board next to the sink. She lifted the serving dishes of chopped tomatoes and shredded lettuce and put them on the table.

Brad trailed after her. “Relax,” he told her. “The heifers are getting hormones to synchronize when they will stand in heat.”

Oh. “Is that why you put them in the barn?” Lainey asked curiously.

“Traveling is hard on them. It’ll be easier to keep them cool in there and let them recover from being jostled around, before we put them out to pasture and let Tabasco Red do his stuff.”

Lainey blinked as she picked up blocks of cheddar and Monterey Jack cheese. “One bull is going to service all those heifers?”

Brad took both cheeses from her and lent a hand with the grater. “One male to every twenty-four to thirty cows is considered normal.”

“Or in other words,” Lainey said dryly, as she added flour tortillas to a skillet, “every male’s dream.”

Brad made a dissenting face. “More like nightmare if you’re talking about humans, and I’d guess—from your tone—you are.”

Time to proceed with her reporting again. “You’re telling me you didn’t enjoy yourself on *Bachelor Bliss*.”

“All those women vying for my attention at once?”

He hadn’t earned his Casanova rep sitting home alone every Saturday night. “It was what you seemed to want back in high school,” she pointed out.

Brad finished his task and lounged against the counter. “That was only because I didn’t want to hurt anyone’s feelings. I was the new kid in town—at least in the junior class at Laramie High—and it seemed like every female my age wanted to date me. I’d never had that before and I didn't know how to say no. So—" he shrugged affably, taking a bite of the cheese he had just shredded "—I started stacking dates one on top of the other."

"I remember." Lainey gave the salsa a taste and added another sprinkling of cilantro and a tad more red onion.

"It was hell when the girls figured it out."

Cocking her head, she offered a spoonful to Brad. He tasted it, nodding his approval. "They tarred and feathered you," she remembered.

"With lipstick and perfume." Brad shuddered in disgust and made her laugh. "I can still remember that awful smell, all those fragrances mixed together. Anyway, I learned my lesson and I never dated more than one woman at a time after that."

Lainey plucked the hot, soft tortillas from the skillet, put them into the warmer and closed the lid. She turned off that burner and leaned against the counter, mirroring his stance and half smile. "How many of those were a one-night-only type of thing?"

Brad looked her up and down, too. "I have no idea."

Aware the meat filling had another ten minutes to simmer, and that the rest of dinner was ready, she bided her time. "How many serious relationships have you had?"

He lifted a brow. "Define 'serious'."

Aware he didn't want to go down this path, but determined nevertheless, Lainey specified, "Where you dated someone more than a couple of times."

Regret crossed his face. "I, uh, haven't."

Just as she had feared. "Which then raises the question, why in the world did you ever go on *Bachelor Bliss?*"

GOOD QUESTION, Brad thought.

"You knew the show was designed to get you engaged and married in six weeks. If you weren't the settling-down type..." Lainey continued.

If he didn't know better, he'd say he was being interviewed. But that was ridiculous. Lainey wasn't a reporter. She was, however, interested in him—her kisses and the way she responded to him demonstrated that. And, as such, maybe there were things she needed to know if this whatever-it-was they were starting was to go any further.

He could deal with that.

Even respected it.

"I am interested in marriage," he told Lainey honestly.

Her green eyes widened. "You really expect me—or any other woman in this country—to believe that?" she asked in astonishment.

"I don't care what the others do or don't believe." I care about you. The thought shocked him, even as he realized it was true. "I'm tired of dating. Tired of not having someone to come home to at night, someone who cares about me—not where we are going or what we might be doing or who we might be seeing that evening." To his surprise, she was listening. Wanting to be near her, he crossed to her side. "I see what other men my age have who are married and have kids of their own. They're happy, Lainey. Content. So, yeah, maybe it was stupid and naive of me, but when I signed up for *Bachelor Bliss* and they told me they would use my answers to the show questionnaire and the information gleaned from the psychologist interview to handpick women who would be just perfect for me, I thought maybe it would work. The old-fashioned way of trying to hook up with a woman by chance certainly hadn't been successful. I figured, statistically, why not give this a try." He paused, aware he had just told her more than he had told any woman. "What about you?" he asked.

Lainey blinked. "What do you mean, me?"

Brad brushed a strand of blond hair from her cheek and tucked it behind her ear. "Are you looking to get married again?" Reluctantly, he dropped his hand.

He wanted to kiss her again. Make his move. Stake his claim. But the thought of Petey or Lewis walking in…

Lainey bit her lip. She looked as vulnerable as she did beautiful, standing there, an embroidered blue denim chef's apron over her clothing, her cheeks flushed from the heat of the stove. "I hadn't thought about it."

Knowing he had to touch her or go crazy, Brad slipped his fingers into the curve of hers and rubbed a thumb over the back of her hand. He studied her until she looked back. "Does that mean you have now?" he asked.

Lainey hesitated. Obviously not sure how much of herself to give away. "Petey wants a father again," she said finally. "That's pretty clear."

Not exactly what he had been fishing for! "You'd marry just to give him a father?" he asked her incredulously, dropping his hand.

"No. Of course not." She stiffened.

"Then why would you marry?" he asked.

That apparently was easy. "One reason and one reason only," Lainey said softly. "For love."

CHAPTER NINE

"MOMMY, THERE'S A MAN outside with a great big tow truck. Come and see!"

Lainey went to the window of the guest house. She saw a man in a garage uniform with a clipboard in his hand, studying the license plate number on the bumper of her SUV. "What in the world?" Lainey stepped outside at the same time as Brad came out of the barn and Lewis stepped out the back door of the ranch house.

"May I help you?" Lainey asked.

"I'm Henry Cross from Dallas Motors." He held out his hand. Lainey shook it. "You Mrs. Carrington?"

Lainey nodded, aware the man seemed nice enough. "That's right."

Henry announced pleasantly, "I'm here to pick up your vehicle for its thirty-thousand-mile servicing."

"There must be some mistake. I didn't schedule anything with the dealership." But her SUV had been purchased there.

Henry took off his cap and set it back on his head. "The other Mrs. Carrington said you might say that," he said uncomfortably.

Lots of thoughts came to Lainey's mind—none of them nice. "Bunny asked you to do this?" she asked, as Brad came to stand on one side of Lainey, Lewis on the other.

"Yes, ma'am." Henry lifted his hat again. "She set it up with the service desk yesterday."

Well then, Lainey thought furiously, Bunny was just going to have to undo it. "I'm sorry you came all the way out here, but you can't pick up my SUV. I won't have anything to drive."

Henry shifted from foot to foot. "Ma'am, you should take that up with your sister-in-law."

Believe me, I plan to. Mindful that Petey was standing right beside her, looking every bit as stressed-out as she felt, Lainey put a comforting hand on her son's shoulder. "We'll just have to reschedule," she repeated as cordially as she could.

"I have to take this SUV back to Dallas," Henry repeated.

Brad stepped forward. "Did you not hear the lady?"

Henry looked at Brad, man-to-man. "If I don't do my job, I'll lose it."

And no one wanted that, Lainey thought. "You know what, fellas? It's fine. Go ahead and do the servicing. When will I get my vehicle back?"

Henry looked back down at his clipboard. "Next week."

"Next week!" Lainey, Lewis and Brad repeated all at once. Petey looked up at Lainey.

Henry shrugged. "Vehicle pickups of this distance aren't easy to arrange," he explained.

"So why don't you just reschedule?" Brad asked again.

"I'd really like to do that," Lainey asserted. "I'll be back in Dallas in another week or two."

Petey's face fell. Lainey had an instinctive feeling that his disappointment had more to do with having to leave the ranch than the missed opportunity of seeing the SUV put up on the flatbed tow truck that would haul it back to Dallas Motors.

Henry paused, really looking like he did not want to be here now. "You'll have to take that up with Bart and Bunny Carrington, since their names are on the purchase papers for this vehicle."

Silence fell.

Lainey felt humiliated. And Petey tensed even more. The boy might not understand the complicated nature of the trust Chip had set up to take care of Lainey and Petey in the event of Chip's death, but Petey knew when his mother was unnecessarily embarrassed.

Seeing no reason to prolong the agony, Lainey forced a smile and swept a hand through her hair. "I guess I knew about this," she murmured awkwardly after a moment, in an effort to comfort her son, who, like everyone else present, was looking more and more upset about the situation.

"I've just been so busy and so interested in everything going on around here I had just forgotten about this," she fibbed, picking up steam as she went. "In fact, now that I think about it, I'm sure Bunny and Bart mentioned it to me last time we spoke."

Lainey felt her son beginning to relax. Hence, Lainey relaxed, too.

They all watched as Lainey's SUV was loaded onto the tow truck. When both had disappeared down the drive and had turned onto the farm-market road that ran past the ranch, Lewis turned to Petey. "Ready to spend another day at the testing facility, playing computer games?" He looked as eager to get out of there as Petey.

Her son's face broke into a broad grin. "You bet!" He high-fived Lewis.

"Then we better get a move on."

IT WAS CLEAR LAINEY DID NOT want to talk about what had just happened, so Brad went back to work, as did Lainey. But when Brad walked into the ranch house an hour later and found her in the family room tearfully organizing boxes of videotapes and DVDs, he knew the time for being circumspect was at an end.

"If this is going to upset you so much, maybe you should have a third party deal with Bart and Bunny for you," he said.

Lainey straightened and swung toward him. Despite the tumultuous events of the morning, she was as lovely as ever. Her honey-blond hair was disheveled, her pretty cheeks glistening wetly. The tip of her elegant nose was red from crying, her green eyes still misty with tears. "It's not Bart, it's Bunny."

Brad crossed the distance between them; he had never been more aware of the differences between them. He was clad in the usual jeans, boots and work shirt. Lainey was wearing a slim black cotton skirt and matching black shoes that had the toe and heel cut out, exposing her cute painted toenails. Her blue summer turtleneck sweater had cutaway sleeves that left her shoulders, and a great deal of her skin toward her collarbone, bare. It was made out of some sort of stretchy lightweight cotton that molded to her figure smoothly and hinted at voluptuous breasts and a slender waist, yet still managed to look classy and refined in that city-sophisticate way. Missing were the pearls and earrings she had worn to the ranch the first day.

"And I can handle Bunny," Lainey insisted, stubborn as ever.

Could she now. Brad sauntered closer, drinking in the floral scent of her perfume. He wished he could just take her to bed and make love to her until all the sadness and uncertainty in her eyes went away. He slid a hand beneath her chin and lifted her face to his. "I don't see how," he told her gruffly, "with Bunny pulling stuff like this."

Lainey's shoulders stiffened. Her back ramrod straight, she moved away from him and went back to sorting DVDs. "She's never done anything like this before. Well, anything this insufferable," she said as she put a stack of them in the bookcase.

Brad glanced at her curiously, trying hard not to notice how seductively her hips moved beneath the trim black skirt as she knelt, stood, sorted, reached. He moved closer to lend a hand. "So what prompted this latest shot across the bow?"

Lainey's pouty lower lip curled ruefully as she sorted movies into categories of science fiction, Westerns and action-adventure. "Me being out here with Petey, instead of in Dallas." She paused, sighing deeply. "Bunny asked us to move in with her and Bart, and I refused. Obviously, she is still angry with me over that."

No joke. Brad studied the unhappiness in her eyes. "Is there anything in your finances you control?"

Embarrassed, she shook her head.

"I still don't understand how your husband could have left you in such an untenable situation," he said, not bothering to hide his frustration.

Lainey ran a hand through her hair and continued to regard Brad warily. "Like I mentioned the last time we discussed this, Chip thought he was doing what was best for Petey and me."

It rankled to hear her continue to make excuses for her late husband. Another silence fell between them, this one fraught with tension. "Now who's kidding themselves?" he demanded. "You're always talking about being truthful and letting the chips fall where they may." He paused, then decided the heck with it—in for a penny, in for a pound. "Your marriage must have had some serious chinks in it if Chip could do something like this to you."

LEAVE IT TO THE BLUNT-SPOKEN BRAD to hit the nail on the head, Lainey thought. She swallowed hard around the knot of emotion in her throat. "You want the truth?"

He lifted a skeptical brow. "Are you ready to tell it?"

Knowing it was past time she talked honestly about this with someone she could trust, and that that person was Brad, she plunged on ruthlessly. "I am angry at Chip for this—and I have been for months now—but I'm angrier at myself for letting it happen because, the truth is, I could have fought the various stipulations and the way everything was set up at the time the trust was established."

Brad took her into the curve of his arm and held her against him. "Why didn't you?" he asked quietly.

Relishing the warmth and comfort of him, so tall and strong beside her, she tipped her face up to his and searched his eyes. "Because I didn't want to face the possibility that anything might ever happen to my husband." She paused and drew in a bolstering breath. "I never imagined he would die in an accident. So, like it or not...this is my fault as much as Chip's."

Brad sat down on the edge of the sofa and pulled her onto his lap. "You could still do something about the way things are set up if you want to." He stroked her hair gently.

Lainey shook her head. "It isn't going to be necessary."

He looked frustrated again, and tapped her tenderly on the nose. "Now who isn't being realistic?"

Aware the tables had changed, and that she was the one running from a difficult situation, Lainey looked at him, her tears gone. "You saw how what happened this morning upset Petey."

Brad nodded, looking unhappy about that, too.

She said frankly, "If he sees me fight with Bunny and Bart over this, he'll be even more distressed."

He didn't argue with that. "So don't let him see it. Have your showdown with your sister-in-law when Petey isn't around."

Lainey rolled her eyes. "A little hard to do now."

"I'll drive you into Dallas right now. We can go see your sister-in-law, tell her you want your car back, and we drive back. By the time Petey comes home tonight from the testing facility, everything will be as it should be. Then you can have your car serviced when *you* want it serviced."

Silence fell between them. "You don't think I'm going to take you up on your offer, do you?" Lainey challenged finally.

Brad shrugged. The look he gave her was more understanding than judgmental. "It's a lot easier to pretend all the bad stuff will go away on its own. I know." His lips twisted ruefully. "I'm an expert on that. At least, lately."

"I'D BE HAPPY TO DISCUSS this with you, Lainey," Bunny said, two hours later when Lainey met with her at Bunny's Dallas home. "But not—" Bunny glared at Brad "—with him here."

Lainey was braced for this and more. "Brad can hear anything we have to say to each other."

Brad smiled casually as he sat down on the elegant sofa beside Lainey. "I promised to be referee or witness, whatever is needed."

Bunny returned the warning with a condescending smile.

With effort, Lainey spoke in a calm, even tone. "These power plays have got to stop."

"Believe me," Bunny promised in a smooth, cultured tone, "I'd like nothing better than that."

"So do it," Brad advised, as Bunny handed out glasses of mint iced tea.

"I can't," she returned with a condescending smile. Her eyes narrowed. "As long as you continue to act so irresponsibly."

Lainey was holding on to her composure—and her temper—by mere threads. "Getting a job is irresponsible?"

"Getting a job Chip would never have approved of certainly is," Bunny shot back disparagingly, her resentment obvious. "And the same goes for dragging Petey out to the country to live in intimate proximity to two young, single men."

Brad gave Bunny a lethal look on Lainey's behalf, saving her the trouble.

"What are you saying?" Lainey demanded coldly.

Bunny lifted her hands. "Simply that a family court judge might very well agree with me that such living arrangements are not appropriate for a widow with a child."

"Unless I'm mistaken," Brad drawled, "I think your sister-in-law just threatened to sue you for custody of Petey."

"I wouldn't *want* to do that," Bunny continued sweetly.

"You would just have no choice," Lainey guessed bitterly.

"I see we finally understand each other." Her sister-in-law offered a chilly smile.

Lainey knew Bunny was never happy unless Bunny was calling the shots, and that her sister-in-law always felt she knew what was best for everyone else. But this was downright ridiculous. Lainey stood and picked up her shoulder bag. Her fingers tightened on the strap until they turned white. "You were right," she said to Brad, never taking her eyes from Bunny's face. Her blood ran hot and cold simultaneously. "This is pointless."

"Now what?" Brad asked as the two of them got back in his pickup. He started the engine.

Doing her best not to appear as if she had been run over by a steamroller, Lainey said, "I need to drop by my house to pick up some more clothes for Petey." Then she wanted to return to the Lazy M. To safe haven. She wanted to be with Brad and Petey and the rest of the McCabes and forget all this.

Brad shot her a concerned glance. "What about your SUV?"

"I'll make do without it," she said wearily, as she paused to direct Brad to her home, located just a few short blocks away. "Maybe when Bunny sees I am not going to be bullied or threatened into toeing her line, she'll stop all this nonsense," she hoped out loud.

But that was before Brad turned into the driveway of the imposing pink-brick Tudor with the gray shutters and white trim, and Lainey saw what else Bunny had done.

"ARE YOU OKAY?" Brad asked, some thirty minutes later, as they stowed the belongings Lainey had collected into the storage area behind the bench seat of the cab. It had been quite a shock to find a For Sale sign in the front yard, a lockbox on the front door and a Realtor inside, already taking a client through. A half-dozen business cards lined up on the kitchen counter indicated others were interested in the property, too.

"Yes."

She didn't look it. She was pale as a ghost. And he understood why. Her sister-in-law was trying her hardest to pull the rug out from under Lainey. He reached over and squeezed her hand. "You were very cordial in there." Brad began to drive in the direction of the freeway that would take them back to Laramie. He didn't know how she had kept her composure. She certainly would have been entitled to lose her temper.

Lainey shrugged, looking very much in need of a hug, a kiss. From him. She forced a vulnerable smile.

"Chip trained me well."

Chip had been a lousy husband, leaving her in a mess like this, Brad thought. Lainey deserved so much better. So did Petey. Silence descended. As they drove through the neighborhood, Lainey drew a deep, bolstering breath.

"I think you may be right about getting a third party in

to deal with Bunny," she said eventually. "Your cousin in Laramie—Claire McCabe Taylor—is a family-law attorney, isn't she?"

Brad nodded. "One of the best."

"You wouldn't happen to have her number?"

"I can get it." Figuring the sooner Lainey took a proactive approach, the sooner she'd feel better, Brad pulled over to the curb and called Lewis at work. Lewis looked up the number and gave it to him. Brad wrote it down for Lainey and she made an appointment to see Claire later that very afternoon. "Claire will be able to help you," Brad said quietly, after Lainey had cut the connection with his cousin.

He was vaguely aware of Lainey nodding as he concentrated on the traffic.

"You don't have to worry," he continued. "We'll get this worked out."

More silence. Wishing he could do more to comfort her, Brad glanced over. Lainey had her head turned away from him, but he could tell by the way her shoulders were shaking that she was crying, silent, wrenching sobs that shook her whole body. He was almost to the entrance ramp to the freeway that would take them back to Laramie, but Brad turned into the first parking lot available. It happened to belong to a hotel. He eased his truck into a spot just beneath the neon sign, released his seat belt and slid across the bench seat.

He undid the clasp of her seat belt, too. She turned, tears streaking down her pretty face. Not caring that it was broad daylight and that they could easily be seen by anyone driving by, he took her wordlessly into his arms and held her close. She rested her head on his shoulder, and he bent his head, burying his face in the soft, fragrant softness of her hair and breathing in the sweet feminine essence that was her. "There, there, now," he found himself saying, as he stroked a calming hand down her back and shifted her closer. "It's going to be okay," he said thickly. "I promise."

Lainey cried all the harder. He felt her despair and it tore him apart like nothing ever had. He wove his fingers through her hair and tipped her head up to his. "Listen to me. I'm not going to let anything happen to you or to Petey."

The need on her face intensified. The next thing Brad knew, they were kissing. And kissing. And kissing. Who knew what might have happened had there not been a gaggle of female voices just outside his truck.

"I told you! It is him!"

"Brad McCabe!"

"Well, that sure as heck isn't Yvonne Rathbone."

Lainey jerked away from Brad at the same time he broke away from her. A chorus of swearwords sounded in his head as he faced their teenage hecklers.

"Hey!" one of the young girls shouted at Brad. The heckler couldn't have been more than nineteen or twenty. "We saw what you did to Yvonne on *Bachelor Bliss* and we're not ever going to forgive you!"

"Yeah! You had no right to go breaking her heart!"

"And now you're making another woman cry! What kind of louse are you, anyway?"

"Guys like you give all men a bad name!"

Brad looked at Lainey. She was white as a sheet, more distraught than ever. He swore. He'd never meant to hurt Lainey. Especially like this, after all she'd just been through.

Brad swore again, more heatedly this time. He put the truck into reverse and eased out of the parking space—not exactly easy to do given the proximity of the hecklers. He drove toward the exit while the girls chased after them. A soda can landed on his bumper and rattled to the ground as he turned back onto the access road running parallel to the freeway. "Sorry," he muttered.

Lainey wiped her eyes. "For kissing me," she asked softly, cautiously, "or for getting caught?"

BRAD FROWNED, a dark shadow crossing his face. "I'm sorry we got interrupted." He glanced at her briefly. "Sorry you were crying. Sorry about, well, just about damn everything."

His disillusionment was painful to see, but Lainey knew that ignoring it and pretending what just happened hadn't, would not make things better. "This won't help your reputation." She plucked the bottle of water out of her bag and took a drink. She hadn't meant to cry on Brad's shoulder, but her minimeltdown had been cathartic. She did feel better. Lots better. Though maybe that had more to do with the way his arms had felt around her, so strong and sure and comforting, and the hot, sexy way his lips had moved on hers. Had those girls not come along, had they been somewhere—anywhere—else, well, who knew what might have happened? she thought, as shocked by her wanton, reckless behavior as by his.

Lainey hadn't expected Brad to want to get involved with anyone else for a good long time, after what had happened to him. And she certainly hadn't expected he would want to get involved with her.

But he obviously did....

And despite all the reasons she knew she should be keeping her distance from the sexy cowboy right now, she realized she wanted to get involved, too.

"It's just a few girls." Brad dismissed the incident in the parking lot with a shake of his head. "Even if they tell all their friends…" He frowned again. "I mean, at this point, with half of America hating me, what does it matter?"

He was exaggerating. Half of America hadn't watched *Bachelor Bliss*, or any reality TV show for that matter. But beneath Brad's deprecating sentiment was a lot of pain. Lainey reached over and touched his arm.

"You should tell your side of the story," she said.

Abruptly, Brad's biceps was as tense as the rest of him. He glared straight ahead as he drove in the increasingly heavy traffic. "Back to that again?"

Lainey swallowed and dropped her hand as swiftly as if she had been burned. She felt pushed away again, the same way she always had when she tried to offer advice to Chip and was rejected for "not knowing what she was talking about." But this time she did, even if she couldn't yet explain to Brad how and why she knew the way the press operated as well as she did.

"I mean it. It's not fair." She continued to look at Brad steadily, glad they were talking about someone's problems other than her own. She wanted to offer Brad the same kind of support he had offered her. "You're such a good guy."

Despite the gentleness of her words, Brad looked even more provoked. "You don't know that."

Aware he had never looked more mesmerizing than he did at that moment, Lainey countered, just as resolutely, "Yes. I do. A bad guy wouldn't do all the things you are doing for me today."

Brad gave a short, humorless laugh. "That's not what the tabloids would say," he told her, looking as if he expected her to argue with him about that, too. His eyes glinted wickedly. "The tabloids would say I just want to get into your pants."

And maybe, Lainey thought, aware it was getting very hot in that truck, that wasn't an assumption very far from the truth. She pulled the neck of her sweater away from her collarbone in an effort to get more air. Still feeling a little breathless, she acknowledged she certainly wanted to get into Brad's pants. Although she doubted she ever would have put it in those terms. But maybe that was the point. Maybe Brad just thought he was bad for her and was trying to scare her off so she wouldn't get hurt.

Had Bunny been right? Was it bad for her to be staying out at the ranch with Brad and Lewis, when every second she was with Brad clouded her perspective more and more, and made her want to be with him—not for the story she was trying to write, but just because she wanted to be with him. And not as his friend. As his woman. She drew a stabilizing breath.

"Perhaps we should move this conversation to safer territory?"

Brad inhaled deeply, too. He reached over to turn the air conditioner to its coolest setting. "Good idea."

Lainey settled back in the passenger seat, determined to get her mind off sex—and that kiss—once and for all. "Tell me your plans for the ranch," she encouraged in the soberest voice she could manage.

"Well," Brad quipped, "first up, is getting all the virgin heifers in heat."

Lainey groaned in mock dismay and real embarrassment and covered her face with her hands. Brad laughed, his old devilry coming back as swiftly as it had fled. He relaxed and went back to teasing her again. "If you're going to hang out on the ranch, you have to get used to the idea that making babies is what we're all about."

Lainey thought about making babies...with Brad.

Another shock.

She really was going to have to calm down.

Brad glanced at her, probably noting the color flooding her cheeks. "What?"

Lainey stammered. No social lie would come to mind. "I—I was just, um, just thinking..." And not very quickly, either.

He reached over and briefly touched her knee. "That you want another baby?"

Her skin tingled where his hand had rested. "How did you know that?" Lainey asked him, serious now.

Brad shrugged, his mood turning contemplative as he continued to drive. "You're such a good mother to Petey," he said, obviously understanding. "You clearly love being a mother. It makes sense you would want more than one child."

Lainey looked out the window wistfully, at the Texas countryside. "I did."

"Then why didn't you have one?" Brad exited the freeway and turned onto the farm-market road that would lead them, first to Laramie, and then to the Lazy M.

"Chip felt one child was enough, particularly since Petey was a boy."

"And you didn't argue with him," Brad guessed, seeming to realize how much that had hurt and disappointed Lainey.

Lainey brushed at an imaginary piece of lint on her skirt. "I tried to persuade him for a while, but when I saw it wasn't working, when I realized how little time he had to spend with Petey, I concluded being mother and father to one child was probably enough of a job for me."

"That was honest."

"Yes, I know. Surprisingly so." Honesty hadn't really been a trademark of her marriage to Chip. The emphasis had been on polite accommodation. Too late, she saw that treating a marriage partner like a guest in your life wasn't the best path to take. She and Chip might have had a better marriage had they stopped being so careful and let their passion…and their feelings…flow. But they hadn't. And now it was too late to rectify that. But she still had a full life ahead of her, Lainey was beginning to see. And room in her heart for love to grow.

Brad gave her a curious glance.

"As you said, I'm always persuading everyone else to be honest and realistic about their particular situation, but not doing it myself." She smiled, for the first time feeling ready to deal with life's thornier issues head-on. "Maybe it's time that changed."

CHAPTER TEN

"THANKS FOR SEEING ME on such short notice," Lainey told Claire McCabe Taylor.

Claire's intelligent, green eyes radiated sympathy. "We attorneys understand family emergencies." Looking every bit the polished business professional in a discreetly tailored suit, Claire took a seat behind her desk. "Why don't you bring me up to date with everything?"

Claire listened intently while Lainey talked. "Sounds like Bunny is really trying hard to get your attention—taking your car, putting your house up for sale, emptying your bank account, and canceling your debit and credit cards."

"Well, she certainly has it now," Lainey lamented with a beleaguered sigh. She reached over and took Brad's hand, glad he had come with her.

Claire paused thoughtfully. The sunlight streaming in through the window blinds illuminated her neatly brushed auburn hair. "What do you think it would take to get Bunny to back off, aside from legal action on your part?" she asked.

Lainey let go of Brad's hand, clasped hers together in her lap. "I think if Petey and I moved in with Bunny and Bart that Bunny would ease up immediately, in a financial sense."

"And personally?" Claire persisted.

"I think it would be unbearable," Lainey admitted honestly. "Bunny means well..."

Brad gave her a look that urged her not to hold back. She knew he was right so she tried again. "Bunny thinks she is doing the right thing."

Claire continued making notes on the legal pad in front of her, then looked up. "And what do *you* think?" she asked bluntly.

"I think," Lainey said, "my sister-in-law needs to get a life and stop trying to live mine."

Lainey's heartfelt exasperation brought commiserating smiles to Claire's and Brad's faces.

"Who set up the trust, do you know?" Claire asked.

"Deloche, Nussbaum and Riker."

"Good firm. They're known for their mastery of estate law. I'll have to take a look at the papers, but I have to warn you—" Claire looked up over the rim of her reading glasses "—the terms may not be able to be overturned. And even if they are, it will be a long, prohibitively costly fight. I'm talking years here, Lainey. Legal fees that go well into the six figures."

"I thought as much," Lainey said, depressed.

"And then there is the emotional damage to Petey and your family," Claire continued practically.

Brad interrupted his cousin. "I thought you were supposed to be helping here!"

"I am," Claire responded with the ease of a respected family-law attorney. "I'm letting Lainey know what's ahead, depending on what path she takes. And it is always best to avoid familial estrangements if you can." She turned back to Lainey. "Have you thought about supporting yourself and Petey on your own? At least during a cooling-off period?"

Lainey nodded. "I've already taken steps in that regard." She knew it was her surest path to freedom, and the best example she could set for her son. Money didn't buy happiness—independence did.

Brad looked at her. "Does that mean you're thinking of staying on at the ranch, as housekeeper?"

"Not exactly," she said. Here it was. The moment of truth. Her chance to come clean with Brad, at least part of the way.

Claire continued taking notes. "Did you work before your son was born?"

Lainey flushed. "No. I wanted to, but we didn't need the money and my husband wanted me to stay home, and so…I did." *I'm not going to be married to a reporter, Lainey. I need a wife with elegance and style, who devotes her life only to me. And in return, I'll provide you and any children we have with everything you've ever dreamed of….* And at that time of her life, Lainey had so wanted to be rescued. Loved. Cared for. Too bad none of it had turned out as she dreamed. Chip had been gone much more than he was ever home. And nothing she had ever done, on her own, had been good enough to really please him….

"So, in other words, you have no practical work experience," Claire concluded.

"Right," Lainey said, feeling a little embarrassed about that. As fulfilling as the roles of wife and mother were, she had always wanted satisfying work of her own, too. Was that wrong of her?

"Except for the professional organizing you're doing out at the ranch," Brad cut in admiringly. "Lainey's a whiz at that."

Guilt flooded Lainey as she realized she had just

passed up her chance to confess all to Brad about why she was really there.

Claire perked up. “Maybe you could turn your organizing skill into a moneymaking operation. I know we don’t have anyone doing that sort of work in Laramie.”

AT SIX O’CLOCK, LEWIS AND PETEY arrived home from the game-testing facility in Laramie. By seven, Lewis was showered and dressed and headed to Austin for business meetings the following day. Travis was on their doorstep with his two younger sons, to pick up Petey for a backyard all-male camp-out on their ranch.

“We’ll keep a good eye on the boys, I promise,” Travis told Lainey as he herded Kurt, Kyle and Petey toward his Suburban.

Lainey smiled. “What time should I—” She was going to say *pick Petey up*, then she remembered she didn’t have a vehicle of her own to drive at the moment, and she didn’t know if Brad’s pickup would be available for her to use.

Travis smiled. Seeming to understand how much her predicament had humiliated and embarrassed her—Lainey had already explained it to Annie when Annie called with the overnight invitation an hour earlier—he offered gently, “Annie will bring Petey home around nine-thirty tomorrow morning.”

“Sounds great.” Lainey smiled her relief. “Thanks, Travis.”

“You bet.” Travis paused to make sure all the boys were safely strapped in, then climbed behind the wheel. “See you tomorrow!”

Petey waved excitedly.

The Suburban disappeared down the drive.

Brad, who had been tending to the herd, emerged from the barn. Aware they were going to be alone together for the entire night, she smiled at him officiously. "Did you want me to make you some dinner?" she asked, aware cooking had become part of the deal. "Or were you planning to go out?"

There was a flicker of concern in his eyes, as if he had something on his mind. Then he shifted gears and said, "How about we make something together?"

Lainey found his casual tone disturbing. Was she reading more into his sympathy—and his passionate kisses of just hours earlier—than there was? This was, after all, a man with a string of abruptly started and abruptly ended romances behind him. Pretending she wasn't the least bit unnerved by her growing feelings for him, she stuck her hands in the pockets of her trim black skirt. "I didn't know you could cook."

"Can't, really. But I can grill. And as you'll note—" he pointed to the box sitting next to the back steps "—Lewis brought home charcoal and a grill for me to put together. So if you can wait for me to get a shower, I'll assemble that and we can cook some steaks out here tonight."

"You don't have to go to all that trouble," she said.

Brad flashed her a crooked smile. "It's no trouble." Without waiting for her to comment further, he disappeared inside the house and up the back staircase.

He returned fifteen minutes later as Lainey was sliding a prepared salad into the fridge. She had two potatoes ready to go into the oven, broccoli ready to steam. And not nearly enough to do given how handsome and sexy he looked in jeans, boots and a navy button-up shirt. His hair was still damp from the shower, his jaw freshly shaven. As he neared her she caught the whiff of his aftershave lotion and her heart skipped a beat.

Brad grinned as awareness roiled inside her. "Don't you look as jumpy as a long-tailed cat around a rocking chair."

Lainey rolled her eyes but did not bother to dispute the truth. She *was* nervous.

Brad plucked the screwdriver out of the toolbox in the pantry, then paused and gave her a hard look. His dark brow arched in surprise. He put down the tool needed to assemble the grill and crossed to her side. "Hey, you're not worried about Petey, are you?"

She felt breathless and confused. *No, I'm worried about being alone with you. Worried that if we spend more time together on an intimate level, I'll end up forgetting why I'm here, get in even deeper.* Assuming she wasn't already in much too deep….

When Brad had kissed her this afternoon, she had moved from impulsively accepting comfort to wanton need in no time flat. Had they not been where they were—in his truck in broad daylight—she knew they would have ended up making love. And once would not have been enough.

"Because I guarantee Travis will keep a good eye on them," he enthused.

He stepped closer, and her skin registered the heat. Hands on her shoulders, he grinned at her in a way that sent her pulse skyrocketing.

"The triplets are going to be out there in the tent with them, camping cowboy-style, too, so…everything will be fine. Petey will have a great time."

"I know and I'm glad." Maybe this was the time to get it out in the open. Talk about what happened earlier.

"But just because Petey's gone, and Lewis is gone… doesn't mean that…"

He drew closer, all six foot three inches of him brimming with a curiosity that was distinctly male. And distinctly disturbing. His gaze traveled over her, the desire in his eyes unmistakable as he gathered her in his arms, aligning her soft body against the harder length of his.

"Doesn't mean what?" he asked playfully, as if knowing what she was going to say.

Lainey mocked him with a toss of her hair and planted both hands on the width of his chest. "That we…" She lost her train of thought as he pressed his lower body against hers. Her hips were lodged against the kitchen counter, making escape impossible, but she angled her head and chest back as best she could. Unfortunately, her evasive movement only served to plant her hips more firmly against his.

"…have to pick up where we left off this afternoon?" He pretended not to notice the traitorous weakening of her knees and the heavy thudding of her heart. Just as she pretended not to notice the strength and heat of his desire.

His eyes lit up as he removed her forearms from his chest, draped them over his shoulders, then brought his head down to hers. Their warm breaths met and blended. "Okay. I'm willing to go back to the beginning. Start over…"

"Brad…"

Lainey never finished the sentence. His lips were on hers in a kiss that exuded tenderness and caring, his sweet yearning to simply be with her. Just that simply, all the blossoming emotion she'd felt for Brad, all the passion, came flooding back. Her reservations receded as she was kissed into silence, seduced by the magnetism that made her want to be his. In that instant, the world fell away, and it was only the two of them, this moment in time. Lainey knew, more than anything, what she wanted from Brad. Closeness and love. The unconditional admiration and acceptance that had always eluded her. The desire only Brad could give her. With Brad, she felt she had the potential to be a whole person. Not just a wife or a mother or a woman who never quite measured up in the eyes of those around her.

"Alone at last," Brad murmured contentedly, kissing his way from her lips to her ear to the slope of her neck.

No kidding, Lainey thought.

He drew back. His gaze turned gentle. He traced the curve of her mouth with his fingertip, the fragile caress heating her blood. "I'm about to make a move on you," he told her softly.

A move she had been waiting for forever, it seemed. Although, it had only been a matter of days since their paths had crossed again, this time in an intimate and meaningful way.

"So..." He framed her face with his hands, the raw vulnerability in his expression giving her the courage to acknowledge what had been in her heart all along. Flashing her a sexy grin, he teased as he tunneled his hands through her hair. "Speak now, or forever hold your peace."

Experience had taught Lainey that moments like this were fleeting, at best. As complicated as their situation was—even if he didn't yet know it!—she wasn't going to bypass the chance at love. "I'm not going to resist," she told him, aware she wanted to make love with him so badly she ached. "I want this, too." *More than you'll ever know….*

"Now we're talking." Grinning, he lowered his head and delivered a breath-stealing kiss that had her middle fluttering weightlessly and her nipples tingling. "Let's get comfortable, woman." He swept her up in his arms in a manner that was all the more possessive and carried her toward the stairs—not stopping until he had reached his bed.

He lowered her to the floor and kissed her again, shattering whatever caution she had left. She surged against him, moaning, her arms coming up to wreathe his neck. He deepened the kiss, his tongue sweeping her mouth, tasting, stroking, teasing, until her whole body was alive, quivering with sensations unlike any she had ever felt. It felt so good to be wanted, so right to be held against him this way. She melted against him helplessly. She could feel his arousal pressing, hot and urgent, through their clothing and yearned for closer contact.

She stepped out of her shoes, then reached for the belt buckle, the zipper on his jeans. "And speaking of getting comfortable," she teased as she eased him out of pants and shirt, shoes and shorts.

His manhood sprang free and proud. The rest of him was just as masculine and beautiful. Rippling muscles. Smooth, satiny skin. Whorls of sable-brown hair. Lainey could have stood there admiring him forever.

Brad had other ideas.

"That, darlin', works both ways." Wanting her "more comfortable," too, he reached for the hem of her knit top, drew it gently over her head. The zipper on her skirt was next. She trembled beneath his questing fingers as he divested her of bra and panties.

Her whole body was quaking as he paused to admire her, before slipping those off, too.

"You are so beautiful, so sexy," he murmured.

Wanting to savor everything about this night, Brad let his glance sift slowly over Lainey, then lowered her gently to his bed. She was stunning, any time of any day or night, but she had never looked more radiant than she did at that moment—her cheeks flushed, her silky cap of hair fanning out across his pillow, framing her beautiful face. His gaze moved over her full breasts, her supple waist, the inches of fair silky skin, before dropping to the shadowy vee. He knew it was way too soon for this to be happening, but he didn't care. He couldn't wait any longer. He had to make her his. He kissed her breasts, the hollow of her stomach, softly stroked the insides of her thighs. Their lovemaking was wonderfully sensual, hot and wild. He took the lead. Lainey responded. Savoring the sweetness of her unexpected acquiescence to him, he stroked and licked and nibbled until perspiration beaded her body and she could barely breathe. She gasped, the whimper of sensation turning into a flood of ever-escalating need. Feeling her tremble uncontrollably, he slid up her body. Hard as a rock, he fit his lips over hers once again, demanding, coaxing, tempting, pleasing. Until there was no holding back, no denying the blistering need. Sensations ran riot through him as she arched her back, opened her knees and wrapped her arms around his back, her legs around his waist. He entered her with a long stroke. Her body closed around him, cloaking him in warmth. Savoring the intimacy and the wonder of it all, Brad moved inside her, slowly at first, then with more and more urgency. Lainey moaned against his mouth, her tongue twining urgently with his, taking up the same demanding rhythm as their bodies.

The insides of her thighs rubbed the outsides of his. And then there was no more holding back, no more clinging to control, and Brad joined Lainey at the edge of ecstasy and beyond.

"YOU REALIZE WHAT JUST HAPPENED is exactly what Bunny thinks has been happening all along," Lainey murmured as they lay together in Brad's bed.

"Smart woman, that sister-in-law of yours," he deadpanned, running a hand down her arm, eliciting delicious tingles everywhere he touched, as well as where he didn't.

"I'm serious."

His expression shifted from playful to compassionate. "I know you are," he said gently. He moved so he was on top of her once again. The possessive look in his eyes made her catch her breath. "But Bunny's not right about everything."

"She isn't," Lainey repeated, knowing if they made love again the way Brad clearly wanted to make love to her, she would not be able to blame their encounter solely on passion and a yearning for intimacy, for connection with someone that went soul-deep. Instead, she would be forced to admit their coming together this way—this soon—meant much more. Joining bodies again would be joining hearts and souls, and she would fall all the way in love with him. The vulnerability of a move like that scared her. Not sure she was ready to let him all the way into her heart, when he had yet to learn everything about her and the terrible fix she found herself in, she tensed.

"No, she isn't," he replied firmly. Mistaking the reason behind her unease, he looked at her with all the gentleness she had ever wanted. "You can trust me,

Lainey. This isn't a fling. It isn't a one-night stand or a temporary thing. What I feel for you is going to last."

Forever sounded pretty good to Lainey, too. But she knew it was too soon to be making such promises to each other, even if she was sure her feelings for Brad weren't ever going to change, either. She let out a slow breath.

"Things happen, Brad."

He continued to watch her in that unsettling way. "What are you talking about?" he asked in a low voice.

I'm going to have to tell you the truth eventually, about the article I'm writing and researching for Personalities. *Heck, I should have already done so,* Lainey thought.

Aware he was still waiting for her to continue, but too selfish to ruin what had been the most wonderful night of her entire life by confessing everything to him now, she merely said, "I'm not sure either of us can know how we're going to feel one, two weeks from now, never mind six months down the line."

"Well, I do," he told her confidently. He framed her face with his hands, his weight on her as soothing as a warm blanket on a winter's night. "I've never felt this way about a woman before." He looked at her lovingly as he traced her lip with the tip of his finger. "I've never trusted anyone the way I trust you." He pushed aside the ends of her hair and kissed his way down the exposed line of her throat to the U of her collarbone. "Never wanted anyone the way I want you."

His heartfelt words only made her feel worse. Lainey splayed her hands across his chest, her fingers sliding through the thick mat of chest hair to the warm smooth muscle beneath. "Brad—"

But it was too late, he was already claiming her body with his hands. Tendrils of white heat swept through her as his mouth moved sensually on the hollow between her breasts, then returned with devastating slowness to her mouth. She gulped in air, aware of the tantalizing warmth spreading through hard muscle and satiny skin, and lower still, the stirrings of his renewed desire. She'd never known such power as a woman. Never felt such an immediate, intense connection. When she was with him like this, the future shone hot and bright as the Texas sun.

"I know my rep as a ladies' man and a heartbreaker," he said, pausing to kiss her full on the mouth again, "but all that's behind me now. I want you, and only you. But if you want me to stop," he murmured, arousing her as he kissed her once. And then again. And again. "I will."

Lainey moaned as his hand cupped the weight of her breast, his fingers closed over the nipple, massaging it into a point. The pleasure was almost as unbearably erotic as his kiss, and everything around her went hot and fuzzy except the seductive pressure of his mouth on hers.

"No. Don't stop." She sighed her pleasure as Brad rolled so that she was lying on top of him.

He brushed the hair from her face. "Sure now?"

She let her lips come down on his, firm and sure. "Very," she whispered back, knowing she was betting everything on the two of them and their ability to meet the very difficult challenges that lay ahead. "I want you," she whispered, aware her heart was beating double-time as she gazed into his eyes. Lower still, where their bodies touched, there was an altogether too-familiar warmth pooling. Need, burning deep inside.

He kissed her back, forcing her lips apart. "Show me how."

Determined to show him she could be as bold and exciting a lover as he was, Lainey kissed him leisurely, then knelt astride his thighs, letting the sheet that had been covering her fall away. Swallowing the rest of her inhibitions, she let him look his fill, then slid lower down his body. Her hands skimmed over his skin, touching, learning, loving, exploring. Aware she had never felt sexier in her life, Lainey shifted once again, using lips and teeth and tongue, taking him to the spontaneous combustion stage. More than anything she wanted this to be a mutual giving of pleasure.

"Lainey," he groaned, his eyes dark with wanting her, dark with need.

He'd driven her mad with desire the first time they'd made love. Now she took him to the brink, until he could stand it no more, until he was reaching for her, insisting, then she was moving astride him once again. Slowly, she lowered herself, taking the hard, hot length of him deep inside. Then she drew herself up, so that she was once again on her knees. He brought her down to him, their mouths mating just as their bodies did, in one long, hot, delicious kiss. Then Brad shifted and she was beneath him once again. Moments later, as their bodies merged, it felt as if he was a part of her...heart and soul. And for the first time Lainey discovered what it meant to come together, as equals. She hadn't known she could want a man like this. She hadn't known she could give and take like this. But she did, she thought, as the passion overtook them once again.

CHAPTER ELEVEN

"WHAT DO YOU MEAN I'M in one of the New York City newspapers?" Brad asked the person on the other end of the telephone the following morning as he and Lainey lingered over breakfast in the ranch house kitchen. They had been up most of the night making love, yet both were still filled with adrenaline and energy. Until now, they hadn't been able to stop smiling or kissing or touching.

Whatever Brad was hearing from the person on the other end of the connection was putting a damper on his spirits, fast.

He grimaced. "I'll check the Internet. Thanks." He hung up the phone.

"What's going on?" Lainey asked, surveying the haunted look in his eyes.

"Come with me and we'll find out." Brad headed for his office, where he fired up his computer. Seconds later, he was on the Web site he'd been told to read. Sure enough, there was a publicity picture of Brad taken during one of the Heart Ceremonies on *Bachelor Bliss.* He was handing a woman an engraved invitation to stay on for future episodes, but where the contestant had stood was a blacked-out silhouette of a woman and a large white question mark, under the caption *His cheating heart.*

Lainey scanned the accompanying article along with Brad.

> Who would have guessed heartbreaking bachelor Brad McCabe would be caught in the arms of a mystery woman in a Dallas motel parking lot yesterday afternoon. Witnesses said the beautiful, blond mystery woman was as distressed as the handsome hunk to be caught canoodling in broad daylight, by a bunch of teenage girls. A check with the motel in question noted Brad McCabe had not checked in yet, nor did he have a reservation under his own name, so no telling what his original plans were for the hot summer afternoon. When contacted, ex-flame Yvonne Rathbone was quoted as saying tearfully, "The secret's out. I think he was involved with her all along!"

"What?" Brad erupted, as he finished reading the nationally syndicated gossip column the same time as Lainey. "I don't believe that witch!"

"Why would Yvonne say you were cheating on her?" she asked, her brain already going into reporter mode.

"Because she doesn't want people to know what really—"

"What?" she demanded, frustrated he hadn't finished. Darn it all, she wanted to be able to clear his name! Get his reputation back for him.

"Never mind," he muttered, his expression becoming closed and unreadable once again.

To her consternation, before she could ask anything else, her cell phone rang. She plucked it out of her pocket, noted the identification of the caller flashing on the tiny screen, and swore silently to herself. Knowing she couldn't possibly take this call in front of Brad, she pointed to the exit. "It's a girlfriend. I'm going to take this over at the guest house, okay?"

"Fine. Whatever." He was still glaring at the computer monitor, as disgruntled as if they had never made love.

Lainey walked quickly through the house and went outside. "Hello?"

Sybil's voice came over the line in a near screech that Brad surely would have been able to hear if they had still been in the same room. "Tell me we are not being scooped!" Sybil said.

Lainey swallowed. She was courting disaster here on so many levels.

"Do you know who the mystery blonde is?" the editor demanded irately.

"I think I have an idea," Lainey muttered, knowing she had done the unthinkable for a reporter—she had become part of the story she was covering.

"Was Brad cheating on Yvonne with this woman while they were on the show?"

Lainey glanced out the window and saw Brad striding toward the barn. "I'm sure he wasn't."

"You have proof? Or you're just guessing?"

"Proof." *Sort of.*

Lainey watched as Brad led one of the virgin heifers out to a pasture located well away from the one where Tabasco Red was grazing.

Silence. "You want to share those facts with me?" Sybil asked tensely.

"When I turn my article in." Lainey hoped by then she would have Brad's cooperation in what she was trying to do for him.

"I'm counting on you to get this story for me, Lainey. Our future career success depends on it."

"I know." Lainey just wished she weren't in such an impossible situation.

"In the meantime, you asked me to see what I could do to get you access to the producers. Well, I couldn't get you that, but I did manage to get you an interview with the show's creator, Gil Hewitt, on behalf of the magazine."

Lainey reached for paper and pen, elated by the coup. Sybil was really helping her out here. "When and where?" she asked.

"Sunday afternoon. You're to talk with Gil, half an hour before you talk with Yvonne. Same hotel."

Well, that was easy. Almost too easy. Lainey wrinkled her brow. "They're going to be there together?"

Sybil paused to say something to her editorial assistant, then returned to Lainey. Paper rustled. "Apparently, Gil and his staff are doing taped interviews of potential contestants for the next season. They have set up some publicity with local newspapers for past stars—apparently Brad was asked but declined to participate."

No surprise there, either, Lainey thought.

"Apparently, the show is attempting to do a little damage control. High ratings of the finale have given way to skepticism about whether people can really find love on a reality TV show. Anyway, Yvonne's going to tell everyone that despite the way things turned out, she would do it all over again, because falling in love…just the hope of a real and lasting romance…is worth it. Blah, blah, blah."

Yes, Lainey thought, true love was worth it. Even if she didn't quite believe that was the case for Miss Yvonne Rathbone.

"I'M JUST GOING TO GO GET the computer games Lewis said I could borrow for the weekend," Petey told Lainey on Saturday afternoon.

Lainey knew once Lewis and Petey started talking software they'd lose all track of time. "I want to be on the road in ten minutes," she warned. "Tell Lewis that."

"Okay." Petey rushed into the house to find the computer-game whiz.

Lainey and Brad were left alone in the guest house as Lainey continued packing up the items she wanted to take back to Dallas. "You're sure you don't want me to go with you?" Brad asked as he watched her fill a wicker basket with laundry that needed to be done.

Wishing she weren't already head over heels in love with Brad—and she suspected that he felt the same about her—Lainey shook her head. In addition to the fact that she knew Brad had a lot to do on the ranch, she needed a little distance to be able to research the story properly. He drove her to distraction when they were in such close proximity.

She still didn't have her car back, but Annie McCabe was letting her borrow one of their ranch vehicles. "Petey and I need to be home for a night or two. I've already asked Bunny to inform the Realtor not to bring anyone through while we're in Dallas this weekend, and I'm taking Petey over to see his cousins tomorrow and spend the day with Bart and Bunny."

"Are you sure that's wise—under the circumstances?" Brad asked.

Touched by his concern for her, Lainey nodded. She'd been thinking about what Claire McCabe Taylor had told her about the emotional and financial costs of lawsuits, and knew she had to give the situation more time to resolve on its own. She wasn't sure yet whether that made her naive or wise, but she knew they would find out by the summer's end, if not before.

Lainey was glad she had Brad on her side. She felt safe and secure and protected by him. He made her feel she had someone to turn to in the storms of life, and that made all the difference. It was helping her regain her serenity.

"I don't want Petey to feel caught in the middle of this conflict between his aunt, uncle and me," she explained, taking Brad's hand in hers and holding it tightly. "We might not be getting along all that well at the moment, but we're still family and always will be. Petey needs to know that with time and patience—and a willingness to compromise—families can work out their problems." She was sure it would be worth it in the end, no matter how much grief she endured in the process.

He looked down at her admiringly. "You have a lot of grace. You know that, don't you?"

"I'm trying to do the right thing—for everyone," she said, knowing it was what her late husband would want her to do. And she was trying to do right by Brad, too. She just wished she hadn't gone about it the wrong way. But Lainey had given her word to follow through on this story. And somehow, some way, she had to carry through on those promises, and discover and make public the truth. And when the time was right, either just before or just after Brad had his reputation back, she had to muster all her courage and come clean with him. Knowing all the while that he might never forgive her if she confessed what had brought her to the ranch in the first place.

If he weren't so darn mule-headed and full of the

McCabe pride, of course, her job would be a lot easier. But no one ever said life was trouble-free.

Lainey smiled, knowing that soon Brad would have his good name cleared of all wrongdoing. Despite his efforts to the contrary. "We'll be back first thing Monday morning."

"Hurry home." He brought her to him for a slow, sensual kiss before she could head out the door.

Home? Lainey thought with wonder as she melted into the warm shelter of his body and kissed him back, as thoroughly and tenderly as he was kissing her. Was that what the Lazy M was to her now? She only knew she wanted it to be.

"LAINEY CARRINGTON, here to see Gil Hewitt," Lainey told the clerk at the Fairmont Dallas hotel the following day.

"We're expecting you." The clerk handed over a pass. "You'll need this to get past the security guards on the fourth floor."

"Thanks." Lainey walked past the groups of beautiful young women congregated in the lobby. It was obvious they were here to interview for the new episodes of *Bachelor Bliss*. They looked nervous and on edge. Knowing what the experience had done to Brad McCabe, Lainey was tempted to stop and tell them all not to do it, but realizing she was already in too deep as it was, she kept right on going.

The fourth floor was also a beehive of activity. Lainey got past security, and made her way toward Gil Hewitt's suite. She was almost there when a short, thick-waisted man garbed in clothing fit for a tropical safari stepped out to greet her. He had a scarf around his neck and a ridiculous hat on his head. She recognized him instantly. "Mr. Hewitt? I'm—"

"I know who you are and you're late."

No, she wasn't. She was fifteen minutes early.

"Do you think we have all day to get through these auditions?"

Lainey swallowed. "I..."

Gil shut the door behind them. Lainey realized for all the attention the other staffers were paying, they might as well have been alone. "You're very beautiful." Gil's gaze roved her face, hair, moved slowly over the tailored linen pantsuit she had on. "But if you want to get anywhere with a bachelor, you should wear a sexy dress. Cleavage is always nice."

Pig. Aware she was learning firsthand how future contestants auditioned, Lainey merely smiled and said, "I'll remember that."

Gil steered her toward a stool set up in front of a photographer's backdrop. "Take her picture and get her basics."

Again, Lainey tried to set the record straight. Gil Hewitt cut her off before she could say a word. "Honey, I already told you, we're behind enough as it is. So just do what you're told and we'll get along fine."

Was this the treatment all potential contestants received? Lainey wondered. Two minutes later, she was up off the stool and headed toward the door with Gil at her side.

"Mr. Hewitt..." Lainey began again.

"Call me Gil."

"Gil. I'm here to—"

"Don't worry, honey-buns. It's a lock. You're in."

Lainey blinked. "I am?"

He whispered in her ear, "I knew the moment I saw you that you were my type. Sophisticated, pretty."

And not at all interested in you. Lainey did her best not to recoil as she caught a whiff of his garlic breath. "Did I mention I'm also the widowed mother of an eight-year-old son?"

He blinked. Thought it over briefly. Shrugged. "Fantastic. Viewers will love it."

He looked at her with obvious interest. Too smart to actually touch her in an inappropriate way, but telegraphing his rather creepy intentions nevertheless. A shudder went through Lainey. So this was what it was like to be sexually harassed on a casting couch. Not pretty.

"And I'm not here to audition for the show," Lainey continued, suppressing her desire to knock Gil Hewitt flat on his keister. She smiled. "I'm here to interview you for *Personalities Magazine.*"

Gil stiffened. "Well, why didn't you say so?" He looked irked.

"I tried."

"You have five minutes." He guided her through another doorway, to a small sitting room with desk and chair.

Lainey set her tape recorder on the table and switched it on. She wanted audio backup for anything she wrote down. "I want to talk to you about Brad McCabe and Yvonne Rathbone."

A second passed. Gil assumed a beleaguered expression. "Poor Yvonne. He really did her wrong."

Lainey looked at her list of prepared questions. "Rumor has it that it's the other way around. Yvonne did Brad wrong."

For a second Gil didn't move at all. "Who told you that?" he asked finally.

Aware she had hit a nerve, Lainey shot back playfully, "Now, Mr. Hewitt, you know I can't tell you that."

He dismissed her theory with a frown. "It's rumor."

Lainey leaned forward. "How can you be sure? Did you see everything that went on between the two of them?"

"Yes. Cameras are on one hundred percent of the time."

Not according to Brad. Which meant Gil Hewitt was lying. And if he was lying about this, what else was he lying about? Lainey was about to ask another question, when Gil abruptly declared the interview over.

"So you talked to Gil Hewitt, too," Yvonne Rathbone said, when Lainey caught up with her. The red-haired beauty looked stunning in a white eyelet-lace sundress.

Lainey smiled, admitted this was so. She put her tape recorder on the table between them in full view and asked a few softball questions as warm-up. Yvonne told her everything she had already said countless times to reporters.

"Did you know anything about Brad before the night you all met him?" Lainey asked.

Yvonne shook her head. "They wouldn't tell us anything! We didn't even see a picture of him."

Lainey looked at her questions. "The first moment you said hello and kissed Brad McCabe's cheek, it looked like you whispered something in his ear, and Brad laughed in response. Care to tell *Personalities* readers what that was?"

"Oh, I just said, 'This is so stupid!'"

Okay, Lainey thought, that was the generic flirtatious

response. Except… "Weren't you afraid Brad would be offended by that, given that he was there to find a wife?" she asked curiously.

"Well, everyone knew Brad wasn't the kind of guy to tolerate such foolishness."

"But I thought you said none of you knew anything about him, at that point."

"We didn't. But we—I—could just tell that was what kind of guy he was by looking at him," Yvonne amended hastily.

Lainey pretended to accept her answer as truthful, even though she knew there was no way anyone could have leaped to that conclusion in the fifteen seconds it took for Brad and Yvonne to lay eyes on each other and walk toward each other for the first time. "Can you tell me what happened the day Brad broke up with you—on camera?" Lainey asked, turning to the next page of her notes.

In front of her she had the transcript of Yvonne's retelling of the event on a network show.

"Well." Yvonne sniffed. Her chin trembled and tears appeared in her eyes.

Lainey watched, spellbound, as Yvonne recounted, word for word, pause for pause, sniff for sniff, even eye dab for eye dab, how Brad had come in, snarled at her and left. It was a verbatim account of everything Yvonne had said before. Which could mean it was all a lie, as Brad said, and Yvonne had memorized it in order to keep her story straight. It could also be that she had told it so many times to so many people and reporters that she had unwittingly memorized her recounting. Bottom line, it was all very dramatic and damning, and if Lainey didn't know a lot more had gone on than what was currently being reported, she would have believed Yvonne and loathed Brad, too.

Lainey moved on determinedly. "Back to Gil Hewitt, the show's creator, and the producers. Did you all get along?"

"Oh, yes." Big smile. "Famously, as a matter of fact. They were very nice to all of us."

"No one got special treatment?"

Yvonne paused, looking like a deer in the headlights. "Not that I saw," she said finally.

"I like Gil, too." Lainey followed a hunch to see where it would lead. "He's very, um, friendly, isn't he."

For the first time that afternoon, Yvonne's smile faltered, then faded all the way. "What do you mean?"

Lainey leaned confidentially close. "I heard he propositioned a number of the girls on the show."

Emotion flared in Yvonne's eyes. Jealousy? "That's not true!"

Lainey sat back in mock surprise. "So he didn't proposition you?"

"He—of course not. Nor did he proposition anyone else," Yvonne reiterated stiffly.

"My mistake," Lainey said. "Now, about your background. I understand you went to San Diego State. And you were interested in theater there?" Another hunch that would be easy enough to follow through on.

"I did a few plays," Yvonne admitted proudly.

"So you wanted to be an actress!" Lainey pretended to be deeply impressed. "How did you end up in marketing and sales instead?"

Yvonne sighed, lowered her guard. "Do you have any idea how hard it is to get an agent…?"

By the time Lainey left the hotel, she thought she had a pretty good idea what had happened. But having an inkling wasn't the same as having the facts. She needed a firsthand account from someone she could trust. The question was, would Brad give it to her?

"I DIDN'T THINK you were coming back until tomorrow morning," Brad said Sunday evening when Lainey arrived at the ranch, a sleepy Petey in tow.

"I thought there would be less traffic this evening," Lainey replied.

"I wanted to come back," Petey said, yawning as he got out of the car Lainey had borrowed from Annie McCabe.

"I'm glad." Brad smiled, looking very happy to have them there.

Lainey's heart skipped a beat as she opened the guest house door and turned on the lights. She gazed down at her drowsy son. "Run on in and brush your teeth and get ready for bed, honey. I'll be in to say good-night in a minute."

"Okay." Petey turned and went back to Brad. He wrapped his arms around Brad's middle. "Night."

Brad hugged Petey back with a warmth that filled Lainey's heart.

"Night, son." He turned to Lainey. "Want me to carry your belongings in?" he asked as Petey disappeared into the bathroom down the hall.

Lainey glanced at the car. "No. That's okay," she said hastily. "I don't have much. I'll get it later."

Brad grinned, teasingly. "If I didn't know better, I'd think you were hiding something in there."

She was. Her notes on the interview work she had done earlier in the day were tucked beneath the clean laundry in the wicker basket. "Ha-ha," she said, wishing she didn't want to forget everything else that was going on, throw herself in Brad's arms and kiss him madly.

"It was lonely around here without you and Petey," he said.

Lainey had been lonely, too. Conflicted. Guilty. Torn between her need to see justice done and have a career, and her need to cater only to Brad, to heck with what anyone else thought. But that wouldn't serve Brad or her need to put the truth about the goings on at the *Bachelor Bliss* show out there.

"Well, we're back now," she said. The amount of uneasiness and guilt she was feeling told her she had no future as a double agent. But then she had never wanted to be a spy. She wanted a future as a reporter.

Chip had once outlawed that.

Would Brad, too?

"Mom!" Petey called from his bedroom.

Deciding this was no time to be thinking about such complex questions, Lainey practically pushed Brad toward the door. "I've got to go."

He stepped out onto the porch, and she hurried back to tuck Petey in. The boy was already under the covers.

"Mom," Petey said sleepily, "can I ask you something?"

"Always." Lainey perched on the side of the bed.

"Is Aunt Bunny upset with you and me?"

Lainey forged ahead carefully. "Why would you think that?"

"I tried to tell her about all the cowboy stuff I'm learning from Brad and Travis, how grown-up I already am, and she acted like she didn't want to hear it."

Lainey imagined that was true. Bunny was losing both her daughters to college this fall. Now, she thought she was losing her nephew, too. Lainey had hoped taking Petey to see Bunny would reassure Bunny that she would have plenty of time with the child no matter where Lainey lived or worked. Obviously, that wasn't the case. Yet, anyway.

"I think she just misses seeing you every day," she said gently, doing her best to maintain a charitable attitude where her sister-in-law was concerned.

"Yeah—" Petey thrust his jaw out stubbornly "—but I'm not her son, Mom…I'm yours."

Lainey smoothed her son's blond hair away from his forehead. "She loves you as much as if you were. You're family to her, Petey. And all she has left of your dad. So, if she's holding on a little too tight, I think that's why."

Petey fell silent once again, seeming to understand better. After a moment, he looked up at her earnestly. "I like it out here, Mom. I want to stay even after you finish all your organizing stuff. Can we?"

Lainey wished that would happen, too, but given what she still had to do, she did not know if that was going to be possible.

"WHAT ARE YOU DOING BACK SO soon?" Lewis asked Brad.

Brad stood in the kitchen, watching Lainey carry her belongings in from the car.

"A gentleman would be out there helping her lug that stuff inside."

Brad did not need to be told that by his nerdy brother or anyone else. He reached into the refrigerator and took out a bottle of beer. "Already asked and was refused."

Lewis lifted a brow as he helped himself to a brew, too. "What'd you do to tick her off?"

"Nothing," Brad admitted in frustration. "That I know, anyway."

Lewis took the bottle opener his brother handed to him. "Not going to go after her?"

Brad shook his head.

"Why not?" Lewis persisted.

Wishing his younger brother would shut up, Brad lifted the bottle to his lips. "Because she obviously needs her space," he explained.

Lewis looked at him, reminding Brad that of all his brothers, Lewis was the most sensitive to others' feelings.

"Sure that's all it is?" Lewis asked.

No. That was the hell of it. Brad wasn't.

Lewis lounged against the counter. "Maybe she heard about that blonde you were supposedly seen kissing in Dallas. Or maybe that blonde you were supposedly seen kissing in Dallas was Lainey," he suggested slyly.

Brad hadn't told anyone he and Lainey had become involved with each other in a romantic sense. To his aggravation, everyone who had seen them interacting together in even the most mundane way seemed to know anyway. Which meant he was wearing his heart on his sleeve. Not smart, he knew. Especially given the fact that Lainey was obviously having second thoughts about making love with him.

"And maybe she didn't like showing up in the papers," Lewis persisted helpfully.

Brad wasn't about to take advice on how to handle a woman from his only brother whose track record with the ladies was worse than Brad's. "Will you shut up?" he growled.

The smirk on Lewis's face indicated he knew what the truth was. "Guess I better be quiet if I don't want to eat a knuckle sandwich." He lifted his bottle to Brad in silent toast. "If you need me, I'll be in my study."

Brad grunted in response and Lewis disappeared.

The lights were on in the guest house. Lainey hadn't closed her blinds. Through the window, Brad watched as she sat down on the sofa, opened up her laptop and got out a sheaf of papers. Then she abruptly stood, went to the windows and closed the blinds. Because she felt herself being watched? he wondered. Or because she had something to hide?

The second thought caught him unaware. He hadn't expected to be suspicious of Lainey. But, deep in his gut, he was. Why? Was it the way Lainey had refused to meet his eyes this evening, when she returned? The way she hurried him out the door and on his way? Or the way she seemed suddenly conflicted and uneasy around him? As if something had happened…something she didn't really want him to know.

All Brad knew for certain was that he was having the same feeling about Lainey he'd once had about Yvonne.

He didn't like it. Not at all.

CHAPTER TWELVE

"READY TO GO TEST SOME more computer games?" Lewis asked Petey on Monday morning.

"I sure am!" Petey hopped up from the breakfast table, where he had been hanging out while Lainey did the dishes from the morning meal.

"We'll probably be home about six," Lewis said.

Lainey nodded. "Don't forget—Annie and Travis and all their boys are coming for dinner."

Lewis had invited them the day before, and Lainey thought it was a great idea. She'd been wanting to return their hospitality.

"Can we play after dinner?" Petey asked.

Lainey smiled. "We'll have to ask Annie and Travis, but I'm sure it'll be okay." Since the "ranchers and rustlers" incident, Petey and his two sweet but mischievous cohorts hadn't gotten into any trouble. "Have fun." Lainey hugged Petey goodbye.

"We will!" Petey beamed as he raced out the door.

Brad walked in, coffee cup in hand, as Lewis's car disappeared down the driveway. As always, the sight of him took Lainey's breath away. He hadn't yet shaved this morning and the hint of beard on his jaw gave him a rugged appeal. He was wearing a pair of worn jeans, boots and a clean but rumpled tan cotton work shirt. As he neared her, she could see the hair curling damply against his nape and smell soap and toothpaste. Desire drifted through her, more potent than any shot of caffeine. His broad shoulder nudged hers as he opened the cupboard and lifted out a mug with a rodeo emblem on the front.

"Any more coffee left?"

Lainey flashed a smile. "I just emptied out what little was left and washed the pot. I'll make some fresh."

He leaned against the counter, making absolutely no move to get out of her way. Letting her realize exactly what he wanted and that he was just waiting for the right moment. His gaze drifted over the clip that held back her blond hair. She hadn't had time that morning to carefully blow it out with her hair dryer, so wispy curls framed her face and the back of her neck. "Did I do something to annoy you?"

"What are you talking about?" Lainey asked, as she filled the water reservoir in the coffeemaker.

Brad backed her against the kitchen counter and clamped a hand on either side of her. "Last night you barely had five minutes for me. This morning you're as jumpy as a frog on a lily pad."

Lainey felt herself blush, embarrassed. He wasn't touching her but she could feel the warmth emanating from his body. It beckoned her like a port in the storm. "I just have a lot on my mind," she said finally.

Brad lifted a brow.

"Well, I do!" Lainey protested.

He leaned closer and looked deep into her eyes. "Somehow I don't think that's all it is."

Lainey gulped as her heartbeat sped up. If only she could tell him everything here, now, and be guaranteed of the outcome….

"And I made myself a promise a while back not to ignore my gut anymore, when it comes to suspecting things are amiss." He paused, letting his words sink in. "So, Lainey, I am asking you, what has changed?"

His low persuasive voice melted Lainey's resistance all the more. He searched her face and caressed her cheek with the pad of his thumb as her guilt increased by leaps and bounds.

"Are you acting this way because we made love?"

"WELL, NOW THAT YOU b-brought it up..." Lainey stammered.

Brad had the impression he was not just being pushed away momentarily, but for good. The thought was damn disturbing. And yet here he was following her around like a lovesick pup. What kind of spell had she put on him? It wasn't like him to pursue someone who did not want to be pursued. "Yes?" he prodded, wishing she would cut straight to the chase.

"I'm not sure that was the wisest course of action, under the circumstances," she recited in a low, battle-weary voice.

Frustrated she was not more talkative—didn't women usually enjoy delving into their feelings?—he dropped his hand and settled against the counter. "I didn't hear you complaining at the time."

Lainey crossed her arms. In the soft light of the kitchen, her classically beautiful features were more pronounced. "Well, maybe I should have protested," she said as her eyes met, then veered away, from his. "We hardly know each other."

"A fact I am trying hard to remedy," he countered softly, "by spending more time with you."

Lainey leaned a slender hip against the counter. "Even so—"

"We know everything there is to know about each

other where it counts, Lainey." Brad moved closer yet, until he was inundated with the sweet softness of her once again. He inhaled the intoxicating blend of perfume and woman. Determined to prove they did know enough about each other to become intimately involved, he put his arms around her. "For instance, I know you love your son and you're one of the best mothers I've ever seen." She lifted her face up to his, gazing into his eyes, and he continued seriously. "I know you have a kind heart and a generous soul…and a sweetness of spirit I can't even begin to find words to describe. I know you make me want to be a better man than I've ever been. I know you're the woman I've been waiting for, the only woman for me," he confessed in a husky voice, feeling as astonished as she appeared to be by the way he was putting himself out there. "And I know when you finally let your guard down, which isn't nearly often enough to please either of us, you're feeling as connected to me as I am to you." Feeling her melt against him, he kissed her cheek, her temple, the delicate skin just behind her ear. "So what else do we need to know?"

Again, something flared in her eyes. She looked as if she had the weight of the world on her slender shoulders. "Brad—"

Resolved they would not lose ground here, he brought her closer yet. "Stop pushing me away, Lainey. Take down those barriers that surround your heart."

He gathered her against him, bent his head and kissed her the way he had been longing to kiss her since she'd come back last night. Determined to make her see what they could have if she would just let her reservations go, he deepened the sweet caress. Then all pretense, all reserve, was gone as she met him, kiss for kiss. Desire thundering through him in waves, he flattened the hard length of his body against the soft pliability of hers. Able to feel how much Lainey wanted and needed him, no matter what she said, he swept her mouth with his tongue, kissing her until she gave him back everything he had ever wanted, everything he had ever expected. Before long, the blood was pooling hot and urgent in his body, and he wanted her more than he had wanted any woman in his life.

When she sagged against him, signaling she felt the same, he broke off the embrace just long enough to slip an arm beneath her knees and lift her against his chest. Her eyes were misty with longing and love as he carried her up the back staircase, and down the hall, to the rumpled covers of his bed. The need to make her his—not just for this moment in time, or next month or next week, but forever—was stronger than ever.

"You've got to promise me something," he whispered as he tugged off his boots and hers and joined her on the bed.

"What?" She watched as he unbuttoned her blouse.

He eased it off her shoulders and away from her body, enjoying the way the uppermost curves of her breasts spilled out of the white lace bra. Beneath the thin fabric, he could see the jutting nipples. "To stop running from me, from us."

She trembled as he slipped a strap off her shoulder and down her arm. "Is that what you think I've been doing?" she murmured as he drew the fabric away.

Brad traced the delicate pink-and-white flesh, luxuriating in the soft, silky feel of her. "I know you're scared." He stared into the turbulent, forest green of her eyes, eyes that were still vulnerable and full of need. Eyes that maybe believed a little of what had been written and said about his allegedly fickle heart. "You don't have to be. This leap of faith we're taking has success written all over it."

She looked like she wanted to trust him, trust the two of them and their impetuous involvement, so much. And he set about showing her that she could, as he removed her bra and kissed her neck, shoulders, collarbone and breasts. They continued kissing—hard, soft, and every way in between—caressing each other until they lay together naked on the bed.

"And I thought I'd given up all my wild ways," Lainey sighed.

Brad grinned as he thought about the sexy dress he had missed seeing her in. He'd have to get her in one again. One he'd purchase for her. "Wild can be good," he whispered, holding her so close they were almost one. His own body throbbing, he moved down the length of her, exploring as he went.

Lainey arched up off the bed. "You certainly make me believe that," she murmured, whimpering and moaning her pleasure in a way that drove him crazy with desire.

"Good."

"In fact—" she turned and draped her body over his "—being wild with you is downright fun."

"Is that so?" Brad drawled.

"Something about letting go…"

Her lips drifted over his skin. "Doing whatever I please…no longer caring about what people think…."

Brad's breath hitched as her lips wooed and seduced. Wondering if he would ever be able to get enough of her, he moved to switch places with her again, so she was beneath him. Parting her knees with his, he braced a hand on either side of her and situated himself between her thighs. "Take it from me—a person's reputation can only go so far in revealing who that person is deep inside."

Lainey ran her hands over the muscles of his back. "You're a good man, Brad McCabe."

Insistent he be the one to set the pace, Brad took her wrists in hand and anchored them above her head. "And you, Lainey Carrington, are not only a good woman, but the only woman for me."

"So what does that mean?" Lainey teased softly, as they locked eyes, playfully and pleasurably delaying the moment when they would come together completely. "We're going steady?"

"Too high school." Brad lowered his mouth to hers once again, lifted her against him and surged into her slick, wet heat, slowly and deliberately. "I prefer something more grown-up."

So did Lainey. "Exclusive?"

"Permanently exclusive," he told her, all the love she had ever wanted to see shining in his eyes, as he entered and withdrew in shallow strokes that soon had her moaning and trembling, wanting, needing. Straining against him, she took up the rhythm he had started, until there was no more delaying, and their hearts thundered in unison. He was surging deeper, harder, claiming her as his. Holding fast to him, she claimed him, too, and then there was nothing…save one secret…standing between them. Their passion was so strong and so right and so filled with tenderness that it didn't feel quite real. But it was, Lainey thought, as she took everything he offered, gave him everything back in return, and soared into the sweet, hot abyss right along with him.

They clung together afterward, bodies humming with pleasure, hearts content. Except for that one thing.

The fact that he did not know she was working as a reporter, investigating him.

She wanted to tell him. She was going to inform him. She should have already done so. Except that if she did, she was pretty sure he would cease all contact with her. And the thought she might lose him when the truth came out about what she had been doing was devastating. So wrenching, in fact, that she burst into tears.

FOR THE LIFE OF HIM, Brad couldn't figure out why Lainey was crying. These didn't look like tears of bliss. They looked like tears engendered by great conflict. "What's wrong?" he asked, unable to understand why she didn't feel as happy as he did, given what had just happened between them.

She just shook her head.

"I can't understand if you won't let me in," he told her tenderly as he stroked a hand down her spine and guided her closer still.

She only sobbed harder.

Frustrated that he wasn't able to comfort her as he wanted, he searched her face and asked, "Do you think I've treated you badly, making love to you so soon?" Damn it, he had known a woman like Lainey needed courting, a lot of it.

She shook her head and avoided his eyes.

"Because I swear, if I thought that was what was hurting you, I'd call a halt to the physical side of our relationship. It'd be hard, but I'd do it—" His voice caught as he realized how vulnerable he'd become to her. "I'd do anything to keep you in my life," he whispered intensely.

She shoved her hands through her cap of tousled hair.

She looked more emotionally inaccessible than ever. "You don't understand."

"Then help me," he pleaded. He hated feeling so helpless.

Lainey wiped the tears from her eyes. She sat up against the headboard, pulling the sheet to her chin, holding the fabric against the nakedness of her body with her bare arms. But to his mounting disappointment, as their gazes met and held, all she did was seem to get further away from him. Finally, she swallowed and took a deep breath.

"I don't deserve you," she said thickly. Fresh tears started as she dabbed at the corners of her eyes with the sheet. "And I want so badly to—" She paused, shook her head miserably, seemingly unable, or maybe just unwilling, to go on.

"Is this because of how your husband made you feel?" he asked as he sat up beside her, really wanting to understand. "Because I swear, if it is—"

She drew in another deep, shaky breath. "It has nothing to do with him," she confessed, finally able to talk more calmly. "It has to do with the fact that I am not the sainted person you think I am."

LAINEY SAW THE LOOK on Brad's face and knew he thought the problem was one of damaged self-esteem. If only it were that simple, she thought unhappily. "It's just…I've gone about this all wrong," she tried to explain in a voice still coated with tears. And she didn't know how much longer she could keep up the subterfuge. She was trying to be all things to all people and succeeding at none of it.

Had she started out telling Lewis and then Brad what she had come to the ranch to find out, Brad never would have spoken to her and Lewis certainly never would have hired her or invited her to stay at the Lazy M with Petey.

Instead, she had let Brad goad her into matching wits with him, and once the sparks had started flying between them, well…it had been as impossible for her to stay away from him as it was for Brad to stay away from her.

And once she had started falling in love with him, the stakes had increased even more.

She'd signed a contract…and Lainey did not make promises she did not intend to keep.

And yet writing a story about Brad and Yvonne and why they really broke up was not something she wanted to do without his permission and approval. But how was she going to get that now…after all that had happened? He was going to think she was just like Yvonne. Pretending to be something—someone—she wasn't.

And worse, he would be right.

How in the world had she ever gotten herself in such a mess?

Despite everything, she didn't regret for one minute loving Brad, because he was the best thing that had ever happened to her.

Brad's glance softened. He wrapped an arm around her shoulders and kissed the top of her head. "Your work for Lewis has nothing to do with my relationship with you," he soothed, still completely misunderstanding the reason for the conflict within her.

"I know that. It's just…" She gulped and started as the sound of a pickup truck rumbled through the driveway.

Brad and Lainey exchanged looks as they realized they were no longer alone. He moved to the window, standing buck naked just inside the curtains, and peered out. "What the...?" He cursed.

Lainey, who knew they couldn't get caught in bed together, was already pulling on her clothes. Brad had enough scandal in his life without adding public knowledge of a dalliance with her to the mix. The truth-telling was going to have to wait until later.

"Who is it?" she demanded, aware she was so distressed her hands were shaking and her knees felt wobbly.

"A girl I used to date."

Lainey blinked, not sure she was ready for this. "Recently?"

"In high school," Brad explained with a frown. "Her parents still live in Laramie but she moved to Dallas after she married and I haven't seen her in...years. She's with her husband. I only know him slightly—he's not from around here—I met him at their wedding."

Lainey blinked and momentarily stopped what she was doing. "You're kidding."

Brad gave her a deadpan look and then went back to observing. "They're headed for the front porch and they both look madder than wet hens." He shook his head, as if his life had gotten so crazy post–*Bachelor Bliss* that he almost expected the sky to fall in, too. "This ought to be interesting," he muttered. "'Cause I have a feeling they aren't looking for Lewis."

Downstairs, someone pounded on the front door—rather furiously, Lainey noted.

Brad opened the window a crack and shouted out, "Hold your horses! I'll be right down!"

Lainey finished dressing as hurriedly as she could, pausing to run a brush through her hair. To no avail. Her lipstick had been kissed off. Her cheeks were flushed, eyes bright, nose red from crying. She was, quite frankly, a mess, she noted as she put the clip back in her hair.

"You don't have to go down there," he said, hurriedly tucking his shirttail into his jeans.

Lainey shook her head. "If I hide, it'll be worse. Everyone in town knows I'm working out here, and that includes her parents. Hence, they are going to expect to see me." She slipped on her red cowgirl boots. "Do I look like I've just made love with you?" she whispered as the pounding on the front door resumed, even more furiously.

Brad paused to kiss the tip of her nose and rub his thumb across her lips. He looked as if he wanted to make love to her all over again.

"Only to me." He took her by the hand. "Let's go."

Lainey went to the kitchen to finish making the coffee she had started assembling earlier, while Brad hurried to the front door.

Both tried to act normal as Brad ushered Melinda Farren, née Evans, and her husband Clint Farren inside. Slim, nicely dressed, with shining blunt-cut blond hair, she could have been Lainey's twin—from the back, anyway. Which was the problem, they quickly figured out as Clint thrust what looked to be a tabloid into Brad's hands.

Lainey stood in the front hall, dish towel in hand, aware she was demonstrating remarkable composure given the fact she had just spent half the morning making love with Laramie's resident heartbreaking bad boy. But maybe that was because Brad had a way of making her feel so loved and cherished, despite the fact he had never once said the words to her.

"Hey, Melinda. Hi, Clint," she said pleasantly, resolved she would not add to the scandal sweeping Brad's life. "What's going on?"

"I'm on the cover of a tabloid!" Melinda wailed.

Lainey blinked. "How did that happen?"

Melinda pointed at Brad. "Ask him!"

Lainey looked at the cover. There was a picture of Brad and Melinda back in high school, going to some prom, and then another of two people kissing, presumably now. It was Brad, all right, in the photo, but all you could see of the woman was the back of a head. The caption above it read, *Yvonne Rathbone tells all! Brad McCabe involved with married high school sweetheart all along!*

"Well, obviously the kissing photo's a fake," Lainey said, studying it closely. "In fact, it looks like one of the publicity photos for *Bachelor Bliss* with another head superimposed where one of the contestants was." She ought to know—she had the picture stored on her computer, along with dozens of others. They were in her "Research" file. "See?" Lainey pointed to the mystery woman in question. "This looks like a wig."

"The whole story's a fake!" Brad growled.

"We know that!" Clint and Melinda said in unison.

"I don't appreciate my wife being dragged into your problems, her reputation ruined," Clint growled. He went chin to chin with Brad.

"I don't, either," Brad said soberly. Sympathy was in his eyes even as he looked at Clint. When Clint relaxed slightly, Brad turned to Melinda. "I'm sorry, Melinda. I'll contact my attorney, Claire McCabe Taylor, and have her demand a retraction and an apology immediately."

"Well, you better do something," Melinda fumed, crossing her arms. "Because I am *not* amused by this. And neither is my family!"

Brad's temper flared. "You think *I* am?" he fired back.

Clint and Melinda stared at Brad. Brad stared back. Then the fight went out of the couple. Brad apologized again, promising to take swift action. The couple, realizing now that Brad had nothing to do with it and was as upset as they were, thanked him and left. But not before Clint Farren offered these parting words: "You better do something to straighten out your life, Brad, or you're liable to drag everyone you know down with you!"

"CLINT'S RIGHT, YOU KNOW," Lainey said as she and Brad retired to the ranch house kitchen for a much-needed cup of coffee. She sat down at the table opposite him. "The situation is only going to get worse unless you come forward and tell your story."

Brad settled more comfortably in his chair. His knees brushed hers beneath the table. "As much as I'd like to, I can't."

She allowed herself a moment to savor the warmth and strength of those denim-clad knees against her own. Aware how close she had come to confessing everything to him in a most ill-thought-out way, she struggled to regain her own equilibrium. Theirs was a situation neither could have predicted. It was going to take careful handling if she didn't want to lose everything—for both of them. And right now, despite how guilty she felt, that was much too high a price to pay.

"Haven't you heard?" she quipped lightly, trying once again to get Brad to do what needed to be done. She looked him straight in the eye. "The truth will set you free."

And that was, after all, why she had first shown up

at the ranch. To track down Brad and help him set the record straight once and for all and get his reputation—and his life—back.

Brad's jaw set in that stubborn way she knew so well. "There's no guarantee anyone would believe me, even if I confessed what happened between me and Yvonne."

"You don't know that," she said.

"Haven't you noticed? Yvonne is quite the actress."

Except, Lainey thought uncomfortably, when Yvonne was being interviewed she always appeared to be speaking from her heart.

Which meant, unless Yvonne suddenly was hit with an attack of conscience and confessed all, it would be a "he said, she said" situation. At this late date, it might look as if Brad were trashing Yvonne publicly out of revenge. That wouldn't help him at all. It would only muddy the waters more. And continue to hurt his reputation.

"No," Brad continued, oblivious to Lainey's thoughts. "The safest way is to proceed through my lawyer, demand a retraction and clarification from the tabloid. Threaten to sue if they don't do the right thing."

"That would take weeks or months to resolve, and in the meantime, lies about you will be spread, your reputation further ruined. You started out a cad, Brad. Now you're a cheating cad," she summed up guiltily, feeling more incompetent than ever. If she had been able to keep her emotions in check, she might have been able to convince Brad to cooperate with *Personalities*. Instead, she had painted herself into a moral corner from which there seemed to be no escape.

Crying about it wouldn't help.

Action would.

She had to put her own selfish considerations aside

and help him see reason. "What's next for you except more of a downhill slide?"

Brad quaffed the rest of his coffee and got up to roam the kitchen restlessly. "You don't know what you're talking about," he accused.

"Oh, yes, I do." Lainey watched him pour more coffee for both of them. "My father worked as a mechanic in San Angelo when I was a kid." Able to see Brad was listening, albeit reluctantly, she continued talking about what she never discussed.

"Tools and parts were being stolen from the garage where he worked, and my dad was framed. He got fired. The owner agreed not to press criminal charges because he felt sorry for my mom and me, but he put the word out that my dad was not to be trusted, and my dad could not get another job because of the allegations. He went on unemployment compensation and when that ran out, he did odd jobs here and there, some janitorial work. But he never got over it, and his attitude on life soured. My mom and dad ended up splitting up because my mom never understood why my dad wouldn't fight to get back what he had lost. My dad died a bitter, disillusioned man." She took Brad's hand. "I can see the same thing happening to you, Brad. False allegations and assumptions like that wear on a person. They rob you of your spirit and your joy."

"I'm sorry your dad and your family had such a rough time," said Brad. "But our situations are not the same, Lainey. I'm already moving on. I've got work. And I don't give a damn what strangers think of me. The people in Laramie know what's true."

"You're kidding yourself." Lainey had seen the look on his face when confronted with the latest tabloid lies about himself, the hurt it was causing the other people in his life. As long as the mystery remained...as long as Yvonne kept flaming the fires to fuel her own need for publicity, then it was never going to stop. Long after national interest died, the curiosity of the locals would remain. The citizens of Laramie were too kind, too protective, to ask Brad about it. But they would always wonder what had happened to cause such a scandal. And Brad would know they were wondering why he had behaved the ungentlemanly way he had on TV. The stigma would eat him alive, just the way it had her father, whether Brad wanted to admit it or not.

"You can't go on this way," she reiterated firmly. His need for the truth had put her in reporter gear again. If he would let her, Lainey knew that she could help him.

"It's not your decision to make. It's mine."

Despite his bullheadedness, Lainey would be damned if she'd see Brad McCabe end up as bitter and disillusioned and heartbroken as her own father. She had one more ace up her sleeve to get him to tell all. "So you're not going to tell me the truth about what happened between you and Yvonne, either?" she surmised softly. With a confident smile, she sat back in her chair, lifted her chin and continued. "Never mind. I think I can guess."

Brad smirked, not believing her for one red-hot second. "No. You can't," he replied, just as implacably.

"Want to bet?"

CHAPTER THIRTEEN

"HERE'S WHAT I THINK HAPPENED." Lainey leaned forward, looking deep into Brad's eyes. "I think you signed on for *Bachelor Bliss,* expecting everything to be on the up-and-up, and hoping to find the right woman for you. Instead, from the very beginning, things just weren't quite right, and there were subtle but unmistakable signs this was so."

Brad stiffened, letting her know she had struck a nerve, and she pushed on. "Yvonne appeared to have special treatment from the show's creator, Gil Hewitt. Plus, she seemed to know things about you that she would have had no way of knowing. And while you no doubt noted this, you were too caught up in taping the show, and playing all the games the producers of *Bachelor Bliss* had you play, to dwell on it. Until that fateful moment of clarity, when, as you said, you realized Yvonne was not who she was pretending to be. My question is—" she paused to let her words sink in "—what happened to help you connect the dots? Yvonne has been running around accusing you of cheating on her, but I don't think that's true. I think maybe the *reverse* may have been true. So what really happened, Brad? Did you think Yvonne had eyes only for you and then discover she had someone on the side?"

Bull's-eye.

"Worse," he said, finally giving in with a weary sigh.

He shoved a hand through his hair, looking ready to confide his troubles to her at long last. Seeming to need her to be not just his lover but his friend. "I caught her in bed with someone."

Lainey could imagine how much that would hurt a man of Brad McCabe's strength and pride. "Gil Hewitt, the show's creator," she guessed, figuring Yvonne was the kind of woman who would gladly hit the casting couch, so to speak, if it meant she emerged the grand-prize winner.

"Yes," Brad admitted reluctantly. Lips pressed together grimly, he continued. "Fifteen minutes before the final taping was to begin, I got a note from Yvonne asking me to meet her in one of the mansion bedrooms. And she was there with Gil Hewitt, in the throes of—well, you can guess."

How awful. Lainey reached across the table and took his hand. She tightened her fingers on his. "Was anyone else around to witness this?"

"Nope, just the three of us." Brad cupped her hand between both of his. He looked at her evenly. "It was obvious they had set me up to get a big emotional reaction from me, although I don't think they were sure what I was going to do during the taping. And that uncertainty added an extra element of excitement." His tone took on a bitter, sarcastic edge.

Lainey's heart went out to him. It was terrible enough to live through something like that, but to have the cameras on him in the immediate aftermath… Rumors swirling. His reputation maligned. "I'm surprised you didn't just walk out," she said sympathetically.

Brad laughed—a short, humorless sound. "I tried, but the producers caught me going out the door and threatened to sue me for five million dollars if I didn't get back in my tuxedo and honor my contract with the show."

Lainey remembered how tense the final Heart Ceremony had been. With Brad staring at Yvonne like he detested her, refusing to deliver the proposal that she—and all the viewers—were expecting. Then simply telling Yvonne it wasn't going to work out, taking off his microphone and walking out. Under the circumstances, she doubted most men could have been even that gallant. "Did you tell the producers what had happened to make you want to bolt?"

Brad let go of her hand. "No. I didn't tell anyone."

"Why not?" Lainey asked, curious.

He stood, roamed the kitchen restlessly. "Obviously, you've never been cheated on." He stared out the window, at the pasture where Tabasco Red was peacefully grazing.

Lainey hadn't.

Brad ruminated in a voice laced with hurt. "Your first response is disbelief and anger and humiliation, and all you—all I—wanted to do was get the hell out of there. And never see or speak to Yvonne again."

Lainey certainly couldn't blame him for that. "You weren't mad at Gil Hewitt?"

Brad swung around. "Sure, I was ticked off, but I'm not sure, in retrospect, that I was really jealous. The whole time I was paired up with Yvonne, I had this feeling that the situation was more make-believe than real, that things were just a little too perfect. There was nothing concrete that would have made me feel that way. Just a lot of little things that triggered an uneasy feeling in my gut. When I found her with Gil, I finally had confirmation that it wasn't my imagination—there really was some reason why I kept thinking I shouldn't trust her."

Lainey knew about gut reactions to people. Her feminine instincts had told her she could trust and believe in Brad from the first moment they had come face-to-face with each other on the Lazy M.

Brad studied her carefully. "No one else has come close to guessing what happened. How is it you know all this?"

Lainey swallowed. The same instinct that had told her she could trust Brad told her this was not the time to confess she was a reporter. She got up and went to stand beside him at the window. She wanted to deepen—not sever—their intimate emotional connection. "I've puzzled over this a lot—first and foremost, because I want to understand you," she said softly. "And what happened on *Bachelor Bliss* obviously devastated you."

"You're very observant."

Lainey shrugged. "You already know I watched the show while it was airing. Since we met up again here at the ranch, I've been paying even more attention to you, listening to everything you've said about your experiences on *Bachelor Bliss* as well as everything you haven't said."

"I never said anything about the show's creator, Gil Hewitt," Brad pointed out, a tad suspiciously.

But Yvonne had. And Lainey had met and interviewed Gil. Treading carefully—she didn't want to alienate or hurt Brad now—she said, "A lot has been written about the breakup and the show. I know how to use the search engines on the Internet. I've been doing a little research on my own."

Brad narrowed his eyes at her. "You're that curious?"

"I want to help you that badly," she corrected.

Brad slid his hands into the pockets of his jeans. "At least now you must see why I don't want the real story to come out," he stated in a low voice.

"Because you're embarrassed."

He smirked. "As well as humiliated, cuckolded, duped, and made a complete and utter fool of."

Lainey could see where that would severely dent the famous McCabe pride. "So you would rather be portrayed as the villain?"

Brad shrugged, some of the walls going up again. "I would rather not be portrayed as anything at all," he stated irritably.

"But the media *is* portraying you," she pointed out.

He turned and looked her in the eye. "It'll fade. A person's fifteen minutes of fame always does."

And if it didn't, Lainey wondered, then what? "What about the people who are still signing up for the show?" she asked quietly, taking another tack to persuade Brad to do what had to be done if he was ever going to be free to live his life again the way he deserved. "Have you given any thought to future contestants and what they might end up going through, because you're too self-centered and cowardly to own up to the truth?"

Her words stung.

He lifted a brow, echoing, "Self-centered...and cowardly?"

"Sound a little harsh?"

Brad nodded, his expression grim. "And then some."

"But true. Think about those poor young women, Brad, the ones who aren't like Yvonne. Who just want to find some guy to love them."

"Or be on TV," Brad countered.

Lainey stepped closer, persisting. "Think about the guys signing up to find the woman of their dreams and having their reputations ruined. It's a travesty." She took both his hands in hers, gripped them hard. "You could set people straight. Prevent it from ever happening again. Or at least make it so anyone who entered the competition on *Bachelor Bliss* would know exactly what they were getting into."

LAINEY'S WORDS STAYED with Brad throughout the day. He had told her before he'd headed out to do ranch work that he would think about what she had said, and he was still thinking about it when Lewis and Petey arrived home that day. Annie, Travis and their five boys arrived shortly after that. By the time Brad got cleaned up and entered the ranch house kitchen, the adults were congregated around the appetizers on the kitchen table, while the three younger kids played outside on the tire-swings Brad had put up beneath the shade trees next to the house.

Talk, not surprisingly, centered on the erroneous tabloid story about him and Melinda.

"What are you doing about it?" Travis asked Brad.

Brad shrugged. He had hoped to talk to Lainey about his decision privately first. "My attorney fired off a letter to the publishers this morning, threatening a lawsuit."

"And—?" Annie asked, all motherly concern.

"We're still waiting to hear back," he admitted. He helped himself to salsa and tortilla chips.

"Did you speak to Yvonne Rathbone about her comments?" Lewis asked, digging into the bite-size tamales.

Brad shook his head.

"Shouldn't you be suing her, too, if what she said about you wasn't true?" Annie asked.

The last thing Brad wanted to do was get in a legal fight with Yvonne Rathbone. He'd be happy if he never saw or heard from her again.

"I'll tell you what I think," Lewis said. "I think you should tell your side of the story once and for all. And I'll tell you what else—" He gulped some mint-flavored iced tea. "If I knew what had happened, I'd put the information out there, even if you got mad at me temporarily."

"But you don't have the information," Brad said, warning his younger brother with a look. "So don't go messing in my life."

"What do you think, Lainey?" Teddy asked, seeming older than his twenty years.

"Do you think Brad should tell all?" Tyler inquired.

"Or keep whatever happened to himself?" Trevor put in.

Brad glanced at Lainey, curious as to what she was going to say. He knew she wouldn't tell what he had reluctantly confided this morning. She had sworn she would never give out that information without his permission, and thus far, he hadn't given it.

"When I think of Brad's situation, I think of my father's situation, when he was alive," Lainey said quietly, after a moment. "He, too, was a victim of character assassination. And he, too, chose to hold his own counsel and not fight. He figured the people that knew and loved him would realize the truth, and those that didn't might not ever believe him anyway." She paused and looked at Brad. "I was just a kid then. I didn't have the means to help him, even if I had wanted to do so."

"And if you had possessed the means?" Lewis asked.

Lainey paused again, her gaze still locked fiercely with Brad's. "You never know, but I would hope I'd have the courage to do whatever needed to be done to help the truth come out."

"TRYING TO TELL ME SOMETHING in there?" Brad asked as he helped Lainey put the chicken on the grill. The rest of the adults would join them shortly, but for the moment everyone was still inside, polishing off the array of Tex-Mex appetizers Lainey had prepared.

"Only that I care deeply about you, and what happens to you," she said quietly. "And I hope you will always remember that—" she briefly touched the region of his heart "—in here."

Brad did. And yet…once again he had the feeling that something was wrong. That Lainey was bracing for something bad, and trying to prepare him, as well. Though what that could be…

"Mommy?" Petey ran over to Lainey's side. "How come that guy is taking pictures of us?"

Lainey and Brad looked in the direction Petey was pointing.

Brad scowled. It was the same guy in tourist garb that had been photographing him and Lainey in the grocery store the previous week. Now he had pulled his car to the side of the road and was using a camera with a long telephoto lens.

"Stay here!" Brad ordered Lainey and Petey. He started off at a run.

The interloper put down his camera, jumped in his car and drove off in a cloud of dust.

Brad came back. Fuming.

"Who was that?" Petey demanded in concern.

"No one we know," Lainey said. Although her tone was reassuring, her expression indicated she was nervous and upset.

"Probably some tourist who wanted a picture of me," Brad explained, doing his best to comfort the frightened little boy. "I'm famous you know, ever since I went on TV."

Petey relaxed, just as Brad had hoped he would. "Yeah. Kurt and Kyle told me about that."

Petey grinned, reminding Brad what big news Brad's stint on TV had been in the extended McCabe family.

"You got to kiss lots of girls!"

"Yuck!" eight-year-old Kyle said, running over to join them, too.

"Yeah, gross!" nine-year-old Kurt agreed.

All three little boys made gagging sounds, and ran off once again.

"Pretty good save," Lainey said.

"Yeah. I just wish I knew who that guy was." Brad didn't recognize him as one of the tabloid paparazzi that had stalked him while he was doing *Bachelor Bliss*. "And who he was taking photos for," he added as two more cars slowed at the entrance to the Lazy M and turned into the drive. One was Lainey's SUV—driven by Bart Carrington—the other was Bunny's Mercedes, driven by Bunny.

Brad turned to Lainey, who was looking a little pale at the sight of her brother- and sister-in-law. "I didn't know you were getting your vehicle back today," he observed.

"That makes two of us," she said, too lightly.

Bart came toward Lainey, keys in hand. Brad could

tell by the expression on the other man's face that Bart had something serious to say.

Petey, Kyle and Kurt were playing along the pasture fence. All were glancing their way, as if wondering what was going on. Petey started toward them, but Brad shook his head and put up a halting hand, letting them know that now was not a good time to be joining the adults. Petey continued staring at them for a minute longer, then the little boys went back to conferencing, their heads bent together.

"For the record," Bart said, "I did not know anything about your car going in for servicing at such an inopportune time. Nor would I have known had I not just happened to be home when the dealership called, saying the servicing was complete and wanting to know if they should continue to keep your vehicle next week. Naturally, I insisted we drive it back to you right away."

Realizing this was none of their business, Annie and Travis—who appeared to be on their way outside—remained inside the ranch house kitchen with their boys.

"It's just as well we had to come back out here, anyway, given what's been going on," Bunny said stiffly, glaring at Brad, as the aroma of grilling meat filled the air. "We saw the tabloid photo of you and that—that woman! And for everyone's sake, especially Petey's, I feel we must absolutely insist that Lainey and Petey leave here immediately."

Brad shot a look at Petey. Although well out of earshot, the little boy looked concerned. Doing his best to protect the child, Brad moved to block Petey's view of the adults, then turned back to Bunny, who was still ranting on.

"...Petey cannot grow up under that kind of influence!"

"First of all, Bunny," Lainey said angrily, stepping forward and waving her spatula, "Brad is a wonderful role model for Petey. And that photo is a fake."

"You're saying you weren't kissing a blonde in Dallas two days ago?" Bunny demanded, as Lainey swallowed, taken aback. "I read it in the New York City gossip columns, too!"

"No, that's correct," Brad answered calmly, looking Bunny straight in the eye. Maybe now was the time to come clean with his feelings for Lainey. Let everyone—including Lainey—know exactly where they stood.

"Then, if it wasn't that woman..." Bunny's voice trailed off. She looked at Lainey, her blond hair.

"As long as we're being honest," Lainey cut in, going on the offensive before Bunny could conclude anything else, "let's talk about the 'tourist' who was just here photographing us with a telephoto lens." Lainey's eyes darkened. "What do you have to do with that, Bunny? Did you send him to spy on me?"

"Me!" Bunny echoed, sounding outraged.

"You threatened to sue me for custody of Petey. I assume you're not standing around doing nothing about it."

"You did what?" Bart asked, stunned.

Finally, Bunny was embarrassed into silence.

Thankful for the reprieve, however short-lived, Brad turned to check on Petey. And swore mightily at what he saw. The little boy was over the fence and in the pasture with the bull.

"Oh, my God!" Bunny whispered, her hand flying to her mouth.

"Petey!" Lainey broke into a run.

"Don't move, son!" Brad shouted, running, too.

Petey glared at them, then looked at Kyle and Kurt, who were standing on the other side of the fence, for once urging Petey not to do whatever it was Petey was trying to do. Petey ignored them, too, and kept moving toward Tabasco Red.

Behind them, Bunny was screaming hysterically—until someone—probably her husband, Brad figured, clamped a hand over her mouth to shut off the sound.

Tabasco Red had been chewing grass, his back to the ranch house, but at the sound of all the commotion he turned around. Still Petey edged closer.

"Oh, no…oh, no…oh, no!" Lainey whispered as they reached the edge of the fence. Tears were streaming down her face as her son squared off with the nine-hundred-pound animal.

"It's going to be all right. I'll get him," Brad said, already vaulting up and over the fence. He landed lightly on the other side. Petey was too far away to hear anything Brad said unless he shouted it, but Brad did not want to yell. Heart pounding, he kept moving.

Tabasco Red stopped chewing and stared at the little boy approaching him slowly and steadily from the front. Brad could see Petey was shaking in his boots. And for good reason, since Petey had never been near the ranch sire. The bull had sharp horns that measured seventy-three inches tip to tip and outweighed him by a good eight hundred pounds or more. Tabasco Red had to look like a behemoth to Petey.

Ten strides later, Brad was even with Petey.

Not about to make any sudden moves under the circumstances, Brad fell in step beside Petey. "Let's turn around, son," he said, placing a paternal hand on Petey's shoulder.

Petey's chin thrust out. He allowed Brad's touch but ignored the directive and kept moving. "Not until I pet him."

Brad looked down into Petey's face, saw the stubborn set of his chin, so like his mother's. Brad could see this was some kind of test of courage.

And what the hell, the kid had come this far.

BUNNY CARRINGTON WAS CRYING hysterically when Petey reached Tabasco Red, held out his hand, let the bull sniff it and then petted him on the nose. There was a brief conference among the three of them, with Brad standing there as calm as could be while Petey said a few words to the giant animal. Then Tabasco Red turned away in boredom and went back to eating grass while Brad and Petey walked over to the fence where Lainey stood, crying her eyes out, next to Bunny and Bart.

By the time both guys had climbed the pasture fence, they were surrounded by everyone in attendance.

Lainey hugged Petey like he'd just come home from the war. She wiped the tears streaming down her face with the heels of her hands, then squared off with him. "There better be a darn good explanation for what you just did," she said shakily.

Petey glanced at Bart and Bunny, and then back at Lainey. "I had to prove to you, once and for all, that I was a growned-up man already."

Lainey blinked. "What are you talking about?" she cried.

Petey swallowed. He waved his small arms expansively. "So Aunt Bunny wouldn't take me away from you and make me go live with them, so's Uncle Bart could teach me how to be a man, 'cause she says only a man can teach a boy how to be a man."

A hush came over the group.

Bart stared at his wife for a long time, then back at Petey. He knelt down in front of the boy. "Is this why you've been so unhappy lately?" he asked gently, showing fatherly concern. "Because you were afraid?"

Petey nodded. He grabbed on to Lainey with one hand, and Brad with the other, and held tight. "I don't want to leave my mommy," he told Bart fiercely.

Bart looked Petey in the eye. "You're never going to have to." He straightened and addressed Bunny. "I understand that you're having a hard time with the girls leaving home for college, but this is not the way to refill your nest."

Bart turned back to Lainey and continued sincerely. "I apologize with all my heart for everything that's been going on. I promise you, every bit of trouble stops now, including the snooping P.I."

"But I didn't—" Bunny protested.

"We'll talk about this at home," Bart said sternly. He took his wife's elbow and steered her toward their Mercedes.

Bunny and Bart departed.

Travis and Annie, who'd been silent up to now, turned back to Kyle and Kurt. "I believe it's your turn to do some explaining," Travis said to their two youngest sons.

"I'M SORRY YOU WERE FRIGHTENED about Tabasco Red," Brad said, hours later, after Petey was asleep and all the guests had departed. Lewis was inside the ranch house, working.

Brad and Lainey were sitting on the front porch of the guest house, enjoying what was left of the summer evening.

"There really is such a thing as a gentle bull?" Lainey asked, for the third time.

Brad wrapped his arm around her shoulders and brought her close. He didn't seem to mind reassuring her. Maybe because he knew how shaken up she still was by all the bad things that could have happened had the situation been just a little bit different. Had Tabasco Red been a rancorous animal. Or Brad not been there.

"You better believe it," Brad said.

Lainey relaxed into the warm and welcoming curve of his body as the glider rocked back and forth. "I always thought bulls were scary-mean and dangerous."

"Some are. Travis's aren't, because he breeds them for temperament." Brad pressed a kiss in Lainey's hair. "And Tabasco Red has lived on Annie and Travis's ranch since he was a bull calf. The boys grew up with him, and they know he's as gentle as a kitten and used to being around little kids. I was going to tell you that when we first brought him here to sire my first generation of calves, but you were so freaked out about cattle in general, I just figured I'd wait and show you later when you got used to being around 'em." Brad paused, shook his head. "I never had any idea Petey would try and go near Tabasco Red."

"So he wasn't in any danger?"

"Right." Brad shifted Lainey over onto his lap. "Although, all the boys know better than to go over the fence unless they are in the company of an adult cowboy. That's what the kids were arguing about before Petey scaled the fence. Kyle and Kurt wanted Petey to do it, but in the company of their older cowboy-brothers. Because they knew that was allowed."

Lainey sighed. "But in Petey's view, desperate times called for desperate measures, and he thought Bart and

Bunny were here to take him away and it was the only way he and Kurt and Kyle could think to prove Petey's manhood in the nick of time." Tears welled in Lainey's eyes as she shook her head. "I should have known something was terribly wrong."

"You did." Brad lifted her hand to his lips and kissed the back of it. "You just didn't know what, exactly."

Lainey laced her arms about his neck. "I should have been able to get him to tell me what was going on."

Brad stroked her hair. "You're a good mother, Lainey. The best."

She choked back a sob, and embarrassed she couldn't seem to get ahold of herself, wiped her eyes. "If anything ever happened to him…" she whispered hoarsely.

"I know," Brad said soothingly. He paused, looked deep into her eyes. "I feel the same way. Which is why, Lainey, the two of you have to leave the Lazy M tomorrow morning, first thing."

CHAPTER FOURTEEN

"W-WHAT? WHY?" Lainey asked.

"Because," Brad retorted heavily, his guilt apparent, "Petey's already been through far too much lately and it's the only way I know to protect you."

Lainey blinked and slid off his lap, onto the seat of the glider. "By sending us away?" she echoed hoarsely. Impossible, how much that hurt.

Brad caught her wrist before she could bolt. His voice was low, intense. "Suppose Bunny is telling the truth and she didn't send that photographer. Then that means he's not after you and whatever dirt he can dig up—he's after me." The haunted look was back in Brad's eyes. "The last thing Petey needs to see is his mother on the cover of a tabloid."

Lainey agreed with that portion of Brad's assessment. Her brief experience as a journalist told her something else about the rest. "I don't think the photographer was from a tabloid. A tabloid would have published the photos of us last week, particularly in light of what that New York City newspaper gossip column published. Tabloids don't necessarily wait to get a whole story—they go with whatever they've got. Speed and scooping all other news outlets via actual photos of whatever is going on is the priority."

Brad frowned. "You think he's freelance?"

"Maybe." Lainey savored the warmth and tenderness

of the hand encircling her wrist. She moved her hand so her fingers were meshed with his. "If that tourist guy had no legitimate connections, he was just trying to get different pictures of us to sell to lots of places…and that might take a little longer."

Brad slouched against the back of the glider as he considered that. "And if he's not?"

"Then I don't know who he is or why he was here unless he's just someone who is plain nosy and wants something to show his friends. In any case, the revelation of our relationship with each other is going to be news…."

He shook his head. "Not if it doesn't come out until interest in me dies down."

Ignoring the feel of his rock-hard thigh pressed up against hers, she looked down at their clasped hands, then back at him. "What are you saying?"

Brad swallowed. He seemed to know she wasn't going to like what came next. "This afternoon I was ready to come clean, go to the press like you suggested, tell my story, and let the dust settle once and for all. But I realize now that speaking out at this point would only generate a whole new wave of public interest in me, and I can't subject Petey—or you—to that, Lainey."

His mind was clearly made up. "So you're breaking up with me?" She did her best to contain her broken heart. Realizing she was suddenly doubting Brad and his feelings for her, when up until now she'd had absolutely no reason to, she stood and moved to the edge of the porch. Her back to him, she looked out at the broad expanse of the Texas night sky. The summer night was clear and warm. A half moon nestled in the stars winking overhead.

"No." He crossed to her side and drew her into his

embrace. "Just putting what we feel for each other under wraps for a while." He stroked a soothing hand down her spine. "We'll still see each other."

"Just not in public." She sighed. "Not where anyone can find out about it."

Brad's mood was as pensive as her own. "Right."

Lainey was silent. She knew it wasn't what Brad was saying, but it felt like he was ashamed of her…and that was devastating. Hadn't she promised herself when she was with Chip that she would never put herself in that situation again? She swallowed, did her best to respond with maturity and grace.

"I see."

"Do you?" Brad asked gently, his gaze lovingly roving over her. He slid both hands through her hair, lifting her face up to his. His heated glance drifted lower and he massaged her shoulders tenderly. "'Cause I don't think you do. What I am trying to tell you here—" he paused to reassure her with another long, direct glance "—is that I want us to be together over the long haul. But to make that happen, we're going to have to protect what we have and keep it secret."

THE ONLY GOOD THING about Brad's sending Lainey and Petey back to Dallas was that she had the time—and space necessary—to honor her promise to her old college roommate well within the required publishing deadline.

Sybil called her Tuesday evening. "I got the article you e-mailed me."

Lainey braced herself for what she knew had to be coming next.

"There's nothing in it about Brad McCabe."

Lainey sighed, glad Petey was already in bed. "Right."

"Nor do you tell why Brad dumped Yvonne," Sybil continued, sounding even more displeased.

Lainey winced. "Right again."

Another pause. Sybil, sounding more boss than friend, continued calmly. "Did you misunderstand what I asked you to do?"

No. Lainey hadn't. She had known exactly what kind of salacious, groundbreaking, cover-level story Sybil wanted out of her. That was the hell of it. Lainey gathered her professionalism around her like a protective cloak. She knew the work she had done on Yvonne—and even Gil Hewitt—was good. She had to concentrate on that and feel proud of it, while at the same time owning up to her own shortcomings. "I can't write about Brad McCabe with any objectivity. I thought I could. But I can't." So she hadn't. Problem solved. Sort of, anyway.

Sybil let out a short, impatient breath. "That sweet-talking Casanova got to you, didn't he."

Lainey told herself Brad's womanizing days were over. Not that they had ever existed beyond his desire not to get emotionally involved with someone he wasn't cut out to be partnered with for life. "What do you mean?"

Sybil scoffed, as blunt and straight-talking as ever. "Brad McCabe has a reputation for making women lose their head, and obviously he's made you lose yours!"

Lainey knew she was in love with Brad. But it wasn't like that. Brad hadn't used her any more than she had used him. It was just a tough situation, that was all. One Lainey was determined to extricate herself from sooner rather than later. "I never should have signed up to write about someone I knew as a kid," she said, excoriating herself honestly. "It's an insurmountable conflict of interest."

"It's also your big chance to catapult yourself into the big-time. Or have you forgotten how much you've always wanted to be a journalist?" Sybil demanded, practical as ever.

Lainey wanted to be loved and cared for more—her relationship with Brad held the promise of that.

"You've been seeing him, haven't you," Sybil pressed, beginning to sound a little angry now.

Lainey didn't want to lie to her old friend, so she said nothing.

"He found out what you're up to and—"

"He doesn't know anything," Lainey corrected.

Sybil made a low, dissenting sound. "I wouldn't bet on that. From what I've heard, Brad McCabe is one smart cookie."

Lainey ran her hands through her hair. "Smart. Dumb. Who cares?"

"*Personalities* readers care. They want to know what happened to make TV's sexiest bachelor go berserk and dump a very sweet and loving girl!"

"As the article I sent you attests," Lainey countered tightly, "Yvonne is anything but sweet and loving."

"I don't care what the other girls or even Gil Hewitt had to say. I want to know when and how and where did Brad find that out? I'm presuming, of course, that is the reason he broke up with her."

"I can't tell you that," Lainey said. She rubbed at the headache starting in her temples.

"Lainey, as it is," Sybil explained patiently, "I cannot—I will not—publish this article. There is very little in it that hasn't been either printed or speculated about before. We're looking for a great big scoop, not a guessing game and a rehash."

She sighed, beginning to feel like she had the weight of the world on her shoulders once again. "It's the best I can do."

"Well, it's not good enough. You still have another forty-eight hours before deadline. There's still time—"

"I've had all the time I need," Lainey interrupted firmly.

"Please don't do this," her friend begged. "Do I need to remind you that you threw away any chance at a career for yourself when you hooked up with Chip? Lainey, honey, I can't bear to see you doing the same thing again!"

"Bear it or not, it's what I have to do," she said. "I'm sorry, Sybil. I know I let you down. Thank you for the opportunity, anyway." And she hung up the phone.

"I DIDN'T THINK STAYING AWAY from each other was going to be this hard," Brad said, four days later.

Lainey walked into the conference room at McCabe Computer Games testing facility in Laramie. Petey was there to evaluate the latest changes in the computer game he had been testing all summer. Lainey was there to see Brad. She went into his arms, glad Lewis had thoughtfully provided the two of them with a conference room where they could talk privately, without having to worry about being caught by someone with a telephoto lens.

"Although—" Brad drew back after a lengthy hello kiss, then another, and another "—you look like you are faring much better than I am in this situation. You look—" he studied her tenderly "—like a huge burden has been lifted from your shoulders."

"It has been."

Lainey smiled at him, feeling a little less sure now.

Nevertheless, she knew what she had to do—tell him everything and then see where they stood, if he was as capable of forgiving her as she deemed him to be. She couldn't go on hiding something this important from him. It was too much to bear. And she needed to make certain that, unlike Chip, Brad could accept that Lainey was not perfect. She made mistakes. Occasionally took a wrong turn. Or made a wrong choice. That didn't mean she was a bad person. Just human. Fallible. Ready and willing to learn from her mistakes and move on.

Lainey was in the market for unconditional love now.

Not a love that hinged on her looking and behaving a certain way, and only that way.

She wanted a love that let her feel free to be.

She wanted Petey growing up the same way.

"How are things with the in-laws?" Brad asked gently.

"Better than you could imagine." She sat down on the edge of the conference table, braced herself and looked up at him. "Bunny's decided to hand over the dispersing of the trust funds to one of the attorneys who drew it up."

"She can do that?"

Lainey nodded. "Chip had a provision built in, in case something ever happened to Bunny or she felt it was too much to handle. She and Bart talked it over and decided it would be best to have the trust administered by a third party from now on."

"That certainly sounds a lot less stressful for you," he said.

She nodded. "Claire set up a meeting. We all talked

at length about my situation yesterday and agreed it would be best to sell our house in Highland Park. I can use the proceeds to resettle in Laramie."

"How does Petey feel about that?"

"He's as ready for change as I am—although," Lainey conceded, smiling ruefully, "he'd prefer to live on a ranch, rather than in town. But I told him he can visit his friends who do live on ranches, so he's happy about that. In the meantime, I'm going to open my own professional organizing business, and probably do some freelance writing on the side, too." She wanted to start living on what she made, and let the money Chip left them be for Petey's education, and any emergencies that came up.

"I didn't know you wanted to be a writer," he said.

She studied the hem of her cotton skirt, where it rode up above her knee. It was time to confess all. Her stomach fluttered with a thousand butterflies as she admitted softly, honestly, "For a long time now."

"Because of what happened to your dad?"

Lainey nodded. "The truth is important. Reporters have the ability to keep things honest and aboveboard."

"When it's done correctly," Brad stipulated.

"Right." Unfortunately, that was a lesson she had learned a little too late when it came to Brad. "Anyway, I studied journalism in college and worked on the Tech newspaper before I dropped out to get married."

Brad looked impressed with her accomplishments, yet wary of her profession. "You know reporters aren't my favorite people these days," he teased, "but I guess I could change my mind about that, if you become one again."

"I hope so," she said. She gripped the table edge on

either side of her, her nerves beginning to get the better of her.

"I know so." He smiled and sat down on the edge of the table next to her. "Because you'd never be the kind of vulture that's been after me since I went on TV."

Guilt swept through Lainey, followed by uncertainty. Was this the time to tell him everything? How could she not?

"Lewis and I've been doing some rearranging, too," Brad said.

Lainey winced, recalling the six boxes she had yet to unpack that were stacked up in the utility room, taking up all the available space. "I'm sorry. I know I'm not quite finished organizing everything there yet." She'd left in such a hurry, at Brad's behest, that she hadn't had time to complete her tasks. "But I promise I'll get to it as soon as you think it's okay for me to come back out to the Lazy M."

"Well," Brad drawled, smiling broadly, looking like he had a secret now, "that all depends."

"On?" Lainey queried.

He reached into his pocket and withdrew a small velvet box. "How fast I can get you to say yes to the idea of marrying me."

LAINEY STARED at Brad, stunned speechless. Her reaction wasn't the one he had been hoping for. Brad gulped and rushed on, telling her all that was in his heart.

"I know it sounds sudden," he said softly as he guided her to her feet and into his arms. "And I guess in some respects it is." He paused and looked deep into her eyes. "But I know you're the woman I've been waiting my whole life to meet. And I want you—and Petey—with me. The only way we can do that in a respectful manner is by making a true and lasting commitment and marrying each other. So…Lainey, will you do me the honor of becoming my wife?"

In place of the jubilant "yes" and kiss he had been expecting, tears welled in her eyes. "Oh, Brad…" she murmured, seeming distraught.

To his dismay, she looked like she wished he hadn't asked.

She splayed her fingers across his shirtfront, his only solace the fact that she did not move away. "If you only knew how much I want to say yes. But I—I need to talk to you about something else—something important—before we discuss that."

"Okay," he said slowly, once again bracing for the worst.

Before she could get another word out, the door to the conference room was flung open. Lewis rushed in so quickly he was practically tripping over his own feet. He had a rolled-up magazine in his hand. He looked at Brad, Lainey, then back at Brad again. "Oh, man!" Lewis said.

Brad glared at his younger brother. "You know, Lewis, sometimes your timing really—"

"Bites. I know." Lewis swallowed hard and shut the door behind them. "Listen, I really don't want to be the one to tell you this, but…you know how I set up that search engine on my computer for stuff about you when you first went on *Bachelor Bliss*?"

Like they needed to be talking about the parameters of Lewis's computer now? "Yes," Brad said patiently, knowing it would be faster to just let Lewis say what he had to say than try to shoo him out.

"Well, it still pulls stuff up every time I get on the Internet," Lewis explained.

"Terrific," Brad muttered, even more irritated when he noticed that Lainey looked upset.

The last thing he needed was Lewis spoiling an already going-downhill-fast mood. "I really don't care what they've written about me," he informed his brother tersely. He sent Lewis a look telling him to leave. *Now.*

"You will care," Lewis countered, just as firmly.

Lainey extricated herself from Brad's arms and moved away.

"Especially when you find out who wrote it," Lewis explained.

Doing his best not to deck his frustrating younger brother, Brad grimaced. "What are you talking about?"

Lewis thrust the magazine at him. "This."

Brad unrolled it. He was not pleased to see it was a copy of *Personalities Magazine.* He swiftly became even less thrilled. On the front cover was a photo of Lainey and Brad in the grocery store. Next to it was a photo of Brad and Yvonne. Below that was a grainy photo of Lainey and Brad kissing, at dusk, on the front porch of the Lazy M guest house. Brad swore at the intrusion into his privacy.

"How did the people at *Personalities* know about us?" he wondered out loud.

"I don't know," Lainey retorted, turning ever paler.

For some reason, Brad noted, Lewis was now staring at Lainey with a peculiar mixture of disbelief and pity.

Which made Brad hope and pray like crazy that the photographer hadn't gotten a picture of him and Lainey in his bed. Brad wouldn't put Lainey through that kind of embarrassment for the world. One thing was certain:

Lewis was acting very peculiar. So was Lainey. It was almost as if they already knew something he didn't.

"The story's on page sixty-seven," Lewis said, already making his way to the exit. Hand on the doorknob, Lewis looked at Lainey. "And boy, oh boy, oh boy, do you ever have some explaining to do."

Lewis left the room, shutting the door behind him.

Brad looked at Lainey. She was now trembling.

"What's he talking about?" Brad demanded.

"Only one way to find out." Lainey snatched the magazine out of his hands and thumbed quickly through the glossy pages until she reached the aforementioned page. She opened it up all the way, so they could both see. The title was written in bold red letters: "Yvonne's Secret Tryst!"

Just below that were the names of the coauthors of the article—Lainey Carrington and Sybil Devine.

Brad stared at it. Read it again. And then again.

Lainey was staring as if she had seen a ghost. She looked as if she might faint, and sat down abruptly in the nearest chair.

Wondering if it was possible—if there was another Lainey Carrington other than the woman he'd been trading secrets and kisses with—Brad moved so he could see more of what was on the page. "Tell me you didn't have anything to do with that," he ordered grimly.

Lainey buried her face in her hands. "Unfortunately," she said reluctantly, "I can't."

For the second time in under four months, Brad's world came crashing down around him. "What the hell is that supposed to mean?"

"It means I did. And then—" Lainey shrugged helplessly "—I didn't."

Brad's jaw clenched. "Lewis was right. Boy, do you ever have some explaining to do."

FEELING THE BLOOD DRAINING from her face, Lainey tore her gaze from Brad's angry expression and quickly skimmed the article. To her dismay, it was all there, even the parts about Brad and his rendition of events that she had carefully omitted from the story she had written on Yvonne and the *Bachelor Bliss* reality TV show.

Aware Sybil had obviously finished the job Lainey had set out to do, she grasped the arms of the chair.

She had to stay calm. Brad loved her. Didn't he? Belatedly, she realized he had never once said the words. He had, however, just asked her to marry him. To commit to a life with him forever. That had to mean something, even under circumstances like these. She swallowed the ache in her throat and met his eyes, determined to do whatever was necessary to make this come out right. "I told you I always wanted to write."

A muscle worked in his jaw. He stared at Lainey, a force not to be denied. Her hot-blooded lover had vanished and in his place appeared a cowboy who always rode away alone.

"You were out at the ranch for two weeks. You never once mentioned you were a reporter."

"That's because I'm not, at least not officially. But when my old friend Sybil called me up and asked me to help locate you, and then do an article for *Personalities*—"

"You agreed."

"No. Not just like that," Lainey said with difficulty, aware he had every right to be angry with her.

"Well, at some point you sold out."

Desperate to salvage their relationship, she defended

herself hotly. "I didn't even expect you to be at the Lazy M Ranch when I stopped by!" With effort she lowered her voice to a more manageable level. "I wanted to talk to Lewis about putting Petey in the game-testing program at his company. And then Lewis asked me to help him get organized—and you walked in. And you sort of taunted me, and the next thing I knew, I said I was going to do it."

He looked at her, sadder and even more disillusioned than before. "And then you conveniently spied on me and pumped me for info, all the while knowing you were going to betray me in the end," he said bitterly.

"I couldn't go back—I had given my word and already signed a contract!"

"So you betrayed me, without batting an eye."

Lainey went toward him, arms outstretched. "Listen to me, Brad. I agonized over the situation I put us both in, and I didn't write anything about you in the article I turned in."

He pivoted away from her. "And what about the rest of it—the tourist with the telephoto lens on his camera?" He gave her a hard, assessing look.

"I swear to you that I did not know the two of us were being photographed by *Personalities*." But that was, Lainey admitted to herself, obviously what had happened. Lainey's sister-in-law hadn't been having her spied on—her editor had!

"Kind of damages your rep, doesn't it, becoming part of the story like that," he observed.

Lainey didn't care about that. She only cared about Brad and how this was likely to affect him. Obviously, it had made him even more cynical and bitter, which was the last thing she had ever wanted. "I didn't tell anyone Yvonne cheated on you," she reiterated evenly.

Brad folded his arms and looked her up and down contemptuously. "Then how did they know I found Yvonne in bed with Gil Hewitt fifteen minutes before the final show was taped?"

Lainey took a careful look at the quotes in the magazine article. Quickly, she put it all together. "Obviously, Sybil got it out of Yvonne. Probably by pretending you had already told all and asking Yvonne if she wanted to tell her side of things." Lainey tapped the pages of the magazine. "Look, it says right here that Yvonne readily admits she only got involved with Gil Hewitt because she knew you weren't really in love with her. She even confesses there was no other woman for you, at that time, that she knew about." Bless Sybil for that much, Lainey thought. "So at least your name has finally been cleared."

Unfortunately, Brad did not look nearly as relieved about that as Lainey had hoped. "Yours, on the other hand, is mud," he pointed out sarcastically. "Since it says here the reason you had to recuse yourself from the article mid-writing was that you became personally involved with me."

Lainey took another look at the photos, of herself and Brad. No denying the intimacy between them.

"I never told anyone that," she said emotionally. She gazed at Brad, embarrassed, miserable. "Sybil must have figured it out on her own."

Brad stood. "So how does it feel to be betrayed by someone you thought was your friend?"

Lainey swallowed at the sick feeling in the pit of her stomach. "Not good."

"At least we're clear on that much." Brad pushed past her and headed for the door.

Lainey moved quickly, barring his way. The happiness

they'd once shared now seemed a million miles away. "I'm so sorry. I tried to tell you..."

He scorched her with a look. "Not hard enough, obviously."

Lainey swallowed as her knees began to shake. If only she had leveled with him much sooner! Shoring up her courage, she tried again. "I know I made a mistake, even agreeing to write the article about Yvonne, but once I had signed the contract I had to follow through."

Brad grunted in contempt. "Your responsibility to tell me or Lewis what you were up to be damned?"

Lainey drew another breath, searched his face. There was so much more she wanted to say but she could see it was pointless. She had wounded his already badly damaged McCabe pride. "You're not going to forgive me for this, are you," she said sadly.

The old cynicism was back in Brad's eyes, more potent than ever before. He leaned in closer, until they stood toe to toe, nose to nose. "Now you've got a clue."

CHAPTER FIFTEEN

SEVERAL WEEKS LATER, BRAD signed on the dotted line his attorney Claire McCabe Taylor indicated. Claire smiled as she collected the papers.

"That should about do it. You're all set. Although, given the fact you have just agreed to do two million dollars' worth of endorsements for everything from your favorite saddle soap to pickup truck, I'd expect that you'd be looking a lot happier."

Hard to be happy, Brad thought, when he had lost the only woman he'd ever dreamed was the one for him.

"This is enough to buy into the Lazy M as a full partner and get the cattle operation up and running the way you wanted to, before all your previous endorsements fell through."

Brad nodded, acknowledging the fact he was a much richer man. "Thanks for doing such a fine job negotiating on my behalf."

"My pleasure." Claire's expression gentled. She'd been married for fifteen years, had two adopted children of her own and knew the value of family. "Have you spoken to Lainey?"

Brad stretched his legs out in front of him. "Not since the issue of *Personalities* with us on the cover hit the newsstands." That was a day that would live on in memory as one of the unhappiest of his entire life.

Claire tossed down her pen and leaned back in her swivel chair. "She cleared your name."

"And muddied her own." To the point Brad figured Lainey's chances of getting a magazine job—at least anytime in the near future—were nil.

Claire shrugged. "True love is selfless."

Beginning to feel increasingly annoyed—Lewis, Annie and Travis were lobbying for reconciliation, too—Brad shot back, "She should have told me what she was up to from the very beginning."

"Right." Claire shot him a telling look. "And you'd have given her the time of day?"

Brad shifted uncomfortably in his chair. Guilt flowed through him. "Well, no…"

"She was a reporter on a story. She had a job to do. Getting involved with you was not in her plans."

Brad knew that much was true. He had seen her struggling with something the entire time they were together. Suddenly it all made sense why she had cried the last time they'd made love and said they never should have gotten involved.

"She still should have stayed away from me," he said.

Lifting a brow, Claire said dryly, "I'm sure you made that easy." Claire leaned across her desk, determined to make her point. "Come on, Brad, who pursued whom here? Who initiated the first kiss? Or teased her into paying attention to you in that distinctly man-woman way?"

Okay, Claire had him there. Brad had pursued her with everything he'd had; he had wanted to make her his woman that badly.

"Had it been anyone else but you putting the moves on her, I'm sure Lainey would have easily kept her distance. But she didn't keep the walls around her heart up because what was going on between the two of you was stronger than any ambition she might have had for herself. So she sacrificed her long-held goal of becoming a reporter, to do the best she could in this impossible situation she found herself in."

Brad slowly released the breath he'd been holding. For the first time since they'd split, he felt a flare of hope. "How do you know all this?" he demanded testily.

"I talked to her last week when I represented her and Petey's interests in a meeting with Bunny, Bart and the lawyer for the trust her late husband left." Claire paused, making sure she had his full attention. "Lainey regrets what happened more than you will ever know. But the two things she is *not* unhappy about are that, thanks to her, the truth is now out there and all future contestants of *Bachelor Bliss* know exactly what they are signing up for—and risking. And, most importantly, that your name and reputation have been cleared."

"CONGRATULATIONS on your promotion," Lainey told Sybil over her cell phone as she drove.

"Thanks." Her friend paused, then continued awkwardly. "I wasn't sure you were ever going to speak to me again."

For a while, Lainey hadn't been sure whether that would happen, either. Then she'd thought about everything that had occurred, and decided this was a rite of passage that—however painful and instructional—she had been destined to work her way through. It was great, she knew, when someone did everything right the first time out of the gate. But a person didn't necessarily learn anything from doing everything right.

When someone made a mistake, on the other hand,

especially a big one, and then found a way to rebound, a tremendous amount was always gained. Those kinds of lessons were the ones a person never forgot. She knew she would be remembering her time with Brad McCabe for the rest of her life.

"I understand why you did what you did," she said finally as she bypassed the road to Laramie and continued driving through the Texas countryside. She knew she and her old friend needed to have an open and honest discussion about what had occurred, and why. "I let you down. You still had a job to do."

Sybil confessed miserably, "I had a feeling you were going to back out on me."

"And you were right." Lainey knew she would do the same thing again. She would always choose to protect the people she loved, even if it meant she had to forfeit—at least temporarily—career success.

"Are we ever going to be friends again?" Sybil asked finally.

Lainey smiled as she drove past Annie and Travis McCabe's ranch. "We never stopped," she said quietly, thinking about a friendship that had spanned twelve years and gotten Lainey through some rough times. She and Sybil were on different life paths now, but they were still connected and always would be. "You gave me a chance you probably shouldn't have. I kept things from you I had no right—as a reporter under your direction—to suppress. You then did what you had to do and managed to uncover the rest of the story in very little time... and gave me partial credit, to boot." Lainey smiled again at the end of her recitation of events. "I'd say we're even when it comes to mistakes made and lessons learned."

Sybil sighed, relieved. "You are something, you know that?"

Lainey just wished Brad thought so, too.

She ended her conversation with her old friend with promises to be in touch soon, and turned her SUV into the Lazy M.

Lewis had assured her, when she had agreed to come out and unpack the last five boxes at the ranch house, that Brad would be in town meeting with their mutual lawyer, Claire McCabe Taylor. However, when Lainey walked into the ranch house, she saw Brad McCabe slouched on the stairs.

For a moment her heart seemed to stall. He was just so handsome, so ruggedly male. So obviously waiting for her. She eyed him cautiously, unsure of his mood. And suddenly, Lainey couldn't risk another encounter that ended badly. She had barely survived the last.

She took several steps backward, reached blindly for the doorknob behind her. "I'll come back later."

He unfolded himself and stood with a lazy, determined grace that jumbled her emotions all the more. "Don't go."

Lainey stared at him, not sure whether to laugh in joy or burst into tears. She only knew that she had never felt more worried or uncertain or full of bittersweet anticipation in her life. And Brad, darn his stubborn, unforgiving heart, was to blame. As their eyes met she drew a deep, bolstering breath, pretended an insouciance she couldn't begin to feel. "I'm not up for another browbeating, so… if you're planning to tell me what a lousy woman-friend I was to you…" *Or an even lousier reporter…*

He swaggered toward her. As he closed the distance, she could smell the spicy scent of his aftershave lotion and the cool mint toothpaste he favored.

His brown eyes were shrewdly direct as they locked

on hers. Triumphant, almost. "You were more than that to me."

Had she been? Lainey lifted a brow, realizing in that instant that he wasn't the only person who had changed. She had, too. No longer was she going to allow herself to have expectations put on her that could not possibly be met. She dropped her shoulder bag on the floor beside her and folded her arms across her chest, more than ready to do battle with him if that was what he wanted. "You didn't seem to have any trouble ditching me," she pointed out.

"I was a fool," he stated matter-of-factly.

"And now you're not?" she asked, a little sadly, aware her throat ached and her knees were shaky and she'd never had so much at stake in her life.

"Only if I lose you." His eyes darkened with sensual intent. His voice dropped a notch. "I don't intend to lose you."

She wanted this. But she had to make sure it would work this time before she leaped in heart-first. "I'm not perfect, Brad."

"I know—" he told her gruffly, his voice catching. "Neither am I."

Tears gathered behind her eyes. She drew a tremulous breath, forced herself to go on. "I have to know… if we ever…resume—"

"I'm looking for a lot more than a resumption, Lainey," he interrupted hoarsely. He stroked her face, cheek, lower lip, until she trembled from his tenderness.

"I need to know that I don't have to be perfect," Lainey continued with a gulp, forcing herself to find the courage to go on despite the fact he obviously was ready and willing to continue their romance. She looked deep into his eyes, knowing this was all-important if they were ever going to be truly happy together. "I need to know that I've got room to make mistakes." She needed reassurance that if she screwed up, he would still love her and want her. That their life together wouldn't be bordered by endless conditions and rigid expectations.

He regarded her soberly, and she saw the love she felt reflected back. "As far as I'm concerned, the only person who needs forgiveness in this situation is me," he told her in a low voice laced with love and hope. "Lainey, you were—are—everything to me. I'm the fool for taking so long to realize that I love you just the way you are, and I always will." His mouth lowered to take hers in a possessive kiss.

"Oh, Brad." She wrapped her arms about his neck and kissed him back sweetly. The warmth and strength of him cured everything that ailed her. "I love you, too. So very, very much."

Contented moments passed as they simply held each other.

He stroked her hair. "I'm sorry it took me so long to forgive you."

She cuddled closer and drew aimless patterns on his chest. "I understand. What I did was…unforgivable."

"No," he corrected, lifting her face to his, "you did what had to be done. You helped put the truth out there—about everything. And you were right, the truth does set you free."

"You really do understand," Lainey marveled. Better yet, he understood—and admired—her determination to set the record straight.

They shared another longer, more leisurely kiss. Relief flowed through her in great, calming waves.

"So, speaking of the facts…you promised me several weeks ago you were going to give me an answer to the question I popped." Brad took a familiar velvet box from his pocket.

Lainey grinned with the promise of the future as he showed her a beautiful diamond ring. "The answer, cowboy, is yes!"

EPILOGUE

"THIS IS GOING TO BE THE best-est wedding ever," Petey said as he paced the room where Annie was putting the finishing touches on Lainey's veil. He had been able to come in, as soon as Lainey was in her dress, and was now waiting to escort her down the aisle and give her away.

"You think so?" Lainey smiled at her son. He looked so handsome and grown up in his wedding attire.

"Brad is even wearing cowboy boots with his tuxedo."

Lainey reached out to give his cummerbund and suspenders a playful tug. "So are you."

Petey grinned proudly. "Aunt Bunny isn't feeling too well, though," he said, continuing his recitation of events.

Aunt Bunny was pregnant. And she and Bart couldn't be happier about the late-in-life pregnancy. Lainey smiled and said reassuringly, "That'll pass, honey."

Petey's eyes widened curiously. "Are you and Brad gonna have more babies, too? 'Cause it would be okay with me if you did. Kurt and Kyle and Teddy, Trevor and Tyler say it's lots of fun to have brothers...and I'd really like to have a brother. Even a sister would be okay."

Lainey grinned. She brought her son to her for a hug. "You are one special guy, you know that?"

Petey smiled back as the music started.

"Are you ready to walk me down the aisle and give me away?" Lainey asked.

Petey nodded, held up his arm to her. "Let's do it."

As they left the anteroom, she saw Brad's whole family gathered on the Lazy M lawn. Lainey's friends from Dallas were there, too. Sybil had even talked them into allowing a photographer from the magazine to take photos.

The sight of everyone close to them filled Lainey with gratitude and peace, but it was Brad, looking so determined and so full of love for her, standing next to the minister at the other end of the aisle, that made her heart race. The joy in his eyes matched her own.

The ceremony itself was a wonderful, happy blur. *"...to have and to hold...from this day forward... forevermore..."*

When the minister announced, "You may kiss the bride," Brad grinned and said, "It's about time!"

The crowd erupted around them and their lips met. Basking in their joy, Lainey and Brad's life together, as husband and wife, began.

* * * * *

BLIND LUCK BRIDE

Laura Marie Altom

For Hannah—
my beautiful baby girl who has grown into a smart, talented and stunning young woman.
I love you *thiiiiiis* much!

CHAPTER ONE

"MITCH, YOU'RE JUST AS DUMB as you look. Why, I could find another bride just like that." Before taking another swig of his long-neck beer, Finn Reilly snapped his fingers to emphasize just how easy the task would be.

Good Lord, hadn't he already been through enough today by being jilted at the altar? So why was Mitch Mulligan, his biggest contracting competitor and pain in his neck still giving him grief? Maybe if he closed his eyes, the three-hundred-pound genetic throwback to the woolly mammoth would vanish. Just in case, Finn blinked.

Damn, his bad luck hadn't changed.

"Oh yeah?" Mitch said—and his beer breath—in Finn's face. "Well, I'm gettin' sick and tired of you thinkin' you're so hot with the women 'round here, Reilly."

"That's 'cause you're jealous."

"Ha! Jealous of what? The way your pretty little filly practically *galloped* out of that church to get away from you?"

Finn rolled his beer bottle across his throbbing forehead. Why did everyone keep bringing up the speed with which Vivian had left the church? While she'd vroomed into the sunset with that leather-wearing, motorcycle-riding bandit she met at the Department of Motor Vehicles, Finn had stood abandoned at the altar. Now honestly, did it seem as if he'd been at fault for their troubles?

Why couldn't everyone at Lu's Bar remember he was the injured party?

"Well, Reilly?" Mitch said. "What've you got to say for yourself?"

"Look, Mulligan." Matt Marshall, Finn's best friend since junior high, hollered above the dart-throwing, off duty firemen. "Give the guy a break. Can't you see he's in pain?"

"Pain? *Pain?*" Mitch laughed so hard he spouted beer all over the bar. "Oh, now that's ripe. I always knew you were the prissy type, Reilly, but Matt here just gave me proof."

"Can it," Matt said. "My bud, Reilly, is no more prissy than your mother."

"What'd you say about my mother?" Despite his size, Mitch scrambled to his feet in two-point-five seconds. "Nobody insults my mother without—"

A loud whistle came from behind the bar.

Finn winced.

Crazy Lu and her settle-down-boys banshee blast were landmarks in the small town of Greenleaf, Utah. She'd owned the burger and beer joint for as long as anyone could remember and while she put up with a lot of things, fights weren't one of them. "Mitch Mulligan, either take it outside or take it up with me." White-haired Lu couldn't have topped five feet wearing heels and a tiara, but the row of ornery guys standing at the bar backed down as if their own mothers had issued the command.

Everyone, that is, except for the woolly mammoth. "Oh now, Lu, don't go gettin' your panties in a wad."

"How do you even know I wear panties, Mitch? I agree with Matt. Just this once, give Reilly a break. Here," she shoved a paper plate heaped with orange-rose-laden wedding cake across the bar. "Put some food in your belly. It'll make you feel better. You prob'ly got gas from all that beer. It's makin' you nasty as a three-headed rattler."

"I don't want any cake and I'm always this nasty. The only thing I want a piece of is that punk sittin' over there shaking in his boots."

"Fine." She winked Finn's way. "Then make him a good honest bet. Just don't mess up his pretty face for the next girl in line for his kisses."

"Why, thank you, sweetheart." Finn winked boldly. At least someone loved him, even if it wasn't the stacked redhead he'd *planned* to be loving right about now.

"Sure thing, angel."

Mitch snorted. "Angel, my—"

"Watch it," Lu warned.

"Ha. All I wanna *watch* is how much crow Reilly here eats when he loses this bet." Mitch pulled a wad of cash from the front pocket of his dingy jeans, peeled off ten hundred-dollar bills, then smacked them on the bar. "All right, pretty boy. I've got a thousand bucks—my entire payroll—says there's no way you can find another woman stupid enough to marry you by the end of the week."

"Mulligan," Lu warned. "There's families depending on that pay. Don't go bettin' away their suppers."

With a wave of one of the massive paws he called hands, he brushed her off. "This here's a sure bet. No one's gonna lose but ol' Reilly here. And seein' how he just got the contract on that fancy new highway motel, he's got plenty of cash to spare."

Finn rolled his eyes. Was Mulligan ever going to get over the fact that Finn's Custom Building consistently got more jobs than AAA Construction?

"Whatsa matter, pretty boy? Too chicken to take me up on a bet you know you're gonna lose?"

That's it. Finn slammed his bottle on the bar, then grappled to his feet.

Nobody called him prissy, pretty boy *and* chicken all on the same night—especially not when his own aunt had called him a *poor, sweet thing* just that afternoon. "By God, Mulligan, I'll not only take you up on that bet—" he pulled honeymoon cash from the chest pocket of his tux, counting out a grand before smacking it beside Mitch's "—but I'll raise the stakes by throwing in my truck."

"Finn," Lu said. "You're a bright boy. Be sensible. This is marriage we're talkin' about. A lifetime commitment—not to mention a brand spankin' new black Chevy."

"All respects, ma'am, but stay out of it—and I'm far from a *boy.*" He took another swig of beer. "I'm Grade A, genuine, *M-A-N.* And if it takes a stupid bet to prove any woman would be thrilled to marry me, then by God, bettin' is what I'll do." He shoved the pile of money toward Lu. "Sweetheart, hold on to this until next Saturday night. If I'm not back wearin' a ring by then...well, then you'd better give all that cash to old ugly over there." He gestured to Mitch. "He'll be needin' it to pay for my funeral, 'cause one thing's for sure..."

"What's that?"

"If I'm not married by Saturday, I must be stone-cold dead."

"NO, NO, NO," Lilly Churchill cried, stomping her white satin pumps in frustration. Unfortunately, all that fussing raised a dust cloud, which caused her to sneeze, which in turn caused her to need a tissue—a tissue that was in her purse.

On the front seat.

Snuggled alongside her keys.

Keys to the car she'd just securely locked.

"Not now," she said to an audience of a million twinkling stars. "Not when I was for once getting things right." Hot tears threatened to spill, but she stoically held them back. This was not the time for a crying binge.

Hiking her heavy white skirts, she teetered across the restaurant's gravel lot.

So, on the eve of her wedding she'd locked her keys in the car? Big deal.

It wasn't an omen that her marriage was doomed. After all, look what'd happened at her big sister Mary's wedding, and four years later, her marriage was still going strong.

Yeah, her conscience butted in, *but don't forget you were the cause of Mary and her three bridesmaids arriving over two hours late for her ceremony.*

And how Robby the groom freaked out because he thought Mary had cold feet. And speaking of cold—remember how the delay caused the reception caterers to run out of Sterno to heat their hot wings, minipizzas, and quiches? Ick. To this day, Lilly could still taste the congealed grease.

Her brothers—and even Mary—assured their *baby* sister that running out of gas on the way to the ceremony hadn't been her fault. That the old Nova's gas gauge had always been cranky—especially below an eighth of a tank. But no matter how many times Lilly told herself the mishap could have happened to anyone, she knew that simply wasn't true.

How? From the disappointment in her mom and dad's eyes. From the looks that said how could such a rotten apple have landed in their perfect bushel?

The truth of the matter was that her sister's wedding wasn't the first time Lilly had seen those looks. They'd been there when she dropped out of the University of Utah after her first semester. They'd been there every time she'd lost her retainer, left the milk out, forgotten to take out the trash or feed the dog, bombed a high school final, missed curfew or lost a job. The list went on and on.

For Lilly's whole life, her older, overachieving, straight-A brothers and sisters had done their best to cover up for her when she failed. They'd treated her like a pet they hated to see punished, but now that all of them were busy leading fabulous careers and marriages, she felt lost and alone in trying to figure out what she wanted to do with her life. She thought she knew, but then this whole mess had happened with Elliot, and now…

Now all she wanted to do was make her troubles go away—a goal easily enough accomplished by marrying Dallas. But then what? Would her parents view her marriage as just another bandage? Or, as for the first time in her twenty-five years, her way of taking responsibility for her biggest ever blunder?

FINN CRADLED his forehead in his hands.

Ugh, had he truly drunk all six of the long-necks standing like a row of not-so-pretty maidens on the bar?

The queasy churning in his gut, not to mention the

sour taste on his tongue, told him that, yes, not only had he downed all those beers, but he'd downed them in a hurry.

What was the matter with him? He knew better than to drink like that—especially over a woman, but darn it all, he was ready to settle down. Seemed like he'd been ready ever since his parents and sister died when he was eight.

This afternoon he'd been damned close to making his dream of starting over with a new family finally come true, but then Vivian had pulled her disappearing act. Not only had she ruined their wedding by walking out right in the middle of it, but she'd stolen their honeymoon tickets to Cancun.

At the very least, he and Matt could have been toasting Finn's sorrows beachside instead of in this stinkin' bar.

He raised his head to look around.

For eleven o'clock on Halloween night, the crowd had grown thin. Old Judge Crawford sat in his usual booth in the corner, and Betty and Bob Bristow, the county's finest line dancers, two-stepped to a honky-tonk tune blaring from the jukebox. They made a cute couple in their alien costumes. Doc Walsh and her house husband wore hospital whites—Mr. Walsh wearing a not-too-flattering nurse's cap and gown.

Though not a single patron currently held a cigarette, a thick haze clung to the renovated barn's ceiling, accompanied by the smell of one too many grease fires.

Finn shook his head.

Yep, after today, he was supposed to have been living the good life. Eating plenty of home-cooked meals. Getting back rubs. Indulging in stimulating conversation and—

What the...

A woman—no, an angel—stood at the red vinyl door. Dressed in a gown of gossamer-white, carrying a bouquet of full pink roses, she looked ready to star in a wedding.

Even worse—or maybe better—she was headed his way.

"Excuse me?" she asked, her melodic voice about as loud as a marshmallow being dropped on a cloud. "But...are you by any chance..."

"Waiting to get married?" This had to be a joke. Mulligan had to have sent her.

"Yes, me too. I'm Lilly and you must be Dallas."

Dallas?

She held out her hand. A tiny, white-gloved affair that when he briefly gripped it, felt lost in Finn's palm. *Lilly.* Such a fitting name for this delicate flower of a woman.

A rush of protectiveness flooded his system.

But wait a minute... Since Mitch had obviously hired this woman to mess with Finn's head, why should he feel anything for her, let alone protective?

Giving the blonde a cool appraisal, in his mind's eye, Finn unfurled the enemy's master plan. Mitch must have met this "bride" at a buddy's Halloween party, then bribed her to feign interest in Finn. Hell, maybe he'd even paid her enough to pretend she was actually going to marry him, then, just when Finn wagged a marriage license in the mammoth's ugly face, Mitch would drop his bomb that this angel was no bride, but someone he hired to cause Finn to lose the bet! To most folks' way of thinking, Finn would have won by marrying, but Mitch wasn't most folks. Mitch was crafty—wily enough to deduce that if Finn wed a bride who was lying about her name, then the marriage wouldn't be legal. Thus causing Finn to lose on a technicality.

And trust Mitch to have not even thought his plan through well enough to tell the woman the name of the guy she was supposed to dupe. "Yep," Finn said with a knowing smile. "I'm Dallas. That's me."

"Thank goodness. I've been driving for hours. I never thought I'd find this place." Her shoulders sagged. "Even now, Dallas, I must say I'm surprised. When you described *Luigi's,* I thought it would be a little more..."

Finn followed her sweeping, and maybe even a bit fearful, gaze as it flitted from face to face to land on old drunken Pete who sat half-asleep and mumbling at the other end of the bar.

"You thought *this* was Luigi's?" That place was the swankiest restaurant for miles. Swallowing hard, Finn blocked the memory of how beautiful Vivian had looked the night he'd taken her there to propose.

"Well...yes. It is, isn't it? I saw the *L-U*-apostrophe-*S* on the sign."

"Sure. This is *Lu*-igi's. I'm glad you found it."

"Me, too." She licked her lips. Kissable lips. Lips that on a good night could drive a man all the way to distraction.

After the day he'd had, did he feel like going for a ride? *Hell, yes.*

"So?" she said. "Shouldn't we get going? I made all the plans. All we have to do is...exchange our vows." She smoothed the front of her satin gown, looking up at him with impossibly wide, impossibly blue eyes.

He gulped.

Mitch had certainly done his homework in hiring this gal. She was a real pro to have almost had Finn falling for her—*almost.*

"I was afraid you wouldn't come," Lilly said, fighting the urge to flee. When Dallas had said in that morning's e-mail that he was suit-and-tie handsome, he'd been way off in his description. Deliciously off.

She couldn't *really* marry a man like him, could she?

Do I really *have a choice?* It wasn't as if guys were lined up around the block waiting to marry a woman in her condition.

"Not come?" He snatched a French fry from a basket on the bar. She tracked his hand all the way to his mouth. A mouth with lips that looked chiseled from the most fascinating stone. "How could I have stayed away from our big day? Or—" another fry in hand, he waved toward a darkened window "—I guess that would be night."

When he spied her gaze lingering on his mouth, he offered her his latest fry, but she shook her head, flushed with heat at the mere possibility of consuming food that had come so perilously close to his lips.

She cleared her throat. "I, ah, don't blame you if you've changed your mind. I mean, this is kind of sudden."

"Nonsense." He swallowed his bite of fry.

"It's okay. Really. I wouldn't be too upset if you want to back out."

"Nope. Not me."

"Great." Lilly released the breath she hadn't realized she'd been holding. In the month they'd known each other via the Marriage of Convenience board on Singles.com, this was what she liked more every day about Dallas. He was a man driven by convictions. Okay, so he wasn't marrying her out of love, but his conviction to succeed in his ultraconservative law firm—the same firm that told him he needed a wife—but she was okay with that. All she needed was a husband—the rest would work itself out in time.

"Let's go," she said. "I set up the ceremony for ten tomorrow morning, but even driving all night, that doesn't give us much time."

"All night? I don't get it."

"Vegas. That's where we'll be taking our vows. Remember? How you told me your mother always wanted to be married there?"

"Oh." He conked his temple. "Of course. *Mom. The Elvis Chapel.* How could I forget?"

"I thought she liked Wayne Newton?"

"Um… Wayne, Elvis, she liked 'em all."

Lilly drew her lower lip into her mouth and nibbled. As relieved as she'd been only a minute earlier to have finally found her man, something now told her riding off into the night with this virtual stranger wasn't one of her brighter ideas. It didn't matter that she and Dallas had talked via e-mail for the better part of a month. His not remembering his own mother's favorite recording artist concerned her. Where was the man who bragged of having a photographic memory? The man who cited countless statistics on the reasons why arranged marriages were infinitely better than the real thing?

The whisker-stubbled, bona fide stud seated before her surely didn't give a flip about dry statistics, and he looked as if he'd be far more comfortable listening to a Garth Brooks song than to *Aida,* his supposedly favorite opera.

Should she ask to see his driver's license?

No. Too direct. Yes, she needed to verify he was who he said he was, but surely she could think of a less combatant way. She cleared her throat. "I, ah, realize this may sound a tad off the subject, but could you please tell me what my favorite food is?"

His eyes narrowed, and he took a long time before saying in a sexy twang, "Aw, now, *angel,* you already know that I know what your favorite food is." He reached for her left hand and rolled down the cuff of her satin glove, exposing the frantically beating pulse on her inner wrist. "Why don't you ask me something a little tougher…."

Oh my gosh! He was actually drawing her wrist to his mouth! He was—oh no. Oh no, he did not just kiss her on the wrist. As an employee of Tree House Books, she read a lot, but in her favorite novel of all time, *Whispered Winds,* the hero, Duncan, kissed his bride's wrist at their third wedding. True, it had taken them three times to get their relationship right, but oh, how right it had finally been. Favorite food be damned. The fact that Dallas remembered how much she adored that scene proved beyond a shadow of a doubt that he was not only who he claimed to be, but that first and foremost, he was the man destined to be her husband.

Closing her eyes, Lilly surrendered to the hot-cold champagne bubbles zinging through her body.

The white-haired woman keeping bar interrupted Lilly's almost-wedded bliss. "S'cuse me," she said to Dallas, "but what in tarnation do you think you're doin'?"

"Mind your own business, Lu, this is my future bride."

"Isn't one bride per day enough for you, Fi—"

"That's it. We've gotta go." Finn nearly fell off his bar stool trying to slip his hand beneath his bride-to-be's elbow while at the same time shooting Lu a would-you-please-hush look of desperation. By God, if she went and ruined this for him, he'd take her to court to cover the small fortune in cash and pride he'd have to fork over to Mitch. He might be able to handle a lot of bad situations, but voluntarily losing a bet to ornery old Mitch Mulligan wasn't one of them. He knew it wasn't neighborly, but he just plain despised the man, and he'd do anything to get the better of him. Even if it meant marrying this loco filly in the morning only to up and divorce her the next afternoon.

While all that sounded real good in theory, a pang of confusion rippled through Finn at the all-too-fresh memory of how badly Vivian had hurt him.

All his life he'd only wanted one thing—to once again be part of a family. So sure, by going through with this marriage, he'd make Mitch look like the fool he was, but in doing that, he'd also be making a mockery of his heart's lifelong ambition. Was that wise?

A whiff of pretty-as-a-spring-meadow perfume wove its way like a love potion through Finn's senses. He took one look at the vision in bridal white standing before him and decided what the heck?

He needed to lighten up.

Besides, what was the worst that could happen on a trip to Vegas?

CHAPTER TWO

"READY, DARLIN'?" FINN SAID, low enough so that hopefully Lu wouldn't hear.

"I sure am." Lilly waved to the still-gaping older woman. "Bye-bye."

Lu might have been willing to let the whole incident slide if only Finn's bride hadn't—from out of nowhere—burst into tears.

"Now, now," Lu crooned, zipping around the corner of the bar. "What's the matter?"

"I—I'm so ha-ha-happy," Lilly blurted in the same kind of hormonal, nonsensical, downright blithering sobs that had taken over Matt's sister the day after she found out she was pregnant. "But I've waited so long for my wedding day, and Dallas, you're even more of a gentleman than I'd imagined, but…I just remembered I locked my keys in my car, and…"

Lu's eagle eyes bored into Finn's forehead like twin laser beams. After pulling Lilly in close for a hug, she said, "Now, honey, 'round here folks lock themselves out of all sorts of things. Don't you worry. Your *groom* knows just what to do."

Never had Finn wished harder that he lived in a less nosy town.

After a few more minutes of what Finn considered award-winning acting, Lilly calmed down, her smile shining brighter than the chrome on Vivian's boyfriend's motorcycle. "I'm sorry," she said. "I don't kn-know what came over me, especially when you had such great news about the keys."

"Emotions'll do that to a body," Lu said, lapping up this rare opportunity to cluck over one of her patrons. "How about you visit the little girl's room. Freshen up while your, ah, groom gets started on your car—if he's sober enough."

"That'd be great," Lilly said through a watery smile. She looked Finn's way. "You don't mind the short delay, do you?"

Mind? Hell, yes, he minded. Not only didn't he like the idea of spending the next hour or so outside with a coat hanger and flashlight, but once he got this human tear-bucket into her car, did that imply driving it and her all the way to Vegas? It was on the tip of his tongue to call off this whole charade when he caught sight of those wide-open skies his bride called eyes. Never had he seen eyes more blue. On manly autopilot, he said, "Ah, sure, I don't mind. You go on and do whatever you need to and I'll just be outside."

"You remember what I drive?" she asked, her voice all breathy, as if his knowing such a fact guaranteed theirs would be a lifelong love.

"Sure, darlin'." *Simple logic tells me it'll be the only spit-shined sedan in the lot.*

More to prove to Lu that he had the woman's best interests at heart than to satisfy his own blazing curiosity as to the feel of her petal-soft lips, he slipped his free hand about Lilly's waist and kissed her hard—not too hard—just hard enough to let her know she was in the company of a real man. Mitch Mulligan might be signing her paycheck, but Finn Reilly was calling the shots.

When she seemed good and dazed by his prowess, with a quick pat to her satin-covered behind, he sent her in the direction of the ladies' room.

But just as he was growing accustomed to the sight of his bride-to-be's backside, Lu grabbed him by the ear and yanked for all she was worth—not an easy feat considering he was well over a foot taller than she. "You low-life, back-stabbin', pitiful excuse for a yellow-bellied—"

"Ouch!" he complained, backing out of her reach. "That hurts."

"Damn straight, it hurts. Almost as much as that alley cat Vivian hurt you this afternoon. Don't you see what you're doin'?"

"What do you mean?"

"You know exactly what I mean. Look, son, and make no mistake, over the years you've been comin' in here, I've grown to think of you as my own son. What you could end up doin' to this girl is the same thing Vivian did to you. You're gonna lead her on, then dump her. Only at least Vivian dumped you for love. You, on the other hand, will be freein' yourself up for a truck named Abigail."

"Slow down, Lu, you don't know the half of what's going on." Challenging her steely gaze with one of his own, he said, "Shoot, Mitch put my *bride* up to this. That woman's no innocent. I mean, come on, unless she was being paid darned good money, what would a gal like her be doing in a place like this? No offense."

"None taken, but, Finn," she said, sounding all too much like the aunt who had raised him—the same aunt who had been living in Miami, blessedly out of scolding distance, for going on five years. "I don't know who this girl is, but one thing I do know just from lookin' at her is that she's not messed up with Mitch. Maybe she has amnesia or somethin'? All I'm sayin' is be careful."

"Lu, like you said, you know me. I'm not planning to hurt anyone."

"No, I'm sure you're not, but you be careful anyway, 'cause now that I think about it, the only one gettin' hurt around here might be you."

"Ready?" asked the angel in white.

"Yeah, I'm—" Finn looked up, only to have his heart lurch at the sight of her. He'd always fancied himself as preferring redheads, but this blond-haired beauty had brushed her curls into an adorable halo that looped and swirled about the heart-shaped contours of her face. She'd applied a light coat of lipstick that accentuated the faint swelling caused by his kiss. Whew, Mitch sure had improved his taste in women! "I'm ready," he said. "Sorry I didn't get a chance to get the car."

"That's okay. Once you get the keys out, probably with what you've had to drink, it's better that I drive. We wouldn't want anything to further delay our trip to the chapel, would we?"

No. Hell no.

To Lu, his angel said, "Ma'am, it was sure nice meeting you, and thank you for—" she held up a wadded pink tissue "—for helping me see that Dallas is the only man for me."

Upon hearing another man's name in association with Finn, Lu's eyebrows shot up like a pair of jackrabbits scared out of their holes. She looked to him, then the woman in white. "You're welcome, child. And the only thanks I need is the promise you two will share a *lifetime* worth of happiness."

That did it.

His bride's waterworks started all over again, but

this time, she turned to Finn for her hugs. Never had he felt more masculine than holding this petite thing in his arms. Never had he felt more in control. This gal was a mighty fine actress, but no one fooled Finn Reilly. He could smell one of Mitch's tricks from a mile away.

Once she broke her hug, Finn slipped his arm around her slight waist and led her out of the bar as fast as his black dress boots could scoot.

Outside, feet firmly planted on the pea gravel driveway, his gaze aimed at the stars, Finn gulped gallons of the crisp fall air. Had there ever been a luckier man than he? Yep, having Mitch arrange for this fallen angel to enter his life was just about the best damned shot of blind luck he'd ever had. Winning this bet was not only going to be easy, but a ton of fun.

Confirming that thought, his bride snuggled close, resting her head on his chest. Her soft curls tickled the bottom of his chin. He'd always liked it when a woman fit him—even a woman he was only pretending to like.

He and Vivian had stood eye to eye. She'd been a bad fit.

"Dallas?" Lilly said.

"Yeah?"

"I just want you to know, before tomorrow, that I really appreciate you doing this for me. And...and one day, I hope we'll not just share a marriage license, but maybe even a special friendship."

A special friendship? Ugh.

Time to raise the stakes.

"Dallas?"

Not thinking, just doing, Finn cinched her closer, planting his lips atop hers for a powerful kiss.

"Mmm, Dallas," she said on a sigh that was more of a purr.

She started kissing him back, but the voltage of their second embrace caught Finn off guard and he pulled away.

Nope.

No way had he enjoyed that marathon smooch to the degree his racing heart implied.

To prove he was still in complete control of not only the situation, but his feelings, he kissed his bride-to-be all over again. When she mewed her pleasure, he fought to hold back a moan. Lord, they were good together.

Had he and Vivian ever been like this? Maybe once, or maybe he'd only wished they could be. Damn, what was happening to him? He knew better than to be sucked into the spell of another conniving woman.

"Mmm, Dallas." She pulled away with a whispery sigh. "I didn't know that outside of the movies a kiss could be that good."

They usually weren't. "Yeah…well, what can I say?"

She smiled and the heartbreaking beauty of it nearly stole the breath from his lungs. "I know what I'd like you to say."

"What's that?"

"Ask me to marry you. I've read it in your letters, but I've never heard you say it. Say it, Dallas. *Please.*" As strong as Lilly had felt only moments earlier, Dallas's kiss had left her that weak. Her knees felt rubbery and her chest strangely tight with anticipation and tingling warmth. Was a marriage of convenience supposed to be this much fun?

"How can I ask you to marry me when I don't know your name?"

"Excuse me?"

"You know, your, ah, *full* name."

Thank goodness. *Her full name.* Of course. She'd almost been back to her original worry that maybe this man wasn't Dallas after all. "My given name is Lillian Diane Churchill. But, please, feel free to keep on calling me Lilly. There's no need for you to get formal on me now."

"Okay, *Lilly...*" He paused after drawling the *l*'s. Never before had just hearing her name brought such heady pleasure. "Will you marry me?"

Would she marry him? She'd follow him to the end of the earth and back—that is, assuming he never lied to her. Elliot had lied, and look what she'd gotten from him. That's why she knew things were going to work out great with Dallas. Their relationship was based upon total honesty.

She licked her lips, took a deep breath and committed every second of this moment to memory. She'd remember the way Dallas smelled, like...well, a little like beer and cigarette smoke, but beneath all that, she detected citrus aftershave and a distinctly delicious scent that was all him—and soon to be all hers! "Yes, Dallas. Of course, I'll marry you."

"Good. Then how about you and me getting this show on the road?"

"Mr. Lebeaux, it would be my pleasure."

"Who's *Mr. Lebeaux?*"

"Oh, Dallas," she said, her giddy laugh carrying across the still night air. "You're so funny."

Not so funny, though, was when, a few minutes later, Dallas calmly opened her car's passenger door to reach for her keys. How could she have been so scatterbrained as to not even check the other door to see if it was unlocked?

"This is embarrassing," she mumbled. She would have added that since finding out about the baby, she hadn't been feeling herself, but the problem was that incidents like this were exactly herself. Good grief, she was soon going to be a mother. She had to start being more responsible.

"There you go," Finn said. Wearing a bemused grin, he handed her a wad of interconnected souvenir key chains. "Guess we'll chalk this incident up to bridal jitters."

"I'm afraid it's more than that," she said, placing her hand protectively over her tummy.

"Oh? Confession time?"

"Only on the matter that you're about to wed a misfit. I thought our marriage would instantly transform me, but so far, I guess it hasn't worked."

"We're not hitched yet," he pointed out. "Maybe saying those all-important vows is all you need to turn your life around?"

"You think?" She looked at him, *really* looked at the man she would spend the next fifty years with. And what she saw wasn't just a handsome face and warm, expressive brown eyes, but for the first time in the month they'd corresponded, she saw that perhaps instead of this marriage being the platonic business arrangement she'd expected, there just might be a chance of something more.

THE NEXT MORNING, after finally pulling into the chapel parking lot for some shut-eye, Finn woke to a delicious weight resting on his chest. From his perch behind the wheel—somewhere around one in the morning he'd taken over the driving—he saw a crown of silken gold contrasting with the black wool of his tux. To test if his latest fiancée was real, he looped his finger around one of her baby-fine curls. She shifted and moaned, granting him a breathtaking view of her profile.

Yep, she was real all right. A real knockout.

Let the games continue!

Warm sun beat through the car windows, illuminating honeyed highlights in her eyebrows and lashes. Her lips looked every bit as plump and kissable as they had the night before, and the brief memory of the way that mouth had felt touching his caused a swelling down south that made his pants even more uncomfortable.

As his future bride again stirred against him, spilling the softest of mews, Finn wondered what the hell he was doing? The marriage license they'd obtained near dawn rested heavy in his chest pocket, as did the fact that he'd had to slip the clerk a hundred while Lilly had been in the courthouse bathroom to fill out the document in his real name.

During the night's long drive, while Lilly softly snored, he'd reconfirmed his belief that her calling him *Dallas* had to be part of Mitch's grand scheme. For if Finn were to marry Lilly using a false name—to insure that she didn't know he was on to her plan—their marriage wouldn't be legal, thus giving Mitch the right to drive off in Abigail on a technicality. But as usual, Finn was one step ahead of his nemesis.

The one thing Finn hadn't counted on was being this attracted to his bride. Still, he supposed his attraction to her would add a certain touch of realism to their ceremony—even if it was just pretend.

"Lilly," he said, deciding the time had come to guarantee his winning the bet. "Hello? Are you ready to tie the knot?"

"Hmm?"

"Hello? Wake up." He softly tickled behind her right ear. "We're at the Wayne Newton Chapel, just like you requested."

She took a second to wake, then eased upright, quickly processing the fact that she'd been using his chest as a pillow. "Sorry," she said, unaware of the adorable red mark on the left side of her face from where she'd pressed her cheek against his lapel.

"How do you feel?" she asked, scooting to her half of the front seat. From the dashboard, she reached for her bouquet, which had wilted during the night. The heavy scent of fading pink roses filled the air.

"Feel?" Even as he said the word, his head pounded. "Oh right. *Feel.*" He flashed her a wry grin, hoping his beer breath didn't smell as bad as it tasted. "Actually, not so hot."

"You don't make a habit of drinking that much, do you?"

He shook his head. "Must have been all the excitement."

"Sure. I understand." Pulling down the visor, she gazed into a small lighted mirror and pursed her lips into a frown. "Ugh, looks like that drive took even longer than I thought." She reached to the floorboard for her purse and dove inside, pulling out a tube of lipstick. After giving her lips a pretty sheen, she eyed him funny. "Are you sure you feel up to this?"

"What kind of question is that? You trying to back out on me?"

If he could have bottled the feeling her grin gave him, he'd be a rich man. Gone was his headache and, oddly enough, all his doubts about the vows he was about to take. How the marriage ended they could figure out later. Right now, he planned to enjoy the moment, starting with appreciating his lovely bride.

Her lipstick was the sheerest of pink and, just as she had at Lu's the night before, she did a fluff-and-tuck routine on her hair that left it a tousled, yet somehow elegant, shoulder-length mess. She capped it with her veil, mesmerizing him with the sight of filmy white lace whispering to flushed cheeks. What was she thinking? Did she find herself in the similarly bizarre situation of being as attracted to him as he was to her?

She lifted her hand to his cheek. Here it came, she was about to tell him how hot she was for him….

"You've, um, got something on your face." His heart plummeted when she brushed at a spot to the left of his nose, then held up a gray lint ball for his inspection. "See? I didn't want you wearing this in our wedding photos."

"Right. Ah, me neither." Damn. Could he have possibly misread that situation more completely? This temptress was so sly that for a second she'd *almost* made him forget why they were there.

Trying to hide his consternation with both himself and his bride, he fumed out the dusty car window. At dawn, he'd parked the vehicle in an alley they shared with a primer-gray Impala up on blocks and two overfilled Dumpsters. What were the odds that he'd smell motorcycle exhaust at his first wedding, then week-old trash at his second? "So," he said, rubbing his palms together. "Should we do this thing?"

"You're sure?"

"Why do I keep getting the feeling you're not?"

Lilly returned her attention to her purse. "I don't

know…because I don't feel the slightest bit apprehensive." Her digging took on a furious pace. Could she really go through with this? Sure, making her parents proud and all was a very big deal, but after what Elliot had put her through, did she feel ready to open her heart to another man?

Whoa.

She scavenged her purse even faster.

Who'd said anything about doing anything with her heart? This was a marriage of convenience. The love-match line formed on the other side of the building.

"What are you looking for?"

"Mints. I've got to have mints. I don't want to say my vows with bad breath."

Grasping her by the wrists, he stilled her hands, then took them in his. "Lilly, you smell fine, you look beautiful. Trust me, there's nothing for you to be worried about."

"Really? I look okay? I don't look as though I was up all night driving?"

He grinned. "How could you when you've been sleeping on me for the better part of the last—" he eyed his watch "—eight hours. It would have been nine, but remember when we dealt with that pesky business of getting our license?"

"Oh, yeah. I forgot. So I slept all that time?"

"Peaceful as a baby."

Smoothing the front of her gown, she said, "Yes, well…"

Finn's stomach took a dive. *Was* she thinking of backing out? She'd better not. He had a lot at stake. Not only a brand-new truck that wasn't even paid for, but a massive amount of pride. He *had* to win this bet. Still, maybe if she was getting cold feet, he should take it easy on her, act as if he had all the time in the world for them to make their vows. "Maybe we should wait?" he suggested. "We could get a room. You could take a nap and freshen up, then, once you feel up to it, we'll get hitched tonight."

"You want to get a room? Now?" There went those eyes of hers again. Big blue saucers brimming with disapproval.

"Well, sure. Why? What's the matter with our sharing a room?"

"I thought you knew how I felt about such things."

"What things?"

"You know..." She ducked her gaze, aiming it on the yucca plant thriving between Dumpsters number one and two. "Premarital—and in our case, even aftermarital—relations."

"Huh?"

"S-E-X."

"Oh. *Ooh.* Well, who said anything about doing the mattress mambo? All I suggested was that we get a room so you could take a nap."

"That's okay. I'd just as soon get this over with."

Get it over with? What kind of a thing was that for a bride to say? Even a pretend bride! "Ah, sure. Let's go."

He bolted from the car, racing around the now dusty sedan intent on opening her door, but he was too late. She'd already done it. Didn't she know she was being paid to let him do manly stuff for her so that she felt more like a woman and he felt like more of a—

Dope.

While he'd stood there contemplating his manhood, she'd already hustled past the weed-choked side of the pink chapel. Coming around the corner, Finn looked up to see a gigantic statue of smiling Wayne Newton. He held a wedding cake in his hands, and an inscription across the top of the chapel read, *Wayne's House of Love,* and beneath that, *Danke Schoen for your patronage.*

Dear Lord, what am I getting into?

"Lilly! Wait up!" He tried shoving the keys into his pocket, but they wouldn't fit. Her massive key chain was loaded down with a pink rabbit's foot and mini snow-globes from every cheesy destination in the West. "Can you please put this in your purse?"

"Sure," she said, pausing to grab the wad of fuzz and plastic from him, then slip it into her white bag. She glanced at her slim gold watch. "We'd better hurry. We're almost late. Do you have the license?"

"Yeah." *Only it doesn't quite read the way you think it does.* How would she take the news when she learned he'd been on to her scam from the start?

"Hello? Dallas?"

"Huh? Oh—right. I'm ready and rarin' to go."

"No, not yet." She approached him, then, standing on her tiptoes, buttoned his collar and retied his bow tie. The warm brush of her fingers against his throat startled him. Her act was intimate—the kind of thing a wife does for her husband before they attend their daughter's wedding. Again Finn's conscience reminded him of how badly he yearned for that kind of lifelong bliss, and of just how far this sham marriage was from the real thing.

"There," Lilly said with a misty smile. "That's better. Come on, let's get married."

On her way inside, for the umpteenth time Lilly wondered if she was doing the right thing. After all, she was still kind of on the rebound from Elliot, and maybe a month wasn't long enough to know someone before she married him.

Yeah, but on the flip side, she'd known Elliot Dinsmoore all her life. Could she help it if, during the brief time they'd both moved away from their hometown, the charming traveling insurance salesman had gotten married—and conveniently forgot to tell her during their whirlwind romance that he *still was* married?

Shameful heat crept up her cheeks at the memory of the horrific day he'd told her his news. The day she'd given him not only her virginity, but her heart. Even now, almost two months after the fact, she knew that if her perfect family, none of whom had ever done a bad, stupid or reckless thing in their lives, found out she was pregnant with a married man's baby, they'd never forgive her.

Well, she thought, throwing her shoulders back at the same time she opened the mirrored-glass chapel door, this was one time she was doing exactly the right thing. After being dumped by Elliot, she feared she'd never find a father for her baby, but after only a few weeks of online chatting with Dallas, she'd known everything would work out fine.

From her first sight of his out of focus—yet still cute in a blurry way—online picture, to the way he promised to be a good dad if she promised to be a good hostess, she'd known theirs would be a lasting relationship. A relationship no one ever need know wasn't based on love.

All her adult life, her family had urged her to go to college, to find a *real* job, yet all she could ever remember wanting to do was raise a big brood of kids—just like her own mom. Lilly dreamed of ruling a rambling Victorian home alongside a loving husband, raising not award-winning kids, but rambunctious kids who got into as many jams as she had growing up.

And just think, finally, within a matter of mere minutes, all those dreams would be well on their way to coming true—well, all of them except for the Victorian house and loving husband, but then Lilly glanced over her shoulder just as Dallas stumbled across the threshold from concrete to red-hot-red shag carpet. Even tripping over his own feet, the man was criminally handsome—maybe even more so now that she'd seen he wasn't perfect, either!

He flashed her a smile of strong white teeth, making her tummy flip-flop. Wow. There may never be love in their future, but if he kept that up, at least on her part there was starting to be a disconcerting amount of attraction.

"Hey," he said. "Great taste in chapels."

"You like it?"

"What's not to like?"

Wayne Newton's voice crooned through hidden speakers and pictures of Wayne coated every available inch of wall. A mannequin resplendently dressed in what a plaque at the bottom claimed was a genuine Wayne-worn suit spun in a slow circle. Everything about the place spoke of fun. Las Vegas-style fun. So why did she feel like bursting into tears?

"Hey?" he asked, cupping her face with his big, work-roughened hands. *When had Dallas—an accomplished corporate attorney—ever done a lick of manual labor?* "You look like you're about to spout another eye gusher. Come on, Lil, don't cry."

His mentioning the word *cry* brought on her waterworks. "It's j-just that I..." She gestured to their surroundings, to the dyed blonde, approaching at eleven o'clock who was dressed in head-to-toe black sequins. "Oh, Dallas…" Lilly threw herself at her groom. "I know I told you this was okay, but I always w-wanted to get married in a ch-church." Wishing she wasn't such an emotional basket case, she flashed him an apologetic look, then hefted her skirts in a mad dash for the door marked Powder Room.

"Are we having a problem?" their hostess asked.

Finn shook his head and whispered, "She'll be fine."

"I hope so, because…" Finn followed her gaze to a mirrored grandfather clock that was on chime number four of ten.

"We've got a big group coming in at ten-thirty. Either you two get the show on the road, or I'm afraid we'll have to reschedule you for—"

"No," Finn said, heading for the bathroom door. "No need to reschedule." At least he hoped not! Not only were Lilly's amazingly accurate fake tears tugging at his freshly broken heart, but visions of Mitch driving his truck screamed at his pride. The more Lilly stalled, the more Finn knew Mulligan was paying her to be with him. All this wailing had to be another part of the plan designed to yank his chain. Mitch must have told her to keep an eye on him while letting the bet deadline run out. That way, by the time Finn caught on to the scam, it would be too late to find another—less calculating—bride.

After a few minutes, Finn heard sniffles, then the door creaked open. His adorable, pink-cheeked bride peeked out. "A-after all my b-blubbering," she managed to say, "y-you probably don't want to marry me, do you?" A single tear glistening on her left cheek pierced his conscience.

Good grief, how had this all gotten so complicated?

Suddenly his scheme to win a thousand bucks and make Mitch look bad had somehow taken a back seat to his desire to once again make Lilly smile. "Of course, I want to marry you, sweetheart." *Sweetheart?* "And listen, I was thinking that with this being Sunday morning and all, we could find a church and do this thing right. I mean, our family and friends won't be there, but…"

"Oh, Dallas!" Although her sobs started anew, he spied a smile mixed in with the tears. His feeling of manly pride almost swelled right out of his chest.

Damn, she was good.

While their hostess gaped, Finn figured he might as well prove to her, too, that he was a grade A, genuine, manly *M-A-N,* so he swooped his bride into his arms. Though he could barely see past the tufts of flowery-smelling lace tickling his nose, he ushered Lilly out of the chapel and into brilliant sun.

CHAPTER THREE

AN HOUR LATER, LILLY BEAMED when Dallas had not only found her a lofty Methodist church to marry in, but an elderly minister with a few minutes to spare between his first and second services.

Standing in sunbeams shafting through decades-old stained glass, never had Lilly felt more sure about one of her decisions. Rich scents of pale pink cabbage roses and fragile lily of the valley wreathed her senses, bringing her to the conclusion that Dallas Lebeaux was a hero among men.

Not only had he found this church, but at a grocery store he had bought her a glorious new bouquet because he had noticed her old one drooping. Then he'd taken it upon himself to make every moment of their revised ceremony complete, all the way down to wonderfully gaudy, gum-ball machine rings. His TLC calmed her bridal jitters, and for the first time since sealing their arrangement, she didn't feel the slightest bit apprehensive. If anything, she felt oddly excited about the years—and especially, hours—to come.

"Do you, Lillian, take thee Dallas as your lawfully wedded husband?" The minister's solemn voice echoed in the lofty space.

"I do," she answered strong and clear.

He turned to Dallas. "Do you, Dallas, take thee Lillian to be your lawfully wedded wife?"

"Yeah…I, ah, do."

"Then by the power vested in me, I hereby pronounce you husband and wife. Dallas, you may kiss your radiant bride."

As he did just that, Lilly thought she'd melt with bone-deep satisfaction. Her family would be so proud of the way she'd mended the broken pieces of her life—that is, they'd be proud if they knew what kind of mess she'd gotten into. Thankfully, now, they need never know. Her pregnancy cover-up was a fait accompli.

TWENTY-MINUTES LATER, Finn sat behind the wheel of his *wife's* car, driving down a main drag, wondering if taking his marriage vows under another man's name had broken any laws of man, or just God? Telling the kindly, rushed for time, elderly minister he'd left their marriage license all the way back in the car probably hadn't been good, either. But hey, if the minister had noticed the discrepancy in names, Lilly would have been clued in on the fact that her groom was onto her scheme. Finn's stomach churned, but one glance at Lilly did the work of a hundred Rolaids.

Lord, she was a sight to behold.

What was he worried about? He'd already won the bet. Now all he had to do was gloat to Mitch.

Sneaking another peek at his temporary bride, Finn noticed how her golden curls perfectly matched a magnolia smooth complexion that seemed more suited to Mississippi than the dried-up West. "Have you always lived in Utah?" he asked, stopping the car at a red light.

She eyed him funny. "Are you feeling okay?"

"Sure."

"Then why would you ask me something like that? You know all about my childhood, goofy."

"Right. How could I forget?" Thankfully, the light changed so he could pretend to focus on driving. "Ready to head back to Greenleaf?"

She shot him a look of horror. "Don't you remember?"

"What?"

"Dallas?" Sounding hurt, she said, "I made reservations at the Bridal Fair Theme Motel and Casino. Remember how you said your mother had always wanted to stay there, but hadn't had the money?"

He shook his head. "Aren't you sweet? Here, we've only been married a few minutes and look, already you're taking care of me to the extent that you're worried about my mother." *God rest her soul.*

That brought the roses back to Lilly's cheeks.

Aha! Again, his earlier assumptions had been right. Her wanting them to stay in Vegas was definitely another facet of Mitch's plan. A form of insurance.

Since Lilly thought he had married her under an assumed name, she still believed she'd won the bet for the enemy camp. The only way she wouldn't win was if Finn realized that although he had lost the bet on a technicality, he still had time to find another bride. In short, Lilly had been told to keep her eye on him while letting the clock run down.

Fortunately, Finn was still about twelve steps ahead of her. And given that he'd always loved Vegas and a good party, he figured why not combine those two loves to not only celebrate his victory, but call Lilly's bluff to see just how far she was willing to go for her boss.

"I've got an idea," he said. "How about since my mother isn't here, we stay at one of the big boys? You know, like Luxor or Bally's? Even better, The Venetian—I've heard it's *very* romantic."

She dropped her gaze. Her bottom lip started to quiver. "Y-you said you preferred intimacy over crowds. I mean, though we discussed taking you know—things—slow, I even booked the Mount Vesuvius Suite."

Mmm, smooth move. Looked like she was definitely willing to go all the way, but playing coy.

Eyeing her lips, he remembered how soft they were. Soft and warm and moist and—

"Look out!"

Finn slammed on the breaks, narrowly avoiding a nasty run-in with a diesel-belching city bus.

Instinctively he shot his arm out to brace Lilly should they crash, but with the danger long gone, he gave himself a pat on the back. Way to go, man—not for saving the car, but for accidentally landing a direct hit atop her left breast. Beneath his palm, her nipple swelled and hardened, returning him to high school to watch one of those slow-motion science films on budding flowers. Right before his eyes, or rather his touch, this flower was blooming, and the sight of her flustered smile filled him with awe.

Whew, he thought, taking his sweet time removing his hand. Good thing he had a handle on this situation or he might have mistaken all this lust for genuine attraction.

"Do you need me to drive?" she asked.

"Nope. I've got everything under control." Except for that nagging issue of forgetting he was parked in the middle of a bustling six-lane road.

FIFTEEN MINUTES LATER in a dark, dank-smelling alcove leading to the bathrooms of Elvis's Hunk o' Good

Cookin' Café where they'd stopped for brunch, Finn had a hard time transferring the numbers from his calling card to a pay phone. He wasn't trembling, was he? The slight shake to his hands must have been from hunger, because he certainly wasn't that upset about his bothersome fascination with his wife.

Three tries later, the other line rang.

"Yeah?" a groggy Matt finally answered.

"You gotta help me, bud. I'm scared."

"Finn? That you?"

"Yep, and I'm treadin' some pretty deep water."

"What's up?"

"You know that bet I had with Mitch?"

"Uh-huh..."

"Well, to make a long story short, I found a bride and this morning...I married her in Vegas."

"You what?" Instantly Matt's voice went from sleepin'-it-off mode to high-noon alert. "Please tell me you're joking."

"Sorry."

"Oh, man. What're you gonna do? Who is she? Where'd you meet?"

Finn gazed at Lilly, at the way sun filtered through the café's tinted front windows, bathing her in lavender. Lord, she was beautiful. Lord, he wanted to fulfill his husbandly duty. But no matter how much he wanted to take Lilly into his arms, there was that matter of her having been hired by Mitch to consider. Not to mention his vow to never, *ever,* get mixed up with another conniving woman.

"Finn? You there? Talk to me, man."

"I'm here. I...oh hell, bottom line, something's happening to me, Matt. I thought this was a joke. You know, to get back at Mitch, but I don't know. Once I won the bet, I figured she'd fess up that Mitch hired her, but she hasn't. And I feel kinda funny when I look at her. And when she talks, I sometimes have a hard time breathing."

"Okay, first off, I'm sure if you're in Vegas, it's the dry air making you breathe funny. And second, if Mitch hired this woman, you can't be *that* attracted to her. Either she's got you under a spell, or this is merely a rebound thing from the wedding. For the sake of this discussion, we'll call it 'the Vivian Effect.'"

"Great. We have a name, but what's the solution?"

"Simple. Go with it. She likes you. You like her. I'm failing to see the problem—unless she interferes with Friday night poker."

Swell.

Finn said a quick *catch ya later* to his friend, then hung up, grumbling, "Fat lot of help you were," as he thumped his forehead against the cool chrome front of the phone.

What was he going to do?

On the one hand, Lilly was not only a hottie, but sweeter than cotton candy. She was exactly the kind of woman he'd always pictured his kids coming home to after school.

Then, as the sun was setting, he'd park his truck in the driveway and his family would all come running out the front door to greet him—a big golden lab named Rover leading the pack—followed, of course, by the three mutts he already had. His four boys would be next to tromp down the front porch stairs. And Lilly would bring up the rear, pausing at the rail, backlit by golden afternoon sun, hugging his infant daughter to her hip.

He'd always planned on having his boys first. That way they could help him keep Charlotte's boyfriends in line—oh, and Charlotte was going to be his first daughter's name. In memory of his mom. His first son would be named Edward in honor of his dad. He'd name his second daughter, Katherine—Katie for short—for his sister.

Okay, so that was the one hand. On the other, he was a fool to think, even for a second, his dreams were about to come true.

For the last time, man, Lilly was hired by your worst enemy to mess with your head. Lilly probably isn't even her real name!

"Dallas?"

Finn looked up to see *her*.

"I don't mean to invade your privacy," she said, "but our brunch is almost ready." She capped her words with a shy, intoxicatingly pretty grin. "After being up all night, you must be starving, and well—" she ducked her gaze "—you know it's not healthy to wait too long between meals."

As if watching himself in a movie, Finn heard the low din of conversation, the chink of silverware against china, the sad strains of a country song playing over hidden speakers. He smelled cigarette smoke and bacon and the sticky sweet scent of maple syrup. And while he was acutely aware of all that, he tried not to be aware of his ridiculous curiosity as to what it might be like to start a family with this woman who *might* be named Lilly.

Cautiously he slipped his arm about her wisp of a waist, gazing deep into her baby blues. Matt's words skipped through his brain. *She likes you. You like her. What's the problem?*

"Dallas? Are you already feeling weak?" She stood

on her tiptoes, skimming cool fingers across Finn's fevered forehead. "You're hot."

For you.

"Maybe we should get you to the motel so you can lie down?"

"You want me to *lie* down, huh?" Steering her toward their table, he held her deliciously tightly.

"Watch it, mister. You know what I mean. You look sick."

"Gee, thanks."

They'd left the dark hall to enter the maze of tables and he took her by the hand to lead her through.

"Congratulations," called out a portly man seated at the counter as they passed. "Have y'all been married long?"

Lilly beamed. "Almost an hour."

"Well, that's just great. Good luck to you both." To Finn he said, "Take care of this little missy. I can tell just by lookin' at her she's a special gal."

"Um, thanks." Finn hardly even slowed on his way to their table.

"Dallas?" she complained once they slid into their booth. "Why didn't you stop and say something to that man? He was being nice."

He sighed. "Sorry. I guess after our long night I didn't feel up to small talk."

"You *are* sick, aren't you?"

"No. Really, I feel fine."

"Then why do you seem different?"

"You're overreacting, *Mrs. Lebeaux.* I'm just tired."

Her eyes narrowed. "Okay, then tell me who you called and what they said that's made you so glum."

Finn took a deep breath. *There you go, man. You'll*

never get a better chance to bring up the bet. Ask her what she's doing hooked up with a slimeball like Mitch—not to mention what it'd take to buy out her contract.

Unfortunately, just as Finn was about to pose his question, a waitress wearing a wig that looked more like tinsel than hair stopped in front of their table. "Who ordered the Graceland Special?"

"Me," Finn said.

"Okeydoke." She slid a double cheeseburger and crinkle fries in front of him. "This must be yours," she said, setting another burger and fries in front of Lilly before stepping back and putting her hands on her hips. "Strange but true observation—the only other couple I know who order burgers for breakfast has been married over sixty years. You two have that same look about you—the one that says you just might go the distance."

"Thank you," Finn's bride gushed, pressing her hands to glowing cheeks. "Including the minister who married us, you're the third person this morning to wish us luck, and you know what they say about the third time being a charm."

"Oh, so then this is your third marriage?" There was barely a rise in the waitress's purple eyebrows.

"Um, no," Lilly said with a cute frown.

Finn hid his grin behind his burger.

"I, um, meant you were the third person to wish us luck on *this* marriage."

"Oh, sure." The waitress sagely nodded. "That's great. Oh—and hey," She reached into the pocket of her short black skirt to draw out two slips of red paper. "Before I forget—The King, also known as my boss, Kenny, gives these to all our newlyweds."

"What are they?" Lilly asked, accepting their gift.

"Complimentary tickets to the matinee performance of Elvis's Bird and Dog Show. You'll love it."

"Yo, Moonbeam!" a burly bald man called from across the room. "My hair's not grownin' any thicker waitin' on you!"

"Keep your pants on, Burt. I'm comin'." To Lilly and Finn, *Moonbeam* said, "Enjoy the show," before heading Burt's way.

"Wasn't she sweet?" Lilly said. "And what fun we'll have with these tickets. A bird and dog show. How exciting. I wonder if the animals perform together?"

Finn suppressed what had to be his hundredth groan of the morning. "As newlyweds, don't we have something else we're supposed to be doing?"

"Don't tell me you mean…you know…" Her cheeks turned a dozen shades of pink.

"Yeah, that's what I mean. So? Doesn't that sound like more fun?"

"Dallas," she scolded. Lowering her voice, she said, "You know my feelings on that subject. I think it'd be best if we got to know each other first." She looked at the tickets, then her watch. "The show starts at noon. It's ten past eleven, which means if we're going to check into the motel first—*just* to guarantee our room and change our clothes—then we'd better hurry up and eat."

Ooh, you're smooth. What an amazing stroke of luck the way Lilly had managed to wriggle her ripe little tush out of sealing their vows just yet.

"This tastes delicious," she said, swallowing a bite of her burger. "I can't stand eggs, so when I was a kid, I told Mom that as soon as I grew up, I was only eating hamburgers for breakfast."

"Are you kidding?"

"No. Why would I make something like that up?"

"I wasn't implying you would, it's just that I feel the same way about eggs—or any breakfast food for that matter. I always figured why not skip breakfast and go straight to lunch." What Finn didn't reveal was that the reason he'd adopted the habit of skipping breakfast was to make the days after losing his parents and sister pass faster. If he jumped right out of bed and went straight to lunch, in a kid's mind, that translated to a lot fewer hours in the day.

His wife sat her *Love Me Tender* special down and flashed him one of her wavering grins that typically preceded tears. "Do you know what our both liking burgers for breakfast means?" Her big blue eyes turned shimmery.

I know what it usually means when you start up your sprinklers. You get whatever you want. But not this time. I'm onto you. I'm—

"It means that we really *do* have a shot at our marriage lasting forever. Everyone knows the more things a couple has in common, the more likely they are to stay together. My oldest brother, David, is a marriage counselor, so believe me, I've heard this from a reliable source. Uh…" She wiped tears from the corners of her eyes. "I'm sorry. I've been so hormonal since—well, you know. Anyway—" she reached across the table for his hands "—all I wanted to say is that Dallas Lebeaux, you are my knight in shining armor for rescuing me not only from the Wayne Newton Chapel, but—no, I'm not going to get emotional again. I just want you to know that if it's the last thing I do, I'll never make you sorry for marrying me."

"AND NOW, ladies and gentle*man*..."

Lilly grinned to see Dallas squirm at Elvis's mention of him being the only other man in the room. And what a room it was. The so-called theater had been set up in an old grocery store. The checkouts were piled high with souvenir T-shirts, mugs and key chains and the raised center deli section was now a stage. The overhead lights had been turned out and the entire perimeter of the massive space glowed with neon outlines of dancing pork chops and milk jugs. The place smelled like a cross between salami and glazed donuts, both of which made Lilly's stomach growl.

"For my next amazing feat," Elvis said, "I'll need a lovely assistant. Do I have anyone out there who'd like to help Sparky the Wonder Dog?"

"Me! Me!" A half dozen pint-size girls squirmed in their seats, itching for the chance to clamber up on stage.

"Hmm, such a tough choice," Elvis said, "You're all so lovely, but I pick...you." He pointed to the only one of the girls not squirming, a pigtailed angel seated in a wheelchair. "Sir," Elvis said, pointing to Dallas. "Could you please help the little lady onto the stage? Her mama looks like she's got her hands full."

Lilly followed the magician's gaze to where the girl's mother cradled a tiny bundle of blue. What a cute baby! But then Lilly caught sight of her groom staring at the infant and found a whole new meaning for cute. Beaming at the tiny face, Dallas's expression had turned to pure mush.

Wow...her heart felt ready to burst.

She'd been terrified that, because he hadn't asked the smallest question about her baby, Dallas had changed his mind about wanting to become a father, but seeing him now, gazing upon a stranger's infant, then taking extraordinary care wheeling the girl toward the stage, Lilly again had her decision to marry him confirmed.

"There you go, sir," Elvis said. "Wheel that darling right on up the ramp, then you can take your seat."

For Lilly, with Dallas back beside her, the rest of the show passed in a blur of jumping toy poodles, squawking parrots and barely contained tears. Never could she remember having been so happy. With the help of the Internet, she'd found a wonderful father for her child.

Yes, but what about a wonderful husband for you?

She swallowed hard and cast a glance Dallas's way.

No. No matter how many times as a young woman she'd dreamed of Prince Charming sweeping her off her feet, she had to keep in mind that, now, it would simply never happen. The current platonic arrangement she shared with Dallas was beneficial for them both. If she were to open herself up to the kind of pipe dreams that had led to her involvement with Elliot, she'd only be inviting more trouble into her life.

All that said, Dallas seemed to be getting a genuine kick out of not so much watching the show, but watching how much the children around him enjoyed the show. Meeting this one-in-a-million man had been a miracle, and while she knew their feelings would never move beyond friendship, at the moment she very much felt that she had already made a lifelong friend. And somehow, she thought, swallowing past the lump in her throat, that would be enough.

She and Dallas laughed at the same corny jokes, she adored his taste in flowers and rings, they'd even eaten the same unconventional breakfast. By the time Sparky the Wonder Dog was readying for his brave fire leap and her husband had taken her hand in his, Lilly no longer felt sorry for herself, but more like the luckiest woman alive.

All too soon the show was over and they were the last to leave the small theater. While Dallas made a quick run to the rest room, she waited for him in the foyer, counting the seconds to his return.

When he strolled out of the makeshift lobby wearing a cheesy grin, she said, "What are you up to? You look like you've been doing a lot more than going to the bathroom."

He shrugged and slipped his hands into his pockets, where she could have sworn she detected the sound of crinkling plastic.

"Dallas Lebeaux, what are you hiding?"

He kissed the tip of her nose. "Can't a guy keep a secret from his wife?"

"Did you buy me a present?"

Again, all she got from him was a maddening shrug, then, "Guess you'll have to wait and see."

"Hmm, sounds intriguing." She didn't press him further, for if there was anything she liked more than her new husband, it was surprises!

"Whoa, it's bright out here," Finn said, holding the door open for his adorable wife as they moved from the dark ex-grocery store to blinding midday sun.

"It sure is." On the way to the car, she brought her hand to her forehead to shade her eyes. Sunbeams shot through the paste diamond in her gumball-machine ring, reminding him for a second of the antique ruby and diamond he'd almost slipped on Vivian's hand. The ring had been his grandmother's, then his mother's.

Giving that ring to Vivian would have been the worst mistake of his life.

But then if marrying his real fiancée would have been *just* a mistake, what did marrying a hired fiancée amount to? Full-out catastrophe?

He eyed the scooped neck of the pink T-shirt Lilly had changed into. No catastrophe there. The full upper curve of her breasts peeked at him, practically sending him an engraved invitation to feel how soft they were and pliable and—

"Wasn't that girl you helped onstage adorable?"

"What? Huh?" Finn, reaching to unlock, then open Lilly's car door, was still focused on the adult entertainment.

"Don't tell me you already forgot her corkscrew pigtails?" she said, climbing inside the car.

Hell no, he hadn't forgotten the girl or her baby brother. It was just that the topic of kids was too painful to bring into this lark he and Lilly called a marriage.

"You're going to make a great father," she said after he slid behind the wheel. "My brother says you can tell a good parent by their patience, and what with all my blubbering last night and the church thing this morning—" she transfixed him with her near-flood-stage baby blues "—what can I say? You're a patient guy. A guy I know is going to make a great dad."

Talk about hitting below the belt. How had Mitch known Finn yearned to be a father? The power Lilly wielded with her body already had Finn losing control. If she started talking babies, too, he'd be a goner.

Figuring the best way to avoid the issue was to ignore it, he started the car.

"Where to?" he said.

"Want to go back to the motel and talk?"

"Nah," he said, backing out of their parking space. "It's too early for *talking.* How about playing a few slots?"

CHAPTER FOUR

"COME ON, BABY… MOMMY needs a new pair of shoes." Lilly pulled the one-armed bandit's lever, then watched in disgust as once again, her nickel investment paid a dividend of exactly squat.

"You're not doing so hot," Mr. I-Can't-Lose said smugly from his stool beside her. His coin tray was heaped with nickels to the point that he'd had to get one of the jumbo-size SlotWorld coin cups to hold his overflow. And wouldn't you know it? Just as she looked his way, his machine hit triple blue sevens *again.*

"Awesome!" he shouted. "That's twenty more bucks! I'm rich!"

Great. You're rich and the chink, chink, chink of nickels spewing out of your machine is giving me a headache. As were the dinging bells of other winning machines—not to mention the cigar cloud haze from the old guy on the next row.

Sighing, Lilly reached into her wallet for another five-dollar bill to slip into the change portion of the machine.

"You know, beautiful," Dallas said with an annoyingly warm smile, "you're welcome to grab a handful of my nickels."

"Thanks, but I've never been too keen on accepting charity."

"We're married. What's mine is yours." Before she

could stop him, he dumped his coin cup into the base of her machine.

"Hey, what'd you do that for?" He was still leaning into her personal space and suddenly she was far more disturbed by his oh-so-male scent than his nickels.

"I did that," he said, leaving his stool to straddle her knees, "because you need to loosen up. This is our honeymoon for heaven's sake and here you are worrying more about beating a stupid slot machine than getting to know your husband."

Lilly gulped. She'd only imagined the heat of his breath on her chest, right? "Um, Dallas…" she managed to say though her lungs felt strangely weak. "I, ah, think you should get back to your own stool. Someone might take your machine."

He flashed her a wicked grin before glancing down one way, then the other of their dead-end aisle. "Looks to me like we've got the whole place to ourselves. Hmm, whatever shall we do with all this privacy?" He slipped his hands to her waist, shocking her with a sudden turn of the tables that put him back on his own stool, landing with her on his lap.

She took a long time drawing her next breath, praying the additional air might still her frenzied pulse. Rats. No such luck. "Dallas, please…"

"Please what?" he said, his breath hot against her neck, her right ear. "Please, kiss you? Please slide my hands up your shirt? Please take you back to our poor, lonely suite?"

Without waiting for her reply, he did slip his hands under her shirt, and such was her shock—not to mention secret, aching delight—she froze, allowing him to skim his open palms up her torso until finally reaching her silk-covered breasts. The heat of his palms caused her nipples to traitorously swell, and she deeply, honestly searched for a reason to push him away. But in the end, the only dizzying thought that sprang to mind was that Dallas was now her husband. She was his wife. And if they stayed their current course, no matter how impossible it seemed, every dream she'd ever had would be well on its way to coming true.

Skimming her hands to his back, she arched into him, licking her lips before darting her gaze to make one last check they were alone. However wary she might have been about ever again opening her heart, the attraction drawing her ever-closer to her husband was a powerful thing. Two seconds later, when Dallas still hadn't crushed his lips to hers, she decided to live life on the edge by cupping the back of his head and drawing him to her, finishing the job herself.

Dear Lord, Finn thought on the heels of a groan. Had he ever partaken of a woman so sweet? Lilly's kisses tasted like ice cream and cotton candy. Bubble gum and red hots. She was the most honeyed, most indescribably delicious thing he'd ever tasted and he couldn't wait for more. Damn Mitch. Finn had won his part of the bet fair and square. Whatever happened between Lilly and him from this point on was gravy—or maybe that should have been chocolate sauce!

"Oh, Dallas," she softly crooned. "You have such a way with kisses."

Screech. There went those damned mental brakes.

Like fingernails on a chalkboard, Lilly's calling him Dallas grated his nerves. That's it. Once and for all, they had to establish the perimeters of their relationship—not that they even had a relationship—but before he made love to her, which he fully planned to do by the end of the day, Finn wanted to hear *his* name spilled from those full, pouty lips.

"Um, Lilly," he said, summoning superhero strength to push her even slightly away. "We need to talk."

"We will," she said, marching a parade of kisses down his neck. "Later."

"I know, but don't you think we should talk now?"

Kiss, kiss. "Now that you taught me how much fun kissing can be, I'd much rather kiss now, and talk later."

Dear Lord. She ducked to kiss his collarbone and the indentation at the base of his throat. She was absolutely right. Now was not the time to talk. Now was the time to stand up, tuck Lilly's legs around his waist and march to the nearest utility closet to finish what this minx had started. Well, technically he'd started this particular escapade, but then at this point, who was going to call him on a technicality? Yep, without a doubt, now was the time to—

"Excuse me," said a graveled voice from behind him. "Are these machines taken?"

Finn looked up.

An elderly couple walked in their direction. They each had spiky gray hair and matching T-shirts that read Alta Vista Seniors Rock!

He groaned.

Lilly giggled. "Nope," she said to the man. "Use any of them you want."

"Way to go," Finn muttered in his bride's ear. "And this was just getting good."

"Shame on you," she said, eyes sparkling. "After our agreeing to take things slow, you did realize my kisses weren't going any further, didn't you? I'm a good girl. I would never even consider indulging in a serious public display of affection."

"Right. After what we just shared, you're a good girl my—"

"Oops…better watch that language." She pressed her fingers to his lips.

"Woman." He gave her saucy behind a light smack before hefting her back to her own stool. "Either sit there and play nice, or I'm going to take you back to our suite and ravage you senseless. What's it going to be?"

Already knowing her answer, Finn scooped the nickels in his machine into a plastic coin bucket.

"What are you doing?" she asked.

He froze. "What's it look like I'm doing? We're going back to our suite ASAP, right?"

"Wrong. You gave me two choices, remember? And I choose to stay here and play. After all," she said, glancing toward her meager pile of coins. "I have a lot of catching up to do, don't you think?"

"No. What I think is that—"

"Oh look, there's a waitress and I am kind of hungry. Ma'am?" she called out with a friendly wave. "Could you please bring me some popcorn and a Shirley Temple?"

THREE HOURS' WORTH of slot-playing later, in a mall attached to the casino, Lilly asked Dallas, "Tell me again why you didn't think to pack a suitcase for our honeymoon?" Her words barely rose above the sound of a barbershop quartet competing with the food court's waterfall.

"I did pack," he said, "but I didn't think to bring my bag to Lu's."

"Lu's? Is that what you locals call Luigi's?"

"Yep."

A trio of belly-ring-baring teens passed by, nearly running Lilly into an ivy-filled planter in their blatant ogling of her husband.

"That was rude," she said after they passed.

"What?" Dallas glanced over his shoulder. "I didn't see them do anything."

"You wouldn't."

"Great. A department store," he said, veering to the right. "I'm a one-stop-shopping kind of guy."

Grasping her hand, he towed her through the mirror-and-glass cosmetic section with all its exotic scents and women, and again Lilly noticed how much attention *her* husband was receiving.

"Evenin', ladies," he said to a pair of sleek brunettes standing behind the Chanel counter. "Nice place you have here."

"Thanks," the taller one said. "Come back and see us when you can stay a while." The woman then had the nerve to pucker up her big, harlot-red lips and blow Dallas a kiss.

A kiss!

"Did you see that?" Lilly complained under her breath.

"No, what'd I miss this time?"

While the two thoroughbreds ducked their heads together and snickered, Lilly slipped her arm around Dallas's waist, making sure her left-hand ring finger—along with its ring—was visible. Honestly, what was this world coming to? Couldn't those two find their own men?

"Did you have to be so polite?" she said, hoping it was overwrought pregnancy hormones and not too many kisses that had brought out this sudden possessive streak.

"Sure, I did. Mama taught me to be polite to all the ladies—" he leaned close enough to finish his sentence in Lilly's ear "—especially the pretty ones. Like you." Before stepping onto the down escalator, he finished his flattery with an enchanting kiss to her cheek.

Wow. Wow. Wow. With a hundred years of composition time, Dallas couldn't have thought of a more perfect comeback. Oh, she knew her breakup with Elliot was far too fresh for her to even think about falling for another man, but honestly, how was she supposed to resist Dallas? He was charming and kind and honest and dependable. No wonder so many women found him tempting.

"What do you think of these?" Finn asked a few minutes later, in front of a rack of khakis, cursing Vivian for locking his suitcase in her car. Probably by the time he got back, her folks would have retrieved her yellow Mustang from the church parking lot and dumped his suitcase in the Lost River. After she'd taken off with Mr. Motorcycle, they'd actually scolded Finn for not chasing after her and bringing her back!

"Khakis are nice. I imagine you get tired of wearing a suit to work every day, huh?"

He frowned. "A suit?" Boy, Mitch had done a lousy job on the dossier he'd given Lilly, but that was all right.

Tonight Finn had big plans, starting with buying a new set of duds, then taking his bride out for a nice dinner, at the end of which he'd force her to come clean or stick her with the bill. Okay, so he probably wouldn't stick her with the bill, but for the hell she'd put his swollen nether regions through that afternoon, the least she could do was pay for his meal.

"Yeah, you know, a suit. As in three-piece or monkey?"

He grinned. "Let's just say Monsieur Levi is my favorite tailor."

She flashed him a funny look before moving on to the next rack. "This is nice," she said, showing him an emerald-green Polo pullover. Holding it to his chest, she added, "Perfect. This color looks great with your eyes."

"You like it, huh?"

She nodded.

"Great. Put it in the cart."

"We don't have a cart, remember? They're all back at the Elvis show holding Sparky the Wonder Dog T-shirts."

"Right," he said with a laughing groan. "How could I forget?"

She wrapped her arms around him in a spontaneous hug, and for an instant, holding her with the shirt she'd selected caught between them, everything in the world felt right. Time stood still and all that mattered was Lilly. Lilly sharing his love of hamburgers for breakfast. Lilly laughing beside him while Elvis coaxed a bunch of poodles and parrots into barking and squawking "Don't Be Cruel." Lilly, kissing him on a slot-machine stool, making him feel like the luckiest—not to mention randiest—man alive.

"We're starting to have quite a shared history," she said shyly, pulling away to move on to the next rack of shirts.

"Oh yeah?"

"Just think of all we've managed to squeeze into one

day. Sheesh, the last guy I dated barely even took me out for dinner before he was expecting me to fall into his bed."

Finn narrowed his eyes. "How did that make you feel?"

"How do you think? Awful. All I wanted was a piece of Elliot's time, but in the end, all I got was a piece of him."

"What do you mean?"

She ducked her gaze. "You know."

No, I don't, and he was itching like hell to ask, but couldn't—or maybe *wouldn't*—would be the more correct term. A second ago, when she'd held up that shirt to his chest, they'd felt cozy again, like a couple, just like when she tied his bow tie at their first attempt at a wedding. But knowing her capacity for deceit, he knew better than to step any further into her spell.

She was an enchantress, weaving a powerful potion about his senses. He knew better than to fall for her, yet every time he smelled her floral perfume, he felt a little more lost. If she had been any other woman, that fact would have thrilled him. But she was hooked up with Mitch, and the day Vivian left him, Finn had promised himself to never, ever get mixed up with another conniving woman.

"What size do you wear in jeans and I'll grab you a pair of 501s," she said, evidently as happy to change the subject as he was.

"Thirty-four thirty-six. Thanks." Finn felt like a dope for not asking her more about this Elliot character. Even though Lilly was hooked up with Mitch, she deserved better than the kind of second-rate treatment her last guy had given.

Trailing after her, he wondered how she knew he

wore 501s. He wished she'd known by some kind of powerful ESP thing they had going between them, but alas, the fact that she knew what kind of jeans he wore could only mean one thing—Mitch had finally gotten one of his facts right.

Once they selected and purchased slacks, jeans, a couple T-shirts and boxers—even a new belt and shoes—Finn changed from his tux to Lilly's green shirt and the khakis, then guided his bride back out into the mall.

In front of the waterfall, the barbershop quartet had been replaced by a group of elementary kids singing "How Much Is That Doggy in the Window?" The sight of them, not to mention their boisterous sound, caused his heart to ache. He wanted to start a family so much, which just made Lilly's deception harder to bear.

If only she were the ultralovable kissing angel she portrayed. Unfortunately, it was anyone's guess who she really was. For all he knew, she could be a professional con artist—available for hire on the Web at Scams-R-Us.com.

"Aren't they cute?" she said, holding her tummy with a misty look in her eyes. "And they're doing such a great job. Their parents must be so proud."

"Yep." If he talked about kids any more his heart would bust in two. Time to get back to business. "How about me taking you out to a swanky Italian place for dinner?"

Her eyes lit up. "Sounds great, but…" Her grin fell.

"But what?"

"All I brought is shorts and jeans. Remember how you said we wouldn't be doing anything fancy?"

"Right, because I wanted to *buy* you something

fancy. Come on," he said, patting himself on the back for quick thinking. "Let's go find the dress of your dreams."

That brought back her smile. "You, sir, certainly know how to charm a girl."

"Hey, they don't—" It'd been on the tip of his tongue to brag that people didn't call him "Lucky" Finn Reilly for nothing when it occurred to him that they were still playing the Dallas charade. Damn, damn and double damn. Well, because he was having such a great time, he'd let this farce continue until dinner, but over a nice bottle of Chardonnay, whether Lilly liked it or not, she was going to confess to the part she'd played in the bet.

"Don't what?" Lilly asked, pausing in front of a store window loaded with dresses.

"Nothing. I forgot what I was going to say."

Oblivious to the battle raging in his head, she flashed him her prettiest grin. "Don't you hate it when that happens?" Her attention back to the dresses, she said, "Which one do you think would look best?"

Why did women do this? Vivian had asked this sort of question with her shoes and, invariably, when he chose the pair he honestly thought looked best, she called him hopeless. Told him he wouldn't recognize a good-looking shoe if it jumped up and kicked him on his—well, anyway, she hadn't valued his fashion opinion.

"Dallas? I'm waiting."

"Um, I like..." He dropped his voice to a mumble.

"Which one?" The children's choir launched into a number about Martians and car horns beep-beeping. "I couldn't hear you over the kids."

Oh hell, he might as well tell her the truth and get

his scolding over with. "I like the simple black one. It looks like that silky fabric would feel good against your skin…and mine." He flashed her his most devilish grin.

"Oh, Dallas!" Flinging her arms around his neck, she gushed, "What are the odds that out of all those dresses, you'd choose the exact same one as me?"

"I did?" He gulped. "Yeah, well, I suppose that's easy for you to say now."

Stepping away from him, she placed her hands on her hips. "Dallas Lebeaux, have you no faith in your fashion sense? That dress is amazing. Any woman would be thrilled to wear it." Grabbing him by the hand, she towed him into the store. "Come on, I want to see if it fits."

FROM INSIDE a fuchsia dressing room that had black feathers lining the ceiling, Lilly peeked between the door slats to see Dallas seated on a hot-pink velvet love seat. Ricky Martin crooned a love song over hidden speakers and the air was thick with rose-scented potpourri. Never had a man looked more out of place or ill at ease, yet there her husband sat, patiently waiting for his personal fashion show.

After slipping off her shorts and T-shirt, Lilly drew the cool black silk over her head, shoulders, breasts and hips, then surveyed her image in the mirror. Wow. The garment clung in all the right places and none of the wrong. It did show far more cleavage than she'd thought she had, but seeing as she was now a married woman, she figured it wouldn't hurt to give her husband a thrill.

After fluffing her hair and applying fresh lipstick, Lilly was ready for her one-woman show.

"Taa-daa," she finally said, throwing open the dressing-room door.

Bull's-eye.

Dallas's slightly dazed expression was exactly what she'd been aiming for. "What do you think?" she asked, knowing full well she looked better than she ever had.

"What I think," he said, clutching his chest, "is that you're trying to do your old man in for the life insurance. Seriously, woman. You look hot."

CHAPTER FIVE

"SO THERE WE WERE," LILLY said later that evening over fettuccine Alfredo at Vicienti's Ristorante. "My best friend, Gail, and I were tossing this diving brick around in the locker room. Swim practice was over, but Gail's dad had called our coach to tell him he'd be late. So anyway, we knew we had plenty of time to head out to the parking lot, so we figured why not start a game of locker-room catch? All was going great until I slipped on a wet spot on the tile and the brick went flying straight into one of the sinks. Crash. The porcelain shattered in at least a hundred pieces."

"Oh, man, what'd you do?" Finn asked, entranced not only by Lilly's latest story of her childhood misadventures, but her captivating features. Candlelight made her skin glow honey-gold and her natural-blond curls kissed blushing cheeks. Her eyes had become inviting seas of blue and no matter how hard Finn tried convincing himself she was the enemy, he feared he was falling for her.

Though the restaurant was crowded, their corner table might as well have been their own private paradise. Roaming violinists played Italian love songs and the air smelled ripe with tomatoes, fresh baked bread, and an aromatic bouquet of herbs.

"What'd we do?" Lilly repeated, filling his soul with her silvery laugh. "What we did was run like the devil.

That night, I stayed over at Gail's and we thought we were home free—at least until, unbeknownst to us, our coach called her father. What we hadn't realized—duh—was that since we were the only two left in the locker room, we were the only kids who could have been to blame for the broken sink. Thank goodness, my folks were out of town that weekend and my brother, Mark, on vacation from law school, pretended to be Dad so I wouldn't get in trouble."

Finn frowned. "So if Mark covered for you, what kind of lesson did you learn?"

"Well…" Clouds passed over her sky-blue eyes and she nibbled on her full, lower lip. "I guess at that time I didn't learn much of anything, other than to be grateful for my quick-thinking brother. But now… since meeting you, I feel reformed."

"How's that?"

"I've finally learned to handle my own damage control. And now that I'm Mrs. Dallas Lebeaux, that whole mess with Mr. Elliot Dinsmoore has gone from being a problem to a blessing."

Reaching for a bread stick, Finn felt as if Lilly were speaking in code. Who was this Elliot Dinsmoore guy she kept bringing up? And since she was no longer with him, what kind of problem did she have? Because from where Finn was sitting, he saw that her biggest problem was being associated with Mitch.

Thoughtfully chewing, Finn figured that maybe she'd been doing so much acting that she'd somehow mixed up her roles.

"Mmm, the music is beautiful isn't it?"

"Not half as beautiful as you." Despite her being a soulless conniver, Finn couldn't take his eyes off his bride. Her eyes, her lips, her golden curls. Why did everything he thought he knew about her have to be a mirage? "Want to dance?" he asked, yet again putting off the inevitable confrontation of calling her bluff.

"I'd love to."

He stood, offered her his hand, and then they swayed as one to Italian love songs as old as time. Her so-called simple black dress dipped dramatically in the back and he couldn't resist skimming the tips of his fingers down her spine. Lilly's skin was magnolia-smooth and she smelled fresh and pure—like soap and a light shampoo that could have been sunshine in a bottle.

With a mewing sigh, she rested her cheek against his chest. Her soft curls tickled his chin. "This is nice," she said. "Makes me think we just might be one of those couples who really do live happily ever after."

He winced. Why did she keep doing this? Acting as if everything between them was as it should be?

Mitch wasn't a wealthy man. How much did she stand to gain by stringing Finn along? Shoot, for all he knew, she could be trading her services in exchange for Mitch's carpentry talents—shabby as they were.

"Dallas?"

"Yep. Our marriage is a fairy tale all right." Only he wasn't talking the typical *Cinderella* or *Beauty and the Beast,* but more of a *Draculette* with him cast as the vamp's victim!

"Ready to go back to our suite?"

"Are you?"

He felt her nod.

"Okay..." Taking her by the hand, he led her through a garden of well-dressed diners. "But do you mind if, before we go, we talk?"

The little minx answered by shyly averting her gaze. "I-if you don't mind, I'd rather go back to the motel. I never thought I'd be saying this, but after that buffet of sweet kisses you gave me this afternoon, I'm kind of hungry for dessert."

BY THE TIME they reached their suite, Lilly wondered if people died from longing?

Her one night with Elliot hadn't been any big deal. At the time, she had thought she loved him, but now she knew better. She had never loved Elliot. She'd only been lured to him by the notion of love that she'd waited her whole life to find. Now, what she felt for Dallas, while it couldn't possibly be love, was at once wild yet safe. Unnerving yet comfortable. How it was possible that, after only one day of marriage, she felt irrevocably drawn to him, she didn't know. Tonight the only thing she truly did know was that her whole life up to this point had been based upon crazy, incalculable risks. But here, in Dallas's arms, she felt grounded and finally, wonderfully mature.

While he struggled to get the card key to work, she giggled.

He turned to her and growled.

"You'd better watch it," he said, after finally opening the door. "I've had about all of your teasing I care to take."

"Ooh, big threats. Bet you can't back 'em up with action." Inside the room, the door closed and locked behind them, she pinned him to the wall for a surprisingly hungry kiss.

"For you being a bettin' woman," he said on a groan, "you sure don't know much about knowing when to fold."

He skimmed his big hands down her bare back and when he reached her bottom, he gripped it hard, lifting her off her feet and against his arousal. Knowing he was as hot for her as she was for him only made him that much more attractive and she deepened their kiss, doing things with her tongue that she'd only read about in books.

"I've got to have you," he said. "Right here. Right now. No more games, Lilly. This is for real."

"Oh…yes…" What games he was speaking of she didn't have a clue. She'd just add his cryptic statement to the ever-growing pile of things they'd talk about in the morning. Right now, though, nothing mattered but that he'd set her on her feet.

Fingers splayed on her hips, he knelt before her, shoving up her dress, revealing her black lace panties.

"Wow," he said on a groan before kissing the barely there, center vee panel. Her blood turned to shimmering honey. Need pulsed between her legs.

He pushed her dress higher, kissed the crown of her belly and ran his tongue in agonizingly slow circles around her navel. She sliced her fingers through his hair, urging him which way she didn't know.

Higher went her dress, and then he was standing, tugging it all the way over her head. The silky garment caught on her left earring. Keeping his touch tender, he separated the fabric from the gold stem, swearing softly under his breath when the task took longer than expected.

Exposed to the room's nighttime chill, her braless nipples puckered and hardened. From somewhere in the depths of the mighty Mount Vesuvius, red light glowed, reminding her, when her husband took her hardened bud into his mouth, of how close she was to the first of her own personal eruptions.

He moved his kisses to her throat and she arched her

head, granting him access to all he desired. "Please…" she said, not sure what she was begging for but knowing, whatever it was, she wanted it to come soon.

Her fingers at the button to his slacks, she nimbly undid it, then slid down his fly. "Come on. Just like you said. Right here. Right now."

He stopped, curved his fingers around her throat, planting his thumb beneath her chin. Searching her eyes, he said, "You're sure?"

"Yes. I need you inside me." *To prove what I'm feeling isn't a dream.*

It took only seconds for him to tear his shirt over his head and toss it to the floor beside her dress. Another second for him to rip the side strings of her fragile panties. "Oops," he said, holding up the wisp of fabric as if it were a prize. "Guess I didn't realize my own strength."

"I did," she said with a knowing smile, skimming her hands up his sculpted chest.

He tossed what was left of her panties to the growing pile of clothes, then once again was lifting her, only this time, he urged her knees around his waist.

"What about your pants?" she asked, entwining her arms about his neck.

"What pants?" With a wink and simple shifting of his boxers, he released himself. One swift, sure thrust later, she sighed when her body swallowed him whole.

Sweating, panting, she clung to him while over and over he thrust and pressure built. She kissed his ear and neck and when the spellbinding torture became too great, she bit his shoulder, frenzied from need.

Higher and higher her spirit soared, and always, just when she felt near the top of a towering peak, there was another mountain to climb, another icy, hot cliff to scale.

She pressed her fingertips into his back, bracing for the elemental rush awaiting her at the top. "Yes," she cried. "Oh, yes, yes, yes..." And then she was there, at the summit, and all around her, sun exploded and angels sang and if only for that instant, her life reached the pinnacle of perfection.

FINN AND HIS BRIDE were lounging in the eerie red glow of the bubbling crater Jacuzzi when she asked, "When you were a kid, what was your favorite game to play?"

"That's a tough question." Especially since she was naked against him, running her short pink nails in slow circles through the hair on his chest. Feeling himself swelling all over again, he tried to stay focused. "Let's see, Monopoly was fun. And playing Matchbox cars." He took another second to think. "But I guess my favorite game would have had to be playing explorer. The area where I grew up had an old silver mine we weren't supposed to mess around in, but did anyway. About a quarter mile down into one of the tunnels, the miner's shaft opened into a cave that was a real freak of nature. There was even a small lake. A gang of us guys would go down there with lanterns and play pirate, or gold miners, or jungle explorer—didn't really matter what the theme was. We always had a good time."

"That does sound fun." She kissed an indentation in his shoulder.

"Come to think of it," he said, gazing at their surroundings, "this suite reminds me of that old cave."

The walls and ceiling had been rounded, then coated in bumpy concrete to resemble the inside of a lava tube. The bed consisted of a huge multileveled platform upon which piles of plush pillows and fake fur rugs had been artfully strewn.

On the wall across from the bed roared a gas log fire—okay, so it might not have exactly roared, but it was putting out a fair amount of light and heat.

"Did you ever take any girls down there with you?"

"One. Her name was Shannon Jowoskiwitz and she waited until after we hiked all the way down to tell me she was afraid of the dark. So, here I'd set up this big seduction scene. You know, mixed up a canteen of extrasugary cherry Kool-Aid, snitched a whole box of saltines, and the second we got to my favorite rock where I planned to wow her with a kiss, she freaked and demanded I show her the passage out."

"I'm sorry," his bride said, and because the mood was right, Finn believed her. "Did she give you a kiss once you brought her back outside?"

"Nah, by then she said she was late for dinner and had to hurry home."

A thoughtful expression lingering on her face, Lilly said, "I've never been afraid of the dark."

"Oh?" Finn placed his hands on her hips and drew her up the length of him for a long, wet kiss. "What else aren't you afraid of?"

"Mmm, not spiders. And I've never been afraid of—" her eyes sparkled with mischief as her fingers dallied beneath the red bubbles "—big snakes."

Finn gasped when she grabbed hold of him and gave him a squeeze. "Ouch. Do you know what you're playing with, little girl?"

"Only my favorite new toy."

That was all the cue Finn needed to take this game

to a naughty new level. With a swoosh, he rose from the water, scooping his bride along with him.

"What are you doing?" she protested laughingly, kicking her legs while he headed for the lowest level of the bed, which was only a few feet from the fire.

"What do you think I'm doing? I'm playing explorer and you're my captured native."

"That's not politically correct," she said with a teasing tsk-tsk.

"Okay," he said, gently setting her on the faux-fur-covered platform and placing a leopard-print pillow beneath her head. "How about if I pay you to be my captive?"

She pretended to look shocked. "That's even worse. Then I'd be like your concubine."

"Yes," he said, eyeing her before kneeling at her side to draw one hardened nipple into his mouth. "But you'd be my *favorite* concubine. And you know, along with favored status always comes special privileges."

"Like wha—" Before she could finish the question, he skimmed his fingertips along her abdomen and between her legs.

"Open sesame," he said, "And we shall see what treasures await us deep inside the sultan's secret cavern."

On a breathless giggle, she did as he asked, only to quickly realize he wasn't finding treasure but creating it. As if an invisible drum beat deep within her, with his fingers and tongue he established a rhythm old as time. Suddenly she was no longer Lilly, but the exotic chief of a long-forgotten nubile tribe.

"I—I think I like this game," she said, her breath coming in ragged spurts.

"Me, too." Like a stealthy jungle cat caught lapping forbidden cream, he looked up and shot her a lethally handsome grin. In the dancing firelight, his dark eyes shone obsidian and his skin was slick with sweat. Heat was building.

In the room.

In her body.

In her soul.

He brought her to climax again and again, and then he was again inside her, only this time, instead of him supporting her weight, she supported him, meeting him thrust for deeper thrust.

Their strange, glowing environment transported them to another time and place when there were no societal rules because there was no society.

They made up their own rules as they went along and fleeting words like *wild* and *unbridled* and *carnal* sprang to Lilly's fevered mind. They licked and nipped, and when exhaustion claimed them, their mating turned softer, sweeter, to touching and whispering and mewing indecipherable yet universally acknowledged words of affection.

Sated, they lay side by side, stroking each other's face and hair.

Right before his eyes, Finn watched as Lilly closed her eyes and drifted into a deep sleep. He instinctively thought to cover her, but the fire's warmth made the idea of using a blanket silly. Tropical heat encased them both, and Finn was in danger of drowsing off as well. The problem was, he didn't want to sleep, not when he was terrified of waking and discovering that this dream woman he knew as Lilly was gone.

In her place would be the real woman Mitch had hired.

Her name would be Sheila or Kimberly, and she wouldn't be soft, but hard as nails, capable of carrying out even this elaborate a hoax for nothing more than a little cash and the knowledge that she'd played him for a fool.

When he could no longer force himself to keep his eyes open, he let them fall closed, but even then, his last thought before losing consciousness was of her.

Of Lilly.

And of the question, how was he going to let her go?

LILLY WOKE SLOWLY, aware of every deliciously sore muscle in her body. Beside her, her husband softly snored.

To the right of the bed, sunbeams shafted through a tiny part in the red flame-patterned curtains, alerting her to the fact that morning had indeed come. What a wild and wonderful night. What a radical departure from the way she'd thought she would be spending it!

Frowning, it dawned on Lilly that no matter how incredibly attracted she was to her husband, a repeat performance of what she and Dallas shared must never happen. For if she spent too much more time in his arms, she was terrified of going that next step further, which was wanting him in her heart. And after the Elliot mess, opening herself up to another relationship simply wouldn't work.

Careful not to wake Dallas, she lifted his arm from where he'd draped it around her waist, then slid out from under him.

In the bathroom, she used the facilities, took a steamy shower, then fished through her suitcase for fresh, albeit slightly rumpled, green shorts and a white T-shirt.

She'd just brushed her teeth when it occurred to her how hungry she was. Knowing a delicious room-service breakfast was only a phone call away, she rummaged through a faux-fur-trimmed desk drawer for the menu, then ordered cheeseburgers and fries for two, along with ice water and carafes of both regular and decaf coffee.

By the time she'd finished blow-drying and curling her hair and applying light makeup, a knock sounded at the door.

On her way to answer it, she glanced at the platform they'd used as a bed, not surprised to find Dallas still fast asleep—not to mention naked as the day he was born. The sight of his sculpted body and the memory of how he'd used it to bring her a glorious amount of pleasure temporarily muddled her thoughts.

What was it she was supposed to be doing?

Another knock, this time harder, rattled the door.

Oh yeah. Breakfast.

She tossed a light blanket over Dallas's sleeping form, then, as the waiter knocked for a third time, she sang out, "Coming!"

"Hey," said a clean-shaven guy in his early twenties from behind a loaded white-clothed cart. "Did you order room service?"

"I sure did. Why don't you let me take it from here."

"No can do, I'm supposed to set up everything for you."

"Really, that's okay," she protested. "My husband's still sleeping."

"Oh. *Ooh.*"

While the kid blushed, Lilly commandeered the cart, capably steering it into the room. "If you'll wait a second, I'll get you a tip." Assuming she could find her purse.

Her gaze skittered from the floor to the bed to the desk, but it was nowhere to be found. What she did see was Dallas's wallet lying on the boulder serving as a bedside table. Figuring that since she was now his wife, he wouldn't mind if she snatched some cash, she opened it wide and drew out three ones she then handed to the waiter.

He said a quick thanks before jogging off down the hall.

Lilly had closed and locked the door and was heading back to the boulder to replace Dallas's wallet when she stumbled over her pile of luggage.

While she managed to catch herself, the wallet yawned, flying halfway across the room to land in a heap of credit cards and cash.

She had crossed over to it, stooping to gather everything into a tidy pile before sticking each card back into its respective leather slot when the name sprawled across the bottom of a credit card caught her eye. *Finnigan Reilly.*

Furrowing her eyebrows, she looked at the gas card beside the credit card. The name read *Finnigan Reilly.*

Heart pounding, hands trembling, she looked at a department store card, a library card, a blood donor card, even his tux rental ticket. All of them—every single one, read *Finnigan* or *Finn Reilly.*

Short of breath, pulse racing, she looked at her peacefully sleeping husband, then back to the wallet. She had to find Dallas's driver's license. Surely, with all those other cards, there had to be some kind of mistake. One look at his license would clear everything up.

Wham!

As if she'd received a physical blow, her worst fear

was confirmed. There, along with the official state seal of Utah, was undeniable proof. The man she had married wasn't trustworthy, mild-mannered, child-loving Dallas Lebeaux, but a total, complete—possibly even dangerous—stranger named Finn Reilly.

Lilly wanted to pull a Victorian stunt like collapsing in a fit of vapors, but she was much too strong a woman for that. Hand protectively over her womb, she marched to the stranger who had somehow become her husband and shook him as hard as she could. "Wake up!" she demanded.

"Huh? What?" He groggily came to. "What time is it?"

"It's time," she said, holding his driver's license a scant two inches from his face, "to tell me who the hell you are!"

CHAPTER SIX

"EXCUSE ME?" FINN SAID, wondering what could have turned normally mild mannered Lilly into this raving lunatic. "You know exactly who I am."

"No, I don't. I don't have a clue who you are other than a man who quite possibly kidnapped my real fiancé." After tossing his wallet in his face, she turned to the window, sobbing as if her best friend had died.

Lord Almighty, he'd had it with the acting. He'd meant to clear up this whole business about the bet long before they'd partaken of each other's many pleasures, but one thing had led to another and, well...

He'd be the first to admit that things had gotten a bit out of hand, but that was no reason for Lilly to go off on him. "Look, lady, you could win an award with all the boo-hooing you've been doing, but enough's enough. Mitch and I had a bet, fair and square, and I know you think you pulled the wool over my eyes, but you didn't. We're married, sweetheart, and I've got the license in my name to prove it."

"Stop." Lilly's head was spinning and she collapsed onto the nearest pile of faux fur. "What are you talking about? What bet? And who's Mitch?" How could this be happening? She'd planned her marriage to Dallas so carefully, covering every possible contingency, but never the scenario where she married the wrong man!

"What do you mean, what bet?" he said, scrambling

to his feet—all seventy-five gloriously naked inches of him! "You sashayed into Lu's telling me you were all ready for a wedding. You even addressed me by the wrong name to lead me off track, but I'm no fool, Lilly—if that's even your real name. I knew all along you were trying to marry me under the wrong name so Mitch could win Abigail on a technicality."

"Who's Abigail? And for the last time, who's Mitch?"

"You know damned well Abigail's my truck—the truck your boss planned to drive off in."

Now Lilly really did feel she was near fainting. The only question was whether it was a hunger faint or panic faint. Either way, she knew she didn't want to do it in front of this virtual stranger—a naked stranger! Had she really only yesterday said she liked surprises?

Reaching for a fry from the breakfast tray, she shoved it into her mouth and swallowed before ducking her head between her knees.

"What's the matter with you?" he asked.

"I'm about to pass out from the shock of all this—as if you'd even care."

"What's that supposed to mean? I'm the injured party here. All along your sole purpose in this marriage has been to scam me, and now, you've decided to play the innocent victim? I don't think so—and would you please look at me when I'm yelling at you?"

"I can't look at you. You're naked!"

"Yeah, well, that didn't seem to bother you much last night, Little Miss Game Player."

That brought her out of her faint. "Why you..." Storming to her feet, she pummeled her fists against his chest, but she might as well have been punching a brick wall. This Finn person was built.

As she remembered all too well in intimate detail!

Furiously blushing, she turned her back on him, but luckily she was at least facing the food tray. Reaching under the plastic lid, she snatched three more fries.

"You might save a bit of that for me," he said, grabbing some fries for himself. "I swear, the only other woman I've seen eat more than you was my best friend Matt's sister—and she was eight months' pregnant!"

It was on the tip of Lilly's tongue to tell this creep that she *was* pregnant, but then she decided against it. Who knew how he felt about babies, let alone the fact that she'd be having one in seven months!

"Could you *please* put some clothes on?" she said, sharply averting her gaze. "You need to tell me who you are, but I'd appreciate you doing it fully dressed."

"By all means, your highness. Anything else your conniving heart desires?"

"Yes." Her lower lip started to quiver and the back of her throat felt tight. She'd never liked fighting with her brothers and sisters and she sure wasn't enjoying this altercation with the man who claimed to be her husband. First one tear fell, rapidly followed by another and another. "I—I want you to stop yelling," she wailed. "A-and put s-some clothes on, a-and tell me who Mitch is...a-and—"

"Okay, okay, I get the picture." Finn put his hands up to stop her midstream. "Just quit crying." Spying his new jeans spilling from a nearby bag, he snatched them out, jerked the tags off and pulled them on, all the while feeling strangely self-conscious. Lord, he had a tough time thinking straight when Lilly was crying, and he sure couldn't find it in his heart to stay angry with her. What he really felt like doing was pulling her into a hug, but that was ludicrous in light of their current situation, which was growing stranger by the minute.

Why did she keep asking such weird questions? If she didn't know who Mitch was, or at the very least who Abigail was, then what did that say about who she was?

The question struck terror in his soul.

Sitting quietly, nibbling on a juicy-looking cheeseburger, she watched him yank the tags off a red T-shirt and pull it over his head.

"What?" he said, his voice rougher than he'd intended.

"Nothing. I'm just wondering how I could have made such a huge mistake? I mean, I've made some doozies over the years, but this one takes the cake. And if you're not Dallas, then where is he?"

Finn's feeling of unease grew by a factor of ten.

"I know I would love Dallas. And he certainly loves me."

"That's some kind of love, lady, when, if what you're saying is true, you obviously didn't even know what the guy looks like or you wouldn't have thought I was him."

"I've seen his fuzzy picture."

"Great. Did you ever think it might be a good idea to actually meet the man himself before you ran off to marry him?"

"We did meet. Through e-mail. And I'm not the one who did something wrong here, mister. You were the one who should have told me right from the start who you were." Flashing him a look of horror blended with disgust, she said, "At least one good thing came out of all this."

"What's that?"

"At least we're not *really* married. Because for us to be *really* married, I would have had to marry you. Which I didn't. My marriage license reads Dallas Lebeaux, and since you're obviously not him, then we're obviously not married."

His stomach hit rock bottom. "Think again." She looked so alone and fragile, holding on to the food cart as if it were her only port in a mighty ugly storm. "Why don't you try to relax?" he said. "I'm thinking this explanation may take a while."

While he told her the details of Mitch's bet, she perched on the edge of the bed. Finished, Finn didn't know whether to be relieved or terrified that the woman he'd married was indeed named Lilly Churchill, or rather, Lilly Reilly.

"This is awful," she said with a pitiful sigh.

"Why? I know this mess would have been a whole lot easier to clean up if we hadn't..." Thoughts of exactly what they'd done caused his face to go all hot. "Well, you know what we did. Anyway, if we hadn't done that, we probably could have gotten an annulment, but now I think we'll have to go with the full-fledged divorce."

"No, no, no," she said, scrambling from the bed to furiously pace.

In the light of day, far from the pleasure den it'd been during the night, the room looked shabby—even tawdry. So, he mused, the night had been a dream after all. A dream that had turned into a genuine nightmare.

"No, we can't file for divorce this afternoon?"

"No, as in we can't file for divorce, period."

He scrunched his nose. "I'm afraid I'm not following you."

Turning her back on him, she headed for her suitcase, knelt before it and started folding like a woman possessed.

"Now isn't the time to do your laundry," Finn pointed out. "We need to be talking lawyers."

"There isn't going to be a lawyer," she said without stopping.

"I know I'm going to regret asking this, but why?"

"Because there isn't going to be a divorce. My whole life I've been either running from trouble or covering it up, but no more. Quite simply, by law—not to mention after what we did last night—we are now, for better, or in our case, worse—married. For life. *Forever.*"

"Are you nuts?" Finn asked. "We don't even know each other."

"Far from being nuts, as you so eloquently put it, I'm merely trying to make the best of a bad situation."

"So let me get this straight, you're calling being married to me a bad situation?"

"Yes. And as for how well we know each other..." She blushed a furious pink, folding all the faster. "After last night there isn't much we *don't* know about each other—except, of course, in your case, I'm still a little sketchy about your name, what you do for a living and, oh yeah, every single thing about you other than how you kiss."

"Ha! You have to admit I do that pretty damned well."

She ducked her gaze. "I will admit no such thing."

Steeling his jaw, Finn worked overtime on keeping his cool. "Excuse me, but were you in the same room as I was last night? Because if you were, I'd say you were every bit as into me as I was into you."

"How could I have been *into* you, when I don't even know you? The man I thought was my partner in the ultimate commitment two people can make is named Dallas. He's a dependable, hardworking lawyer in Salt Lake City and he loves both me and my—" She put her hand to her mouth.

"So just because you don't know me, I'm not dependable or hardworking? I'll have you know I've owned and operated my own highly successful construction business for the past ten years. I'm the very definition of dependable."

Lilly pulled the zipper around her suitcase, then stood, rewarding this Finn person's speech with a slow round of applause. "Bravo. That was very convincing. Now, if you'd care to prove how dependable you really are, could you please take me home?"

"Sure, if you tell me where you live."

"That's easy. As your wife, I guess I'm stuck living with you, Mr. Reilly."

STUCK LIVING WITH HIM?

Finn cast a narrow-eyed glance across the car's front seat at his sleeping bride.

How dare she act as if being married to him was some kind of hardship? After all, a lot of the women in Greenleaf considered him to be one heck of a prize.

Right. Which must be why Vivian ran off with Mr. Motorcycle.

Fuming all the harder, Finn chose to ignore his conscience's latest sarcastic remark.

With his elbow propped on the open window, warmed by bright Utah sun, and a dry desert breeze ruffling his hair, were it not for the company of his current companion, he would have been content. Just what kind of prize did she think she was? Sitting over there snoring for the past six hours, she was about as much fun as talking to a potato.

His gaze accidentally strayed to the curve of her cute tush encased in a pair of minty-green shorts. Admittedly she was one hell of a prize in the physical department, but that was it. Other than the eye candy she provided, she was a royal pain in his—

He gripped the steering wheel harder.

Of course, yesterday, he had sort of enjoyed her company.

Sort of, my horse's behind. I couldn't get enough of her. I liked her laugh, and the way she looked out for me. Tying my bow tie. Ordering my breakfast. Picking out my clothes...kissing me like she wanted me more than any other man in the world.

Eyebrows furrowed, it occurred to Finn how much he'd grown to care for Lilly over the past two days. How many times, when he thought she'd been hired by Mitch, had he wished things could be different between them? How many times had he longed for her to be the woman she'd pretended to be?

Talk about being careful what you wished for.

Every single thing he'd grown to adore in Lilly was the real deal. Even better, she was his wife.

His wife!

For years, he'd prayed to be in this very situation.

Well, not the part where his wife hated him and thought he was the worst lowlife to ever walk the planet, but the being-married part was still good.

He eyed Lilly again, noting the way her silky gold curls danced in the warm breeze, tickling her cheeks, making him green with envy that they were allowed to touch her and he wasn't.

Dammit, this was stupid.

The fact of the matter was that, even though their meeting was a colossal mistake, Lilly could deny it all she wanted, but they did have chemistry. He hadn't been with that many women, but he'd been with enough to know that nights like the one they shared were hardly the norm. He'd felt things with her he hadn't even believed were possible.

Best of all, she was one hundred percent trustworthy—unlike certain other women he'd almost married. A female who had enough moral convictions to remain married to him on a matter of principle was a hard thing to come by in this day and age. That fact alone told him that one thing he could always count on hearing from her was the truth.

Stirring beside him, she asked, "Are we almost there?"

"We've still got another forty-five minutes."

"Oh." Her tone sounded flat, as if she'd rather be scrubbing toilets than seated in a car beside him.

"You don't have to sound so excited."

"Good, because I'm not."

Finn raked his fingers through his hair. "Have you considered the fact that, aside from my name changing, I'm the same guy you were all over yesterday?"

"Ugh," she said, cradling her face in her hands. "Don't remind me. The things I revealed to you—and I'm not just talking about..." He caught her in a deep blush. "About, you know—last night—but stuff I've never told anyone but Dallas—the man I love."

"Yep, I can see where e-mailing could lead to true love."

"It did," she said, shifting on the seat to face him. "Whether you believe it or not, Dallas understood me in a way no other man ever has. He's my soul mate…" She reddened. "Well, at least he used to be."

"Which thoroughly explains why you don't want to divorce me to be with him."

Crossing her arms, she said, "You don't understand anything."

"Why don't you try explaining."

"Because after what you did, you don't deserve an explanation." Lilly turned her gaze to the window, to the same unremarkable stark, brown landscape they'd been passing through for hours. Without Dallas's safety net, she might as well consider the rest of her existence as void of love as this landscape was void of life.

"I'll probably regret asking this," Finn said, "but what exactly did I do that's so awful?"

"You married me under false pretenses. From the moment we first met you knew full well I had no intention of marrying you. Not even once did you question why I kept calling you Dallas."

"I already told you, I thought somebody hired you to dupe me. And if you're wanting to play the blame game, how about accepting some of it yourself? The bar and grill you walked into is called Lu's—not Luigi's. And the second you walked up to me, you should have asked to see my ID."

Finn looked to see how she liked them apples but soon wished he hadn't. Her big blue eyes were filling up and it'd been quite a while since the last time they had spilled. Now that he knew every tear she'd ever cried was real, he worried they'd be that much harder to take.

Before, when he thought she worked for Mitch, he'd had a good reason to harden his heart, but now, he felt kind of sorry for her—not because she'd wound up married to him, but because she was too stubborn to see him for what he was—a great catch!

"HERE WE ARE," Finn said while steering her car onto a winding, blacktopped driveway. "Home sweet home."

"Gee, don't strain yourself making me feel welcome."

"Believe me—" he flashed her a caustic smile "—after the way you've treated me today, I won't."

Ignoring him, Lilly watched three dogs that could only be described as mutts, ranging in size from a chicken to a mountain goat, tear around the side of a freestanding garage.

"Here comes the welcoming committee."

"Do they bite?"

"Nope. They might try kissing you, though." He shot a scorching wink Lilly's way before putting the car in park.

It was then she saw the house.

In a million, trillion years, she wouldn't have guessed that the stranger she'd somehow married lived in a carbon copy of her dream home. The Victorian castle was like something out of a movie. The yellow-and-white gingerbread-laced structure boasted twin turrets and even a widow's walk.

"You live here?" she said, wishing she could have erased some of her obvious awe.

"Yeah, *I* live here," he said, turning off the engine. "Why? Did you peg me for more of a shack kind of guy?"

"No, it's just that, I..." *Dreamed of living in this house my whole life—not with you, of course—but with a man who loves me.* She licked her lips and eyed the three adorable furry faces smacking their chops to get at her husband. "Let's just say you have a lovely home and leave it at that."

"Thanks," he said with the warmth of ice. Climbing out of the car, he sent the dogs into a fit of barking pleasure.

While Finn's attitude tempted her to demand he take her to her old apartment in a neighboring town, Lilly squared her shoulders and climbed out of the car, ready as she'd ever be to face her future. Hand on her tummy, she reminded herself that her whole life she'd been getting into bad spots and either covering them up or running away, but this time, this problem, she'd face dead on. Over the years, she'd put her parents through a lot of trauma, but this disaster took the cake. If they discovered she'd virtually hired a husband, only to end up not marrying him but a stranger, she wouldn't blame them for washing their hands of her.

"Ready to head inside?"

"Sure." As the biggest of the mutts, what looked to be an odd cross between a sheep dog and a dachshund, approached for a cautious sniff, she patted him between his ears. "What's his name?"

"Moe. The middle-size beagle mix is Larry, and the oversize Yorkie-terrier is Curly Sue."

"Nice to meet you all," she said, giving Larry and Curly Sue pats, too. As much as she tried holding her anger toward Finn intact, she'd always loved dogs and knew that any man who'd take in three such downright goofy looking beasts couldn't be all bad.

She gestured toward the trunk. "Shouldn't we carry in the luggage?"

"Leave it," he growled. "I'll get it later."

On a meandering brick path, she fell into step beside him. "Any time now, feel free to thaw your arctic chill.

I mean, I wasn't the one who doctored *my* marriage license by adding *your* name."

"Thanks," Finn said. "I'm feeling so much better now that you've pointed that out."

"You're welcome. I'm just doing my part to keep you on the straight and narrow."

"Oh, that's ripe coming from you, Miss Misfit."

"Yeah," she said, edging past him on the path, "but thanks to you, my correct title would now be, *Mrs.* Misfit." Eyeing the grand home up close, Lilly froze. "Not that you should take this as any reflection as to the way I feel about you, but again—wow. Nice house."

"Thanks, again. I think." Had she only imagined his voice softening?

"Did you build it?"

"Nah, the house is over a hundred years old, but I did restore it to its original grandeur. It's been in my family for all that time, but…" Finn couldn't bring himself to tell her that when his mom, dad and sister had died, he'd had to abandon this special place to live with his aunt in her mountain home located roughly forty-five minutes west of Greenleaf. The house was uncared-for through the years it took him to turn eighteen, and by the time he moved back in, he'd practically had to gut the entire structure.

Climbing the stairs leading to the wraparound porch, his feeling of pride choked him up. Eight white wicker rockers sat amongst red-impatience-topped side tables. That was one oversize rocker for him, one for his wife, and six for their kids. Leafy ferns hung from each of the porch's arches, drinking in what was left of the unseasonably warm Indian summer day.

Though you couldn't have paid him to admit it, he liked the way his bride stood gaping.

"This place is incredible," she said. "I can't get over how neat and tidy everything is. When my brothers were bachelors, their houses were always wrecks."

"What can I say? I run a tight ship."

"Can we go inside?"

"Might as well." He reached for her legs, but she squealed and backed away.

"What are you doing?" she demanded.

"Carrying you over the threshold. That's what newlyweds are supposed to do, isn't it?"

"Normal newlyweds, but we're hardly that."

Sighing, he crossed his arms over his chest. "So let me get this straight. because you don't believe in divorce after a couple sleep together, that means we're stuck with each other for the next fifty or so years, right?"

"Y-yes."

"And in all those fifty years, you plan on wielding this cold shoulder of yours as weapon?"

"I didn't say that. All I said was that I'd prefer you not carry me over the threshold. It's such a romantic, old-fashioned custom that if we were to take part in it, I'd feel guilty."

"Even though we'd have seven years of bad luck if we don't do it?"

"That's if you break a mirror. I don't think the threshold thing carries any cosmic punishment if you don't follow it, do you?"

"Beats the heck out of me, but at least I got you to think about something other than how awful I am." He thought he spied a glimmer of a smile behind her shadowed eyes and touched his index finger to the corner of her mouth. "I'm not making you laugh, am I?"

"No."

"Then how come that dimple in your left cheek is almost showing."

"I don't have a dimple," she said, grinning all the more.

"You do, too. During Sparky's big clown routine, I saw that dimple peeking quite a few times."

"Okay, okay," she said, now fully laughing. "I admit it, I have a dimple, but I got sick of my brothers teasing me about having a hole in my face, so don't you tease me, too."

He made grave business of marking an *X* across his chest. "Cross my heart and hope to—"

"Leave that last part off," she said. "I never like to hear people casually mention dying."

"Should I take that as a positive sign that at least you don't want me to croak?"

"Ha-ha."

"Wow, was that two laughs in a row from Miss Uptight?"

"Remember? All put-downs should now be in the form of a *Mrs.* And no, that wasn't a laugh, but sarcasm—there is a difference."

"Great. Now that we've cleared that up, how about it?" He lunged for her legs. "Will you let me carry you over the threshold?"

Something deep inside Lilly longed to say yes, but the practical side of her said, "No. I just wouldn't feel right." The minute she saw the crestfallen expression on Finn's face, she regretted turning him down, but then why should she care about his feelings when he'd so callously played with hers?

This whole mess could have been easily avoided if only he'd admitted not knowing her from the start, but now… Now she wasn't sure what to do, other than get through life minute by minute and try to string those minutes into some semblance of normalcy.

The playful spirit that had been present only a few minutes earlier had been replaced by a chilly north wind that had nothing to do with the day's sunshine and everything to do with her new husband.

Turning from her, he placed his key in the door's lock and turned it. With a lonely creak, the door swung open and he stepped aside. "After you."

"Thanks." Before her eyes even had a chance to adjust to the interior's gloom, she heard Finn stomp down the porch stairs. "Are you getting the luggage?" she called out. "Want me to help?"

"Nope. I'll get it later." He headed across the velvety green lawn—not toward the car.

"Where are you going?"

"Doesn't matter," he shouted without slowing or looking back. "Make yourself at home."

Home. Despite the day's heat, she rubbed her suddenly chilled forearms. Why was it that the beautiful house didn't seem nearly as welcoming without Finn?

CHAPTER SEVEN

"FINN!" LU CALLED OUT THE minute he stepped up to the bar. "It's good to see you. None the worse for wear, I suppose?"

"I wish." The beer-cryin' music playing over the jukebox hardly lightened his mood.

"Ah now, what's got you down? Did that cupcake you left here with get some sense in her head and decide not to marry you?"

All he could do was laugh, for if he didn't laugh over his ever-worsening situation with Lilly, he'd end up crying, and he was much too manly to indulge in tears.

Lu set a long-neck beer in front of him before wiping her hands on the tea towel she kept hanging behind the bar. "Don't look so glum. Surely Mitch isn't really going to take Abigail, and even if he does, at least that pretty little bride didn't run off with your heart. That's the prospect that had me worried—that and the fact that you'd be off the market to a gal who'd truly love you the way you deserve to be loved."

"Sorry to disappoint you, Lu, but you're wrong on every account. Care to join me in a toast?" He raised his beer to the few other folks at the bar. Old drunken Pete was sawing logs at his usual spot, and since Finn figured the old guy needed his beauty sleep far more than he needed another drink, he didn't bother waking him.

Lu's eyes narrowed to slits. "What is it we're toasting?"

"What else? My new bride."

"Congratulations," said a long-haired fellow Finn didn't recognize from a few stools down. His girl echoed those sentiments before they both raised their brown bottles to him and his wife.

Far from being happy about his news, Lu scowled. "Please tell me this is a joke. You didn't really marry that girl, did you?"

"Oh, yeah. I sure as hell did."

"Oh, Finn. Have your aunt and I taught you nothing over the years?"

"Guess not," he said, after taking another sip of beer.

"Good gracious gravy," the bartender said to no one in particular. "If this don't beat all. So? Where is she?"

"At the house."

"Her house, or yours?"

"Mine."

"And how do you feel about finally havin' a woman in that shrine to a future family you call home?"

He shrugged, took another sip of beer. "I could be better."

Elbows on the bar, she asked, "Feel like talkin' about it?"

He shook his head. "I'd rather drink about it."

"Don't you mean think?"

"Nope. I'm thinking clearer than ever, and I definitely meant *drink*."

Lu made a clucking sound. "Aw, now, Finn, you don't really mean that."

"What doesn't pretty boy here mean?"

Finn groaned.

Mitch. Just the guy he *didn't* want to see.

"You ready to hand over my money?" Mitch said, heaving himself onto the stool beside Finn.

"Sorry, old pal, but you lose."

"The hell you say. It's only Monday. What woman in her right mind would up and marry you after only knowin' you a day?"

"Her name's Lilly," Lu said, setting a draft beer in front of Mitch. "Pretty little thing, too. Saw her myself Saturday night—not an hour after your own girl practically had to wheelbarrow your drunken behind outta here."

The big man snarled. "I don't believe it. Show me proof."

Finn reached for his wallet and drew out the marriage license that had him in such hot water with Lilly. Showing the license to Mitch should have been a defining moment of his life, so how come it felt flat?

After a few minutes of careful reading, Mitch slammed his fist on the bar, rattling everyone's beers and Lu's few fancy wineglasses. "Damn you, Reilly. I know this is a trick."

At that, Finn laughed. "Trust me, old pal, the only trick here is being played on me. I'm the one stuck with a wife who's gonna hate me for the rest of my life."

THE KITCHEN CLOCK STARTED to chime in exact harmony with the hall grandfather clock. When the duo reached ten, Lilly, lingering over a pot of peppermint tea at the oak kitchen table, sighed, trying not to let the quiet in the rambling old house consume her.

Where was her husband?

Had her not allowing him to carry her over the threshold hurt his feelings that badly? She hadn't meant anything personal by it. It was just that her whole life she'd dreamed of partaking in the quaint old custom, only a big part of that dream had been making it come true with a man she loved.

Yes, Finn Reilly had been perfectly pleasant to her over the past two days, but that didn't bring her any closer to even liking him, let alone loving him. Without a trace of conscience, he'd tricked her into marrying him. And now, because of her own overblown conscience—not to mention fear of being caught in yet another disastrous mess—she was legally and morally bound to him forever. Which, considering how nice his house was, shouldn't have been that bad, but somehow the realization didn't make her feel any better.

The kitchen was a cook's dream with its stainless steel fridge and stove that boasted four gas burners and a grill that would be perfect for Saturday morning burgers. The countertops were made of cobalt-blue tiles and the backsplashes had contrasting yellow-and-white tiles with blue flowers. All the cupboards were incredibly well stocked with not only food but dishes, china and flatware—all services for eight.

Upstairs, there were even sleeping spaces for eight—ten counting the sunny guest room where she'd unpacked her belongings. The king-size master bed could have slept four, but every time she even thought about sharing the bed with Finn, her insides turned to mush.

That morning, when he asked her what kind of a kisser she thought he was, she'd lied when she told him he wasn't all that great. And maybe what they'd done in the big fur-piled bed in Vegas was partially what had her so upset. All her life, she'd tried so hard to be prim and proper—the kind of daughter her parents would be proud of—but how could a proper woman do what she'd done with a man she didn't even know?

But I do know him. He's my husband.

Ugh, he might have technically been her husband, but seeing how she hadn't even known his real name at the time she'd slept with him, somehow that made their magical night seem soiled. She wanted so badly to fit in with the wholesome, perfect, overachieving image the rest of her family portrayed, but yet again, she was the square peg trying to squeeze into a round hole.

She was the one who'd set fire to the family kitchen by leaving Jiffy Pop sizzling on the stove to answer a much-awaited call from Phil, her high school boyfriend. She was the one who'd lost jobs as both a grocery store clerk and a bank teller because she kept forgetting to set her morning wake-up alarm. Worst of all, she was the one who'd believed Elliot when he told her he loved her and would marry her and then, only *after* she slept with him, had he told her he was already married.

By now, the cumulative pain of a lifetime spent messing up had taken its toll and Lilly started to cry. She'd never flat out bawled as much as she had the past two days.

Was this normal?

Was she normal?

Was her baby normal?

The more she fretted the more she cried, and when the back door opened and Finn came rushing in, asking

"Lilly, honey, what's wrong?" It only seemed natural to stand up and go running into his arms. "I've ruined everything," she sobbed against his chest. "I've ruined your life and mine and—"

"Shh," he said, smoothing her hair. "You haven't ruined anything. In fact, in marrying me, you did an extraordinarily, extra superspecial thing."

After drying her eyes on his red T-shirt, which smelled faintly of cigarette smoke and beer, she sniffled, then asked, "What?"

"By marrying me, you won the bet. Look, Mitch paid me a thousand bucks cash." He fished a wad of ten hundred-dollar bills from the back pocket of his jeans and handed it to her. "If it'll cheer you up, this is all yours."

"I don't want that money. It's tainted, just like our marriage."

Finn frowned. "That's what Lu said you'd say, but I figured you to be a whole lot smarter than that."

"Oh?" She raised the golden arches she called eyebrows. Funny, but in the time he'd been at Lu's, Finn had forgotten how pretty his wife was. Pretty as the sunrise on that calendar his accountant gave him every year for Christmas.

"Have you been drinking?" she asked, hands on her saucy hips.

"Not that much."

"Uh-huh, and how did you get home?"

"I brought him." Matt strolled through the back door. "Figured he wasn't fit to drive."

"And you would be?" Lilly asked.

"I'm his best friend. Matthew Marshall at your service, ma'am. I was outside putting those mangy mutts to bed in the barn." He removed a green Greenleaf

Lumber ball cap before reaching forward to shake her hand. "Finn and I here have been through everything together. I thought it was only right that I meet his bride as soon as I had the chance."

"Thank you for driving him home, Matthew. I'm Lilly Churchill—or I guess that's Lilly Reilly now, huh?"

"And what a sweet name it is," Finn said, resting his head on his wife's shoulder. He gazed at the ceiling. "Yo, Matt-o, when did I install a rotating chandelier over this table?"

"You didn't, bud, which is why it's probably a good idea if I get you up to bed." Though Matt was a few inches shorter than his friend, he put Finn's right arm over his shoulder and guided him toward the stairs.

"Do you need help?" Lilly asked, trailing after them.

"Nah, I should be able to handle him. My buddy here never drinks more than he can handle unless he's upset over a woman—and even then he's only been this drunk three times in his life."

"When was that?" Lilly couldn't keep from asking.

"Well, let me think. One, would have to be the day Linda, his old high school flame, left Greenleaf to go to some fancy college out east. Two, would be last Saturday night when he was so upset over Vivian doing what she did. And three, well, that's right now."

"Aw, now, don't go tellin' her all my secrets," Finn protested midway up the stairs.

"I didn't tell all of them," Matt said, casting Lilly a wink. "Just the ones I knew you'd be most embarrassed about."

A FEW MINUTES AFTER Matt had left and Finn had fallen asleep spread-eagled in the center of his king-size bed, Lilly removed her husband's work boots and covered him with a wedding-ring quilt.

The room's forest-green walls were soothing, and sitting in a corner rocker, immersed in only the yellow glow of a bedside lamp, Lilly closed her eyes, breathing deeply of the lemon oil Finn must have rubbed into the antique dressers.

From outside came the faint sound of a few hardy crickets. Inside, all was quiet save for the creaking of her chair rails against the hardwood floor and the sound of Finn's fitful snoring.

She opened her eyes to gaze upon his sleeping face.

Finn. Her husband. The man who would hopefully be a good father to her baby. Despite the fact that he was sleeping, his expression was weary, as if life had dealt him far more than he could comfortably handle.

Abruptly she stopped rocking and went to him, perching beside him. Tentatively she touched his face, traced the fine lines around his eyes and mouth. Did those lines mean he'd led a hard life? Or were they laugh lines earned by more happiness than sorrow?

Could what his friend said be true? That Finn had been this drunk only two other times in his life and both those times had been over a woman?

Vivian. That was his fiancée, who'd run out on their wedding. Her lips turning up in a melancholy smile, Lilly couldn't say she blamed Finn for turning to beer to soothe that kind of pain. His wedding day must have been humiliating. So humiliating in fact, that in retrospect, she could almost understand the rationale behind his taking this Mitch character up on his bet.

Okay, so she understood Finn's bet, but that didn't mean she liked it. And that understanding did nothing to answer one more question she couldn't get out of her head. The question of how he felt about her. For if she'd been the third woman who'd driven Finn to drink, had he been drinking because now that she was in his life, he wanted her out? Or because she was out of his life and he wanted her in?

FINN WOKE to merciless sun spearing his eyes. The scent of frying hamburger ambushed his nose. With his gut in a too-much-beer uproar, he couldn't tell if the meat smelled bad or good. And for that matter, who in the hell was cooking it? He lived alone.

"'I'm gonna wash that man right out of my hair, I'm gonna wash that man right out of my hair, I'm gonna wash that man right out of my hair, and send him on his waaaaay!'"

Correction—he *used* to live alone.

From the sounds and smells of it, his bride was in the kitchen cooking breakfast.

Washing his face with his hands, he groaned.

His mother used to sing while she cooked. Finding a woman who sang had always been at the top of Finn's must-have list for a wife. Hearing Lilly belting out a show tune only made him wonder that much more if maybe they could make a go of their marriage. If Lilly would just forget about his bet and start thinking about the real him.

Sometime during the night, he'd dreamed she was beside him. He'd even slipped his arm around her waist to hold her tight. Then that dream had turned nightmare when she'd left. For a brief time, his lifelong goal of filling his home with a new family had been poised on the brink of coming true, but now, he wasn't sure what to think.

Even if Lilly wanted kids, that didn't mean she'd ever again let him close enough to make any!

Footsteps sounded on the stairs and for a minute he was so confused about seeing her that he almost feigned sleep. But it was too late for that now.

She stood in the open door, hands on her hips, lips pressed into a tight frown. "You're up."

"Barely."

"Do you know it's after eleven?"

"It's my honeymoon," he fired back with a half-hearted grin. "What's the harm in a man sleeping late?"

"None, I suppose." Her expression softened and he detected a glint of a smile in her eyes. "I came up to tell you that if you're hungry, breakfast is ready."

"Thanks." He rolled onto his side. "You didn't have to cook anything, you know."

"I know, but seeing as how I was starved, I figured I might as well fix extra for you."

"Gee, that's the nicest thing you've done for me since you found out who I really am. This doesn't mean I'm starting to grow on you, does it?"

"No." Even as she said the word, Lilly couldn't help but remember where she had awakened, spooned against her husband with his arm snug around her waist. During her first few minutes of consciousness, she'd felt indescribably content, then she remembered this wasn't kind and compassionate Dallas she was cozied up to, but a man who'd tricked her into marriage.

So, Lilly Reilly, if you're so all-fired certain Dallas Lebeaux is the true man for you, why not go to him? Explain everything? Surely, he'd understand? He'd have you out of this house and away from this stranger who makes your pulse race, faster than you can say Oops, I messed up again.

Lilly swallowed hard and raised her chin a barely perceptible notch. No. That had been the old Lilly thinking. For the new and improved Lilly, running away wasn't even an option. Nope, for the baby, and most importantly, for herself, no more running from her problems. The new Lilly faced them head-on.

The soulful look her square-jawed, whisker-stubbled, dark-eyed god of a husband currently graced her with should have made her feel better about that decision, but all it really did was serve as a flustering reminder of their long, hot Vegas night.

He cleared his throat. "About last night," he said. "I never meant to come home in that condition."

"It's all right." Toying with one of her curls, she added, "These things happen."

"Not to me, they don't. Like I told you Sunday morning, I'm not a drinking man."

"Yet this is the second time I've seen you drunk. Sorry," she said. "I didn't mean that to sound so harpy. I guess it's none of my business what you do."

"The hell it isn't. You're my wife, and if you're so all-fired determined for us to stay married, then we might as well start acting like we're married, don't you think?"

She shot her gaze out the window, glad he wasn't in on her secret that, very much like a wife, she'd fallen asleep beside him and stayed with him all night.

"Lilly?"

"I'm sorry," she said, already on her way out of the room with her hands cupping her tummy. "I can't deal with this right now. You. Us. It's all too much."

Ignoring the pounding in his head, Finn went to her, grasping her by the shoulders and gently urging her around. "If not now, when are you going to deal with this, Lilly? Obviously, as we both saw last night, I'm not dealing with our sudden union too well, either. I'm not saying that me knocking back one too many beers was your fault, because it wasn't. What I am saying is that maybe we ought to spend some time together over the next few days. You know, getting to know each other. Talking about our childhoods."

"How is talking about what we did as kids going to make me trust you? Don't you see? I entered this marriage believing you were one man and you turned out to be another. How will I ever know if what we share is real, or another one of your games?"

Releasing her, Finn let out a harsh sigh. "For the last time, Lilly, I never would have gone through with our wedding if I hadn't believed you were every bit as determined to dupe me as I was you. My whole life I've wanted to be—" He looked her way to see that, instead of focusing on him, her attention was aimed somewhere around their feet. "Never mind," he said, heading for the shower. "I can see you could care less about anything I have to say."

"Finn, I—"

It was too late for apologies. He'd already slammed the bathroom door.

CHAPTER EIGHT

"I DON'T KNOW," MATT SAID late that afternoon while he and Finn went over the latest changes to Mrs. Kleghorn's master bath. "I thought she seemed nice—not to mention hot, in a June Cleaveresque sort of way."

"You talking about Mrs. Kleghorn or my wife?"

"That's pretty funny," Matt said, delivering a sucker punch to Finn's left arm. "Even hungover, you're a stand-up kind of guy."

"I'm not hungover," Finn growled, using his red pen to savagely scratch out the lines on the blueprint showing where his client wanted her bathroom fridge. "And who the hell ever heard of putting a minibar in a bathroom?"

"You can't blame her for being upset with you, bud. After all, finding out you've been the butt of a joke would be tough for anyone to take, let alone a sensitive woman like Lilly."

Finn counted to four and a half before he blew. "You think she's so great, why don't you marry her? Now, if you don't mind, could we please get some work done? If this fridge is going to be in the bath, we're going to have to reroute all of Arnold's wiring through the master closet." He pointed to the spot on the plans.

"If I were you," Matt said, leaning against a framed-out window, staring at the mountain view, "I'd woo her."

"*Woo* her? Mrs. Kleghorn doesn't need wooing, just a dose of reality." He rolled up the plans and slapped the paper tube against Matt's gut. "See that Arnold gets these changes. I've got a meeting with the motel folks."

"Can you say please?"

"Watch it," Finn warned, already on the way to his truck.

"Hey," Matt shouted. "I thought you were taking this week off?"

"I was. Then a woman named Lilly moved into my house and now I never want to go home again."

"Cool. Does that mean we're still on for Friday night poker?"

LILLY PICKED UP the kitchen phone, took a deep breath and managed to punch in a whole three numbers before she chickened out and pressed the disconnect doohickey.

"Come on, Churchill—I mean, Reilly," she coached. "You're never going to get a grip on your future if you don't at least try tackling the past." Calling Dallas had to be done.

Later.

Marching to the side-by-side fridge, she opened the freezer section and happily discovered a stash of goodies. Super Duper Commando Trooper Popsicles, Drumsticks, Minnie Mouse shaped ice-cream sandwiches and even a half gallon of Rocky Road. Selecting a Drumstick, she unwrapped it, then went to work gobbling all the chopped nuts and chocolate from the top.

Midway into the cone section of her snack, she wondered what in the world a manly contractor was doing with a bunch of kiddy treats in his freezer. She could see a guy enjoying a bowl of Rocky Road after dinner, but a Commando Trooper Pop?

She tossed her wrapper into the trash can tucked beneath the sink.

"You can do this," she said, once again picking up the phone. "Dallas deserves to know the truth."

Yeah, and my stomach deserves some peace.

Confrontations had never been her strong point and while she didn't think for a second Dallas would be rude, the mystery of not knowing how he would react was starting to get to her.

"Okay, you big chicken," she said, taking one more fortifying breath. "You've had chocolate. You've had ice cream. It's do or die. Crunch time."

After punching the numbers to Dallas's office in real fast, she closed her eyes, halfheartedly praying his secretary wouldn't pick up. Unfortunately, she did, and seconds later, the woman patched her through.

"Lilly," Dallas's rich voice was laced with concern. "What happened to you? I've been worried sick."

"I'm sorry," she said, twisting the phone cord around her pinkie. "Some things kind of happened."

"What kind of *things?*" Was that a pencil she heard tapping in the background? "You haven't fallen ill, have you? Is your baby all right?"

"The baby and I are fine, but I've run into a bit of a snafu where our, um...engagement is concerned."

"Oh?"

"Yeah, you see, I'm, ah...kind of, sort of already married."

For a long time, there was just silence, then a chuckle. "This is a joke, right?"

"Um, no." She drew her lower lip into her mouth for a quick nibble.

"Lilly, I'm in line for partnership—a partnership that hinges upon my having a wife. I've told the entire firm all about you. How we had this whirlwind Miami fling, and now—"

"We never went to Miami!"

"I know, but my bosses don't have to know that. Besides, I was just laying a little foundation work for when I told them about the baby."

"Oh."

He sighed. "You've ruined my life and all you can say is 'oh'?"

Hot tears pooled. While she told him the details about what had happened, Lilly blinked to fight back the tears. "I'm sorry, it's not as if I married the wrong guy on purpose. I mean, your directions to Luigi's were awful, and it was dark, and I've never been good at finding my way at night."

"Lady," he said in a cruel tone, "from where I'm sitting, you're apparently not good at anything. Good riddance."

Hands trembling, Lilly carefully hung the phone back in its cradle. Dallas's words hurt. The old Lilly would have sought comfort by telling herself what he said wasn't true, but deep down, she feared it was. Was she kidding herself with all this hyped-up talk of starting over and facing her problems head-on? Was such a transformation even possible?

One tear fell, and then another and another, until they were coming so fast Lilly could hardly see. In the back of her mind, she'd used the idea of running back to Dallas as a sort of safety net, but now that net was gone. Even worse, she was married to a man who couldn't stand the sight of her.

Boy, she thought with a hiccuping sigh. Being responsible sure wasn't fun.

IT WAS PUSHING SIX by the time Finn finished with the owners of the motel he'd be constructing by the highway. The Good-night Inn would be pretty much a run-of-the-mill roadside place. No frills, with the exception of an indoor pool, which, considering how tight his neck was at the thought of seeing Lilly again, would have been damn nice to jump into.

Pulling into the driveway of his house, he did his usual double horn-honk and by the time he parked Abigail beside Lilly's sedan, two dark-headed kids and all three dogs had come running through the miniforest of firs dividing the neighbor's yard from his.

"Finn! I mithed you!" said Chrissy, the youngest, with a huge grin as he stepped out of the truck. She'd lost both front teeth the previous week and hadn't quite gotten the hang of speaking without them yet. When she gave him a fierce hug, his heart swelled with affection for the runt.

Her nine-year-old brother, Randy, who everybody called Rambo because of his affinity for anything to do with the hot new line of toys called Super Duper Commando Troopers, was quick to follow with a hug of his own. "Mom said Miss Lu told her you already got married again," he said. "But I thought Vivian rode off with that motorcycle guy at the wedding?"

"Randy," Chrissy scolded. "Mommy said Finn's senthative about motorcycles."

"Not motorcycles, you dork. Girls."

"I'm a girl."

"You're a dork."

"Whoa," Finn said, stepping in to referee while ushering the two through the tail-wagging dogs and around the side of the house to the back door. "Your sister's a princess, Rambo, not a dork."

"Ew, gross…" Randy made a face that looked like he'd swallowed a spoonful of maggots. "She's a princess all right, Princess Dork."

"Finn? Did you hear what he thaid? That ithn't nithe."

"Come on, gang," Finn said on the back porch steps. "Let's call a truce, okay? Rambo, your mom's right, I did get married, not to Vivian, but to a woman named Lilly." *Who hates my guts, but hopefully she'll be perfectly pleasant to you little beasties.*

"Ith she pretty?" Chrissy asked, melting him with her big brown eyes.

"Very. Now, I mean it, you two. Be nice."

"Do you kiss her?" Randy asked as they stepped through the door.

As luck would have it, Finn's bride was sitting at the table reading a book that she quickly shut then shoved beneath a pile of glossy magazines. "You're home," she said. "And you brought company." Pushing back her chair, she stood to crouch before the kids. "Hi, I'm Lilly."

"You *are* pretty," Chrissy said. "Finn thaid you were and he callth me a printheth and I think you're a printheth, too. Oh—and my name's Chrithy."

"It's nice to meet you," Lilly said, solemnly shaking the girl's hand. She took a quick peek at her husband to find him glancing toward a ceiling vent.

"Is your hair color real?" Randy asked. "My aunt

dyes her hair blond and wears *reeeaaallly* long fake fingernails. My dad says she looks like a—"

"This is my good friend, Randy," Finn said, saving them all the embarrassment of hearing Rambo's dad's assessment of his sister-in-law.

Grinning, Lilly said, "Yep, my hair is real and so are my nails." She held them out for inspection.

"Cool," the boy said. "Did you remember our surprise?" he asked Finn.

"Yep, you both have a treat waiting for you in the freezer."

"Awesome." He was already racing across the room with Chrissy close on his heals.

Lilly said, "I wondered who the Commando Pops and Minnie Mouse bars were for. Somehow, Finn, you didn't strike me as the Minnie type."

"Gee, thanks," he said with a grimace. "I think. Hey, what smells so good?"

"I hope you like broccoli, chicken and cheese casserole. Not knowing what time you'd be home, I thought that and a salad would be the safest choice for dinner. It'll be ready in about—" she eyed the small clock built into the oven control panel "—twenty minutes."

"That sounds delicious. Thanks."

"You're welcome."

"Chrissy threw her wrapper on the floor!"

"Did not! It wath an accident!"

"Liar!"

"You're a liar—and Mommy thaid don't call me that!"

"Takes one to know one."

"Aren't they charming?" Finn said to Lilly before breaking up yet another squabble. "Come on, kids," he said, shepherding them to the back door. "I think I hear your mother calling."

"No she isn't," Randy said. "She's busy watchin' *Young and the Restless.* She had to tape it today because my aunt's car's busted and she needed a ride to the auto shop. Dad says that bum she's dating burned up the transmiss—"

"Man, would you look at the time," Finn said, nudging them out the door. "I'll see you again tomorrow."

Chrissy gave him a fierce hug. "Bye, Finn. I love you."

Kissing the top of her head, he said, "I love you, too."

"Bye, Finn." Randy was also quick with a hug, but instead of kissing him, Finn gave him a noogie. Lord, he loved these two. They could be a real pain in the neck sometimes, but he didn't know what he'd do without them. If he felt this connected to the neighbor kids, he couldn't even imagine the joy having his own son or daughter would bring.

The second the kids left, awkward silence crept in like a third person in the room.

Finn was almost ready to call Randy and Chrissy back when Lilly said, "I, um, guess I'll set the table."

"Why don't you let me?"

"That's okay. I'm sure you'd like to wash up before we eat. Anyway, I feel kind of antsy after staying home all day. I'm usually just now getting home from work myself."

"What do you do?" Finn asked, heading for the sink to wash his hands.

"I'm a bookstore clerk. At least I used to be." Lilly took a bowl of already mixed and washed greens from the fridge. "Last Friday was my last day. Dallas is part of a big law firm in Salt Lake City. Once we were married, I planned to stay home and do the housewife thing."

"Aren't you going to miss your work?" Finn asked above the running water.

I do now, but I'm sure I won't once the baby comes.

"I'd go nuts sitting around the house all day."

"It has been a pretty strange day, but not so much because I couldn't find anything to do, but because of the way you left this morning."

Drying his hands on a cobalt-blue tea towel, he said, "I meant what I said this morning, about us needing to spend time together."

Her back to him, she set the salad bowl on the table. "I know."

He stepped behind her, softly cupping his hands over her shoulders. To keep from leaning deeper into his touch, she tensed. Why, when her head knew Finn thought so little of her feelings that he'd used her as the object of a bet, did her body trill just being near him?

"Do you know, Lilly? Or are you just paying me lip service? Telling me what I want to hear?" He gently spun her to face him and tucked his fingers beneath her chin, urging her to meet his gaze.

Her heart pounded and her breathing stalled.

"Because if that is what you're doing, it needs to stop. I can't be in a relationship with a woman who won't even look me in the eyes. I deserve more than that and so do you."

She nodded.

"I've been a bear all day to everyone I work with. And about thirty minutes ago, I even gave Mitch, my biggest competitor and worst enemy, his cash—the cash

I won because I married you. Don't you see? I'm trying to make up for my mistakes, Lilly. Can't you at least try to forgive me for making them?"

Again, all she could do was nod, because her throat had grown too tight to speak.

The oven timer went off and she sagged with relief at the intrusion.

"Can't that wait?" Finn asked.

"No," she said, already reaching for hot pads. "Dry casserole is the worst."

A sad chuckle fell from his lips as he muttered, "Dry casserole doesn't sound half as miserable as fifty years worth of dry marriage."

LATE THAT NIGHT, long after their silent meal and an endless succession of watching meaningless sitcoms, Lilly had gone to bed in the guest room and Finn let her.

Truth be told, he thought, roaming the big house, locking up and turning off lights, he'd been relieved to see her go. Trying to keep his mood on an even keel around her was a lot like dealing with Mrs. Kleghorn.

In other words…impossible!

For the life of him, Finn couldn't figure out why Lilly even wanted to stay married to him. Was she a masochist? Because even though his whole life he'd dreamed of marrying and raising a family, he'd never wanted a marriage on these terms.

His gut, remembering how right things had felt between them in Vegas, told Finn to take it slow with Lilly and she'd eventually come around. But his heart told him that logic was flawed. What they had shared in Vegas hadn't been real, but an illusion. The reason Lilly had come across as so relaxed and comfortable with him was because she thought he was that Dallas guy. Now she realized that being married to Finn was the equivalent of being told she had to suffer through a fifty-year blind date!

Yeah, buddy, and that was some kind of suffering *you two did Sunday night.*

Finn cursed under his breath.

He was about to flick off the light over the kitchen table when a pile of magazines on the floor beside the chair Lilly had sat in caught his eye. He remembered her putting those magazines over a book she'd been reading when he walked in with the neighbor kids. Curiosity had him kneeling to scoop up the whole pile and set it on the table.

The magazines were all fairly standard stuff. Vivian's past issues of *People, Cosmo,* and *National Enquirer.* The book on the other hand, was a dog-eared copy of *What to Expect When You're Expecting.*

Wondering if his bride could be pregnant, Finn's heart nearly surged out of his chest, then he remembered the crazy night Matt's sister had gone into labor.

They'd all been playing poker around the kitchen table when Rachel's water broke. Her entire pregnancy, she'd carried that book with her everywhere, consulting it as if it were her pregnancy bible. In all the excitement over getting her to the hospital, she forgot the book and once the baby arrived, she switched from *What to Expect When You're Expecting* to a thick tome on baby psychology and feeding habits.

But Lilly wasn't pregnant. She must have just been bored. Since Finn haphazardly stacked reading material into the big wicker basket his aunt gave him for laundry, he figured his wife had come across the book there.

Kicking himself for being such a hopeless dreamer

when it came to the topic of starting a family, Finn flicked off the kitchen light.

Only in the shadowy moonlight could he find the courage to admit how much all of this hurt. Here he was, finally married, and not only was his wife sleeping in the guest room, but when he tried starting a conversation, she wouldn't say more than five words.

Hell, he thought, walking by rote through the darkened front hall, then climbing the stairs. He of all people knew their relationship had been built on a foundation of sand, but he was a contractor specializing in renovations. He'd asked her if she wanted to spend this week getting to know each other all over again, but she'd turned him down flat.

Beyond Lilly's great looks and bod, he was as intrigued as hell by her morals and mind. Unlike Vivian, Lilly—aside from the fact that she despised him—was Finn's ideal. Loyal, intelligent, trustworthy, dependable—she even sang while she cooked. She'd make a great mom, would never keep secrets, and best of all, she'd never, ever lie. He'd once thought all of that of Vivian, but look how she'd proved him wrong. Now, with Lilly, just by the way she'd reacted to the news of his bet, he knew beyond a shadow of a doubt that she was as genuine as a woman could get.

At the top of the stairs, he flicked on the dim hall light and eyed the closed door to her room.

What did the woman want from him? A bended-knee apology along with chocolate and a few dozen roses?

If I were you, I'd woo her.

From out of nowhere, Matt's suggestion appeared like a beacon in the night.

Was that it? Could the solution to his dilemma be that simple? Was romancing Lilly the key to transforming her into a real wife?

WHEN LILLY WOKE the next morning to another brilliant fall day, she frowned. Why was it, when her mood felt edgy as an approaching storm, the weather refused to cooperate?

Squeezing her eyes shut, she tried falling back asleep, but it was no use. She was wide-awake and, judging by the sound of the shower being turned off across the hall, her husband was awake, too.

Was today the day to tell him about her baby?

He'd seemed fine about the neighbor kids traipsing through the house, and the fact that he even bought them special treats told her he wasn't a complete ogre when it came to the subject of children. And talk about a character witness—when Chrissy gave Finn that hug and told him she loved him…

Ugh, just thinking about how sweet the moment had been made Lilly's eyes well with tears.

Okay, so at the moment, all signs were positive that Finn, unlike Elliot, the baby's real father, would make a great dad—assuming she gathered the courage to tell him.

She sat up only to have a wave of nausea hit like a tsunami.

Hand over her mouth, she raced to the end of the hall, wishing the whole way that when she'd chosen a bedroom, she'd picked one with an adjoining bath.

Just in time, she made it to the porcelain throne.

At the sink, holding a wet washcloth to her head, she glanced in the mirror. The face staring back looked tinted a shade between gruel and wallpaper paste.

Speaking of wallpaper…the burgundy-and-gold paisley pattern on the wall behind her was doing nothing to calm her already frazzled nerves.

A knock sounded on the door. "Lilly? You all right?"

Looking to the ceiling, she sent up a one-word prayer.

Why?

"Um, yeah," she said, holding the cloth to her forehead. "I'm fine."

"You don't sound fine. Can I come in?"

"No."

"Why not? You sounded pretty sick. Maybe I can help."

Help? Not unless he knew of a magical method to get her into her second trimester. The pregnancy book she'd been reading said that was typically when morning sickness let up.

Earlier in her pregnancy she'd experienced a bout of the dreaded malaise, but nothing like this. In fact, maybe this wasn't morning sickness at all but flu?

"Lilly? I'm not leaving until either you come out or let me in."

Glancing one more time at her ghoulish reflection, Lilly opened the door. "There, now that you've verified I'm still alive, will you leave?"

"Wow, you really are sick. You look awful."

"Thanks."

"Sorry," he said, shoving his hands into the pockets of his faded jeans. His broad chest was encased in a mossy green T-shirt that did amazing things to his soulful brown eyes, and his hair was still damp from the shower. In short, he looked disgustingly handsome and she looked worse than death! "I didn't mean to ruffle your womanly feathers," he added. "Just making an observation."

"Yeah, well, next time you feel like observing, keep your comments to yourself." Holding tight to her few remaining shreds of dignity, she tugged the hem of her brother Mark's red football jersey as low as it would go, then shuffled past Finn, ignoring the numbness of her feet caused by the cold hardwood floors.

A minute later, climbing into bed and drawing the covers up to her neck, she planned on going back to sleep, but unfortunately, the stranger who just happened to be her husband sauntered into the room.

He took the liberty of feeling her forehead, then said, "You don't feel like you have any fever."

"Thank you, doctor."

"You're welcome."

Clutching her stomach, she wished more than anything—even more than she wished Finn would leave her to suffer in private—that she had the heating pad from her apartment, but it was in storage along with the rest of her belongings that she'd planned to have shipped to Dallas's house after their wedding.

"Wait right here," Finn said, heading for the hall. "My aunt knew exactly what to do to make me feel better after I tossed my cookies."

"Let you die in peace?" Lilly muttered.

"I heard that!" he said from the hall.

She heard rustling and guessed the source of the racket to be Finn rummaging through the hall closet.

A few minutes later, he was back, wielding his prize. "Taa-daa."

She'd closed her eyes and now opened them. Could it be? Did Finn really hold in his hands what she thought he did, or was she hallucinating?

"That's a heating pad," she said. "How did you know?"

"How did I know what?" He knelt beside the bedside table to plug it in.

"That whenever I'm sick, that's the one item I can't live without?"

He shrugged. "I know when I was a kid it always made me feel better. I've got an iron stomach now, but..." He pushed back her covers and tenderly set the flannel-covered square against her tummy before pulling the yellow floral comforter back in place. "Well, let's just say this baby got me through some rough times."

"You were sick a lot?"

Finn's jaw hardened as he stared out the window at the fir-dotted foothills surrounding his home. "Not sick in the traditional sense." *Just heartsick over the loss of my parents and sister.*

"Then how?"

He took a deep breath and sighed, turning his gaze back to her. "I'd rather not talk about it, okay?" Skimming her bangs from her forehead, he asked, "Can I get you anything else? Sprite? Saltines? Thick socks?"

Grinning, she said, "You know, Dr. Finn, all of the above sounds surprisingly good."

BY LATER THAT MORNING, Lilly felt strong enough to take a shower and style her hair.

The one thing she couldn't do was dwell on how much of her renewed health was due to Finn's nursing.

Just when she thought she had him pegged as an unredeemable scoundrel, for a split second, she'd almost thought she could care for the man. But then she'd probably feel the same about Donald Duck if he not only brought her a heating pad and pair of his own cozy white socks, but made a trip to the store for pop and crackers.

Forehead furrowed, she slowly descended the stairs and made her way through the entry, down the hall and into the sun-flooded kitchen. Finn stood at the stove, stirring a heavenly smelling concoction in a huge Dutch oven.

"What smells so good?" she asked, stepping behind him for a quick peek.

"I thought my patient could use a bowl of chicken soup for lunch. My aunt swears by this recipe. And I'll have you know I had to call her in Florida to get it."

"You did that for me?"

"Yep, and you owe me for the grief I went through. My aunt couldn't quite grasp the concept of me needing chicken soup to heal my *new* bride."

"I take it she didn't know about your bet?" Lilly pulled out a chair at the kitchen table and had a seat.

"Nope. Her boyfriend had tickets to some fancy golf tournie in West Palm Beach for Sunday, so she flew back to Miami late Saturday afternoon."

Looking to her nails, Lilly noted that they needed a fresh coat of polish. Good. Focusing on routine was a great way to keep from asking a zillion more questions about Finn's aunt. "I'm, ah, sorry about what Vivian did to you. That was pretty low."

He shrugged, set the wooden spoon he'd been using on the blue tile counter. "Surprisingly enough, I'm over it. When it happened, I thought I'd die, but now, I guess her leaving was for the best."

"How so?" She looked up and for a second was caught off guard. In all their fussing, she'd forgotten Finn's extraordinary good looks. His square and true jawline. His soul-penetrating dark eyes. And those lips... Her pulse quickened, remembering the feel of them on her breasts.

Swallowing hard, she looked away.

"Easy," he said, crossing the room to pull out the chair beside her. "If I'd been married to Vivian right now, I wouldn't be married to you." He sat unbearably close. Close enough that if she dared, she could cup his cheek and they'd no longer be strangers, but that perfectly-at-ease couple they'd been in Vegas.

Reminding herself to breathe, Lilly licked her lips. "But you must have loved Vivian terribly if you'd planned to marry her."

He reached for her hands and why she didn't know, but Lilly let him. "I thought I loved her, but now, I'm not so sure. Maybe I never even knew what love was."

"And do you now? Know what love is, I mean?" She boldly met his stare and for a moment time stood still. She felt him searching her face for answers, answers to what she didn't know, and she was terrified of the implications of her asking.

"Maybe."

She swallowed again. "What do you think it would take to make you know for sure?"

"A sign."

"What kind of sign?"

"Something that proves that this time, I'm not putting my faith in the wrong woman."

"Knowing how I feel about the subject of divorce, what will you do if you find I'm not the right woman for you?"

With the pads of his thumbs, Finn caressed the sides of her index fingers. "I think that's the least of our worries, don't you?"

Funny, but from where Lilly was sitting, the heat Finn strummed into her fingers made it feel like just the start of her worries!

CHAPTER NINE

THE NEXT MORNING, LILLY rose cautiously, testing her equilibrium before committing to action. But even that motion was evidently too much. Her stomach roiled and once again, the mad dash to the bathroom was on.

Blech.

Once again, she made it in time, but didn't manage to shut the door.

"Good Lord, woman," Finn said a few seconds later, kneeling beside her with his hands cupped around her shoulders. "I thought we had this thing licked, but you must have picked up one heck of a bug."

When she felt stable enough, Lilly plopped onto her rear, resting her back against the cool claw-footed tub.

"Let me get you a washcloth," he said, already on his way to the sink. He first made her a cold one, then hot.

"How is it," she said, leaning her head against the tub as well, "that you always seem to know what I need?"

He flushed the commode and lowered the lid before taking a seat. "It isn't as if it takes any great psychic powers to know that a sick woman needs looking after."

"Yeah, well, psychic powers, or not, I appreciate what

you've done. I enjoyed the soup last night and..." She lowered her gaze. "I'm enjoying your company now."

"It's my pleasure." After they sat in silence for a few minutes, Finn softly stroking her hair away from her forehead, he said, "Feel like getting back in bed?"

She nodded, tried grappling to her feet, but before she could, Finn stood beside her, crouching to place one arm beneath her knees and the other behind her shoulders. In a smooth glide, he scooped her into his arms and carried her to her room.

Lilly's mind was so tired and limbs so weak that it didn't even occur to her to fight. Instead, she rested her cheek against his chest, relishing Finn's quiet strength.

Then, tucked in bed with a pile of downy pillows beneath her head, another pair of her husband's thick socks on her feet and Finn in the kitchen fetching her more Sprite and crackers, it once again occurred to Lilly that for a man she'd so callously accused of caring nothing about her feelings, he sure as heck was doing a bang-up job of proving her wrong.

Funny how the men she thought she'd loved—Elliot and Dallas—had turned out to both be creeps, yet the one man she professed to hate...

Memories of the sweet care Finn had taken with her caused her cheeks to flush.

When he returned, he held a sweating glass of clear soda to her lips and helped her take a sip. Setting the glass on the bedside table, he said, "I'm going to call a doctor. It's weird how this thing keeps coming and going. Last night, I thought you were getting better, but this morning—no offense, you look worse than ever."

"Thanks," she said with a feeble grin.

His quick smile stole what little was left of her breath.

Beyond being sick, what was happening to her? She wasn't falling for her husband, was she?

"KNOCK KNOCK," Finn said later that afternoon at her bedroom door. "Lilly? Are you decent? I brought company."

"Company?"

She tucked the tattered copy of *What to Expect When You're Expecting* beneath her pillow and straightened in the bed.

Finn ushered in a bright-eyed woman Lilly guessed to be in her early fifties. Her hair was styled in a chic blond bob and she wore tailored navy slacks and a matching blazer over a white silk blouse. An elegant strand of pearls hung at her throat and in her right hand she clutched a classic black leather doctor's bag.

Lilly's heart pounded. *A doctor's bag?*

Oh no, was her secret blown?

"Hello," the woman said with a kind smile, setting her bag on the foot of the bed, then holding out her right hand. "You must be Lilly. I'm Dr. Walsh."

"Nice to meet you," Lilly said, returning the woman's firm grip and hoping the physician hadn't noticed the sudden sweating of her patient's palm. "But I told Finn that I'm feeling much better and don't need a doctor."

"That's okay," the woman said, reaching into her bag to pull out a stethoscope. "I live up the road, so it was no big deal for me to stop by on my way home. Now, can you tell me what seems to be the problem?"

Drawing her lower lip into her mouth, Lilly looked from the doctor to her husband, who had made himself at home on the empty half of the bed.

"She hardly keeps anything down, Doc."

"Um, Finn," Lilly summoned the nerve to say. "Do

you mind if I have a few moments alone with the doctor? This is after all, kind of a private thing."

"What do you need privacy for to be checked out for the flu? I should be here just in case. Right, Doc Walsh?"

"Wrong. Skedaddle," the doctor said with a wave of her manicured hands. "Lilly's right. We women don't always need our men listening in." When Finn finally left, closing the door firmly behind him, the doctor said, "You had something to tell me in private?"

Swallowing hard, Lilly nodded. "I'm, um, pretty sure I'm not really sick…just pregnant."

The doctor gasped. "How wonderful! Our Finn's finally going to be a daddy!" Lowering her voice, she said, "Sorry for the unprofessional outburst, it's just that for as long as I can remember, Finn has been caring for everything around here from those stray dogs of his to elementary-school kids. Finn Reilly will make the best father imaginable."

While that was certainly great news to Lilly, the fact still remained that Finn wasn't *her* baby's father. Sure, most any man would love his own child, but to love another man's child? That took a special breed.

Narrowing her eyes, the doctor checked Lilly's blood pressure. "Why do I get the feeling there's something else you aren't telling me?"

"The, ah…" Lilly looked to the door, confirming that it was solidly closed. "The baby isn't Finn's. In fact, he doesn't even know I'm pregnant."

"Oh?"

"Our marriage isn't exactly a match made in heaven. We met in a pretty unorthodox way."

The doctor glanced at her slim gold watch. "I have almost an hour until my husband has supper on the table. I'm sensing you carry a burden you'd like to get off your chest, but please, if that isn't the case, know you won't offend me by telling me to mind my own business." Her genuinely warm smile put Lilly at ease while the doctor settled onto the rocker Finn had placed at the head of her bed.

"No," Lilly said. "You're right. I guess I have been hungering for another woman's point of view." Being careful to only convey facts and not to lay blame, Lilly shared every detail about how she and Finn had come to be married.

"Hmm, that *was* quite a story," the doctor said when Lilly finished. She leaned forward in her chair. "I see how telling Finn about your baby could be rough, but believe me," she said, taking Lilly's right hand in hers and giving it a gentle squeeze, "I've known Finn since he was a boy. He's been through so much pain, and deserves so much happiness. You'll never find a better husband for you, or father for your baby. But as attentive and respectful as he'll be to you and your child, you owe him that same respect. I was at his wedding when Vivian walked out. I saw the anguish in his eyes. Right now, talk around town is that he trusts you implicitly. Were he to lose faith in you as he did Vivian, I'm not sure how he'd react." She took a deep breath and sighed. "Lilly, in my professional and personal opinion, I think you should tell him the truth—preferably before he makes a few deductions of his own."

IN THE KITCHEN, Finn was pouring a cup of coffee when the doctor said, "Your bride is going to live."

His shoulders sagged with relief. "What's wrong with her? Should I go get her some medicine?"

"No, I don't think she needs a thing other than a nice,

long rest." Gesturing to Finn's mug, she said, "Would you mind pouring me a cup? We have to talk."

"That doesn't sound good," he said, snatching another blue mug from the rack hanging beneath the cabinets. "There *is* something seriously wrong with her, isn't there? I knew this whole almost-wedded-bliss thing was too good to be true. She's dying, isn't she? How long do we have?" As he poured the coffee into the mug, his hands trembled and he spilled some of the scalding liquid onto his hand. "Dammit. Why is it that when I find someone I think I could love, they either run off or die on me, Doc?"

"Oh, Finn." She crossed the room to envelope him in a laughing hug. "I'm sorry for planting that seed in your head. Lilly has nothing medically wrong with her. What I want to discuss is the way you met." Releasing him, she took a step back to wag her finger in his face. "I wanted to say, shame on you for ever accepting Mitch's bet in the first place." She shook her head. "You know better."

A second rush of relief turned Finn's knees to jelly. "I'll gladly take your scolding and then some, just promise you'll never scare me like that again."

"I promise." She stepped to the counter to add cream and sugar to her coffee. "Since you've been like one of my own sons for as long as I can remember, Finn, I'll tell you what does scare me about Lilly."

"What's that?"

They both took seats at the table.

"The suddenness with which this whole marriage came about. She seems like a sweet woman, but you do realize that just because she feels morally bound to the marriage, that doesn't mean you have to agree? You deserve the entire package, Finn. Happily ever after with all the trimmings." Placing her hand on his, she added, "Are you sure Lilly is the woman who will make all those dreams of yours come true?"

Flashing his longtime friend a smile, Finn said, "That's the strangest part. Yeah, I think she is my dream woman. Before either of us knew who the other was, we had a chemistry I can't begin to describe. And at the moment we said our vows, I had the craziest feeling that I really did want to be with her for the rest of my life."

"Even though you hadn't yet known her a full day?"

Leaning back in his chair, he sighed. "Doc, as hard as I've tried denying it, I wanted to marry Lilly after being with her for only ten minutes."

The older woman beamed. "That's all I needed to know. In that case," she said, pulling him into a quick hug. "I guess congratulations are in order."

Wincing, Finn said, "I'm afraid your well wishes are premature."

"For heaven's sake, why? You've already admitted to being head over heels for her and I can't imagine why any woman wouldn't feel the same about you."

"That's just it," he said. "She can't stand me."

"Oh, apple dumplings. I don't believe it for a second."

"It's true. She can't get past the fact that I only married her to win a bet."

"Well, then it seems to me your job is clear. You have to make her get over it."

"How? Matt said to woo her with flowers and candy and stuff, but she's been so sick, all I've been able to do is bring her Sprite and crackers—oh, and a heating pad."

The doctor's smile grew even brighter.

"What? I know it's corny, but she really did like it."

"Of course, she did. A woman like Lilly doesn't want flowers—well, I'm sure she'd enjoy the occasional dozen roses—but what I suspect she truly wants is security. The knowledge that she'll always find a home in your arms."

Finn laughed. "Right. How am I supposed to make her feel all that when she won't come near any part of me, let alone my arms?"

Leaning forward with her elbows on the table, the doctor said, "Here's what you're going to do."

FRIDAY MORNING, a quick glance outside—not to mention the nip in the air—told Lilly that their streak of luck with unseasonably warm weather was over. Driving rain pebbled the windowpanes and clouds hung low to the ground, making it seem as if a huge gray lid had been placed on the usually expansive view.

On the table beside her, an antique clock ticked, but Lilly was so afraid of suffering another bout of nausea that she didn't even want to look at the time. She needn't have looked anyway, though. The grandfather clock chimed ten.

Ugh, she thought, pushing a few stray curls clear of her eyes, she'd never been prone to sleeping this late. Married life and motherhood were turning her into a slug.

Since her battle with morning, afternoon and evening sickness, Finn had been extraordinarily kind. Always seeing to it that the few creature comforts that brought her relief were on hand the instant she needed them.

Even better than all the Sprite, saltines, and socks he'd supplied, was his being there. Not since she'd been a kid staying home sick from school had she felt so utterly cared for. And she had to admit, seeing this nurturing side of Finn was going a long way toward changing her attitude about him.

Could he truly be the man she'd fallen for in Vegas?

A knock sounded on the door. "Hello?"

Just hearing Finn's voice made her heart flutter.

"Sleeping Beauty? You awake in there?"

"Barely."

"Are you at least decent?"

"Yes."

"Damn," he said, creaking open the door. His rakish grin was all it took to turn her gray skies blue. "I was hoping to see a little skin."

She touched her palms to her cheeks. "You mean this battleship-green stuff that used to be my complexion?"

"You look gorgeous to me."

"Thanks. Flattery will get you everywhere."

When he perched beside her, it dawned on Lilly how comfortable they'd become over the past few days. "So, sicky? Feel like getting out of bed?"

"I'm not sure. So far I feel pretty good, but I'm afraid if I move I'll end up in another race for the commode."

"How about if I carry you to the living room sofa? Think you'd be all right there?"

The mere prospect of being in his arms brought instant pleasure, which she quickly squelched. Lowering her eyes, lest he see the heat that had risen to her cheeks, she said, "Thanks for the offer of transport, but I can probably make it on my own. Why?"

His only answer was a maddening grin. "Pull on some sweats and meet me downstairs. I have a surprise."

CHAPTER TEN

FOR THE LIFE OF HIM, FINN couldn't figure out what the doc's plan was supposed to accomplish, but he was willing to give it a try. Matt's sister, Rachel, had been pretty keen on the idea, too.

After making the drop-off—a thirty-minute process by the time they'd unloaded all the gear from the minivan—Finn was already exhausted, but it was a good exhaustion. One he hoped would get even better by day's end.

"Lilly?" He hollered up the stairs. "Are you dressed yet? I could really use your help."

"Coming!" she shouted from the upstairs hall. "Let me put my hair in a ponytail and brush my teeth."

Finn glanced at the jumble of pink stuff cluttering his living room, then shouted, "Hurry!"

"I am hurrying," she finally said at the top of the stairs. "You forget, this is the first time I've walked under my own steam in three whole days. So? Where's the fire?" she asked on the bottom step.

"Surprise..." He pointed toward a lacy pink basket on the river-stone hearth. "We're baby-sitting."

Lilly's mouth dropped open, then she snapped it shut.

Some friend Dr. Walsh had turned out to be. She'd told Finn everything, hadn't she?

Tears started at the back of her throat, spilling from

her eyes in two seconds flat. Doing an abrupt about-face, she marched up the stairs as fast as her weakened condition allowed. "How could she do this to me?" she cried. "What ever happened to doctor-patient privilege?"

"What are you talking about?" Finn asked, checking to make sure Abby was still contentedly sleeping, tiny fist in mouth, before chasing Lilly up the stairs. "The doc had nothing to do with this." *Liar.* But why would Lilly suspect Dr. Walsh of playing a part in his plan? "Matt's sister Rachel called this morning and said she had some kind of lady's thing down at her church and that the woman who runs the nursery was at an aunt's funeral in Salt Lake."

"How come Rachel's husband isn't watching her?"

"He's a teacher. He couldn't get off work."

"And you could?"

He shrugged. "I'd already made plans to take this week off for my honeymoon. Remember?" Reaching for her hand, he said, "Come on, help me out, will ya? It'll be fun."

He was encouraged by the fact that she clung to his hand. "Do you promise the doctor didn't put you up to this?"

He gulped. "Sure."

"Okay. I suppose spending the day with a baby would be fun."

"WAAAAAA!"

"What do we do now?" Lilly asked Finn, hoping she didn't look half as panicked as she felt. Why, oh why, didn't babies come with instructions? Cradling squalling Abby to her chest, Lilly patted her tiny back.

"That's it," Finn said. "Burp her. She probably has gas." He warily eyed the half-full jars of baby peas, chicken and blueberries that were supposed to have fed the infant, but somehow more of it had landed on their clothes than in Abby's tummy. "I know if I had to eat that stuff, I'd be feeling under the weather."

"Waaa-waaa-waaa!"

"Finn, do something. Whatever's wrong with her is getting worse. Maybe we should take her to the emergency room?"

Maddeningly calm, he flashed her a grin. "Give me that kid. All she needs is Uncle Finn."

"Waa-huh-waaa!"

"What she needs is a qualified emergency room staff. What if she has internal bleeding? A tumor or blockage?"

Pffft.

"Eeew," Lilly said, wrinkling her nose. "What's that smell?"

Patting Abby's suddenly thicker rump, he said, "I imagine that smell is her *blockage*." Holding the now-smiling infant at arm's length, he said, "Were you having a Maalox moment, Princess Abby?" Zooming her through the air, he headed for the living room to change her diaper.

"Put her down, Finn." Lilly charged after them. "If her tummy was already upset, who knows what cruising through the air at subsonic speed could do."

"Would you relax?" Finn grinned up at her from the changing pad where he'd already removed Abby's diaper and was competently wiping her clean. "I've got this under control. Abby and I are pals. Aren't we, sweetie?" He blew a raspberry on her plump belly.

Collapsing onto the overstuffed washed-denim couch, Lilly watched in awe as her big husband took amazing care of the itty-bitty baby. Realizing that had she been in charge, she'd have already been halfway to the emergency room, her throat tightened. Swiping a few relieved tears from the corners of her eyes, she wondered if now was the time to tell him he was going to have a little bundle all his own?

Well, sort of his own.

She licked her lips. "Um, Finn?"

"Abby, girl," he said, eyeing the baby's muck-encrusted pink jumper. "Instead of putting all this dirty stuff back on you, how about we find out if your pretty face is hiding somewhere under all those peas and blueberries?"

The infant did a coo and gurgle combo that wrenched Lilly's heart.

Tell him, her conscience fairly screamed. *You'll never have a more perfect chance.*

"I'm sorry," Finn said, glancing her way. "Did you say something?"

Summoning a bright smile, she said, "Nope. Want me to gather all her bath gear?"

"Sure. If you feel up to it."

For once, Lilly's body felt fine. Her heart was another matter entirely.

"SHE'S BEAUTIFUL, isn't she?" Lilly snapped Abby's lavender overalls before scooping her up from the bathroom counter to cradle the baby against her shoulder.

"She's a doll all right," Finn said, his heart full at the sight of his beautiful wife and child. Sure, Abby wasn't their baby, but if he had any say in the matter—soon, *very* soon—he and Lilly would start making rugrats of their own. "She's not the only girl in this room I've got my eye on."

Lilly's blue gaze snapped to his.

"I'm talking about you, you know."

"Thanks, but with my hair and clothes coated in pureed peas, I'm sure I've never looked worse."

"You're wrong. See for yourself." His fingers beneath her chin, he steered her gaze toward her reflection in the mirror. No—correction, he wanted her to see all three of them in the mirror. He selfishly wanted her to see that playing house with the right man could be fun. "You look like an angel," he said, not gazing directly at Lilly, but at her mirror image as he wrapped one of the curls that had slipped free of her ponytail round his right pinkie. When he released it, it sprang softly against her cheek. "You make a great toy, you know."

"We should, ah, go downstairs," she said, hastily looking away from both the mirror and him.

"Why?"

"Rachel will be by soon to pick up Abby and we have a lot of packing to do. There's the swing to disassemble and all the dishes and bottles to wash. If Rachel shows up with the house looking the way it does, she'll think we made awful temporary parents."

"And that matters to you? What kind of mom my friend Rachel thinks you'll one day make?"

"Of course, it matters. Doesn't it matter to you?"

Tucking his hands into his pockets on his way out the door, he said, "Personally, I could give a flip what Rachel thinks about my fathering skills. It's you I've been trying to impress."

Abby's downy-soft hair tucked beneath her chin, the smell of the freshly soaped and lotioned baby overwhelming her senses, Lilly didn't know whether Finn had truly said the words or she'd dreamed them.

As he whistled his way downstairs, she held tight to the baby and chased after him.

Halfway down the stairs, she shouted, "Finn Reilly, you can't say a thing like that and then just walk away!"

"Why not?" he asked, already in the living room.

She followed him in there, too. "Because it leaves all kinds of questions racing through my mind."

"Like what?" With him on one side of the sofa and her on the other, he said, "Fire away. I'd be happy to answer anything you'd like."

She licked her lips and hugged Abby even closer for support. "Okay, um, why do you care if I think you'd make a good father?"

Resting his knees on the sofa cushions, he held on to the back of the sofa for balance. Facing her, his mouth close enough to her breasts that they swelled from the heat of his breath, he said, "I care because, even in the short time we've been acquainted, I've grown to care about you, Lilly Reilly. For better or worse, you're my wife. It's important you not only think of me as a good future father, but as a provider, and ultimately, as a man you could grow to love."

"Oh." She drew the lower of her quivering lips into her mouth and nibbled.

"Do you think you ever could?"

"What?"

"Love me?"

"Well, I—"

The doorbell rang, then a muffled voice from outside the front door called out, "Yo, Finn! Open up! It's me!"

"Damn," Finn said, already off the sofa and headed to the door.

"Who is it?" Lilly asked, peering across the living room toward the door.

"Matt."

"That's nice. What with trying to put you to bed, last time he was here we didn't get a chance to talk."

Finn shot her a look before opening the door.

"Hey, man," Matt said, strolling past him to barge right on into the house. "Did you ever ask Lilly if Friday night poker was still—oh, hey, Lilly. How's it going? And I see my little Abster's here, too."

Abby cooed when her uncle tickled her under her chin.

"No," Finn growled. "I didn't ask my wife about poker. And even if I had, you're four hours early."

"Touchy, touchy," Matt said, taking off his coat and tossing it to the Shaker bench by the door. "I didn't have anything better to do, so I thought I'd help you set up."

LILLY YAWNED, closing the front door on the last of Finn's poker guests. "That was fun," she said, heading for the kitchen to clear the table of cups and sandwich plates.

"You're being sarcastic, right?" Finn cleared one side of the table while she tackled the other.

"Not at all. I have four older brothers, and Saturday nights they played poker in the basement. If one of them had a date, I got to sit in."

"Which explains why you beat the pants off all of us."

"You wouldn't be a sore loser, would you, Finn?"

"Hell, yes," he said, rounding the table. "Fifteen dollars and thirty-seven cents in loose change is hard to come by. How am I going to pay the electric bill?"

"I've got money set aside," she said with a wink. "Just this once I can float you the cash, but it's gonna cost you."

"How much?" he said, stepping even closer.

Was he going to kiss her?

When he didn't, she swallowed hard, ignoring her racing pulse and the voice in the back of her head urging her to demand a shocking fee. "I, um, haven't thought that far," she said, lying through her teeth.

"Yes, you have. You know exactly what you want from me. Spill it."

She snatched a beer mug from the table and tried making a getaway, but her husband was too fast, lassoing her around the waist. Aside from carrying her to bed, or holding a cloth to her forehead when she'd been sick, this was the first time since their night in Vegas that he'd purposely touched her.

In a heartbeat, the night came back. The achingly familiar scent of his breath. The feel of his big, open palms covering her breasts. It was too much. The memories were coming too fast, too intense. If she thought of that night for even a second longer, she'd be in danger of telling him not only what she wanted in payment but ever so much more.

This perfect day had made her drunk on life.

The time with Abby, the hours spent laughing with Finn's friends. It only seemed right they should end the perfect day with the perfect kiss.

"Lilly," her husband said, cinching her close. "If you don't name your price, how can I possibly pay it?"

She licked her lips. Swallowed hard. Was it possible for a woman's heart to beat right out of her chest? Giggling at the mental image, she said, "All right, all right, you've worn me down. A kiss is what I want from you." Hopelessly embarrassed, she closed her eyes. "I know, it's a stupid thing to ask for, isn't it? Especially when we—"

"Hardly know each other?" Finn finished her sentence with his mouth less than the width of a poker card from hers.

Her limbs drugged with an unidentifiable need, she somehow found the energy to nod.

"I think a kiss is a perfectly acceptable demand in light of the pleasure you've given me."

"I have?" she squeaked.

Now he was nodding.

"So, um, what kind of kiss should it be? A polite peck between friends?"

"Does that mean you've started to think of me as a friend?" He touched his mouth to hers so softly, so fleetingly, if it hadn't been for the stirring deep in her soul, she wouldn't have believed he'd touched her at all.

At this moment, her heart cried, remembering not only the way they had been in Vegas, but the way he'd treated her here in his home—their home—*I'm not only thinking of you as a friend, but so much more.* "Y-yes," she said, scarcely trusting herself to speak. "I think of you as my friend."

"Good." He touched his lips to hers again, this time, grazing her with a whispery touch that felt like a warm feather against her lips. "Friendship is good. But do you think we could ever be more than friends?"

He pressed his mouth, that finely tuned instrument of exquisite torture, against her neck, giving her no choice but to arch her head, granting him access to whatever he desired.

Friends. Husband and wife. Lovers…

With each passing day, he was opening her mind and heart to the delicious possibilities their future held in store.

"Lilly?"

"Hmm?"

"You didn't answer my question." His lips hot, tongue moist, he pressed an urgent, openmouthed kiss to the base of her throat.

"Uh-huh…"

"You do think of me as more than just a friend?"

Oh, yes.

He'd murmured the words into her left ear and the heat of them sent chills scurrying up her spine.

"That's great, sweetie." He pressed one more kiss, an unbearably chaste kiss, to her cheek, then released her. "I'm glad you're starting to feel more comfortable around me." Whistling a happy tune, he strolled out of the kitchen. "Would you mind locking up?" he called over his shoulder. "I'm hitting the sack."

GRRR.

Lilly gave her pillow a good punch before wedging it beneath her head.

That mind reader she called a husband had known all along she wanted a kiss. The big creep.

Why did he have to be so handsome? And nice? And sexy? And even good at changing diapers?

Was there nothing the man couldn't do?

Staring out the window at the starless night, for the first time since stepping foot in Finn's house, she realized it was starting to feel like home. She liked the layout of the kitchen and the way all the tea towels and dishcloths matched. It was almost as if Finn had readied this house for a wife years before they ever met.

A pang shot through her heart.

Of course, he'd readied this house for a wife. Vivian. Who knew, maybe she'd been the one to add all the decorative touches that made the house such a welcoming home?

Ugh, this line of thought was crazy.

Vivian's loss was Lilly's gain. Finn Reilly was a wonderful man. By the hour—no, minute—he attracted her more than Elliot or Dallas combined. And seeing Finn interact with Abby proved that what Dr. Walsh had said about him one day being a great father was true.

What else had the doctor said might be true?

Were he to lose faith in you as he did Vivian, I'm not sure how he'd react.

Squeezing her eyes shut tight, Lilly fought a wave of panic. She had to tell Finn about her baby. A half-dozen moments this afternoon, the timing couldn't have been more perfect. So why hadn't she summoned the nerve?

Fear.

Plain and simple, she was terrified of losing him. If he didn't want to raise Elliot's baby, she'd understand. He had every right to desire children of his own.

If Finn left her, not only would she be raising a baby all alone, but she'd have to bear the shame of her disapproving family. And it was that fear which had prompted her to seek a husband in the first place.

Perhaps even worse than all those other fears combined was that the past few days with Finn had felt so gloriously right. Her marriage to Dallas would have been based upon mutual convenience, but she suspected that if she gave Finn half a chance, their marriage could be based upon love.

What would become of her if she were to toss wide-open the doors of her heart to this man? What if telling him about her baby, far from pleasing him, gave him cause to send her packing? Could she bear the pain?

No.

Which was why, even though she knew telling Finn was the right thing, the *only* thing, for her to do in order to base their burgeoning relationship upon mutual trust, she couldn't.

Not yet.

But soon.

Cupping her hands to her womb, she felt not the stirring of her child but the ticking of a clock. Just as her affection for Finn was growing, so was this baby. And with every passing day, her window of opportunity to come clean with her husband passed as well.

"WHAT ARE YOU DOING?" Lilly asked Finn the next morning in the kitchen.

"What's it look like I'm doing?" he said, patting the side of an old-fashioned wicker basket. The inside was lined with red gingham and even had matching red plastic cups secured to the side with worn leather straps. "I'm packing a picnic lunch."

The previous day's storm had passed and Indian summer was back, flooding the room with golden sun that washed away Lilly's nighttime fears and filled her heart with hope.

"Can I help?"

"Sure. Grab a couple apples and some pop from the fridge." He'd just finished piling shaved deli ham on two pieces of wheat bread.

"Where are we going?" she asked from inside the fridge.

"It's a surprise."

"Oh no," she said. "As much fun as I had yesterday, this doesn't involve Abby again, does it?"

Slapping cheese and the top piece of bread on the

sandwiches, he said, "Thankfully, no. That little angel wore me out."

"So then?" she said, setting the drinks and fruit in the basket. "Why the mystery?"

He shocked her with a sweet kiss to the tip of her nose. "I like a little mystery now and then. Adds spice to life."

"All right, I'll willingly go along on this magical mystery tour of yours under one condition."

"What's that?"

"Do you also promise we won't be seeing any poodle or parrot juggling?"

"Promise," he said, crossing his heart before setting the sandwiches into the basket beside bags of chips and cookies. Looking at their meal, he frowned. "There's something I forgot, but I can't remember what."

"Hmm," Lilly teased. "Could it be the kitchen sink?"

"Har-de-har-har. Oh, I know. The wine."

Wine?

She couldn't drink. Alcohol was bad for the baby, but how was she going to explain that to Finn?

Again Dr. Walsh's words haunted her. *…you should tell him the truth—preferably before he makes a few deductions of his own.*

CHAPTER ELEVEN

"THAT'S, OKAY," LILLY SAID, "I've never been all that big on wine. Gives me a headache."

"Really? This is good stuff. Made locally. You sure you don't want to at least give it a try?"

She shook her head.

"All right, then. Let me grab a couple of sweatshirts and we'll head out."

The ride to their mystery destination couldn't have been more relaxing. Finn was the consummate host, pointing out spots of interest along the way and sharing funny stories about his childhood. The one thing he never brought up were his parents, and though Lilly wondered why, she figured her husband had his reasons and left it at that.

Greenleaf was nestled in the foothills of the Wasatch Mountains and with each foot in elevation Abigail climbed, the sweeter became the air and view. Majestic firs lined the winding road and snow-covered peaks cradled glistening sapphire jewels far too pretty to be called mere lakes.

Finally Finn pulled the truck off the paved highway and onto a dirt road that was more of a track.

"Now I'm getting suspicious," she said. "This doesn't look like any picnic ground I've ever seen."

"Just wait." Holding tight to the wheel, he steered

the truck around tooth-jarring potholes. "I promise, the destination is well worth this rough ride."

"I hope so," she said, shooting him a grin. "Dentures don't come cheap!"

True to his word, ten minutes later, her husband parked Abigail in an alpine meadow. Tall grasses swayed in a light breeze and when Lilly climbed out of the truck, she was first struck by the difference in temperature, and then by the quiet and smells. The air was crisp, and clean enough to have a taste. Spicy firs, sweet late-blooming alpine willow weed, and the thirst-quenching scent of water from a pond about a hundred yards to the north, its rippled surface reflecting the grandeur of a neighboring, snowcapped peak.

"That's Mount Neebo," Finn said, climbing out of the truck to stand beside her.

"Why's it called that?"

He shrugged. "As kids, we used to call it Mount *Neemo* after the famous submarine captain."

"Makes sense."

"You ready for a hike?"

"That depends. We're not climbing Mount Neebo-Neemo, are we?"

"What's the matter, Mrs. Reilly? You're not chicken, are you?"

Not only that, but every minute I happen to be falling a little more for you, Mr. Reilly. If they had their picnic in the meadow, not only could they be lazy, but she'd have more time to stare at him. In teasing her, he'd lightly wrapped his arm about her shoulders and flashed her his widest smile of strong, white teeth. His eyes shone the deepest shade of brown, reminding her of other yummy brown things such as cocoa and Hershey bars. As if all that weren't enough, there was his body to contend with. His broad shoulders and washboard abs, clad in a faded green Greenleaf High T-shirt, and his long, strong legs in worn 501s. Whew, she'd married quite a stud.

"Bawk, bawk," she finally said once she'd recovered from the gorgeous view—the view of her husband, that is! "Can't we eat here in the meadow? That long ride was tiring, and I am kind of hungry."

"No way are you getting off that easy. I brought you up here for a reason." At the back of the truck, he pulled their basket from the bed. "Come on, woman, march."

"Where to? That lovely boulder over there?" Sweetly smiling, she pointed to a rock not three feet from the truck's chrome fender.

"Nice try. Thatta way." He pointed to a well-used trail winding into a stand of firs and golden-leafed aspen.

The hike was taxing, yet the beauty more than made up for Lilly's aching joints. In the years since she'd been to the mountains, she'd forgotten how much fun a day spent communing with nature could be. The pungent scent of evergreens invigorated her senses. The sight of sunbeams slanting through feathery pine boughs invigorated her soul.

"This is my favorite part of the hike," Finn said, slowing to match her pace while enfolding her hand in his. "It feels like a church, don't you think?"

"Mmm-hmm." She gave his hand a knowing squeeze.

They hiked about ten more minutes, cushy pine needles absorbing their footsteps and voices, then emerged from the forest and into another meadow. At the far end, massive pine timbers framed the opening to a mine shaft that had been blasted into the face of a rocky bluff.

Stopped at the head of the trail, Lilly put her hands on her hips. “Why does this scene strike me as familiar?”

His grin looked the teeniest bit guilty. “Beats me.”

“Finn Reilly, fess up. Is this the same mine where you took Shannon Jowoskiwitz in the hopes of scoring?”

Aiming his gaze toward the blazing blue sky, he said, “Could be. If it is, I’m too much of a gentleman to ever tell.” With a brazen wink, he added, “I’m impressed. You remembered her name.”

“That’s not all I remember. I know firsthand what you like doing in caves.” The moment she said the words, Lilly put her hand to her mouth. That last thought was supposed to have only been for her!

Her husband set their basket at his feet before crossing the short distance to where she stood. Hands loosely on her hips, he said, “Seems to me I wasn’t the only one who enjoyed our game of cave explorer.”

Trying to hide her smile, she pushed free of his hold. “Yeah, well, that was when I thought I knew you.”

“Are we back to that old excuse?”

“What’s that supposed to mean?” She spun to face him. “It’s the truth, Finn. That night, I thought you were Dallas. If I hadn’t, I never would have…well, let’s just say we would have had separate rooms and leave it at that.”

“I’d rather leave it at this….”

Hands back on her hips, he tugged her close. Too close. Her traitorous body instinctively melded against him. Her coursing pulse muddled her normally good judgment. Before she could tell him to slow down, he pressed his lips to hers for the sweetest of kisses. No pressure, just promises. Promises that he'd give her the life she'd always wanted. Babies and a wonderful home and good friends and the respect of her always perfect siblings and parents.

All too soon, he released her and, without his support, she felt fragile as dandelion fluff being ferried by the wind. It was at that moment, when she realized without his arms around her she no longer knew which direction her life should go, that she made the heart-stopping realization that she could be falling in love with him. The bet no longer mattered. Truth be told, he'd been as confused about their meeting as she had. All that mattered now was that they were meant for each other in every conceivable way from them both liking hamburgers for breakfast to the fact that she was a perfect fit in his arms.

All she had to do was tell him about her baby and their lives would be complete. If he felt half for her what she did for him, he'd welcome her child with loving arms. He could have insisted upon obtaining a divorce, but he hadn't. He'd stuck by her and she could only pray he'd stick by her baby as well.

"Are you ready to enter Finn's Cave of Love?" he teased, holding her with one hand and the basket with the other.

"Is it safe?" she said, her maternal instincts overriding those dying to once again be in the dark, alone with her husband.

"Absolutely. I bring scout troops up here every year, so each fall I have a structural engineering buddy help me shore it up."

"You do a lot for kids, don't you?"

"What can I say? I'm a sucker for the little buggers."

Tell him now, her heart urged. *You'll never have a better chance to break the news about your baby.*

He led her into the mine shaft and it took a second for her eyes to adjust to the change in light. The temperature dropped ten degrees and the musty smell transported her to a time when the place would have bustled with men seeking their fortunes.

Again Finn set down the basket. This time though, he opened the lid and withdrew a navy-blue sweatshirt and powerful flashlight.

Holding the shirt up to her, he said, "Lift your arms and I'll put this on for you."

She did as he asked, luxuriating in the feel of his expert care. His knuckles grazed the sides of her breasts, tickling her with an erotic jolt. "Thanks for thinking of me," she said.

"Hey," he flashed her his sexiest grin. "I learned the hard way, through Shannon, that cold girls are a lot less likely to put out."

She made a face. "Is you-know-what all you ever think about, Finn Reilly?"

Drawing her close for a swift kiss, he said, "It is when I'm with you, Lilly Reilly. So how about it? Care to get lucky in an old silver mine?"

Her heart flip-flopping with what she half hoped and half feared was love for this incredibly tender, sweet and sexy man, Lilly said, "Lead the way. You never know what treasure we might find."

"THIS PLACE IS like something out of another world…"

After following a maze of tunnels, they'd entered a cavernous room complete with stalactite chandeliers and an orchestra of dripping water. Crystals sparkled in the flashlight's powerful beam, and the surface of most rocks had taken on a pale, milky glow. Stone pillars formed a natural gate to a clear lake and where most caves she'd been in had smelled as if a bear had been using it as his winter condo, this one smelled fresh, of water and soil, and miners' faded dreams.

"From what I've read about these kinds of rock formations," Finn said, "we practically are in another world. For Utah, this is pretty amazing stuff." Finn found himself once again swelling with manly pride. He loved making Lilly happy, and to think that she was enjoying this unique spot as much as he did made the moment that much more special.

"Shannon Jowoskiwitz was crazy not to have kissed you in here."

"That's what I thought," he said, kneeling to light an oil lamp he kept stashed in the room. "But since her rejection, you're the first girl I've brought back."

Pressing her hands to his chest, she said, "In spite of my cold nose, I'm honored. So?" she asked, lightly stepping from one side to the other of the gurgling stream feeding the lake, "When do I get my kiss?"

"Patience, my dear. No kissing until after we dine." On a massive flat stone, he arranged their picnic atop a red flannel blanket.

After the long hike, Lilly was plenty hungry and never had sandwiches tasted so good. "You're a great cook," she said.

"Thanks. I've been using this top-secret recipe for years. Honey ham and provolone. Don't tell a soul." Even in the wavering lamplight, she saw his eyes sparkle with devilish charm.

"Why didn't you ever bring Vivian here?" she asked after taking a drink of frosty root beer.

He shrugged. "She was pretty high maintenance.

Spending an afternoon traipsing around an old mine wasn't her cup of tea. Come to think of it," he said, popping his last bite of sandwich into his mouth. "We never had that much in common."

"Then why did you ask her to marry you?"

Finn frowned. Was now the time to tell his wife how desperate he'd been to start a family? How weary he'd been of casual dating? "She was gorgeous and said she loved me. I guess I naively thought the rest would work itself out." Snatching a Nutter Butter, he asked, "Speaking of our exes, you never did tell me how Dallas took the news that you'd gotten hitched."

"At first he was nice, said he'd been worried about me. But then I told him what had happened between you and me and he turned cold. Said some pretty harsh things."

"Sorry." Giving her hand a squeeze, Finn said, "I know back in Vegas you thought the guy hung the moon. Discovering you'd rather kick him *to* the moon must've hurt."

"Yeah, well..." Her lips curved in a slight grin, she shrugged. "Honestly, I think it's best he showed his true colors. When I first found out that you weren't him, I toyed with the idea of divorcing you to go ahead and marry him."

"So? What stopped you?" Waiting for her answer, Finn's heart caught in his throat.

"Principle. I remembered I already was married. As you'll find out when you meet my folks over Thanksgiving, they're all about family. Perfect family. There's never been a divorce in our family tree and I wasn't about to be the first to break a branch."

"Even though following that so-called perfect example may mean spending your entire life in a loveless marriage?"

She swallowed hard. "Who said ours was destined to be a loveless marriage?"

"Don't tease me about something like that, Lilly."

"I'm not. These past few days have, well...you've showed me in a hundred tiny ways what kind of man you truly are. I love how you buy ice cream for Chrissy and Randy. I love how you cared for me when I was sick and for Rachel's baby when she needed a sitter. You're constantly caring for everyone around you, Finn Reilly, but never yourself."

Not knowing what to say, he remained silent.

"Well, you know what?" she asked, silently clearing a path in their remaining food to creep to his side of the blanket.

"What?"

"It's about time someone started caring for you, and I nominate...me." In the dancing lamplight, she kissed him. Soft at first, testing, seeing if he understood what she'd been trying to say. But then he groaned and slid his work-roughened hand under the fall of her hair. Leaning back, he pulled her on top of him. And then there was no more need for words when their actions spoke eloquently for them both.

Finn sighed, drawing strength from the woman he found more intriguing by the moment. What an amazing twist of fate meeting her had been. "I know this may sound crazy, but knowing that you're now one hundred percent committed to our marriage is such a turn-on. So is knowing you'd never even think of hurting me like Vivian."

"Oh, Finn..." *Tell him about the baby,* Lilly's conscience urged. *Before it's too late.*

He took her half-crazed moan to mean that she was ready for more kissing, and when he proceeded to do just that, she felt powerless to stop.

Being with him felt so good, so right.

It wouldn't have mattered if they were in this cave or on Mars, she never wanted to be anyplace other than in his arms. But therein lay the problem. What if she told him the truth about her baby and he rejected her? What if she not only had to deal with her family's disapproval, but the heartache of losing her husband?

His voice hoarse from emotion, he said, "I want to make love with you. Right here, right now."

Resting her cheek against his chest, she heard the thunder of his heart. "I want that, too," she said. "You'll never know how much, but I can't."

"Why?"

"I—"

"Look at me, Lilly." He leaned back, granting himself a view deep into her eyes. She might have been fully clothed, but his stare made her feel stripped to her soul. "I just admitted how much I care for you. I thought you felt the same?"

"I do, it's just that—"

"What? Why don't you want to..."

Lilly fought for air. Though his words trailed off, they both knew what he meant.

Time. She needed time to figure out how to best tell him about the baby. Then they'd make love, because only then would her affection be coming from a pure place.

"Lilly?"

She sighed. "Please, Finn, don't spoil what has been a beautiful day. I promise you, we will make love again, but I need more space. Admitting the extent to which

I've grown to care for you was a big step. Making love to you will be even bigger. We've already come so far. Please, *please* be patient just a short while longer."

THAT EVENING, Finn turned off the downstairs lights and was climbing the stairs when Lilly realized she had a tough decision to make.

The night had turned blustery. Outside, a fierce wind sent branches scurrying against the windows, begging to be let in. The wind's lonely howl reminded her how more than anything, she wanted to join her husband in his big bed, spending dark hours cuddled in the light of his arms, but her heart wouldn't let her.

She hadn't yet told him about the baby and with every passing minute, she grew more terrified of what his reaction might be. If she resumed her marital relations with him and he did send her packing once he heard her news, wouldn't the fact that they'd been a husband and wife in every sense of the word make her leaving that much harder?

Pausing at the top of the stairs, Finn said, "Come to bed with me, Lilly."

"Finn, I—"

"We don't have to do anything you don't want. We'll talk. Hold each other."

Her lower lip started to quiver and she longed for the strength to hold her tears at bay. "I wish I could share a bed with you, but I can't."

"Why?"

"I'm not ready. I told you, I need more time."

"Time for what? What is time going to do other than make what we're feeling that much stronger?"

"Nothing, I—"

"What, Lilly?" His fingers beneath her chin, he held

her gaze steady on his. "What aren't you telling me? Are you still upset over the part I played in that stupid bet?"

No. "Yes, okay? You say you feel you can trust me, but I still need to trust you." *Trust you not to break my heart when I shock you with my news.*

"But I thought. This afternoon, the things you said..."

"I meant every word, but can't you see? I need more time to process all of this, what I'm feeling. It came about so quickly. My mind is spinning. Please," she said, pressing her hands to his chest. "Please, Finn, give me room to think."

"Okay." He pressed a tender kiss to her lips. "But as of now, consider yourself on notice."

"For what?" she asked, her heart thudding with dread when he took her hands in his.

"Notice that I'm about to make you the happiest, most contented woman who ever lived. Mark my words, by Thanksgiving, you are going to not only be sharing my bed, but every aspect of my life."

Promise?

He pulled her close for a mind-shattering kiss that not only weakened her knees but her resolve. Yes, she should go with him, to his bed, to his soul...anywhere he wanted to go.

"Before I forget," he said, releasing her to fish in the front pocket of his jeans. "I meant to give this to you today, but the timing wasn't right." He pressed a plastic key chain and key into her open palm, then closed her fingers around it.

"What does this unlock?" she asked.

"Nothing much. Just my home and heart. Good night," he said, his breath hot against her swollen lips.

"Good night."

In the shadowy hall, she felt rather than saw his gaze, and then he slipped away, entering his room and quietly shutting the door.

Take me with you, her heart cried as she squeezed the cold key until it sliced into her skin, but her conscience reigned supreme.

Opening her fingers, in the dim light of the hall sconce, she studied the plastic key chain. It was a big red Sparky the Wonder Dog souvenir, and on the back, Finn had engraved *How about adding me and Sparky to your key chain collection?*

She'd forgotten all about the surprise he'd purchased for her in Vegas. Despite its minimal cost, never had a gift touched her more.

Instantly her old friends the tears were back and she sniffed her way to her room, shut the door and climbed into bed. The sheets were cold and a pine bough swept incessantly against her window.

Tell him, the howling wind urged, never giving her a moment's peace. *Tell him the truth. He's a compassionate man. He'll understand.*

But for every argument in favor of telling him, there was a stronger one against.

What if she told him and he rejected her completely? Thought her despicable for having an affair?

Yes, but you didn't know Elliot was married until it was too late. Elliot told you he loved you and you believed with all your heart you loved him.

Okay, but what if Finn wants nothing to do with raising another man's child?

Nonsense. Finn loves every child. He would never reject an innocent baby any more than he would reject you.

On and on her turmoil raged, as did the ceaseless wind.

She would tell him in the morning.

She wouldn't tell him in the morning.

Like plucking petals from a daisy, the decision went around and around her head. Sometime after the grandfather clock chimed twelve, still clenching Finn's key in her hand, sheer exhaustion granted Lilly sleep, but even in her dreams she was unable to find peace.

If anything, her dreams of what might have been, made the agony of what would most likely happen hurt all the more. Once she told her husband the truth about why she'd been so eager to not only get married, but stay married, he might never speak to her again.

CHAPTER TWELVE

THE TWO WEEKS LEADING to Thanksgiving were the happiest of Finn's life. Yes, the times he'd spent with his parents and sister would always hold a bittersweet place in his heart, but this time with Lilly was different. Not just about cherishing old memories, but making new ones.

The weather had finally changed for good and with each passing day, Old Man Winter knocked harder on their door.

Every afternoon after work, Finn returned home to find Lilly singing show tunes at the stove. She was an amazing cook, and after the two of them lingered at the table discussing their day, he'd build a fire in the living room hearth to warm them as they whiled away the hours until bedtime playing Scrabble or cards, or sometimes doing nothing at all besides lounging in each other's arms, staring into the flames.

The only thing still troubling Finn about their marriage was that Lilly refused to move into his bedroom. He could care less about the sexual aspects of her move. It was the lack of trust that bothered him, the lack of intimacy holding each other through the night would bring.

The day he'd taken her to the mine, he'd been certain they'd reached a changing point in their relationship, and they had, but now he had to wonder how much further they had to go?

Finn wanted all of Lilly, but evidently, that was more than she was ready to give. Still, that was okay. He'd waited a lifetime to find her and if that was what it took to keep her, he'd wait a lifetime more. She meant everything to him. He'd give her all the time she needed to insure she never felt pressured.

"You're going to adore my family," she said to him over a delicious spaghetti dinner the night before Thanksgiving. Outside, cold rain nipped at the windows, but inside, the tropical blue heat of Lilly's eyes made Finn all warm and toasty. "I can't wait for you to meet my brothers and sisters."

"You think I'll fit in?" he asked, his mind spinning at the prospect that he was about to go from having almost no family to so much family he'd have a tough time learning all their names.

"How could they not like you?" she said, setting down her glass of milk to give his hand a reassuring squeeze. "You treat me like royalty and that's all that matters to them."

"Does that mean," he said after swallowing a bite of spaghetti, "you're starting to feel comfortable here, princess? Like this is your castle?"

Not trusting herself to speak, Lilly nodded. If only Finn knew how comfortable she truly felt, and how terrified she was of her deep contentment being snatched away.

After dinner, since she'd cooked, Finn had established firm rules about him cleaning up.

While she sipped an after-dinner cup of peppermint tea, he not only washed dishes but entertained her with hilarious stories about his construction jobs.

Finished washing the last dish, he held out his hand and said, "Mrs. Reilly, shall we retire to the living room?"

"By all means," she said, taking his hand and letting him guide her out of the room.

In the cozy cinnamon-red living room, while Finn built a fire in the river-stone hearth, Lilly took her usual spot at the end of the washed-denim sofa. The cushions were sinkers—meaning they were so comfy that once she plopped down, she was loath to get back up. Which explained how more than a few times she'd fallen asleep, only to wake being carried to bed in her husband's arms.

Adding to the room's warmth were built-in bookshelves lined with current bestsellers and classics. After the first frost, Finn had brought in the porch ferns and they now sat in elegant brass stands tucked into the living room's corners, and throughout the house.

"What's your pleasure?" Finn asked when the fire merrily crackled, fighting off the outside chill. "TV? Letting me beat you at a game of Scrabble?"

"You've never beaten me at a game of Scrabble."

He winked. "That's because I've been letting you win."

"Oh, sure. And that same losing instinct is why it was so important to you to win that bet against Mitch?"

"Ha-ha. Okay, you got me. I'm a loser when it comes to word games, but do you dare play me a game of Monopoly?"

"That depends," she said, stretching like a lazy cat. "Do you deliver?"

He rolled his eyes. "Woman, if I let you, you'd be in bed by seven every night of the week."

"And your point is?" she said with a wide grin.

"You're hopeless." While returning her smile, he shook his head before digging the Monopoly game from the bottom tier of the bookshelf.

Within the hour, Finn was beating her soundly. "Is this some kind of Scrabble revenge thing you have going?" she asked, for the third time landing on Baltic Avenue, and having to pay rent on his supposedly low-budget motel.

"Just pay me your four hundred and fifty bucks and quit whining," he said, fanning himself with a stack of orange five-hundred-dollar bills.

She mortgaged all her property, counted her meager amount of cash, yet it still wasn't enough. "I can't pay. You wiped me out."

"Already?"

"*Already?* You've been trouncing me for the past thirty minutes and you're complaining that it hasn't been long enough?"

A playful sparkle in his deep brown eyes, he leaned across the coffee table, toppling his red-and-green empire to press a kiss to her lips. "Ouch," he said, rubbing his back as he lowered himself to the floor. "I'm getting too old for stealing quick kisses."

"Want me to give you a massage?"

His eyebrows lifted. "Would you? My back hurts *really* bad."

Already rising from the sofa, she said, "Why do I get the distinct impression I'm being bamboozled?"

"'Cause you are?" Finn's rakish grin didn't look the slightest bit sorry as he rolled onto his stomach on the thick rag rug in front of the fire.

"Great," she said, kneeling beside him.

"Hey, can you blame a guy for wanting a rubdown after a long day's work?"

"No, I can't, which is why I'm down here, rubbing you all over, you big lug."

"Mmm..." Her small hands worked magic on his lower and middle back. "Rub me all over, wife. I do like the sound of that."

"You would." She gave him an extra hard squeeze.

"Hey, what'd you do that for? I took good care of you when you were sick."

"Yeah, but I really was sick."

"I am, too. My back is killing me from sitting on the floor while you sat up there on your throne."

"My throne?" Where only a second earlier, she'd been firmly rubbing, she now twinkled her fingers beneath his arms, tickling him senseless.

Rolling over to thwart her attack, he tried tickling her back, but years of practice in escaping her brothers had made her an expert at the arts of both dodging tickles and giving them.

"Okay, okay," he finally yelped, out of breath and laughing. "I surrender."

"And you apologize for that throne comment?"

"Never," he said, a wicked gleam in his eyes.

"Apologize," she said, hitting him with a surprise attack between his ribs.

"All right. You weren't sitting on your throne," he said between laughs. "Just being lazy!"

"Ooh, that's even worse!"

The teasing went back and forth for another five minutes until they were both too exhausted to put up a good fight. Deciding mutual truces would be their best course of action, they collapsed side by side in front of the dancing fire, comfy throw pillows beneath their heads.

"Finn?" Lilly asked after a few minutes of their listening to the rain.

"Yeah?"

"A little while ago, when you mentioned how you nursed me when I was sick?"

"Yeah? What about it?"

"I was wondering," she said, taking a deep breath. "Why did you take such good care of me?" Turning onto her side to face him, she added, "At the time, you hardly knew me."

"You're wrong about that." With his index finger, he lazily reached for her, tracing her eyebrows, cheeks and nose. "I've known you my whole life, Lilly Reilly. I've been waiting for you for as long as I can remember."

"You lost me," she said with a slow smile. "What does that mean?"

Finn was once again on the verge of keeping his most painful experience a secret, but then he saw the warmth in his wife's eyes and decided if she couldn't know the truth about his childhood, then who could? She was the cause of his present happiness. Shouldn't she be let in on the reason he'd previously felt so much pain?

Taking a deep breath, he said, "There's something I haven't told you."

"O-okay…"

"You don't have to look so stricken," he ran his finger along her quivering lower lip. "It's not anything bad—at least not to you. It was to me, but…"

"Whatever it is, tell me. You're scaring me."

He eased himself into an upright position, sitting cross-legged with his back to the fire. "I grew up in this house. When I was a kid, I lived a storybook life. While Dad went off to earn the bacon, Mom cared for my sister and me. The cookie jar was always full of fresh-baked goodies and the kitchen always smelled of home-baked bread."

"That sounds wonderful," she said, her eyes shining with what he prayed might someday be love. "I can't wait to one day meet your parents and sister. Where do they live?"

He swallowed hard. "In heaven."

Still lying on her side, she scrunched up her nose. "Is that in Utah?"

"No, baby," he said, toying with one of her curls. "It's in the clouds."

Realizing his family wasn't a couple hundred miles away, but forever gone, her smile slowly faded. She searched his face for confirmation that what he'd told her was true and when she got it, she scrambled to her knees, only to shuffle the small distance it took to wrap him in her arms. "Oh, Finn. I'm so sorry. What happened? How long has it been since they died?" Waiting for him to answer, she tucked her legs beneath her and sat on her heels.

Finn swallowed years of pent-up grief. "They died when I was eight. I was camping with my scout troop near the mine where I took you. They were on their way to Denver to visit a friend of Mom's who'd had a baby." His words caught in his throat, but still he went on. "They were on Colorado I-70, traveling up Vail Pass when a freak summer snowstorm hit. The storm claimed not just my mom, dad and little sister, but fourteen lives in all. Not thirty minutes after it hit, I've been told that the sun was shining."

"Oh, Finn," she said, taking his hands in hers. "I wish there was something I could do, something I could say."

"But don't you see?" he said, his eyes watering over. "That's what I've been trying not-so-successfully to show you. By agreeing to be my wife, you've already done more than anyone else ever could."

"What do you mean?"

"I mean, my whole life, I've been trying to get back the sense of belonging to a family."

"But you are part of a family. From what I've seen, this whole town loves you."

"I know, and I love them, but as selfish as it sounds, it's not enough. It's never been enough. After my parents died and I had to leave this house to live with my aunt, I always swore I'd come back. I'd fill this house with love the way my parents did for me. I'd bring home a wife who'd sing while she cooked and keep me company on cold winter nights. We'd make lots of beautiful babies and live happily ever after. That's why I fell for you so fast. That's why I knew from what felt like the moment I met you that we were meant to be together, because we were. Angels sent you to me, Lilly."

Her eyes glowing with warmth and unshed tears, she gave his hands a squeeze. "Y-you've got that backward," she said. "Angels sent you to me."

"How's that?"

"Finn…I'm pregnant."

"You're what?"

"Pregnant. I'm going to have a baby."

While Finn stared at her for what felt like forever, Lilly's heart pounded. What was he thinking? Why wouldn't he say something? And then, in one crushing hug, he answered her every question.

"Do you have any idea how happy you've made me?" he asked, drawing her to her feet to hug her all over again. "This explains so much. Your drinking milk all the time and falling asleep. Reading Rachel's baby book. You didn't have the flu, you had morning sickness. Why didn't you tell me then?"

"I—"

"I know. It happened so fast, it must have been a shock to you, too. Oh, Lilly, this is wonderful. And finding out like this, the day before Thanksgiving. Now, when I meet your folks for the first time, we'll really have something to celebrate."

"But, Finn, I—"

"Does Doc Walsh know?"

She nodded.

He lightly smacked himself on the forehead. "No wonder she told me to ask Rachel if we could baby-sit. She wanted us to practice being a mom and dad."

"So Dr. Walsh told you I was pregnant?"

"No, no," he said, cupping her face with his big hands. "She would never divulge a confidence like that. What she did do was give me a few tips on how to make you fall for me like I already had for you. Showing you I'd make a good father was at the top of her list."

"She's a smart woman," Lilly said, reveling in the arms of this wonderful man. Why hadn't she told Finn about the baby sooner? They could have been this happy for weeks.

"I'll say. Did she have you take a pregnancy test that morning? I mean, we'd only just…you know, that weekend. You couldn't have been more than a few days along."

"Um, yeah." Like curtains rising on a stage, revealing the bad guy at the end of a play, it dawned on Lilly why her husband was taking this news so well.

Finn thinks my baby is his.

"Oh, man," he said, running his fingers through his

hair. "This is such a buzz. Like winning the lottery. I can't believe it's finally happened. I'm going to be a dad." After letting out a joyous whoop, he pulled her into his arms, whirling her around and around, kissing her and laughing and making her feel as if, far from her marriage almost being destroyed, it was growing stronger by the second.

Again he was cupping her face with his hands, pressing his lips to hers, sweetly, urgently, begging admittance not only to her heart but her soul. Tears came fast and hot.

Tell him! her conscience cried. *Tell him about Elliot. He'll understand.*

"This also explains all those tears," Finn said, tenderly brushing them away with the pads of his thumbs. "Are these happy tears you're crying now?"

Oh, Finn, think what you're saying. Think back to how I've been this emotional since the moment you first met me. Think of what that implies!

"Babe? Are you okay?" His hands about her waist, he pulled her close for a hug. "Are you still upset about how our relationship began? Are you afraid that because our feelings sprang up so fast they won't stand the test of time?"

She shook her head. "No, I—"

Tell him. Tell him.

"Because if that is the case, it's not true. Think back, Lilly." He lightly pushed her away to look deep into her eyes. "Think back to those first few hours we were together. Our first kiss. Our vows. As much as I tried denying it, I knew even then you were the woman for me. I had that crazy fear you were mixed up with Mitch, but deep down, I knew. I knew angels had handpicked you for me."

"Y-yes, Finn," she said, hardly able to speak through her tears. "Yes. Oh God, yes. I've never wanted anything but you." And she meant it. Lord, how she meant it. It was her turn to explore his face with her hands, the angular planes of his stubbled cheeks and squared set of his jaw and forehead. His deep brown eyes, which never failed to blanket her in security. His eyebrows. His lips. In such a short time, she'd grown hopelessly, wonderfully attached to him. Could this be love? The question terrified her. How many times had she fancied herself in love with Elliot or Dallas, yet look how those relationships had ended.

True, but Finn was different. Finn was infinitely kinder, gentler, all around better.

Through a miraculous twist of fate, he'd become her everything and she couldn't bear to let him go. Not yet. Not when her dreams were so close. She'd tell him the whole truth after Thanksgiving. Then she'd feel strong enough to withstand the pain should he ask her to leave, but until then, she needed time to think. Time to figure out the best way to break his heart by telling him this child wasn't his.

"Make love to me," she sobbed, fisting handfuls of his blue flannel shirt, desperately afraid that if she let go of him for even a second, her house of cards would come tumbling down.

"Are you sure you're ready?" he asked, his voice raspy with tender concern.

She nodded. "I've never been more certain of anything. Make love to me, Finn. I don't want to spend another night outside your arms."

Far from the urgency of the first time they made love, this time, her husband took it agonizingly slow. "I adore you," he said, undoing the buttons one by one on her simple burgundy peasant dress. Though the air by the fire warmed her back, her breasts reacted to the cooler side of the room. Her nipples swelled and hardened as much to the chill as to Finn's appreciative stare.

"You're so beautiful," he said, angling her toward the fire, immersing the front half of her body in its radiant glow. "You're everything I've ever dreamed of and now so much more." He drew her dress off her shoulders, smoothing it down until it fell with a whisper to the floor, pooling at her feet.

He lowered himself to his knees, cupping her behind with his big hands while with his mouth he paid homage to her womb. "I'm going to love you so much," he said to the tiny being inside. "You're going to have everything a kid could ever want."

With her husband's every word, Lilly's heart broke more.

After raining soft kisses upon her tummy, then ringing her navel, Finn moved upward, skimming his tongue along the center of her midsection while with his hands he cupped and kneaded her breasts through her scrap of an ivory silk bra.

As his explorations continued ever higher, he swept aside the lace covering her left nipple. He took that hardened bud into his mouth, then the other, drawing with such ardor that all Lilly could do was arch her head in fevered, dizzying pleasure. The heat of the fire and that of her husband's mouth combined, sending velvety chills coursing through her body. She slid her fingers into his hair, holding on with each new havoc he wrought.

Then he was standing, kissing her hard, soft, plundering her with a fervency that set her soul on fire.

Her fingers shy at first, she slipped them in between

the buttons of his blue flannel shirt. The fabric was soft, the skin beneath, rock hard and hot. After each button, she planted a kiss to the flesh she'd exposed, and when she reached the bottom, she stretched her arms high, drawing the garment past his shoulders and arms and onto the floor.

She wanted all of him.

Now.

She wanted to skim her palms over his ridges and planes. She wanted to trace her tongue along his abdomen, his nipples, take teasing bites of his beefy shoulders. She wanted to do all that and more, so she did, and when she'd had her fill of his chest, she nimbly unfastened the buttons of his 501s, drawing them down, pooling them on the floor where they caressed her dress at their feet.

Slipping her hands into the waistband of his blue plaid boxers, she slid those down as well, helping her husband lift one foot then the other as she brushed them past his feet.

He stood before her gloriously naked, lit by the fire's hypnotic glow, looking so perfect he could have been carved of stone. "You're the beautiful one," she said, taking the silken steel of him into her hand and giving him a squeeze.

"What are you trying to do to me?" he asked through a groan.

"Make you the happiest man alive."

"Yeah, well, you're succeeding."

She took him into her mouth, wanting to grant him as much pleasure as he'd given her in Vegas. He meant so much. The world. If she never had more than tonight, she wanted it to be perfect.

"Stop," Finn finally said, his fingers in her hair. "It's my turn to have fun."

"I thought you were?" she teased.

"Woman," he said with a playful growl. "You know damn well what I mean." Kicking the clothes aside, he grabbed a colorful quilt from the back of a nearby chair, then tossed it in front of the fire, piling the pillows at one end.

"Care to join me beside the fire, Mrs. Reilly?"

"Mmm, Mr. Reilly, I thought you'd never ask."

He looked at her and frowned.

"What's the matter?"

"You still have your clothes on."

"Not many," she said with a giggle.

"When it comes to you, any clothes are too many."

"Well then, since you've appointed yourself the leader of this expedition, what do you propose I do?"

Pretending to think, he scratched his head. "You could take your bra and panties off."

She defiantly shook her head. "Too simple. I want to see what lengths you're willing to go to have me."

"Hmm," he said, pressing his lips tightly together. "Are you wearing a front- or back-clasping bra?"

She looked down at the scrap of ivory lace. "Back."

"Damn. I was afraid of that. This significantly increases the difficulty of my mission."

"Oh well," she said with a saucy sigh. "If you haven't been properly trained, I guess I'll have to carry out the mission on my own." Reaching behind her, she unhooked the clasp.

"You didn't just do that," he said, his gaze appreciably warming at the sight of her slowly baring her breasts.

Before removing the bra all the way, she said, "I'll put it back on if you'd like?"

Swallowing hard, he said, "Nah…go ahead and finish."

"What if I'm too tired?"

"That's it," he growled, surprising her by snatching the silky scrap and tossing it somewhere behind the sofa. "I've had enough games. Show me your treasure or else…" He'd affected a pirate's brogue and lunged for her, holding her close while ravishing her breasts.

Giggling at his antics, she said, "Pirate Finn, are you *ever* going to make a real woman of me?"

He froze, cocked open one eye. "Is that complaining I hear out of you, ye saucy wench?"

"You'd better believe it. There's a whole burning continent in my southern hemisphere dying to be explored."

"Well, now, we can't have that, can we? Who knows what kind of treasure I might find." He touched her right hip. "Is it here that needs further exploration?"

She shook her head. "Lower."

"Here?" he asked, cupping his open palm over the swell of her tummy.

"Nope." The anticipation of how good it would feel when he finally found the damp, pulsing island between her legs drove her wild. Still he mercilessly played on.

Touching her knee, he said, "This wouldn't happen to be the spot, would it?"

"Higher."

"Here?" He'd reached her inner thigh.

"Higher."

"Here?" He covered the silken mound beneath her panties.

"A tad lower."

"Hmm, to explore that region, as lovely as they are, I'm afraid these panties will have to go." Just as he had in Vegas, he effortlessly ripped the garment at the sides before tossing it.

"I hope you're a rich pirate," she said.

"Why's that?" he asked, urging her legs apart while he spoke directly into the place yearning for his touch. The heat of his breath on her most intimate region had her nearly weeping with need.

"B-because all these panties you keep ripping are expensive."

"Maybe you should stop wearing them." He skimmed his fingers along a particularly hot section of skin. Urging her legs still farther apart, he said, "Because really, what good did that bit of lace do you anyway? It's not as if you need to protect all of this tropical paradise from me. After all, I'm just your everyday, average pirate, doing my best to satisfy my demanding wench."

"Grrr," Lilly said, need driving her close to the edge of sanity. "If you're supposed to be satisfying me, dear sir, then quit yakking and take me to bed!"

LYING IN BED the next morning, light snow falling outside the windows, his wife snuggled beside him, Finn couldn't remember having ever been more content—or exhausted! It had been a wild and wonderful night.

"Woman," he said, toying with one of her blond curls. "You wore me out."

"Are you complaining?" Blue eyes sparkling, she aimed her impish grin straight for his heart.

"Nope. Just stating the facts." After a few minutes

of companionable silence, he said, “Tell me again how many brothers and sisters you have?”

“Seven. In descending order from oldest to youngest, David, Kathy, Ben, Mark, Michael, Kristen, Mary, then me.”

“Then you? You’ve got that all wrong. You should have said and finally, wonderfully, you. After you, your parents must have realized they already had the best so why try for any more?”

“Yeah, I never thought of it that way. I’ve always been kind of the misfit. Getting rotten grades. No interest in college. Never finding a career that fit. All I’ve ever wanted to do is raise a family.”

“Sounds like a noble profession to me.”

“Yeah, but you’re biased.”

“Only because I love you.” He planted a soft kiss to her forehead. “Which reminds me, have I told you lately how much you mean to me?”

“Not in at least an hour or so.”

“Then it’s time for an update. Let’s see, I’ve already told you how much I adore your lush little body.”

She playfully rolled her eyes. “Only about a dozen times.”

“And I’ve expressed my excitement for our bundle of joy,” he said, smoothing his warm hand over her tummy.

“That was about two dozen times.”

“Can’t be. I’ve only been playing this game since midnight.”

“Mmm,” she said, snuggling close, her naked body pressed to his beneath the heavy down comforter. “And what a fun game it’s been.”

“Hush, woman. I’m trying to think of a new way that I love you besides the physical.”

Her stomach growled. Looking toward that region, she said, "I've got a great appetite."

"True, but I'm looking for something splashy."

"How about the fact that if you'd let me out of this bed, I could whip us up a couple of mean cheeseburgers?"

"Nope. I've got it. I know I've told you this before," he said, combing stray curls from her blue eyes, "but this is so good, it bears repeating."

"In that case, I'm all ears."

"Actually, you're all smart mouth. Where was I?"

"Singing my praises."

"Oh yeah. All joking aside, one of my favorite things about you is knowing how incredibly principled you are."

"Finn, I—"

"No," he said, pressing his fingertips softly to her lips. "Let me say this. After what Vivian did to me, I never thought I'd trust a woman again, but you've proved that not all women are out to work their own agendas. With you, I know that you're every bit as devoted to me as I am to you. I know that you're not going to lie to me or play silly head games. You're too good for that kind of childish nonsense. In short, you're perfect." He ended his speech by drawing her into a deep kiss.

What Finn hadn't admitted was just how grateful he was to have found such an on-the-level woman. He'd been hurt so many times in his life, he didn't think he could live through it were someone to hurt him again. But then what was he thinking? Here it was Thanksgiving Day. He was about to meet more family than even he'd imagined having. Not only would he have his wife by his side, but his growing child. Life didn't get any better.

Even though it was snowing outside, for once in a

very long time, Finn Reilly had nothing but sunshine in his heart. And after twenty-five years of eternal winter, spending the rest of his days bathed in Lilly's warmth was exactly where he wanted to be.

CHAPTER THIRTEEN

LILLY STARED OUT THE truck's window, watching Mother Nature transform the usually brown landscape alongside I-15 into a winter wonderland. This should have been one of the happiest days of her life, ranking right up there with her wedding day, but the daunting task she had ahead of her in telling Finn about Elliot being the real father of her baby scared her to the core.

Even worse, since Elliot's parents were friends with hers, what if she ran into him? What would he think of her all of the sudden being married? Would he suspect she'd married for a reason? If he did, he surely wouldn't tell anyone what that reason was, would he? After all, he had as much to lose by blabbing about their brief relationship as she did.

Squeezing her eyes shut, Lilly tried clearing her mind of anything but how delicious her mother's meal would taste and how good it would be to once again chat with her siblings. Even if they were perfect, she loved them.

"You're awfully quiet over there," Finn said from behind the wheel. "Quarter for your thoughts."

"A quarter, huh?" She flashed him a grin. "I doubt they're worth that much."

"Try me."

Shifting on the bench seat to face him, she said, "For

the first time ever, I'm finally on an even keel with my brothers and sisters."

"How so?"

"I'm married to a wonderful husband, have a baby on the way. I've quit my job at the bookstore that they always secretly thought was beneath me."

"How do you know that's what they thought? To my way of thinking, you had a job and were making your own way in the world. Even better, it was a job that allowed you to live life on your own terms. You had plenty of time to read. No stress. All in all, it seems like a pretty great gig to me."

"But not to my family. David—the oldest, is a marriage counselor with at least ten degrees after his name. Kathy's been married forever. She has a high-profile accounting job, four great kids and is head of the PTA, both Boy and Girl Scout troops, teaches Sunday school and still manages to keep an immaculate house. Ben is an award-winning policeman. He has a sweet wife who runs a needlepoint store and raises twin daughters. Mark is a lawyer. His wife is a judge and their son just won—"

"Okay, okay, I get the picture. Your family sounds pretty daunting, but then look at all your accomplishments."

She raised her eyebrows. "Mind telling me what those might be?"

"You caught me, didn't you?" Reaching for her hand, he gave it a quick kiss.

"Yeah, but the only reason I caught you is so you could save your truck. Face it, Finn, you married an only recently reformed misfit."

After scowling her way, he steered the truck onto the paved shoulder, then moved the gearshift to park.

Her purse slipped from the seat to the floor and, while picking up everything from keys to lipstick to her wallet, she asked, "What's wrong? Did we have a blowout? Was there an animal in the road?"

"None of the above." Setting the emergency brake, he unfastened his seat belt and turned to face her. "The only emergency here is the state of your self-esteem."

"I'm all right," she said. "Really, sometimes I just get a twinge impatient for my own life to start. I want to show off my baby pictures and ribbons my cookies won at the county fair." *And I'm terrified that once we get home and I tell you the truth about Elliot being the father of my baby you'll never speak to me again. All these dreams of mine that are finally within reach will go poof, back to the realm of fairy tales that failed to come true.*

"You'll do all of those things you want and so much more, Lilly. Give it time. You're young. How much older are these paragons of accomplishment you keep raving about?"

Sniffing back tears, she said, "David's eighteen years older than me."

"Well, there you go," Finn said with a laugh, pulling her close. "I would hope he'd have accomplished something in all that time. You have your whole life ahead of you to have babies, be my wife, work at a job you love. Don't you see? Now that we've found each other, anything's possible. All we have to do is dream it and it's ours."

Trying harder than ever to hold back tears, Lilly painfully added to her thoughts. *Does that mean if I wish hard enough, you'll not only forgive me for hiding the truth about my child from you, but accept him or her as your own?*

GAZING DOWN THE LENGTH of the cloth-covered plywood-and-sawhorse table lined with loving, laughing, family—*his* family, a feeling of bone-deep satisfaction filled Finn's soul. Lilly had been right. Her mom and dad, brothers, sisters and in-laws were amazing people. The majority of them had Lilly's blond hair and rosy cheeks—even her bold blue eyes. His dark hair and sudden appearance clearly should have set him apart as a stranger to this boisterous crowd, but nothing could have been further from the truth. From the moment his wife introduced him, they'd welcomed him as if they'd known him their whole lives.

The rich scents of turkey and ham, mashed potatoes, sweet potatoes, gravy and buttered rolls all mingled together, reminding him how hungry he was and how the coming feast would be the first Thanksgiving that hadn't felt empty since the death of his own family.

Swallowing hard, he prayed, *Mom, Dad, Sis...thank you. Somewhere up there, I know you're smiling down on me. Though no family could ever replace the love I feel for all of you, finally, I feel as if I've found another home.*

Finn's father-in-law clanged his fork against his wineglass, then, from his seat beside Lilly's mom at the head of the table, he stood. "Before we eat this magnificent meal, I'd like to say a few words."

Good-natured groans abounded.

Midway down the table set for nearly thirty, Lilly's brother David said, "Be quick, Dad. Mark's got his eye on the drumstick."

"Luckily, the good Lord saw fit to put two legs on that bird, which means you have no reason not to sit there and listen to every word I say."

Turning to his daughter and Finn, he said, "Lilly,

I've always been especially fond of you—not that I don't love every single one of my brood, but you're my baby, and as such, you will always hold a special place in my heart."

"Aw," Lilly's sister, Mary, said from the seat beside her, eyes shining with unshed tears. "You're my baby, too."

Lilly's mom, nodding, placed her hand on her husband's arm.

"Okay, so I'm assuming it's fairly safe to say that we all feel extra special about our little Lilly who's not so little anymore."

"Here, here," David said, raising his glass high. "To Baby Lilly!"

"To Baby Lilly!" everyone cheered.

"I'm not finished yet," her dad complained, "but what the heck, this toast'll be a warm up. To Baby Lilly!"

While some laughed, others openly shed happy tears.

"Okay then, where I was headed with this, I have no idea. I just wanted to say how pleased I am for you, sweetheart. I'm still peeved about missing my chance to walk you down the aisle, but your mother assures me that if your wedding day was special for the two of you, then that's all that matters."

"Here, here," David said, "Let's toast Baby Lilly's marriage."

Lilly's dad shot his son a look.

"What can I say? I'm hungry?"

While everyone else laughed, David's wife gave him a good-natured whack.

"In conclusion—"

"Grandpa Tom," piped Mary's daughter, three-year-old Erin. "You talk too much!"

"All right," Grandpa Tom said, a twinkle in his blue eyes—Lilly's blue eyes. "I get the message." Raising his glass one final time, he said, "Here's to Finn Reilly, the newest member of our family and hearts. May you and our little girl live happily ever after!"

"To happily ever after!"

Lilly's mom said a blessing for the food, then all pandemonium broke out in a mad grab for grub.

"Um, I know you're all hungry," Finn said above the clang of serving forks and spoons, "but I do have one more quick announcement—and I do mean quick."

"Go ahead," Tom said, a bite of turkey poised at his lips. "But we're going to hold you to your promise to be quick. Mother, here, makes the best turkey around and I've been waiting since last Thanksgiving for another taste."

"No offense to your cooking, Mrs. Churchill, but since my wife here has been shy on this matter, I thought I'd go ahead and tell you the news myself."

Lilly dropped her fork to her plate. *No! Finn, don't tell them I'm pregnant. If they don't know, then there won't be any way of Elliot knowing, either.*

Standing, wrapping his arm around Lilly's shoulder and giving her a squeeze, he said proudly, "Your daughter and I are already expecting."

All food forgotten, Lilly was stampeded by hugs and well wishes. While her mother burst into joyful tears, her sisters began planning a baby shower and her brothers patted Finn on his back.

While she should have told them all right then and there the truth about the baby, the look of pride on her husband's face was too precious to publicly shatter. She'd tell him the truth the second they got home. Until then, not only would she let him revel in this moment, but she'd indulge in a small slice of happiness, as well.

All her life, she'd celebrated her siblings joys, but now, finally, it was her turn to be lauded. What could it hurt to hold on to her secret a short while longer?

"HE'S A HUNK," Lilly's sister Mary said an hour later, scrubbing a rose-adorned plate, then passing it to Lilly to rinse while her sister Kathy dried.

David's wife, Stacie, hard at work on leftover disbursement at the kitchen's center island said, "And did you ever see such broad shoulders?" Closing her eyes, she sighed. "He's like Jean-Claude Van Damme and Tom Cruise all rolled into one. Mmm, your baby is going to be adorable."

"Would you guys knock it off," Lilly said.

"What's the matter with you, squirt?" Mary flicked her sister with bubbles. "We're all happily married. What's it hurt to let us dream about your guy for a while instead of our flabby couch potatoes?"

"Speak for yourself," Heather, the policeman's wife, said. "Ben is buff."

"That's true," Mary conceded. "But the rest of our guys could use a couple years' worth of workouts."

"Mary," Lilly's mom said, stepping in from the living room to supervise the cleanup. "That's enough yammering about how cute Finn is, although—" she looked over her shoulder to see if any of the guys had followed her into the room "—he is a real stud, isn't he?"

"Mom!" Lilly's cheeks pinkened in horror. "Where did you even learn the word *stud?*"

"I know all kinds of words," she said with a wink. "In fact, just the other day your father and I were making out when he said I was a—"

"No!" Mary cried. "No more sharing of Dad's and your sex lives. I can't take it anymore."

"Why not? I should think you'd be glad that your father and I still lust for each other."

"We are, Mom," Stacie said from her center-island post, wrapping the turkey tray with foil. "We just don't want to hear about it."

"Yeah," concurred the rest of the women.

Mary said, "It's kind of depressing to know your mother gets more action than you do."

"Speak for yourself." Lilly's grin was wide. "Last night was pretty amazing."

Mary was back to flicking suds.

"Hey!" Lilly cried. "Can I help it if, like Mom said, I married a stud?"

"You just wait," Stacie said. "Before you know it, your baby will be here and then you and that stud muffin of yours can kiss your intimate nights goodbye."

Mary washed the last plate, then handed it to Lilly. "You know," she said, "I used to be so envious of you. Frittering away your time in that quaint bookstore, dating, doing whatever you wanted with your time. But now, you're just like the rest of us, little sis. Welcome to the grown-up club."

Mary, envious of her? "In case you haven't noticed, I've been a grown-up for quite some time now."

"Yeah," Stacie said, sliding a bowl of cranberries into the fridge. "But you've been a grown-up without all the hassles. No orthodontists, no surprise plumbing bills."

"No cooking for last-minute business parties," added Janine, Michael's wife.

"But don't you see?" Lilly said. "I've been envious

of what all of you have. You all lead the perfect lives and I've just been sitting at home, night after night."

"Poor Lilly," Mary said. "Soaking for uninterrupted hours up to her neck in hot bubbles."

Stacie added, "Not having to share the remote."

"Jeez, guys," Lilly said, drying a china gravy boat. "You're scaring me. Is married life that much drudgery?"

"Don't you listen to them, baby." Her mother gave her a quick hug from behind. "Married life has its ups and downs. Believe you me, there have been plenty of times I've felt like sending your dad packing, but looking back over the years, I wouldn't have traded a second. It's those moments late at night, when the kids are finally asleep—or blessedly moved out of the house—and you're lying on cold sheets and find those warm, familiar arms reaching out to draw you close. That's when you truly appreciate marriage. Well, that and the fact that having a man around means you don't have to take out the trash."

"Oh, Mom!" Laughing, Stacie playfully threw a dishrag at the older woman. "And here I thought you were about to impart some genuine pearls of wisdom."

"I did. I can't help it if you don't hold the proper appreciation for what it'd be like to haul out your own trash." She plucked the dishrag from the floor and slipped into the utility room to toss it into the washer. "Anyway, what I originally came in here for was to hurry you along. The Dinsmoores have invited us over for cookies and caroling at six and I don't want to be late."

Crash.

Lilly's great-great-great-grandmother's china gravy boat—the one that had been brought to Utah in a covered wagon all the way from Boston—slipped from her hands, shattering on the hardwood floor.

"Lilly!" her mom called out, rushing to her side. "What's the matter with you? All of the sudden you look white as a ghost."

"I'm sorry about the dish, Mom. I didn't mean to break it." Kneeling, she began the heartrending process of picking up the larger pieces of china. How could she have been so careless? That dish was an heirloom she could have passed on to her daughter. Yet again, Lilly felt like the family misfit. This time, because of Elliot. She couldn't go to his parents for caroling. She wouldn't.

"Here, let me do that," Mary said. "You go lie down."

"I don't want to lie down," Lilly said. "This is my mess, I'll clean it."

Mary backed away. "Was it something we said that has you upset? We were kidding about all those bad points of marriage, you know. I wouldn't trade Robby for anything."

That's just it, Lilly's heart cried. *You would never have to because your marriage is based upon truth. Mine, however, is built upon nothing but lies. Lies that if Elliot is at his parent's house tonight could blow up in my face.*

Still picking at the china, Lilly said, "I'm not going."

"Why?" her mother asked, her voice laced with concern. "You love the Dinsmoores. They've always been like a second family to you."

"I don't feel good." Putting her hand to her pounding forehead, Lilly stood.

"Nonsense," her mother said. "A second ago you told

us you felt fine. Now I don't know what's the matter with you all of the sudden, but caroling with the Dinsmoores is a family tradition."

"Yeah," Lilly fought. "One we usually don't participate in until a couple weeks before Christmas."

"Lillian Diane Churchill-Reilly. You're going to the Dinsmoores for caroling and that's final."

CHAPTER FOURTEEN

IN THE DINSMOORES CROWDED, two-story entry hall, Finn leaned close to Lilly and whispered, "Who are all these people again?"

"Remember back in Vegas when I told you about Elliot? The guy who played me for a fool?"

"Yeah?"

"Rose and Harold Dinsmoore are his parents."

"Is he going to be here?"

I hope not! A few more neighbors entered the cramped space, forcing Finn and Lilly against the oak stair railing. Mrs. Dinsmoore had already put up her Christmas decorations and the fragrant pine boughs wrapping the newel post stabbed Lilly's behind. Stepping a few inches away from the prickly decor, she said, "Probably Elliot won't be here. He got married not too long ago, so most likely he's at his wife's family's house."

"I hope he *is* here. I'd like to sock him in the gut for what he did to you."

As perversely pleased as she was at the thought of Finn beating the tar out of Elliot, Lilly said, "Whoa, there, fella. You might want to tone down the testosterone."

"Why? He hurt you."

"Yeah, but I was stupid enough to let him."

He sighed. "You're completely missing my point.

Anyway, how long do we have to stay? I was kind of hoping to try out that old twin bed of yours."

"Finn!" she muttered under her breath, blushing furiously at the thought of what the two of them could do in that teeny-tiny bed.

"What?" he whispered back. "Are you telling me you don't think it might be fun to see how quiet we can be while at the same time seeing how bad we can be?"

"Grrr, what I'm saying is—"

"There's my pretty Lilly." Elliot's mom, Rose, called out, easing her way through the crowd to pull Lilly into a hug. "When Elliot married Missy, I thought my heart would break. She's a lovely girl, but you know I always had my hopes set on my boy marrying you. You two could have raised my grandbabies right next door."

Lilly flashed her a weak smile. "You know what folks say about things having a way of working themselves out for the best."

"I suppose, but I still say you would have made the perfect daughter-in-law. So," she said, eyeing Finn, "is this that handsome husband of yours your mother told me about?"

"He sure is," Lilly said, growing more relaxed by the minute. Surely if Elliot was in the house, Rose wouldn't have dissed his choice in wives? "Mrs. Dinsmoore, meet my husband, Finn Reilly."

"Reilly," she said, pursing her lips into a frown. "I knew some Reillys who went to the Presbyterian church on Maple. Are you any relation?"

"No, ma'am, 'fraid not," Finn said, warmly shaking her hand.

"That's a relief. I never did care for Helen Reilly. She made this horrible sucking noise through her dentures. Like to drove me batty during our women's prayer meetings. Anywho, it's nice meeting you, Finn." She gave his shoulder an affectionate pat. "You two young people go mingle. Elliot and Missy are around here somewhere."

Lilly's heart stopped, then started up again, racing at an unfathomable pace.

"Hon? Are you okay?" Finn asked.

"Yes, I—no. I think I need some fresh air. I—" The space was so cramped and the smells of spiced cider and cinnamon potpourri and fresh pine cuttings combined to bring on an even fiercer headache than she'd had earlier while washing dishes.

"Rose?" Lilly's mom called out. "Did my daughter and new son tell you their joyous news?"

"No?" Rose said, her thin eyebrows arched high. "Don't tell me? You two aren't expecting, too?"

"You'd better believe it," Finn said, snugly wrapping his arm around Lilly's waist. "No messing around for us. We both wanted to start a family right away, and bam—that's exactly what happened."

"How wonderful," Rose said. "Wait right here while I go get Elliot and Missy. They're expecting, too, you know."

"I need to go," Lilly said to Finn, clutching his arm. "All these people. The heat."

"Let's stay a minute longer," he said. "I want to get a load of this chump Elliot's reaction when he hears you're already carrying my baby."

"Finn," she tried warning. "I don't think that's such a good idea. We should—"

"Lookee who I found," Rose sang out. "Elliot, hurry. It's your old flame, Lilly Churchill, from next door. And look how much prettier she is with that expectant glow of a new mom."

The look Elliot cast Lilly could have frozen over hell. “Congratulations,” he said. “Mom, told me you’d recently gotten hitched. Is this the lucky guy?”

“I sure am,” Finn said, holding out his hand for Elliot to shake. “We’ve been married almost a month now and neither of us have ever been happier.”

“That’s real niii-ce,” Elliot said, his voice squeaking when Finn shook his hand.

Lilly cringed. Finn, almost a full head taller than Elliot must have shaken her former beau’s hand harder than necessary. Still, so far so good. Despite the fact that her heart felt ready to pound right out of her chest, Lilly took Elliot’s chilly demeanor as a sign that he too was reluctant for anyone to discover their affair.

The day would come when she’d have to tell him her baby was his, but if everything went as planned, she wouldn’t be telling Elliot until *after* she told her husband.

“GATHER AROUND, everyone!” Rose called from in front of a crackling fire.

Trying desperately to pretend she didn’t even know Elliot, let alone that he was standing a mere ten feet away, Lilly put on a brave smile and snuggled closer to her husband. At the rear of the room, they shared a cozy padded bench.

“I hope we do ‘Silent Night,’” Finn said. “Mom used to sing that in our church choir and every year her solo blew the congregation away.” Wrapping his arm about Lilly’s shoulders, he said, “Have you ever sung in a choir?”

Her throat tight, thinking of the heartsick boy her husband must have been when he’d lost his whole family at such a young age, she shook her head. Now was hardly the time to tell him she'd been blackballed from her church's third-grade choir for gluing the hymnal pages together of the songs she didn't like.

"You should, you know. You have a beautiful voice."

"Thank you." His compliment warmed her like a steamy mug of cocoa.

"You're welcome."

With Finn's arm still around her, making her brave, Lilly gazed across the room at the way Elliot affectionately nuzzled his wife's neck. The pretty brunette cast him a smile of pure devotion, and it sickened Lilly to know that not only could her own marriage be blown apart by news of her baby's parentage, but Missy's, as well.

Rose started off the caroling with a rousing rendition of "Jingle Bells" and finally Lilly relaxed. Elliot no more wanted to make a scene than she did. Besides, what motive would he have? He didn't even know her baby was his.

"I love you," Finn whispered in her ear at the end of the song. "This is nice."

"Caroling?"

"Yeah. You forget, it's been a while since I've done something like this. Sure, I usually throw a big Christmas bash for my construction crew down at Lu's, but somehow drinking beer with the guys while singing 'Rudolph the Drunken Reindeer' isn't the same."

"I'm glad you're having fun," she said, her tone perhaps too heartfelt. Lowering her gaze, she said, "That's all I want, Finn, is for you to always be happy."

"Hey," he tilted her chin, forcing her to meet his gaze. "You okay?"

“I’m fine. Just tired and a little thirsty. Mind if I sit this next song out in the kitchen?”

“Nope. In fact, now that you mention it, I’ll come with you. I could use some punch.”

“Okay, everyone,” Rose called out. “It’s time for ‘Silent Night!’”

As Lilly stood, Finn gazed her way. “I’ll meet you in a sec,” he said. “I’d love to sing along to this one. You know, for old time’s sake.”

“Want me to stay?”

“Nah, you go on ahead.” His eyes looked suspiciously full. “I’d like to do this on my own. Take a second to give thanks for you and our baby coming into my life.”

“O-okay,” she said, even though the heavy ache in her chest was anything but okay.

She quickly slipped from the room, hoping no one noticed her using the backs of her hands to wipe away sentimental tears. She was so happy it hurt.

The kitchen was blessedly quiet and looked much the same as it had when she’d played there as a child. Mrs. Dinsmoore took pride in her baked goods and every day after school, while Elliot and Lilly played board games or watched cartoons, she presented them with trays of cookies or blueberry muffins.

“Do you mind if I have a word with you, Lilly?”

She spun around. “Elliot,” she said, putting her hand to her chest. “You startled me. I didn’t hear you come in.”

“I startled you?” he said. “Ha! That’s rich. Come on, we need to talk.” Casting a wary gaze over his shoulder, he pulled her into his mother’s king-size pantry, flicked on the dim light and shut the door. Inside, the air smelled of flour and nutmeg and a multitude of other homey spices that felt out of sync with Lilly's pensive mood.

"What do you want?" she whispered. "Because as far as I'm concerned, we have nothing more to say."

"The hell we don't." Even through her heavy red sweater, his hold on the soft skin of her upper arm hurt. "For starters, why are you here?"

She raised her chin. "To visit my parents. Is that a crime?"

"Not at all. I just don't want you getting any ideas in your head about telling my wife about our affair."

"*Our* affair?" She laughed. "Correction. Make that *your* affair. I had no idea you were married. I was horrified. And once I discovered I was preg—" Her hand flew to her mouth.

Tightening his grip on her arm, he said, "Are you telling me the baby you're carrying is mine?"

Dizzy. Hot. Nauseous. The words didn't come close to describing the anguish gripping her body. What had she done?

"Answer me, Lilly." From the living room came the faint voices of their family and friends starting "Deck the Halls." "Is your baby mine?"

"Yes, but—"

"Damn," he said, letting loose of her to pound his fist against the wall.

Lilly jumped.

The force of his blow rattled the neat row of homemade pickles lining the shelf behind him.

"This isn't good. Not good at all." Eyeing her, he said, "You're not expecting me to play a part in this kid's life, are you?"

"No, in fact, I—"

"That's good. Damned good. I don't even know how I'm going to support my own kid, let alone yours."

Bravely swallowing back tears, Lilly said, "That's fine with me, Elliot. As far as I'm concerned, my husband will be this child's father in every sense of the word."

"So he knows the kid isn't his?"

"No, but—"

Elliot clutched his stomach, laughing. "You married that guy because you were pregnant and needed a father for your baby, didn't you? Priceless, Lil. This is priceless." Slapping her on her back, he said, "I always knew you were a resourceful gal, but this beats all. You're nothing but a con artist with an angel's face."

"Elliot, I—" She started to tremble, and silent tears streamed down her cheeks. She had to get away from this man. This place.

"Quit the innocent act. As sure as I'm standing here, you purposely duped this guy, didn't you?"

"No. He means the world to me and believe me, more than anything, I wish this baby was his."

"Right," he said with a cruel snort. "And I'm the pope. So? When were you planning on springing this news on my wife?"

"Never."

"You're damned right," he said, gripping her arm again and squeezing harder than ever. "She *never* needs to know any of this. What the two of us shared was for fun and if you had any experience at all, you'd have been on the pill."

"Stop," Lilly sobbed.

"Oh, I'll stop all right, as soon as you get it through your head that I don't want to see you or this kid ever again."

"Okay," she said. "Just go. Leave me alone."

"My pleasure." After giving her a mock salute, he mercifully left.

Finn. She needed him. His strength, his warmth.

Never would she have guessed Elliot had the capacity to be so cruel.

Quivering with relief that the ugly scene was over, her legs felt like soft sticks of butter. Yet as hurtful as Elliot's words had been, they could have been so much worse had Finn overheard. What she needed to do, Lilly thought, smoothing her hair and dress as if bringing order to her appearance would bring order to her mind, was calm down. Just because Elliot was upset didn't mean she had to be. His outburst had had no effect on her plan to tell Finn everything as soon as they got home.

She knew her husband better than she'd ever known anyone. He had to understand about her baby. He had to. She couldn't survive if he didn't.

Forcing her breathing to slow, she reached into a plastic sack of red Santa napkins, drawing one out to use as a tissue.

Everything will be all right.

Everything will be all right.

In preparation for blending back into the crowd, she took a deep breath. If Finn asked why she looked as if she'd been crying, she'd say she'd been caught up in the holiday spirit.

Hand poised on the pantry's doorknob, she reminded herself that she was strong. After what had just happened, she could handle anything. She was no longer Lilly Churchill—misfit, but Lilly Reilly. Strong, intelligent woman. Fully capable of cleaning up her own messes.

Spirits bolstered, she straightened her shoulders, threw open the door and marched right out of the pantry and into her husband. "Finn! You startled me."

"I'm sure I did."

She wrapped her arms around him, hugging him tight. He felt so good, but why was he stiff? Holding his arms to his sides instead of returning her hug. "How was the song?" she asked. "Did it sound as good as you remembered?"

"No."

"Why not?"

"Probably because I wasn't listening."

"Oh?" What was wrong? He'd steeled his jaw and his eyes looked cold instead of filled with their usual warmth. "I thought you were looking forward to singing along."

"I was, but I was worried about you. That's why I came into the kitchen instead of singing. When I heard raised voices, I started to leave. I figured a personal altercation wasn't any of my business. But then I heard your name and I realized what was being discussed was very much my business, wasn't it, Lilly?"

The room spun.

Her blood ran hot and cold.

Dear God, no. Please, God, don't let Finn have heard.

She licked her lips. Fought for air. "Finn, I—I can explain."

"I'm sure you can," he said, his voice icy and expression not much warmer. "The problem is, I'm no longer interested in anything you have to say."

"Y-you don't mean that," she said, searching his face for any sign of forgiveness. "I know you, Finn. I know you'll understand." She reached for his hand, for his reassurance, but he jerked away.

"I'm sure that's exactly what you'd like to believe, isn't it? Good old trustworthy Finn. He'll buy your story hook, line and sinker. He's so desperate for a kid, he'll take in anybody's baby." Grasping her firmly by the shoulders, he gave her a slight shake. "Lies, Lilly. Every single damn thing we've ever shared has been nothing but a lie, hasn't it?"

"No, Finn," she said, sobbing into his chest. "It wasn't like that. If you'd just listen. Let me explain." She clung to him, fisting his shirt. "Let's go back to my parents' house. It'll be quiet there and we can talk. I was planning to tell you all of this on Monday. I wanted to wait until we got home. I thought this was something better discussed in private."

"Sure." He let out a short, sharp laugh before turning down the dark hall leading to the back door. "You were going to tell me Monday, huh? That's easy to say now that the damage is done."

"Please, Finn," she begged, throwing herself against him, trying futilely to make him understand. "Take me with you. We'll go home to Greenleaf tonight. We'll leave my parents a note."

"Don't touch me," he said from between clenched teeth, pushing her away. "I'm leaving all right, but you're not coming with. As far as I'm concerned, as of this moment, you're a stranger to me, Lilly. I wish I'd never met you and I sure as hell never want to see you again."

FOR THE LONGEST TIME after Finn left, Lilly stood in the cold, dark hall doing what she didn't know. Waiting for Finn to come running back to apologize for the hurtful things he'd said? Then it occurred to her that she was the one who'd hurt him. If anyone had apologizing to do, it was her.

And so she swallowed what tiny bit was left of her pride and ran after her husband, oblivious to her family and friends singing a rowdy "We Wish You a Merry Christmas." Unless she somehow made her husband understand she never meant to hurt him, Lilly feared she might never have another merry Christmas.

Without her coat, oblivious to the biting wind, she ran across her parents' snow-covered yard. All that mattered was Finn. Would she reach him in time to beg him to take her with him?

Bursting through the front door, her mind and body filled with renewed hope, she cried, "Finn? Finn, are you still here?" She received no reply, but that didn't necessarily mean anything. He could be upstairs, packing.

Chasing up the winding staircase she'd sledded down as a kid, she now only had adult matters on her mind. Matters like how to save her marriage.

"Finn? Sweetie? Are you up here?" At the top of the stairs, she raced for her bedroom, knowing he'd still be there, and thankfully, just as she'd prayed, he was.

After shoving the rest of his clothes into his duffel bag and zipping it shut, he looked up. His eyes were red. "I told you back at the Dinsmoores that we have nothing more to discuss."

"How can you say that? We have everything to discuss. I can't believe it took me this long to realize it, Finn, but I love you. Please don't let Elliot's few words change your entire outlook on what we've worked so hard to build."

"Have *we* worked hard, Lilly? Because I don't see

it that way. Looking back on it, I spent this past month doing everything in my power to atone for making you the object of a bet. Only the joke was really on me, wasn't it? Because you'd been playing me all along. From the night you strolled into Lu's looking for a husband, you didn't give a damn who that husband was, just that he'd make a good father for Elliot's child. You knew Elliot wanted to stay with his wife, so unless you wanted your baby born a bastard, you had no option but to get married. That's why you didn't want a divorce back in Vegas—not because of some deeply felt moral convictions about once a man and woman sleep together they're bound forever, but because plain and simple, you'd found a daddy for baby and a provider for you, and you weren't about to give up that meal ticket."

Tears streaming down her cheeks, she went to him. "Oh, no, Finn. How could you think that? When I thought I was marrying Dallas, he knew he was getting not just a wife but a child. After we married and you never brought up my baby, I thought you'd changed your mind about raising another man's child." Wringing her hands, she said, "And then, when I found out you weren't Dallas, I was afraid you never wanted to have kids. But then we got to Greenleaf and I saw how wonderful you were with Chrissy and Randy and Abby. Can't you see? I've grown to love you, Finn. Not because you could give me and my baby a nice house, but because you're you." Her hand to his dear, familiar cheek, she said, "I love you. Maybe I've always loved you. That's why I had such a hard time telling you the truth about the baby, because I was terrified of how you'd take the news. And see? Your reaction is proving me right. You don't love me enough to raise another man's child. I knew it all along."

"No, Lilly," he said, snatching his bag from the bed and heading for the door. "I would have gladly accepted both you and this child for the miracle you both were if only from the beginning you'd told me the truth. As it is, I don't know whether you're the woman I married or another coldhearted creature like Vivian who never really loved me at all, but thought of me as a good time. And again, just like Vivian, you played me for a fool not just in private, but in front of family and friends—people I instantly cared for as much as you. Do you know how that makes me feel, Lilly? Do you have any idea what a jackass I must have looked like playing the role of proud papa when you knew all along I wasn't your baby's real father?"

"Please forgive me," Lilly said, following him to the door. "Take me home with you. We can talk about all of this on the ride back."

"Not a chance. Fool me once, shame on you. Fool me twice, shame on me." Aiming his index finger at her chest, his hard stare boring into hers, he said, "It's time for me to grow up. I'm not the eight-year-old boy who lost his parents anymore. I'm a flesh-and-blood man who offered you everything any woman could ever dream of on a silver platter. The absolute only thing I asked of you was to be straight with me, yet you couldn't do even that. Well, now I'll be straight with you. Starting right here, right now, our marriage is over."

CHAPTER FIFTEEN

"WHAT ARE YOU DOING?" Lilly's sister Mary asked an hour later, seeing Lilly lugging her suitcase down the stairs. "I noticed you'd left the caroling party and when I couldn't find Finn, either, Mom sent me to check on you."

"Something awful's happened, Mary, but I don't have time to explain. Can I borrow your car?"

"Why? It's nearly ten o'clock and the roads are a mess. And where's Finn? He's not ill, is he?"

"Not in the way you mean." Lilly tugged her bag the rest of the way down the stairs.

Hands on her hips, Mary said, "Then tell me how."

"We had a fight, okay? Now, can you give me the keys to your car, or should I take Mom's car?"

"Neither," Mary said, blocking Lilly's path to the door. "You're not going anywhere until you tell me what's going on. I mean, I know newlyweds fight, but one minute you two couldn't keep your eyes and hands off each other and the next he's left you here with him chasing off to God only knows where?"

"Mary, please, just let me go."

"No." Softening her voice, she said, "Let me fix you a cup of tea. Once you tell me why you need my car, if I deem it necessary, I'll ask Mom to watch the kids and Robby and I will drive you wherever you want to go, but first you have to tell me why."

Thirty minutes later, seated at the long pine kitchen table, just as they had years earlier when discussing dating problems, Lilly spilled all to her big sister. The *whole* story, starting from how Elliot had taken her virginity to how desperately she'd grown to love Finn, to how terrified she was of never again earning his trust.

A dozen hugs and three mugs of tea later, Mary said, "Oh, honey, you have gotten yourself into one heck of a jam, but you know what?"

Lilly shook her head.

"I don't care what he says, Finn loves you. He can deny it all he wants, but I saw the way he looks at you. He's lost, down for the count, and the only woman who can bring him back into this fight we call life is you."

"Exactly," Lilly said, "which is why I have to go to him tonight. To make him understand that I kept the truth from him not out of a desire to hurt him, but out of a selfish desire not to hurt myself."

Mary sighed. "Look, you may not want to hear this, but I'm going to say it anyway. You've botched this situation from the start. From the instant you found out you were pregnant, instead of developing some harebrained scheme to marry this Dallas guy you'd only met through e-mails, why didn't you come to us for help? You know how much we love you, Lilly. We're your family. We'd do anything for you."

"But that's just it. All my life, you've been bailing me out of jam after jam, but after this, I thought for sure Mom and Dad would disown me. I mean, isn't it about time I grew up and learned how to save myself?

If only Elliot hadn't confronted me, I'd have had this all worked out."

"You think so, huh? You've been sitting on a potential powder keg for weeks, and you think that's *worked out?*"

"No." Lilly glanced at her watch. "Which is again the reason why I have to go to Finn—now."

"You're not going anywhere," Mary said with renewed conviction. "As for your fear of our parents disowning you—that's just plain silly. And I don't blame Finn for being upset. What he found out purely by accident tonight must have been one heck of a blow to his pride. What he needs is time to come around. If he truly loves you…as I believe with all my heart he does, he'll be back."

"DAMMIT, PETE, if I'd wanted this bathtub green, I'd have ordered it that way." A week before Christmas, Finn looked at the offensive special-order whirlpool tub that was going to cost him at least a thousand bucks in lost labor and shipping fees to send back to the manufacturer and felt like kicking it.

"Yeah, but, boss—"

"I don't wanna hear excuses, just rip the damn thing out and get a white one ordered ASAP."

"But, boss—"

"For cryin' out loud, Pete." Finn slashed his fingers through his hair. "Just do it. I don't have the patience for this kind of amateur screwup."

His plumber for the past seven years stormed off, mumbling a string of curses that'd make a sailor proud.

The morning was so cold that as Pete walked, tool

belt jangling, a cloud of white rose from his mouth. For a split second Finn wondered if Lilly was warm enough at the house. Then he remembered to call himself a fool for caring, because she wasn't at the house.

Dammit. How much longer until he forgot Lilly Churchill's existence? When would he forget the smell of her hair? Her breath? The sound of her laugh after they made love?

Time, man, he thought, giving himself a pep talk. *All I need is enough time and I'll forget about her just like I did Vivian.*

Heading for the thermos of coffee he kept in Abigail, he snorted.

If time was so all-fired important, then how come he'd gotten over Vivian's leaving in a day and here it was going on a month since he'd last seen Lilly and it still hurt to breathe? Everything hurt from his head to his heart to his soul. If the woman had been so hell-bent on destroying him, why hadn't she gone ahead and finished the job instead of leaving him in limbo like this?

He yanked open the passenger-side door of his truck and swore he caught a whiff of her perfume. He'd been doing that a lot lately and the habit was making him crazy.

Fumbling with unscrewing the cup and then the lid to the thermos, he set them both on the edge of the seat and took a swig of lukewarm black coffee.

"Drinking straight from the bottle's hard core for this early in the morning, isn't it?" Matt strolled up behind him. The soles of his boots crunched on the frozen earth.

"Unless you have something work-related to say, with all respects, leave me the hell alone."

"No can do, bud." His best friend patted him on the back. The motion caused Finn to jerk away, in the process knocking the thermos lid off the seat and onto the truck's floorboard.

"Thanks a lot," Finn said, already bending to retrieve it, but Matt shot out his arm to stop him.

"Get that later. We need to talk."

"I already told you, I—"

"And I told you," Matt said, his voice uncharacteristically rough. "We need to talk and by God, if I have to move your lips myself, that's exactly what we're going to do."

"If this is about Lilly, I—"

"Your damned right it's about Lilly, but not how you think."

Finn hardened his jaw, furious at his friend for this invasion upon his private pain.

"Finn, man, you've gotta either get over her, which would be pretty stupid considering how much fun she was at poker night, or go get her—wherever the hell she went—but this black funk of yours can't go on. We lost three good men over at the motel site yesterday because they couldn't hack your temper."

"Yeah, well," Finn said, gazing out at the expansive view of rolling snow-covered foothills and the Wasatch Mountains beyond that. "If their egos were that fragile, we probably didn't need 'em anyway."

"Bull. They were good men, Finn. Men who have been with us for years. They were family men who appreciated the fact that you willingly gave them time off to take their kids to the dentist or go see a school play, but you're not that man anymore. Whatever happened with Lilly has changed you."

"I told you," Finn said, his teeth clenched, "I don't want to talk about her."

"If you don't want to talk about her, maybe you'll talk about this—that green tub you jumped Pete for mistakenly ordering?"

"Yeah?"

"While you were on your honeymoon, Mrs. Kleghorn wrote out a sixty-eight-hundred-dollar check for that monstrosity. She said some fool thing about it matching her favorite gemstone. Anyway, bottom line is that whether you like it or not, the tub is stayin'. Unlike Pete. He quit not three minutes after you called him an amateur."

Groaning, Finn put his hand to his forehead. "Crap. Go after him for me, would ya, Matt? Give him a five grand bonus and tell him I'm sorry."

"No can do," Matt said, standing his ground.

"Why the hell not?"

"Because if you've got an apology to make, the words should come from you. And while you're at it, I could use one, too."

Before Finn had a chance to say anything, Matt stormed off, hopped in his red Chevy truck and aimed it toward the motel site.

Damn.

Finn hated losing a good plumber even worse than he'd hated losing a bad wife.

Leaning into the truck to fetch the fallen thermos lid, he hit his head on the door frame, which did nothing to soothe his already bearish mood. Cursing a blue streak, rubbing his head with one hand while reaching beneath the seat with the other, his fingers grasped not the plastic lid but cold glass. "What the…"

Eyebrows furrowed, at the same time he pulled the cylindrical object out, his heart broke anew.

It was a perfume bottle.

Or to be more precise, Lilly's perfume bottle. The fragrance was called Wildflower and he yanked off the lid, closed his eyes and held the bottle under his nose. The achingly familiar fragrance filled his eyes with tears.

Had she planted that bottle the night he'd left just to continuously torment him with her scent?

The practical side of him quickly squelched that irrational thought. He vaguely remembered her purse falling to the floorboard Thanksgiving morning. He'd been the one who'd abruptly pulled to the side of the road, so he was at fault for Abigail smelling more like his wife than his truck.

Could he be at fault for other things as well?

CHRISTMAS EVE, while the rest of the Churchill gang sat around the fire swapping holiday stories over cookies and cocoa, Lilly sat at the kitchen table, staring at the kitchen wall phone, willing it to ring.

Mary, a red Santa mug in hand, entered the room and sighed. "I thought you said you were going to the bathroom and then you'd be right back to the party?"

"I lied."

Pouring a fresh cup of cocoa, Mary said, "You've got to stop this moping, honey. If Finn is even half the man we all believe he is, he'll come around. But believe me," she said, and pulled out the chair beside Lilly's and sat down. "As an officially old married woman, I know firsthand how fragile a man's ego can be. Hearing the news about Elliot being the father of your baby didn't leave Finn much room to maneuver. He feels tricked, and only through time will he hopefully begin to see that wasn't the case."

"Yes, but what if he never sees me as anything but a conniving woman out to—as he so bluntly put it—find my baby and me a meal ticket? And *is* that what I was doing, Mary?"

Her sister took a sip of her steaming drink, taking her time to formulate an answer. "I guess maybe you were, little sis. And from what you told me about Dallas, he would have been using you to some extent to give himself an instant family to help his image at his law firm. The arrangement you'd made with him—while I deplore it—at least was based upon mutual understanding. For Finn, though, once he told you about his bet, he was never anything but straight with you. In return, he expected that same honesty."

Bowing her head, Lilly sighed. "I really messed up this time, didn't I?"

Mary set her mug on the table and pulled Lilly into a hug. "I'd be lying if I said you hadn't, but I'll make a deal with you." Pulling back, she brushed two tears from Lilly's cheeks.

"What?" she asked with a sniffle.

"If Finn hasn't come back to claim you by Valentine's Day, I'll drive you to Greenleaf myself and see what we can do about talking some sense into that man."

"Valentine's Day?" Lilly's eyes widened in horror. "I'll never survive that long without him."

"Oh, yes, you will. We Churchill women are strong." Tucking a fallen curl behind Lilly's ear, Mary said, "You've grown a lot in the past month. Mom and Dad just this morning told me how proud they are of you for owning up to your mistakes. We all think you deserve a second chance. In short, you've been very, very good." She winked. "Who knows, maybe tonight Santa will put Finn in your stocking?"

CHRISTMAS EVE, Finn sat on his favorite bar stool at Lu's, nursing a beer. The place was packed full of either partiers or loners like him who had no place else to go. Elvis crooned "Jingle Bell Rock" on the jukebox and Betty and Bob Bristow were dancing up a storm in matching red satin Santa suits.

Sighing, Finn tried his damnedest to block the noise and smelly cigar smoke, but it was no use. He'd come here to get his thoughts off Lilly, but the harder he tried forgetting her, the more she was on his mind.

The Elvis music took him back to that zany dog and bird show in Vegas and the way his wife had flashed him her adorable dimpled grin. The bar's smooth surface reminded him of the feel of her silky curls. Even the cigar smoke reminded him of her sexy slot playing.

"Can I get you a turkey dinner to go with your beer?" Lu asked.

"No, thanks. I don't much feel like eating."

"Come on, Finn, it's almost Christmas. Can't you give me even a puny smile?"

Only to please the woman who'd been like a second mother to him, he raised the corners of his mouth a fraction of an inch.

"Sorry to break this to you, son, but that wasn't a smile, but a frown."

"At least give me credit for trying. It's not my fault that my damned mouth doesn't work anymore."

"Judging by the foulness of your language, you're

darned right it's not working and I'll bet I know the reason why."

"Hey, Lu!" Mitch called from the other end of the bar. "How about lettin' that loser rot in his own self-pity and gettin' me another beer?" He waved his empty mug.

"How about you shuttin' that hole in your face," she hollered back, "then gettin' off that big rear end of yours and fetchin' it yourself!"

Turning back to Finn, she said, "Where were we? Ah, yes, the reason why you've turned more crotchety than a two-legged dog tryin' to scratch a flea."

Finn rolled his eyes.

To which Lu promptly swatted him with her bar towel. "Don't you sass me, boy. You're still not too big for me to toss over my knee." Cracking a grin, she said, "Now, if the thought of little old me tryin' to wrestle you onto my lap didn't make you smile, I don't know what will."

"How about finding a woman who won't lie." He downed his last swig of beer.

"Funny, but I thought that was exactly what you'd found in that sweetheart, Lilly?"

"Are you kidding me? You know how she kept the real father of her baby from me, Lu. Even you can't deny that was a downright despicable thing to do."

"And you haulin' her off for a quickie Vegas wedding to save your truck wasn't?"

Eyes narrowed, he said, "You know what I'm talking about. She made a fool of me."

"No, the way I see it is, you're makin' a fool of you."

"I'm probably going to kick myself for asking, but how's that?"

"Because you've become a dawlgoned coward when it comes to love, Finn Reilly. Granted, what Vivian did to you was a cryin' shame, but Lilly is a far cry from Vivian. Since the first day you came in here, I've been hearin' these sob stories of how you want a wife and kids. Well, now you've finally got a beautiful, loving bride who every time she looks at you bursts into happy tears, and as if that weren't good enough, she comes complete with a baby on the way."

"Yeah," he said with a snort. "Some other guy's baby."

"If that's truly how you feel, then you're not half the man I thought you were. What? Just because that child's not yours, is that going to make him or her any less lovable? If anything, knowin' its real daddy would so shamelessly up and abandon his own flesh and blood and Lilly like he did should make you love that mother and child all the more."

"If you're done scolding me," Finn said, waving his empty bottle, "may I please have another beer?"

Hands on her hips, she said, "No, you may not. And don't interrupt me when I'm on a roll. Just because your wife had a hard time tellin' you what was obviously a sensitive subject, are you honestly pigheaded enough to give up the dream you've spent your whole life tryin' to find?"

"What dream is that?"

"Ugh!" She threw her hands and the towel in the air. "I give up."

"Good."

"Good? That's it. Not only are you *not* gettin' another beer tonight, but either you come back with your bride in tow, or you're no longer welcome on these premises—ever."

"Aw, now, Lu, you don't mean that."

Jutting her chin as high as a barely five-foot-tall woman could, she said, "Try me."

CHAPTER SIXTEEN

AT HOME, FINN FED HIS three mutts, made sure their heating lamp was on in the barn, then, since the small box by the road had been overflowing on his last drive by, he loped back across the snowy yard to grab the mail.

In the kitchen, he kicked off his work boots at the door, making sure not to look anywhere near the direction of the table, for if he did, he would see *her,* laughing over a plate of one of her delicious casseroles. But then if he looked toward the stove, he'd see her singing over a pot of spaghetti, and the memory of her angelic voice—not to mention the harmony she'd briefly brought to his home—would make his soul weep.

Unable to look anywhere but straight ahead without pain, he shuffled through the mail to find mostly sales circulars. A few bills and Christmas cards. He was about to set the pile on the counter before heading to bed when a small red envelope caught his attention. The return address read simply Vivian. The card had been postmarked in Galveston, Texas.

Frowning, he tossed the rest of the mail to the table before slipping his finger beneath the envelope's seal.

Hey Finn,

I guess sorry doesn't come close to making up for me running out on our wedding like I did, but with it being Christmas and all, I had to at least try explaining why I took off with Ray. Make no mistake, I did love you, and probably a part of me always will. But the way you put me on a pedestal, expecting me to be the perfect wife in that perfect house of yours, trying to be the living incarnation of all your dreams. It was just too hard. I knew I'd never live up to your standards, so I ran.

I'm doing fine. I found a job waitressing at a swanky place with a view of the beach, and Ray and I are still together. I'll always have a special place in my heart for you, Finn, and hope more than anything that one day you'll not only forgive me, but find that perfect woman you've been dreaming of—Vivian

Whew. By the time Finn finished reading, tears welled in his throat.

For all the reasons he'd imagined Vivian fleeing their wedding, never had he thought his high standards could be to blame. After all, what was wrong with a man expecting certain things from his wife? Namely, that she wouldn't ride off with a stranger on a motorcycle at their wedding, or that she'd have the decency to tell him if she was pregnant with another man's child *before* they tied the knot.

Tossing Vivian's note onto the stack of mail already on the table, he stormed through the silent house, intent on building a fire. Since early that morning, cold had gripped him and wouldn't let go. But even when he had the fire crackling hot, Finn was still chilled to the bone. Only then did it dawn on him that the kind of warming he needed didn't come from outside, but inside.

Here it was Christmas Eve and he was all alone.

He had more friends than he could shake a stick at who'd invited him to share in their family festivities. Shoot, if he'd wanted, he could have walked the half mile down the road to Doc Walsh's, or for that matter, barged in on Randy and Chrissy's celebration, but he figured what was the point in celebrating when any glimmer of cheer he'd ever had was in a house over a hundred miles north?

Gazing out the darkened window, he wondered what Lilly was doing.

Singing around the fire with that wonderfully wacky family of hers? Had her mother made any of her caramel pecan rolls? For Christmas dinner would they be having turkey, ham or maybe even goose? And was Lilly showing yet? He'd always loved the sight of a pregnant woman. She'd be especially cute. If the baby was a girl, would she have her mom's thick head of curls? If it was a boy, would he have the straight Churchill blond hair Lilly's brothers had?

So many questions, he thought, washing his face with his hands. But perhaps the biggest question of all was the one Lu had posed.

Just because your wife had a hard time tellin' you what was obviously a sensitive subject, are you honestly pigheaded enough to give up the dream you spent your whole life tryin' to find?

Was he that pigheaded?

In the days he'd been away from Lilly, he'd gone over their time together with a fine-tooth comb. He searched his memory for ways she'd deliberately tried deceiving him, but no matter how hard he tried, he found none. In fact, if he were totally truthful, he remembered times she must have tried to tell him about the baby, but for different reasons, he'd cut her off.

Like the ghost of Christmas past, Vivian's words haunted him, too.

...you put me on a pedestal, expecting me to be the perfect wife in that perfect house of yours, trying to be the living incarnation of all your dreams. It was just too hard. I knew I'd never live up to your standards, so I ran.

Could Vivian be right? Had he held not only her, but Lilly to impossible standards? Could Lilly have been telling the truth when she'd told him repeatedly Thanksgiving night that she'd wanted to tell him about her baby but had been too afraid?

In the hall, the grandfather clock struck twelve.

Christmas Day. The ultimate day for forgiveness and new beginnings.

Looking back on all the kids he'd loved over the course of his life, he remembered countless Cub Scout troops, Randy and Chrissy, baby Abby. None of those children had been his, yet that technicality hadn't made him love them any less.

So why should it be any different with Lilly's baby?

A baby who, if Finn would only open his heart, would love him like a daddy—or maybe even more.

And Lilly. As much as he'd told himself Vivian had ruined him for life in the love department, he'd been wrong. He did love Lilly. He loved her more than he'd thought it was possible to love, which was why it hurt so damned much having her gone. But it didn't have to be that way. Yes, during the course of their whirlwind relationship, they'd both made huge mistakes, but what if they wiped the slate clean? What if starting right now, on Christmas Day, they started over? All their secrets out in the open. All their love ready and willing to give.

Anticipation filling his soul, he raced up the stairs.

In the back of his top dresser drawer, he kept his mother's jewelry box. If he was going to do this thing, he might as well do it right, starting by proposing to Lilly this time as Finn—not Dallas. And in order to do that, he needed a piece of his past to form a shining bridge to his future.

By God, Lilly might have entered his life via blind luck, but if he had anything to do with it, she'd be staying in his life via determination!

BOOM.

Boom boom.

Lilly, fitfully sleeping, thought she must have dreamed the odd sound, but sure enough, there it was again, a solid thumping against her window. Slipping out from under her floral down comforter, she went to the window to have a look.

Finn? Throwing snowballs?

Now she knew she was dreaming. She was heading back to bed when a voice stopped her.

"Lilly!" he shouted. "I'm sorry! Meet me at the front door!"

Heart pounding, she didn't bother slipping on a robe or slippers over Finn's Greenleaf High T-shirt and thick white socks. All she knew was that the sooner she got to the front door, the sooner she'd know whether or not she was still asleep.

Racing down the stairs, turning the lock, then yanking open the big front door, at first, all she saw was swirling snow, but then he was there, brushing past her to enter the front hall.

"Hi," he said, blowing on his bare hands. "It's cold."

"It usually is on Christmas."

He grinned. "You look gorgeous, and I'm glad to see my foolishness hasn't caused you to change your taste in fashion."

Though she wasn't sure whether to laugh or cry, she said, "What are you doing here? It's got to be one or two in the morning."

"Actually, it's almost three, but I figured, what the heck? I might as well get a head start on my holiday gift giving."

"Is—is that why you're here?" she said, tucking flyaway curls behind her ears. "Because you want to give someone a gift?"

"Not just someone, Lilly…*you*."

"Santa?" said a sleepy child from the living room. "Is that you?"

"Go back to sleep, Erin," Lilly said to her niece. To Finn she said, "All the kids are bedded down in the living room and den. Why don't we talk in the kitchen?"

"Sure. Lead the way."

She did, feeling self-conscious about the length—or rather lack of length—of her borrowed T-shirt. Why was he here? Was he coming to make up? Was he willing to accept Elliot's baby as his own? Could she really be so lucky?

In the kitchen, she flicked on the light over the sink, then asked, "Can I get you anything? Cocoa? Tea?" *Me?* He looked even more handsome than she remembered, his dark hair all mussed and made darker by melting snow. He wore faded jeans and a hip-length brown leather jacket that did heavenly things to his eyes.

"Thanks," he said, "but all I really need is for you to sit down."

"O-okay." She did as he asked, pulling out a chair at the table, trying to tug her T-shirt lower on her way down.

"You must be cold," he said, shrugging off his coat and placing it over her bare legs. It smelled of leather and him, and still radiated with his warmth.

"Mmm, that feels good," she said. *Almost as good as once again being with you.*

"I'm glad, you know, that you're warm." Turning his back to her, he rubbed his face with his hands before spinning back around. "On the ride up here, I had all this worked out, but now I'm not sure where to begin."

"How about if I start?" Lilly said, her voice quiet in the cold, still night. From upstairs, she heard a floorboard squeak and in the kitchen, she jumped when the refrigerator motor clicked on. "Look at me," she said with a nervous giggle. "I'm even more jittery now than when you left."

"I'm sorry about the way I took off like that. You were right, we should have talked."

"No, I was wrong. We should have talked all right, but back in Vegas when you first told me you weren't Dallas. I'm so sorry, Finn, I never meant to hurt you that way. I..." She wrung her hands. "Once I realized how much I loved you, I was afraid if I told you the truth about Elliot being my baby's father you'd stop loving me."

"Never," he said, crossing the short distance to her and kneeling on the hardwood floor to draw her into his arms.

"But you did stop loving me, Finn. Exactly what I was afraid of happening happened."

"Because I'm a fool."

"No, don't call yourself that. I understand why you were upset."

"But being upset didn't give me the right to run out on you like I did."

"Okay," she said with a nervous laugh, "we've both made mistakes, but what should we do about them?"

Reaching into his front pocket, he withdrew a black velvet ring box. "I don't know about you, but this is what I want to do." Popping open the box, he took out a ruby and diamond ring. Holding it between his trembling thumb and forefinger, he said, "This was both my grandmother's and mother's engagement ring. I wanted to give it to you on our wedding day in Vegas, but, well, you know how that turned out. Anyway, I'm giving it to you now in the hopes that you'll forgive me, then marry me all over again. This time, with your dad walking you down the aisle and your mom baking us a great cake, your sisters acting as bridesmaids and hopefully, I can borrow a few of your brothers to stand beside Matt as my grooms."

Lilly was sobbing so hard with a mixture of joy and relief that she couldn't even speak.

"Angel? I know the baby makes you overly emotional and stuff, but I'm dying here. Is that a yes or no?"

She sobbed all the harder.

"I, ah, know our first marriage was built on a weak foundation, but I am a contractor, sweetheart. I specialize in renovations. If you'll give me a yes, I promise to spend the rest of my life building the perfect marriage for us both."

"Oh, F-Finn," she said. "I love you…."

"Then that's a yes?"

"O-of c-course it's a yes."

"Okay then, whew." Finn felt dizzy with relief. He'd come so close to throwing this wondrous relationship away, that now that he'd officially saved it, he felt like joining in on Lilly's latest batch of tears. "I guess that settles it. We're going to have a wedding and a baby."

"Does that mean we can all join in on the celebration?" Mary asked from the kitchen door.

"How long have you been standing there?" Lilly asked.

"Long enough," she said, running across the room to crush her sister, then brother-in-law in a hug. "Congratulations. When Erin came and told me Santa wasn't here, but Uncle Finn was, I took the liberty of waking the rest of the troop."

One by one, the rest of Lilly's pajama-clad, sleepy but happy family filed past, shaking Finn's hand and patting him on the back.

On the ride up, he'd feared them holding a grudge, but nothing could have been further from the truth. They all shared stories of times during their marriages that they'd been through rough patches and expressed their joy that he and Lilly had survived theirs.

Around five-thirty, Lilly's mom took fresh caramel pecan rolls from the oven before passing around a fragrant pot of coffee. From his seat across the room from his wife, Finn caught Lilly's gaze and held it.

Crooking his finger, while the rest of her family happily chattered around them, he beckoned her to him. When she perched on his lap, it took his body less than half a second to recall other times she'd been this close, and how nearly every single one of those times had turned out.

"Merry Christmas," he whispered in her ear.

"Merry Christmas," she whispered back.

"Think anyone would notice if we slipped away for our own private celebration?"

Seeing that her brothers were engrossed in the prospect of the Utah Jazz having a winning season and her sisters and mom were planning her second wedding, she shook her head. "Nope, looks like the coast is clear."

Finn gave her a swift but passionate kiss, then scooped her into his arms.

They were about to make a clean getaway when Mary called out, "Sleep tight, you two!"

"We will," Lilly said with a wave.

"The hell we will," Finn said in the privacy of the hall, giving her one more kiss before mounting the stairs.

His mind spinning with joy and relief and even sadness for the time they'd lost, Finn couldn't help but remember how long he'd dreamed of this very moment. Best of all, it hadn't taken a bet to find true love…just blind luck.

EPILOGUE

A YEAR LATER, CHRISTMAS NIGHT, after the gifts had been opened, the turkey eaten and the good china put away, Lilly drew her husband into the laundry room. Granted, with both the washer and dryer chugging, it wasn't the most romantic spot to give him one more gift, but considering how many people filled her parents' house, it was the most private.

"Mmm," he said from his perch against the dryer. "Now that Charlotte's finally asleep, you're stealing me away for a little hanky-panky, are you, Mrs. Claus?"

"Brilliant deductive reasoning, Mr. Claus." She lightly jingled his Santa hat's bell. "But in this case you're wrong."

"Oh?" Hands on her hips, he cinched her close, slanting his lips atop hers for a mind-blowing kiss. When he succeeded in turning her mind to needful mush, he pulled back. "Well, Mrs. Claus? Wasn't there something you needed to be doing other than ravaging your poor, helpless husband?"

"Yeah," she said with a grin. "Bonking you on your big head with that giant candy cane you gave the baby—like she can really eat something that big, Finn."

"Hey, she's got teeth."

"Two!"

"Tell me," he said, stealing a quick nibble on her ear. "Have I committed any other fathering sins? Have

I scalded her with too hot bathwater? Poked her in the eye with a rogue *bumblebee, bumblebee* spoon?"

"No."

"Okay. And how many times have you had her over to Doc Walsh's for ridiculous reasons?"

"Hey," she said, giving Santa a poke in his belly. "She said it was perfectly normal for me to be concerned about Charlotte's early penchant for Minnie Mouse shaped ice cream sandwiches. What if she chokes on a stick?"

"Never happen. Remember? I hold on to the sticks."

"One might gag her."

"Nope."

"Stab her?"

He sighed. "Give it up, sweetie. Let's face it, I am the perfect dad."

Even in teasing, Lilly couldn't find fault with that statement, so standing on her tiptoes, she gave him another lingering kiss.

"Wow. What did I do to deserve that?"

"You're you. I love you, you know."

"I love you, too. We have a great life, you, me and Charlotte."

Too choked up to speak, she nodded.

"What's wrong? You look close to spouting one of those gushers you used to when you were pregnant."

"Uh-huh. It's just that I'm so h-happy. It's Christmas and we're here with all our family, and I'm finally pregnant again with—" Tears really flowing, she flew her hand to her mouth. "No, no, no. I can't believe I spilled my own secret. The new baby was supposed to be a surprise. I have gift-wrapped booties stashed in the washer and everything."

"Sweetie, I hate to be the bearer of bad news, but sounds like the washer just kicked into the spin cycle."

"Oh no!" Lunging for the lid, she raised it, but by the time the barrel stopped spinning, it was too late. Her prettily wrapped package with its pink and blue ribbon was ruined. "Why does this kind of thing always h-happen to me?" she sobbed against her husband's chest. "Why am I constantly messing things up?"

Far from being upset by the incident, Finn worked hard to hold back a laugh, but didn't quite succeed. "Can you believe it? I'm going to be a father—again!"

"This isn't funny. I wanted this announcement to be a special moment for you."

"Baby—or I guess that would be, *Mommy*," he said, his mouth frozen in what he feared would be a nine-month-long grin, "You've just given me the happiest news of my life and you think a pair of wet booties is going to ruin it?"

She shook her head and dried her eyes on the tails of his red flannel shirt.

"Look at me," he urged, softly nudging her pouting chin upward. "Haven't you figured it out yet?"

"What?"

"I love you. I love the way you turn all my white T-shirts pink. I love the way the slightest peep out of Charlotte sends you into a tizzy. Hell, I even love the way you've somehow fertilized-to-death over ninety percent of my ferns."

"I have not!"

"Have, too," he said, drawing her into yet another fervent kiss. "Mmm, and I especially love your way with—"

"Knock, knock." Mary stood at the laundry room

door, a cooing, wide-eyed Charlotte in her arms. "Sorry to interrupt this late-night smooch-a-thon, but I caught this kiddo trying to escape her crib." She eyed Finn. "*Someone* must've sneaked her too much candy and now she's ready for action."

"Give me Daddy's girl," Finn said, his heart so full of love for his wife and daughter and the new addition to their family on his or her way, he felt ready to burst. Mary handed him the baby, and with the munchkin already cooing, he bounced her a few times to really get her juices flowing. "No kid can ever have too much candy on Christmas, can they, my little pumpkin pie?"

Hands cupping her tummy, Lilly cast her daughter and husband an indulgent grin. As usual, Finn was right, but far from being upset by the fact, it only made her love him—and their life—more.

Never had she felt happier. More complete. It was as if up until finding him, a piece of herself had been missing. But now, Finn's love shone in her heart like a beacon, lighting the way to his loving arms, finally making her see that while she might always be a misfit, as long as she had Finn for a husband, best friend and lover, she was the luckiest misfit in the world.

* * * * *

JEMIMA yanked open a drawer in the sideboard to find Alfie's birth certificate. Her son was her husband's child. It was a question of telling the truth whether she liked it or not. She extended the certificate to Alejandro.

"This has to be nonsense," Alejandro asserted.

"Well, if you can find some other way of explaining how I managed to give birth by that date and Alfie not be yours, I'd like to hear it," Jemima challenged.

Alejandro glanced up, golden eyes bright as blades and as dangerous. "All this proves is that you must still have been pregnant when you walked out on our marriage. It does not automatically follow that the child is mine."

"'I know it doesn't suit you to hear this news now and I really didn't want to tell you. But I can't lie to you about it. Someday Alfie may want to look you up and get acquainted."

"If what you have just told me is the truth, if that little boy does prove to be mine, it was vindictive and extremely selfish of you to leave me in ignorance!"

Jemima paled. "When I left you, I had no idea that I was still pregnant."

"Two years is a long period of time, yet you made no attempt to inform me that I might be a father. I will want DNA tests to confirm your claim before I make any decision about what I want to do."

"Do as you like," she told him curtly. "*I* know who Alfie's father is and there has never been any doubt of his identity."

"I will make arrangements for the tests to be carried out and I will see you again when the result is available," Alejandro drawled with lashings of dark Spanish masculine reserve.

"I'll contact a solicitor and start the divorce," Jemima proffered in turn.

Alejandro's eyes narrowed in a piercing scrutiny that made her uncomfortable. "It would be foolish to do anything before we have that DNA result."

"I disagree," Jemima flashed back. "I should have applied for a divorce the minute I left you!"

Alejandro quirked an ebony brow. "And why didn't you?"

Jemima dealt him a fulminating glance but said nothing, merely moving past him to open her front door in a blunt invitation for him to leave.

"I'll be in touch," he delivered on the doorstep.

What is Alejandro's next move? Perhaps rekindling their marriage is the only solution! But will Jemima agree?

Find out in Lynne Graham's
exciting new romance
JEMIMA'S SECRET

Available March 2011
from Harlequin Presents®.

HPEXP0311